# The LUCINO File

## S. J. Garrett

Other Titles by S.J. Garrett

**CHRONICLE Series**
Chronicle of Destiny
Chronicle of Summer

**ETERNITY Series**
Ghost Eyes

**DESCENDANTS Series**
Shadow on the Sea

**3rd DISTRICT Series**
The Shaughnessy File
The Carmichael File
The Dease File

**Stand-Alones**
Until the Dawn Breaks

# PROLOGUE

There was a place known as the 3$^{rd}$ District.

When viewed from a plane, it resembled a small triangle located in the edge of New York City, New York. From space, it could not be seen. It was not a landmark. It was not a place of great historical import. It was, for all intents and purposes, a backwater area in a bustling city of hundreds of thousands of people.

It was also the place where magic lived. If your life crossed the roads of 3$^{rd}$ District, it was said, then you would find true love and live happily ever. You would find a true faerie tale story.

This story is one of them.

Folder One
ISABELLE & GABRIELLE

# CHAPTER ONE

*(Two years ago)*

"Why do we have to have bodyguards?" Isabelle Lucino muttered at her elder brother as they walked down the hall to their father's office. At nineteen, she was four years younger than her brother's age of twenty-three. She was also a whole foot shorter. She blamed their mother's genes; she had been short too.

Rafael sighed deeply. "I am not happy about it either, Bella," he admitted, "but Papa was insistent that it is needed. Do you remember the embezzlement sting that he and I helped the police set up? It worked, but the man we caught is certifiably nuts. He made some rather serious threats against us."

"Have the cops caught him?" She fought a chill.

"He got away before they could." He opened the door to their father's office and walked inside. "We have our wardens, do we?"

Antonio Lucino smiled wryly. "Rafe, I would not do this if it was not necessary. You should have heard your grandfather when I told him. I think he wanted to hire hitmen. I managed to talk him out of it, but if you see any mushroom shaped clouds in the general direction of Italy, hide under the table."

"Have I mentioned that I am glad we are in NYC and not Rome?" Isabelle sat down on the edge of her father's desk. "When do we meet the poor saps who have to follow us everywhere?"

He lifted a brow. "Right now."

Rafael glanced at the door and winced good-naturedly as he saw the two males standing there. One was a young man who couldn't be much older than himself, and the other looked to be in his late twenties. "My apologies."

The younger male grinned. He had an interestingly androgynous face, lively baby blue eyes, and unruly short blond hair. He appeared tall and slender but stood with a casual confidence that Rafael most often saw in exceptionally talented street fighters and martial artists. "I would resent things too, if I was in your shoes," the bodyguard said dryly.

Even his voice seemed an interesting blend of male and female, as if nature simply hadn't been able to decide which to give him. Rafael liked him instantly. "My shoes would not fit you."

"And it's a good thing. My feet complain when inside anything other than sneakers or boots." He gave a slightly cocky salute but his smile looked genuine. "Tori Li."

"Rafael Lucino." He gestured to his sister. "Isabelle."

Isabelle eyed the taller male beside Tori warily. He stood the same height as Rafael, and was roughly the same size, so he would easily tower over her. He was also uncomfortably handsome with dark red hair and chocolate colored eyes. Morosely, she sighed mentally. She could all but see her hormones jumping up and singing hosannas in Italian. They would make things so much more troublesome. "Hello." It was all she offered.

"Hi." His voice sounded calm and amused, and very masculine. The way he stood beside Tori made them into a study in opposites. "My name is Alexander LaGuardia. Everyone calls me Alex."

"Your friends do at least," Tori murmured. "Have you heard what your enemies call you?"

"It's no worse than what *you* call me."

Antonio just smiled. "Alex, you will be in charge of Isabelle's safety. Tori, you will be in charge of Rafael's."

"What on Earth made you decide *that*?" Isabelle demanded. She pointed at Tori. "He is shorter than Rafe!"

Rafael stepped closer to Tori and held a hand out from the top of his head to over the top of the shorter male's. "It is by only half a foot or so. Besides, it is not your size but how you use it. He looks as if he knows what he is doing, and an easily underestimated bodyguard works for me." He eyed Alex. "Yours looks like he eats nails for lunch."

"As a matter of fact," Antonio offered, trying not to smile, "part of the application process included a personality quiz. Not only were Alex and Tori the ones with the highest qualifications, they also had the best matches to your personalities."

"A personality quiz?" Rafael asked warily. "They are our bodyguards, not our dates."

"Very true, but if I want peace in my household, I want to be sure you will get along with each other." Antonio lifted his brows. "Is that understood?"

Isabelle sighed. "*Sì*, Papa."

"Yes, sir." Rafael offered a hand to Tori. "I will try not to make your life too hard."

"That's okay." He shook his hand with a smile. "I need to earn my pay."

Alex walked closer to Isabelle and held out his hand. When she reluctantly took it, he bowed gracefully. "Don't worry," he said sympathetically. "It shouldn't be too long to endure. As soon as the threat is gone, I'll be out of your hair."

"Are you sure we cannot let *Nonno* hire hitmen?" Isabelle muttered at her father. He just laughed, and she withheld another sigh. Dealing with a bodyguard would be bad enough. Dealing with one she was attracted to would be worse. Their personalities matched? What a joke. The sooner things ended, the better.

*(Present)*

"I was just talking to your *nonno* on the phone," Antonio said wryly from the head of the table. "He wants great-grandbabies."

As one, Isabelle and Rafael groaned and dropped their heads onto the dining room table. Antonio didn't blame them in the slightest.

It was a beautiful Saturday morning in October. The Lucino household was in full swing as usual. Though a weekend, there were fifty million things to be done. Isabelle had a fitting for her wedding dress. Rafael had a luncheon with clients. Antonio had to go in to the office to put out the fires that had cropped up over his day off. Both he and his son were in charge of the family advertising business, Just In Time, Inc., and though they had tried to coax Isabelle into coming on board as well, she had declined. She had no head for art of any kind.

"Who was he aiming his ire at this time?" Rafael asked dryly.

"Well, certainly not Bella since she is engaged, so presumably he meant you, my boy." Antonio grinned when his son groaned anew. "He married your grandmother when he was nineteen. He assumes things are still the same these days. I tried to explain, but you know he never listens to me."

"Does *Nonno* know that Isabelle probably will not be giving him grandbabies either?" Rafael asked dryly. "It is just a business marriage." One that he hoped would eventually be a marriage of love as well, but he kept his thoughts to himself. His sister acted a bit touchy on the subject of her pending nuptials.

"Do I look mad?" his father asked politely. "He does not even believe in business marriages." He cleared his throat and then said passionately, "It is about love, 'Tonio! Love is what is great in this world! Passion drives people and gives your poor father his *bambini* to hold and cherish! I married your mother for love, and we have stayed together more than fifty years!"

Isabelle dissolved into giggles. "You sound just like him!"

He laughed. "After fifty years, I would hope I could make my impressions credible." He glanced over as the door opened, and he smiled instantly. "Ah, there you are. We were waiting to eat until you got here."

"Hey, Tori." Rafael grinned as he saw his friend walking over to sit beside him. Tori had been his bodyguard for two years now. They were the same age, and Tori was slightly smaller, but Rafael had seen him in action. He knew he could be no safer with anyone else. "Did you oversleep again?"

Tori snorted softly. "That would be Alex's shtick. I was just sneaking in an early workout." He took his seat beside Rafael. "Alex is the over sleeper."

Alex just lifted a brow as he sat beside Isabelle. He was ten years her elder, thirty-one to her twenty-one, and after two years, there was nothing he didn't know about her. Because of it, he said dryly, "I was just testing to see if Isabelle's temper would flare, and she'd come track me down. You keep swearing she has a temper and I've yet to see it."

Her elbow landed sharply in his side. "Be glad," she countered haughtily. "My temper is a force to be reckoned with."

"You're Italian," Tori noted. "It's a force of *nature*."

Servants came in with breakfast and began to serve dishes. All wore smiles. The Lucinos did everything loud and passionately. It was one of the reasons it could be so much fun to work for them. The other was the fact that *Signor* Antonio always gave them holidays off with generous bonuses. Even just working for the Lucinos made you part of the family.

After breakfast, Isabelle escaped the table as fast as humanly possible. She hurried upstairs to her room, threw herself onto her bed, and screamed as loud as she could into her pillow. If people didn't stop talking about her marriage, she would *kill* someone! She liked Roberto, but he was as much a brother to her as Rafael. She didn't want to marry either of them!

When Alex stepped into the doorway, he felt entirely unsurprised with the scene. He walked with surprising silence over to the bed and sat on the side. Her ashy brown hair was coming out of its braid, and he resisted an urge to help it be even freer. "Would you like to talk?" he asked her. "I think we're friends too, aren't we?"

She lifted her head, her piercing blue eyes both resigned and reluctant all at once. She was, in his opinion, one of the most beautiful women in the city. It wasn't a passive pretty or a normal lovely. She had a fierce and striking beauty, a nearly sultry one in fact, that turned heads wherever she went. It was mark of her Lucino bloodline being enhanced by her mother's genes; the gene pool had been covetously guarded for centuries until Antonio had married a Caucasian woman and finally brought in some diversity.

"We are friends," she told him, "but you work for Papa. I know you spy on me for him!"

"To some extent," he admitted readily. "Your safety is, first and foremost, my primary duty. But if you told me something in private that had nothing to do with your safety, it would go nowhere else, Bella." He offered a hand to help her sit up. "Now, talk to me."

She sighed deeply as she sat beside him. To be honest, she liked talking to him. In fact, she liked far too much about her bodyguard for her own sanity. His height, his strength, his heart, and his handsome face that just could not be ignored. Two years had done nothing to make her attraction ebb for him; in fact, it had only gotten worse.

The curious thing was that he didn't even technically look that handsome. She had never been able to put her finger on it. He had red hair and chocolate brown eyes—he blamed the combination on a combustible Irish/Italian combined bloodline—and his features went together nicely, but he wasn't classically handsome like Roberto or strikingly beautiful like Rafael. He was just . . . Alex.

He was also as immovable as a mountain, stubborn as a mule, and gentle as a kitten. She had been beating her head against the brick wall of his over-protectiveness for two years. She would be doing it for many more at their current rate. The idiot who had caused all the trouble by making threats against the family still had yet to be caught.

"Is it Roberto?" Alex asked her.

"Yes and no. I mean, I like him. I would not hesitate to say that I love him. He has been Rafe's friend since they were five. But . . . I am not *in* love with him. I know that it is just a business marriage, and that he would not pressure me to become his—his lover, but . . . ."

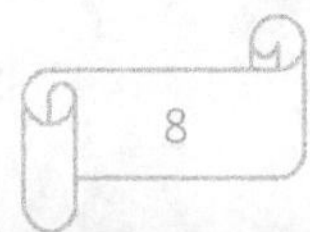

"You're not happy at not marrying for love," he noted shrewdly. "I think you have more of your grandfather in you than you thought."

"Is it too much to ask?" she muttered.

"No," he decided after a moment of thought. "Have you tried telling anyone?"

"Ha. You imply they would listen. They are too happy at making the merger between our companies. 'We have to keep up with that Dease family, Bella. Ever since those boys took over, they have taken some of our clients!' Feh!" She fell onto her back and covered her face with her hands. "I could scream!"

"You did. But I won't tell anyone I noticed."

"*Grazie.*" She groaned when she heard the doorbell ring. "Roberto."

"It's bad form for a bride to be so underwhelmed by her groom's presence."

"Do you have sisters?" she shot at him.

"Two."

"Contemplate marrying one of them and tell me how you would feel!" She reluctantly let him pull her to her feet and crossed her arms tightly as she followed him downstairs. Somehow she found a smile as she saw the dark-haired man waiting for her at the bottom of the steps. "*Ciao,* Roberto."

Roberto Viani smiled and leaned in to kiss her cheek. "*Ciao, Bella.*" He tweaked her nose lightly. "Do not look so happy to see me. It is not good for my heart."

She smiled suddenly. "You are going to be miserable married to me. You know you are. You always hated me nagging you, and now I will have a *legal* reason to do it."

"Yes, but I will have a legal reason to tell you to shush." He hugged her with one arm and smiled at Alex. "Hello, Alex. How are you today?"

"Despite Tori poking fun at me and Isabelle accusing me of treason, quite well." He smiled as he said it. He liked Roberto despite the fact that he had an urge to rearrange his too handsome face. Ever since the marriage had been decided months before, Alex had been struggling to keep his jealousy hidden.

"When do we leave for the bridal shop?" Isabelle asked Roberto. "The fitting is in an hour, correct?"

He raked a hand through his black hair. "Isabelle . . . Hell. I told Rafe I did not want to be the one to tell you."

"Tell me what?" she demanded. "Now what are you going on about?"

"Isabelle." Antonio stepped into the doorway to his study. "I am sorry, *cara*, but you are being put on house arrest for an indefinite time." When her mouth fell open, he held up his hands. "I am afraid I do not have a choice. There was a very specific threat that arrived only minutes ago. I have called the police, but there is not much they can do right now."

"What threat?" Alex asked very softly. His hands lightly settled on Isabelle's shoulders protectively.

"'Don't let her out of your sight, old man,'" Rafael quoted from where he leaned in the doorway to the parlor. "'You never know what might happen to such a pretty girl.' The detective that we talked to said that we need to take it very seriously. It could be a prank, but it might not. We would rather find out later it was a prank and have overreacted than see something happen to you because we assumed wrong."

"Your dress is being delivered here for your fitting," Antonio said firmly. "And you do not step foot out of this house unless we are sure the immediate danger is past."

Isabelle's hands slowly curled into fists at her side but she withheld her temper as carefully as she could. Calling the men names and throwing things would be entirely undignified.

Satisfying, but undignified.

Less than ten miles from the Lucino villa, there was a small area of New York City known as the 3rd District.

You couldn't find it on a map. It didn't show up on Google. Even most of NYC was unsure if it really existed. Those who knew of it spoke of it in hushed whispers. The 3rd District, it was said, was the place of magic. No one who lived there was normal. No one who was born there was entirely human.

It was overseen by an immensely large corporation known as the Enforcers. The company had existed since before the Revolutionary War, and some suspicious historians felt sure it had been there in some form even before Columbus had landed on North America's shores. To be sure, Enforcers had a very great amount of power, both corporate and political. People suspected they might even have federal backing, but no one was gutsy enough to ask.

Among the many other things they did, Enforcers' main duty was to watch over the District. Every business in the District was either overseen or owned by Enforcers. In fact, quite a few immediately outside the District were as well, but not as many people knew about those.

The District was mostly commercial, and the people who worked there lived in homes attached to their place of work. The entire place looked like a slice of history; none of the exteriors had been modernized except for Enforcers Headquarters. The purely residential area always looked rundown, but it was deliberately done. No one wanted outsiders coming in. If you wanted to stay, you had always belonged.

It was that simple.

Gabrielle Wisteria was one of the ones who had been born there, but she would have belonged regardless. She was half water elf, and as such had some rather . . . interesting powers over water, and an interesting physical trait she strove to hide by deliberately keeping her ashy brown hair long in the front so that it covered her ears. They were *just* pointed enough to cause lifted brows if seen. She also wore headbands made by a weaver in the District if she was unsure her hair would stay where it belonged.

At twenty-one, she was a legal adult, which was to her advantage because she was also an orphan. She had lost her parents years before in the 9/11 attack on the World Trade Center. She would have become a ward of the state, but Rhianna Taber and Eric Mason from Enforcers had smoothly stepped in and made sure she stayed in the District.

Brie had paid them back in as many ways as she could. She had worked part-time as front desk support, and she still went in willingly if they needed an extra pair of hands for anything. Normally, however, she worked as a waitress at a small restaurant that catered to the tourists who came through the Gentle Brook Inn, the District's primary hub.

"Brie!"

She looked up from collecting empty plates and smiled as she saw her manager. As always, he looked far too rushed and far too preoccupied. "Yes?"

"Kitchen, now." He took the plates from her. "Please!"

She just shook her head and headed for the kitchen. She knew, even before walking in, what she would see. And sure enough, the sink was on strike again. Water spewed in the air and pooled on the floor. The cooks were trying desperately to protect their food by using umbrellas to block the spraying water.

"Oh geez." She walked over to the sink and put her hand over the fountain. "Grab that tub." When it was brought over, she held her hand over it. The water flowed obediently up one arm and then down the other into the tub. In moments, the spray had stopped. "When is he going to replace this thing?"

"When you quit," another waiter said with a grin. He was mopping up the mess on the floor. "If he doesn't have to worry about it, he won't."

"He should pay me extra. Sheesh." She fixed the broken spout on the faucet and turned the water back on. Everything worked fine. "I should have been a plumber. But nooo. I had to be an artist."

The sink incident set the tone for the entire morning. It was a very busy morning, and she found herself practically running to clear dishes from one table before serving people at another. It wouldn't have been so bad if she hadn't been doing the job for two years. She felt so *bored* with it. Nothing ever changed.

"Brie, help!" It was the manager again.

She sighed. Nothing *ever* changed.

Isabelle was in the parlor reading a book when Rafael walked in with a cheerful seamstress from Bridal Dreams, the wedding boutique, following him. "Here you go," he told her with a smile. "And ignore her if she snaps at you."

"I do not take out my anger on the innocent messenger," Isabelle muttered as her brother walked out whistling. She found a smile for the other woman. "I am sorry that you were called out here on such short notice."

"I get paid either way," she assured her. The tag on her blouse said her name was Demi. "Now let's get this gown on you and see if the last alterations are exactly what they need to be. You're so lucky," she added on a sigh. "I'd kill to wear a B. R. Matthews dress down the aisle."

"It just seemed made for me," Isabelle admitted as she locked the parlor door. She didn't trust her brother, or her fiancé, to not pull a prank on her. They could be fifteen, twenty-five, or fifty-five, and they would still be tormenting her.

The alterations were perfect. The dress gathered just right at the bust and fell in shimmering waves past her ankles. As much as she didn't want to marry Roberto, she couldn't help but love her wedding dress. She would have been happier to wear it to marry a man she was in love with, but she would take her enjoyment where she could find it. "The sleeve is a little snug," she noted.

"Let's see . . . ah." Demi used a pin to mark the spot. "The seam was taken in just a bit too far. We can get that fixed just fine. And since it'll be your last fitting, as long as you don't decide to go on a sundae binge, you shouldn't have any more problems."

Isabelle had to laugh at that. "I am allergic to chocolate, so there are no worries about sundaes for me." She got back out of the dress gingerly to avoid the pins and then pulled her regular clothes on once more. Once she had, she unlocked the parlor door. "I do not trust my brother," she explained.

Demi smiled. "I have one too. I know how you feel." She sighed as she gathered up her things. "Your fiancé is so handsome."

"Yes. He is." Isabelle crossed her arms as she followed Demi out into the foyer. Alex and Rafael were waiting for her, and she narrowed her eyes on them both. "What? Is some mysterious person going to attack me in the parlor?" She shot a look at Tori as he approached. "What, are you here to babysit me too?"

Tori backed up carefully, hands in the air. "Easy. I'm unarmed. I only just got here." He bumped into Roberto as the other male came up behind him. "Careful. She's out for blood."

Roberto walked over to Isabelle and caught her shoulders. "It will be over soon, Bella," he said soothingly.

Her blue eyes began to simmer with temper. "The threat or the wedding?"

"Both," he responded calmly. "You are just starting to get nervous."

"I am getting pissed off!" She knocked his hands off her shoulders fiercely. "I do not want to marry you!" she shouted. "I am tired of being told what to do! Did I have a say in any of this? No!" She backed up when he stepped toward her. "Just leave me alone!"

She darted around him and ran up the stairs two at a time. The

men remained silent for several moments before, wryly, Tori said to Rafael, "I owe you ten bucks. You're right; she *does* have a temper worse than yours."

A sinking feeling suddenly filled Alex. He got to his feet and swiftly ran up the stairs toward Isabelle's room. The door was locked. "Bella, open the door!" he ordered. There was no response and he cursed softly.

"Let her be," Rafael suggested from the bottom of the stairs. "If she has not come out by dinner, I will get the key from Marco. He has the master key to all the rooms."

Alex sighed and headed back downstairs. There was no way to explain the feeling he had. It was just a feeling that told him Isabelle was getting herself into trouble somehow. He had become acquainted with the feeling; he just didn't understand how or why he had it. "I need a drink," he muttered.

Roberto laughed at him. "I think we all do. Isabelle certainly keeps things entertaining."

By the time Brie had her lunch break, she was at the point of tearing out her hair. "Ooh." She stalked down the street away from the restaurant before she gave in to the urge to kick her boss. "What I wouldn't give to just get a single day away from here!"

She swung around the corner blindly and walked head-on into someone coming toward her. Both of them fell onto the sidewalk. "I'm so sorry," she started to say, but the words disappeared as she stared in shock at the young woman she had run into. The other female stared at her with just as much astonishment.

From the length of their ashy brown hair to the tilt of their clear blue eyes, the two women were perfectly identical. "*Dio,*" Isabelle breathed, her eyes slowly widening further.

"Whatever you just said," Brie managed to say, "I probably

concur. Holy shit." She got to her feet carefully and offered a hand to Isabelle. As the other woman stood, she felt her head spin. They were the same height, the same build . . . Anyone looking at them would easily think that they were identical twins.

"I think we might need to talk," Isabelle said. She gave a shaky laugh. "This is surreal!"

"Tell me! C'mon. My apartment is near here." She studied Isabelle, noted the quality of her clothes and the way she walked, and smiled wryly. "You're so not from around here." She pulled off her hat and plopped it on her companion's head. "Here. So people don't stare at us until we get there. I'm less noticeable than you are."

"Talk about a coincidence," Isabelle said softly.

Brie laughed out loud. "You're *definitely* not from around here. Let's go. I think this is going to be one heck of a tale, and I've absolutely got to hear it."

# CHAPTER TWO

Brie lived in an apartment in a complex only blocks from where she worked. Isabelle had heard rumors of the rundown state of this portion of the District, but she was a little puzzled to see that it didn't look nearly as bad as it had been made out to be. Something felt oddly welcoming about the area.

The apartment itself was on the smaller side, and it had been filled with all manner of furniture and art. The warm tones in the color and wood both reminded Isabelle of her home with its distinctly Tuscan flavor. "This is wonderful," she told Brie.

"Thanks." Brie shrugged out of her jacket and tossed it casually over the back of a chair. "Grab a seat. Want a soda?"

"*Sì.* I mean, yes, thank you."

"Okay, what the heck is that you're speaking? Spanish?"

"Italian." Isabelle sat at the kitchen counter with a smile. "My name is Isabelle Lucino. I am usually called Bella."

"Gabrielle Wisteria, but Brie for short or I'll smack you." She smiled as she said it. She passed the soda to her companion and had to laugh. "This is so weird. It's like looking into a mirror! We even *sound* alike, except for your accent. But we're definitely not long lost twins or some such junk."

"Can you be sure?" Isabelle asked curiously. "I mean other than the obvious that my parents never divorced; my mother died a few years ago from pneumonia. And there was no reason for her or Papa to give up a child. We like big families."

"Well, that would be one reason. The other is your ears."

"My *ears*?"

Brie pulled off her headband and tugged her hair up and away. "Now don't go freaking out on me."

Isabelle stared in disbelief at the obviously pointed ears on her double. "*Dio*. You are not human?!"

"You make it sound like a bad thing." Brie grinned. "I'm half, thank you, and very proud of my water elf half." She took a sip of her soda. "My mom was the human. My dad was the elf. And my mom was Italian too, by the way. You're a halfsie with something else?"

"It certainly is not elf, I assure you. I know they say everyone has a double somewhere; there is no such thing as perfect genetic uniqueness, but this is truly crazy." She laughed suddenly. "But it is too amazing not to enjoy! It is like finding a sister. I always wanted one. I am surrounded by men all the time!"

Brie offered a hand. "I could use one too. I've never had a lot of friends. I get along with everyone, but I'm not really close to anyone, you know?" When Isabelle took her hand, she smiled. "So what's your life like, Bella? You've got that 'private school' thing imbedded in you, so I know you grew up on the 'right side of the tracks' as it were. How old are you?"

"Twenty-one. Recently, actually. My birthday is in July."

"Heh. April here. I'm older than you by four months." Brie hopped up and sat on the edge of the counter. "Thank god for it, too. It would be too much if we had like the same birthday or whatever."

"Agreed. And, yes, I did grow up in a good family. Have you heard of Just In Time, Inc.?" At the nod, she smiled. "My father is the owner and CEO. My brother is slowly stepping in, though. They pretty well co-run the place now. They tried to get me onboard, but I have no artistic skills." She looked around the apartment wistfully. "Clearly, you do."

"More's the pity. I traded all my practical genes for it." She grabbed a cookie from a jar and offered it. "Chocolate chip?"

"I am allergic to chocolate."

Brie looked at her in horror. "How do you *live*?"

Isabelle laughed. "Quite well as long as I avoid it. It will not kill me, actually. It just makes me very sick. And I get a rash. It is hard to determine which is worse."

"I eat the cookie on your behalf then." She took a big bite and thoughtfully chewed. "So rich girl comes wandering into the District, huh? What gives with that?"

"I lost my temper with my family." Isabelle dropped her head onto her arms with a sigh. "I am getting married to someone who might as well be my brother. It is a business marriage so our companies can merge. I have known Roberto my entire life. I do not want to marry him. And on top of that, there is some sort of death threat against the family. It became personally aimed at me, and I was confined to the house."

Brie winced in sympathy. "Making you a time bomb with an Italian temperament. You go out your bedroom window?"

"Yes." She propped her chin on her hands. "I should be able to get home before they get the master key from our housekeeper. I just needed to *breathe*, Brie. I had heard that the 3$^{rd}$ District was where people went to escape."

"The irony being that when I ran into you, I was trying to escape my life too." Brie grimaced. "I like my boss well enough, but I feel so . . . underwhelmed there. I'm a waitress," she offered. "And since I can fix most problems in the kitchen, I'm pretty vital. But I'm so bored. It's that artsy side you envied. I want challenge and creativity."

"No college?" Isabelle asked curiously.

"No funds and no desire to be indebted to the federal government. Enforcers offered me a scholarship, but it just didn't seem worth it. I told them to give it to someone who needed it more." She sighed. "I'd give anything to be someone else for a day."

Isabelle slowly began to grin. "I think I might know how to solve both our problems. Let us switch!"

"Let us *what*?!" Brie stared at her. "Are you nuts? We'd SO get caught, and we'd get in so much trouble!"

"No, no. I think we can do it! Would your boss mind?"

"No," she said slowly. "He'd probably be amused by it. You wouldn't have to pretend with him. But me . . . your family'd go nuts!" She winced. "And I don't want to kiss your fiancé."

"Do not worry," Isabelle assured her. "It is only a business marriage. I have never kissed Roberto. Come on, Gabrielle. It would be fun!"

"Don't call me Gabrielle," she muttered. She blew out a breath. "I somehow know we're going to regret this, but I can't help but be tickled by the idea. Okay. Hit me with the facts. Tell me what I need to know to pull this off."

"How good is your memory?"

"Good enough, I hope!"

Isabelle started at the top with all the servants and made sure to describe them as best she could. If Brie messed up even once, then they would both be in a lot of trouble. Isabelle had absolute faith in Brie's ability to pull this off, though. "And do not forget," she added, "that I do not talk quite like you do."

"I'll try not to sound like a peasant," Brie retorted dryly. "I'm fairly decent at mimicking most accents, too—remind me to show off my Irish accent I learned from one of the co-owners of the Gentle Brook Inn. Now describe your family."

"Papa is named Antonio. He is on the taller side, over six-foot, and his hair is half-gray and half-dark brown. Brown eyes. My older brother, Rafael, Rafe for short, looks like Papa twenty-five years younger except his eyes are blue like mine. My fiancé is Roberto Viani. He is only slightly shorter than Rafe, and his hair is black. His eyes are a rather interesting shade that is not quite blue. Almost lavender, really."

"Is that it?"

"No, there are two more people. One is Tori Li. He is Rafe's bodyguard. About five-ten, blond and blue-eyed. You cannot miss him. He is this fascinating blend of male and female in just about everything, except perhaps strength. He was amazing when saw him in a delightful co-ed mixed martial arts tournament. He took down almost everyone! The other person is my bodyguard." Her voice softened unconsciously. "Alex LaGuardia."

Brie slowly lifted a brow. "Alex, huh?"

"Same height as my brother, but more powerful. Red hair and brown eyes. Not your normal handsome, but he is . . . breathtaking." Belatedly, she saw how Brie was looking at her. Her cheeks slowly turned pink. "Uhm."

"Bella . . . do we have a bit of a crush on our bodyguard?"

"No!" She waved her hands in the air. "Of course not!"

"I get the feeling I definitely won't be bored," Brie decided dryly. "Your family sounds nuts."

"*Grazie.*"

"You're welcome. I think."

Isabella laughed. "I will have to teach you some words eventually. Well, what do you say? Can we switch?"

"Well . . . we need to tell Enforcers first," Brie said reluctantly. "I wouldn't want them to call you thinking you were me and then getting mad because they didn't know. I owe them a lot, Bella. And besides, it never hurts to have someone watching out for you, right?"

"You mean ask them for permission?"

"Let's put it this way: I might be able to fool your family, but there's no way you'll fool anyone here. Better that we tell Enforcers than have them find out accidentally." Her doorbell rang suddenly and she blinked rapidly. She cautiously went over, peeked out the spyhole, and then sighed as she opened the door. "Don't do that, Gwyn!" she complained. "It's creepy!"

The white haired young woman on the other side of the door just grinned, her gray-purple eyes twinkling merrily. "You can't be surprised. A lot of people saw you two meet, and word came to us." She shot a cheerful smile at Isabelle. "Hi, I'm Gwyn Vincent. I'm from Enforcers."

Isabelle found herself smiling. There was something so likeable about Gwyn that she put everyone around her at ease. "I am Isabelle Lucino."

"Of course you are." Gwyn walked in and put down a tote. From within, she pulled out a stack of papers. "Rhianna says it's perfectly fine to switch, but she wants it formal so that if anyone tries anything with Isabelle, then we, Enforcers, can claim she's under our protection as well. People might mess with most anyone, but no one is dumb enough to mess with us."

Isabelle hesitated only briefly before smiling and signing the bottom of the contract. Brie signed next to her. Gwyn curiously studied their handwriting. "You guys even write similar. That's pretty nifty. I mean, I have two twins and we're not even that much alike."

"You mean triplets," Isabelle said, confused.

"No, she has two twins," Brie corrected dryly. "It's a long story. Thanks, Gwyn!"

"Don't mention it." With a wink, Gwyn collected the contract, stuffed it in her tote, and left the apartment.

"She is *tiny*," Isabelle observed the instant the door shut. "I mean, we are only five-three and I felt *huge* next to her. What is she?"

"Different."

Accepting that, she laughed. "Let us switch clothes and then go talk to your manager! This is going to be so much fun!"

Mr. Prost was understandably puzzled when the two women showed up, but he had as good a sense of humor as anyone born in the District did, as well as a good understanding of how the universe worked. He also liked Isabelle a great deal, finding her to be lovely, personable, and quick to learn. "It's hard work," he warned her.

"I look forward to it. I have never had to work for anything. I think it is time I tried. Brie will get her pay for what I do, right?"

"Naturally." Mr. Prost winked at Brie when she stared at him. "It's not like you're leaving me in the lurch. I think we can get Bella to do a fine job." He sighed heavily. "I suppose I better get that sink fixed though."

And thusly, Brie found herself catching a taxi to the Lucino villa. Following Isabelle's specific directions, she snuck around to the back, climbed up to the balcony, and crept inside the bedroom. Fascinated, she studied the design and décor and found it to be very similar to her own choices at home. It was tidier, though. She wouldn't mind the house arrest if it meant being in a place like this. It was gorgeous! And she had Isabelle's computer logon and password, and Isabelle had hers, so they could exchange emails at night just in case.

They always ate dinner together, she remembered, and they dressed for it. No pajamas allowed. After a quick perusal of Isabelle's closet, she decided on a slim black skirt and a pretty blue blouse. Didn't her partner own any *jeans*? Not a single t-shirt hung anywhere either. It wasn't that her clothes weren't lovely, but Brie knew she would miss her comfy clothes before very long.

They even wore the same size shoes, and she pulled on low-heeled black slippers. She had never worn heels in her life and could only pray she wouldn't break her neck going down the stairs.

A loud knock sounded on the door and made her heart leap. "Bella," a man called through the door. "Open the door this minute. You have sulked all day and Papa is getting worried."

He had to be Rafael. Bracing her shoulders, she hurried to open the door. Sure enough, the male on the other side could have been *her* brother. He looked exactly as he had been described. "I was not sulking," she informed him, mimicking the family accent with surprising ease. "I was resisting an urge to throw something at your hard head."

His brows shot up, then he grinned. "It would do you good. You simmer so long that I am always worried you will blow entirely like you did this morning." He leaned down and kissed her cheek. "Dinner is ready, Bella. And try not to kick Roberto under the table. Last time he tried to retaliate, he kicked *me*."

Having been without a family for years, the obvious love and affection from him acted as a balm to her soul. She followed him downstairs and tried to not be obvious about the way she was trying to take in everything. She wasn't entirely successful since he cocked his head at her and said, "You look like you have never seen the place before."

Carefully, she said, "I suppose I was just realizing how lucky we are."

"I cannot argue with that." He hugged her lightly and grinned when he saw Alex approaching. "Look what I found, Alex. I lured her out with promises of *Nonna*'s fettuccini recipe."

Alex came to a sharp stop as he stared at the young woman before him. She had Isabelle's face. She had Isabelle's eyes. She even had her smile. But she was *not* Isabelle. He had been so used to feeling a gut kick of desire if he so much as caught a glimpse of her that it was shocking when he didn't feel it this time.

Brie searched his eyes and her heart began to race madly. He knew. She could see he knew. She moved forward quickly and caught his arm. "Alex, can we talk? I owe you an apology as much as I owe one to Roberto. Please?"

"Of course." He led her into the parlor. "We'll be right there, Rafael," he called as he shut the door. As he heard the other male's footsteps fade, he turned toward Brie and narrowed his eyes slightly. "So. Who are you?"

"Gabrielle Wisteria, Brie for short." She took a deep breath. "Isabelle and I met a few hours ago. We thought it would be fun to trade places. She's doing my job as a waitress in the 3rd District. I'm here to spend some time with her family. Please don't tell anyone!" she pleaded. "We were both bored, and we thought it might be fun! It knocked both of us for a loop when we met!" She frowned suddenly. "How did you know I wasn't Isabelle, anyway?"

"I would know my Isabelle anywhere," he said simply. "You are as beautiful as she is, but I'm not attracted to you as I am to her. I suppose it is her soul that I want most."

She studied him intently and a smile began to tug at her lips. "You been in love with her all this time?" Geez, and Isabelle had a crush on him in return. They were both idiots in her book. If she'd had a hot guy like this who loved her, she would have been ecstatic.

"I have." He suddenly smiled. "Isabelle uses little to no slang, so you had better watch your speech. You say she is in the District?"

At the nod, he sighed deeply. "I had better find an excuse to take a weekend off to go find her. It is my duty to protect her."

"And your honor. And your desire. And . . ."

"Yes, yes. You've made your point." He shook his head in bemusement. "You are identical in the face, but not the personality. Perhaps you can learn from each other. She could use your relaxed air."

"And I could use some polish." She grinned. "Don't be embarrassed to say it. I don't deny the truth." She blew out a breath as she heard someone calling 'her' name. "Don't abandon me yet. Help me get through dinner, I'm begging you."

"Certainly." Wryly amused at the entire situation, he escorted her from the parlor and led the way to the dining room. In a voice so low only she heard, he said, "Go to your papa and kiss his cheek. Then take the seat to his left, beside Roberto."

She took a deep breath and hurried to the older gentleman sitting at the head of the table. She bent to kiss his cheek and smiled. "I am sorry, Papa. I did not mean to worry you. I was having a snit." She shot as lofty a look as she could at Rafael who was sitting to Antonio's right. "It's certainly different from a sulk."

Antonio laughed and kissed her forehead. "*Sì*, Bella, and you are entitled. You have been too well behaved your whole life. Papa is convinced you are a changeling. '*Miei bambini* need more passion, 'Tonio!' Or so he claims."

She bit back a giggle as she turned to take her seat. To her surprise, a dark-haired hunk with seductive lavender eyes was holding her chair. Her breath wedged in her lungs even as her blood heated happily. The sudden fist of desire started somewhere deep and spread outward sharply. She swiftly averted her eyes, feeling the heat in her cheeks. Holy crap, she was lusting after her friend's fiancé. She would burn in hell. "Thank you," she said softly as she sat down.

Roberto stared at her intently as he sat down beside her. She sounded like Isabelle. She looked like Isabelle. She even mimicked most of her mannerisms. Yet he was absolutely positive that she was *not* his fiancée. When he had looked up to see her in the doorway, he had nearly been felled by a sharp hunger to taste her smiling lips and feel her silken skin under his hands.

He watched her intently as she sat beside him. There was a slight hesitation in her hands as if she wasn't entirely sure of which utensil was for what. Her speech, though formal enough, just didn't have the same polish as Isabelle. And with every passing second, his hunger for her grew. Who was this mysterious changeling that seemed to be made of magic in her soul?

If the others noticed anything, it was simply that Isabelle acted suddenly a little more open. Her smile came much quicker, and she laughingly exchanged quips with Tori and Rafael, much to their delight as she had never really verbally sparred with them before. "I think your seclusion did you good, Bella," Rafael told her laughingly. "You are a little different now. A good different."

"Am I? I hadn't noticed a difference." Brie told herself to shut up before she got in deeper. It was just so easy to relax with these people! It was like finding a long lost family. Maybe she and Isabelle could switch again sometime. At least, before she got married. Brie didn't like the way her pulse scrambled at Roberto's every steady look, and he was watching her a *lot*.

His knuckles grazed ever so lightly down her leg and she jolted. "Is something wrong, Isabelle?" Antonio asked curiously.

"Roberto kicked me." She turned up her nose, trying to hide her rapid heartbeat. "I would kick him back, but my legs aren't long enough."

Somehow, she made it through dinner. Making it through the weekend would be *hell* at this pace. As they were adjourning from the table, Alex suddenly said, "Antonio, may I have a word with you and Isabelle? We'll need Tori as well."

Puzzled but amiable, Antonio said, "Certainly, Alex. Rafael, Roberto, please excuse us?"

"Of course." Rafael smiled at Tori. "I will wait for you in the billiards room. I want to win another ten dollars."

"In your dreams."

Roberto studied Brie intently. "I would like to speak with you as well, Bella. I will wait in the parlor."

She absolutely did not want to be alone with him, but she knew she couldn't get out of it. "Of course." As soon as she got upstairs, she would call Isabelle and demand they call this off. There was way too much going on in this weird family!

In Antonio's study, Brie gratefully sat down in one of the chairs. Antonio went around behind his desk and sat down with a wry smile. "Do not tell me you want to quit, Alex. Isabelle cannot have finally made you reach your limits of patience."

"Of course not." Alex lightly rested a hand on Brie's shoulder. "Unfortunately, I have had a family emergency come up. I would ask for the weekend off to make sure everyone is all right. I will come back on Monday morning. Since Isabelle is under house arrest, it should be simple enough for Tori to watch over her as well."

"Absolutely," Antonio agreed. "I do hope everything is well."

"So do I, which is why I'm leaving as soon as I pack a bag." He smiled down at Brie. "Don't cause too much trouble for Tori."

Lacking a more appropriate response, she simply sniffed disdainfully. It was the right response since it made Tori laugh. "Don't worry, Isabelle," he said cheerfully. "I won't be dogging your every step inside the house. Just don't go near the doors or windows else I have an urge to pull you away like we're in some sort of spy movie."

She barely kept from grinning. She really liked Tori. He was so easygoing! She just felt comfortable with him in a way she didn't usually with other people. He felt very real, and very natural. No wonder he and Rafael had become such good friends.

With that meeting done, she very reluctantly went to the parlor for another. She nearly asked Tori to go with her but knew that she had no way of explaining why. She opened the door and peeked inside, and there was no sign of Roberto. Glad he hadn't gotten there yet, she walked over to the fireplace to warm her chilled hands. Hazards of her power: when she became nervous, her hands got as cold as ice.

The door suddenly shut behind her and a lock clicked. She whirled sharply and caught a breath as she saw Roberto leaning against the door. "You startled me," she managed to say.

"Fair enough, *cara*." He crossed his arms as he watched her. "You certainly startled me when you walked into the dining room."

What the hell was *cara*? Isabelle hadn't given her a crash course in Italian terms! She resisted an urge to edge backward. There was really nowhere to go, and he wasn't even that close to her. "You would think you hadn't seen me before."

One side of his mouth kicked up in a lethal smile. "I do not believe I had." He straightened and slowly began to walk toward her. "I do not think we have been introduced, *cara*."

"You're being silly." She found herself backing up to escape his approach. "We've known each other for years." He couldn't have guessed like Alex did. Not unless he was in love with Isabelle too. God, this was just getting more and more complicated!

"No. We have not." He leaned in and caged her against the wall with his hands on either side of her head where she could not escape. As he bent his head, the scent of her curled up and dug into his lungs. She smelled like pure water and magic, and it was a scent that most assuredly did not belong to Isabelle. He would know this mysterious beauty anywhere. "You are not Isabelle," he said very softly near her ear.

A shiver rippled through her body at the heat of his breath, felt even through her headband. He had seemed such a gentleman during dinner, but she realized then that it only acted as a façade. He was no more tamed than she; he just hid it far better. "Of-of course I am."

Just how far would she take the farce? He lifted her chin until she was forced to look at him. "Then you will not mind kissing your fiancé, will you?"

Isabelle had sworn she wouldn't find herself in this predicament! She tried to turn her head away. "You've never wanted

to kiss me before." At least, dear god, she hoped he hadn't! Maybe Isabelle hadn't realized her fiancé wanted more than business. "Let me go!"

"That, *cara*," he murmured huskily, "I find I cannot do. You walked into the dining room and took my breath. It is only fair that I take yours." His lips brushed across hers lightly, temptingly, and he savored the sound of her breath hitching. Whoever she was, she wanted him as badly as he wanted her. Mutual madness. "It should not be so alarming," he murmured as he pressed soft kisses along her jaw, "to want your fiancé."

She pushed at his shoulders. "Stop. Please, stop." She wanted to sound forceful, but the breathless tone gave her away. It seemed as if she was going weak all at once, every muscle turning pliant as his incredible mouth traced her face.

His lips settled over hers gently, and his tongue softly teased her lips to open. She gave a shivering little moan and it raked across his body like velvet claws. When her lips parted, he took what she offered, deepening the kiss with a hunger that had simmered for hours. He pressed closer, let her feel how badly he wanted her, and was rewarded with another delicious shiver.

They slowly parted and he stared into her clouded blue eyes. They seethed like the restless surf on an ocean shore. She slowly pressed her trembling fingers to her lips, something like fear moving to replace the desire in her gaze. "You are not Isabelle," he told her roughly. "I never wanted her the way I want you. Who are you?"

"I knew this wouldn't work," she whispered. Her head dropped onto his chest as her shoulders slumped. "I just knew it."

"Easy." He ran his hands softly over her arms to soothe. "Let us sit down and talk." He eased back and drew her over to the settee. He made sure to sit close beside her and left one hand on her knee while his other arm rested across her shoulders. She would run before he got his answers if he didn't hold onto her. "Now then. Will you tell me who I just kissed?"

"Gabrielle Wisteria." She didn't look up at him and kept her gaze on her hands in her lap. "Brie for short. I'm from the 3rd District." She did peek at him then, but he looked more speculative than alarmed. "Isabelle was running away when we met. We thought it might be fun to switch places."

"No wonder Alex took off," he murmured. "He always knew her best. He knew instantly that you were not Bella. I wonder what clued him in."

She kept her mouth shut. Things were awkward enough without telling the man that his fiancé and her bodyguard had the hots for each other.

He studied for several moments, his gaze lingering on the headband she wore. It might as well have been another clue. He had never seen Isabelle wear one before, and it seemed more like a disguise than a fashion statement on Brie. "Gabrielle." He said the name slowly, savoring it. "I like it." He skimmed his knuckles across her cheek. "Would you let me get to know you, Gabrielle?"

"Brie," she muttered.

"Why? Gabrielle is a lovely name."

"Only those close to me can call me that."

"Then I will call you Gabrielle, as I very much wish to be close." He leaned in and tugged lightly at the headband. She went very still, her eyes widening. "What are you hiding, *cara*?" He lifted her chin. "I will kiss you again," he said softly, decisively.

"You're engaged." She broke out of his grip and scrambled to her feet. "I don't *care* if it's 'just a business marriage.' You're still engaged. I'm not a cheater. And if you are, then you're a jerk. Isabelle deserves better than you." Temper lit her eyes when he lifted a brow. "You gonna tell me that you wouldn't take me to bed if I offered? That makes you a jerk."

"I have no intentions of seducing you while I am engaged, *cara*. But I do wish to get to know you. You are here this weekend, yes?" When she nodded, he got to his feet. "Then I will 'court' you. If any ask, we can simply say that we are trying to see what being a couple is like. When Isabelle returns, we will see what we will see then." A little smile crooked his lips. "Tell me, did Alex tell you why he knew you were not Bella?"

"The opposite of you," she muttered. "He *didn't* want me." She studied his face. "You're not surprised."

"Oddly, I am not." He stepped closer but stopped when she retreated. "I am not going to kiss you, Gabrielle. Give me your hand, please." She very cautiously offered her hand, and he drew it to his lips. "My name is Roberto Viani," he said softly. "I am delighted to meet you."

The man was *dangerous*. She freed her hand and rushed out of the parlor as fast as she could unlock the door. If only he hadn't been engaged to Isabelle! Business marriage, nothing. An engagement was a promise, and she refused to be made to feel like she had helped break one.

As Roberto walked out of the parlor, Rafael was coming down the stairs. His brows lifted through his bangs. "Well," he said. "You are looking a little . . . stressed, friend."

Roberto sighed. Though it would have been simple enough to tell Rafael everything, doing so would mean that Brie left. He most assuredly did not want to let her out of his sight until he had no choice. "Something seems to have happened to Bella and I."

Rafael grinned. "That is one way of putting it. Thank *Dio*, that is what I say. I was hoping you two would be happy."

"Well, that remains to be seen. I have decided that I have been a bit lax in the fiancé department, Rafe. I will see if I can court your sister this weekend. She certainly cannot run from me, can she?"

"Not right now, no." He shook his head. "No wonder she seemed so different at dinner. She must be floundering right now since this is so sudden."

Roberto hid a smile. "That is one way of putting it, yes."

# CHAPTER THREE

As the oldest of three, with his younger siblings both being sisters, Alex was well used to the fascinating way many women could be as different as night and day between their internal and external personas. He appreciated it, even admired it. Certainly he had been admiring Isabelle for the last two years as much mentally as physically. She came across as being a little distant, a little aloof, but there was a smoldering passion inside her that he had always been helplessly drawn toward.

While he wanted any threat removed from her life, he couldn't help but hope it took longer so that he could build up memories. As soon as she married Roberto, she would be forever beyond his reach. He had once hoped that as soon as he was freed of his duties, he could court her. Now he knew it would never happen.

Finding her in the 3$^{rd}$ District wasn't hard. It seemed that everyone there knew what was going on. He very shortly walked into the restaurant where she was working, though he took great care that she not notice him. It was easy enough to blend into the crowd since it was the dinner rush.

He started smiling within a few moments. Isabelle was having the time of her life. She laughed and smiled as she waited on tables or cleared away dishes. She helped out with the register, learning patiently how to work the machine from another waiter. She obviously worked hard, but she was also clearly enjoying every minute.

He caught another waiter's eye, and when the man walked

over, Alex said softly, "I don't suppose I could request the blue-eyed waitress."

The man grinned. "You and nearly every other male here. Sure. Her table list isn't too big. I'll switch with her." With a whistle, he headed over to where Isabelle was stacking receipts. "Hey, Bella. Table Two asked for you specifically. Betcha get a good tip if you flutter your lashes."

She laughed. "You mean Brie would get a good tip. I am making money for her, remember?"

"She'll make you keep the tips, trust me."

"You are probably right." Amused, she grabbed her order pad and headed for Table Two. It was tucked into a quiet, shadowy corner. The man was reading a newspaper, so she couldn't tell his identity yet. "I am Brie," she said cheerfully as she reached the table. "Can I get you some water or coffee?"

Alex put down the paper and grinned when her eyes widened. "And you look surprised, Isabelle. Did you think I wouldn't notice the switch?"

"I do not have time to talk to you right now. I am on the clock, and it is Brie's paycheck." She looked at him pointedly. "Water or *caffè*?"

"Water." He offered the menu from the table. "Just the house soup special, please, and a small side. I already ate dinner."

"Side potato, mashed." She had written it down before realizing she should have made it a question. The simple fact was that she knew him almost as well as she knew herself. All his likes and dislikes. "Uhm, butter?"

"You know I prefer sour cream," he said softly.

"*Sì*." She sighed and took the menu. "Just . . . stay there and do not cause me trouble, Alex!"

"When have I ever?"

"If you only knew," she muttered as she walked away. The man caused her trouble every time he looked at her. Every time he smiled. His casual way of touching her shoulder or tugging on her hair. Her whole family was physically affectionate, but Alex was assuredly *not* like her brother or father, or fiancé.

Thankfully, he seemed to be aware that it was actually Brie's job on the line and he didn't make a scene. He thanked her when she brought over his meal, declined an offer to refill his water, and spent a humorous two minutes trying to decide on dessert. "Cheesecake or pie. Hmm."

She shook her head at him. "You have been spoiled on Peggy's cooking!" she scolded lightly. "It is a wonder that you have not gained fifty pounds over the last two years with the way you inhale her tiramisu!"

He grinned. "I work out with Tori. The kid is a slave driver. He frightens me, really. He's half my size and he drops me on the mat regularly." He put down the dessert listing. "Cheesecake," he decided. "But don't put chocolate on it."

"Why not?" she asked curiously.

"I can share it with you if you don't."

Feeling her cheeks heat, grateful for the low light, she hurried toward the kitchen. As she was coming back out with the dessert, Mr. Prost caught up with her. She smiled as she saw him. He was such a funny man; he seemed to be the rooster whose feathers were always ruffled. "Hello."

"Ah, Bella. Brie will be very happy with how hard you worked." He clapped her on the shoulder lightly. "It's quitting time for you, my girl. You go on home and get some rest. You have the morning shift tomorrow, alright?"

"Very well." She held up the dessert. "Let me just deliver this and then I will clock out. Actually," she put down the plate to take off her apron, "I know this man, so consider me off the clock now, alright?"

"Of course."

She picked up the plate again and carried it over to Alex's table. She put it down in front of him and slid onto the seat across from him. "I am off duty now," she explained when he arched a brow. "And

thank *dio*. My feet are killing me." She picked up a fork and broke off a piece of the cake. "What are you doing here, Alex? Did not anyone wonder why you were running off while I was in grave danger?"

"I told them I had a family emergency and since you were supposed to be indoors, Tori could watch over you for me." He crossed his arms and sat back. A dark frown filled his face. "Isabelle, what were you thinking? Running off as you did, you're lucky it was Brie you met. We can't know if anyone is watching the villa."

"I am tired of being a Lucino," she retorted fiercely. "Just once I wanted to make a decision for myself."

He glanced around, saw that the place was preparing to close, and got to his feet. "Let me pay for my meal and then you can take me where you're staying so that we can talk."

"Fine."

Minutes later, they were walking through the lamp lit streets of the District. Even at night, the place felt welcoming to Isabelle, and to Alex as well. People were only just shutting down for the evening. Someone who sold woodworks was carting all manner of items into her home. At another house, a pregnant woman helped her husband carry in beautiful articles of clothing. When she spotted Isabelle and Alex, she waved cheerfully.

Isabelle waved back with a smile. "It is so lovely here. I envy Brie a little." She led the way to the apartment complex and into the small home itself. "This is Brie's place, but she said I could stay here. I guess you can as well."

"How gracious you are." He shrugged off his jacket and hung it up on a hook near the door. He glanced around the apartment and had to smile as he realized that Brie and Isabelle shared more than matching faces. They had similar tastes as well, although Brie's living space seemed to shout that someone with creative talent lived there. Sadly, Isabelle had none.

She sat down on the couch and kicked off her shoes. "Ooh. My feet. I have never stood for so long before! I have an entirely new respect for servers of all kinds."

He sat down beside her and resisted an urge to offer to rub her feet. He wasn't sure he could keep his touch impersonal right then. She looked rumpled and flushed, and much softer and more approachable than she ever had before. The soft golden light in the room just made her beauty more seductive, more alluring.

Unaware of his scrutiny, she asked, "How did you know, Alex? Did Brie get caught?"

"No," he said softly. "I simply knew she was not you. I asked her about it and she told me you two had decided to walk in each other's shoes for the weekend."

"Yes, we did. Now go home." She aimed a glare at him. "You are going to ruin everything if you keep following me!"

"My duty," he reminded her quietly and firmly, "is to see to your safety. I'm not going home until you do."

"I do not want you here!" she shouted at him. "I am so sick of being a Lucino and being so in need of protection! Consider yourself fired, Alexander! I want nothing to do with you!"

Something volatile lit his eyes. "You think I care this much because you're a Lucino. Ha!" His hands closed around her shoulders and he jerked her closer so that she sprawled across his lap. "I don't care what you are, Isabelle. I never have. But thank you for firing me. Now I can do something I've wanted to for two damned years!"

She took a breath to curse at him, but the words were lost when his hungry mouth covered hers. Her eyes went wide with shock for an instant before a searing wave of desire swept through her body. It was so sharp, so compelling, that she found no will to resist it. On a low moan of need, she curled her hands into his shirt and pressed up to deepen the embrace. She had wanted him so badly for so long . . .

His hands released her only to bury his fingers in her hair and pull her ever closer. His mouth was hard and wild, not merely asking for her response but demanding it. When her lips parted, he immediately thrust his tongue inside to taste her. She reminded him of the sweetest of grapes, like the kind made into the best of wines.

Addicting. Arousing. She was everything.

He released her as sharply as he had grabbed her. Roughly, he said, "That, Bella, had nothing to do with my being your bodyguard or your being a Lucino. In fact, it was probably the stupidest thing I've ever done in my life." And if she didn't stop staring at him with her slumberous blue eyes, he was going to do it again.

She shook her head sharply and pushed at his shoulders. "Let me go, Alex."

He did so reluctantly though his fingers glided across every inch of skin they could. He was entirely unsurprised when she scooted away from him down the couch. "You can't make me go away," he said quietly, "any more than you can change who you are. And I wouldn't want you to try." A little smile suddenly tugged at his lips. "And since your father hired me, you technically can't fire me either, Bella."

"I am also engaged," she shot at him. "Let us not forget that either!" She raked her hands through her hair. It seemed as if she was shaking from the inside outward. 'Want' was too mild a word for what she felt. 'Lust' was much closer, but even that fell short. She *needed* his touch in a way that was dimly terrifying. If only he hadn't kissed her! Now she knew exactly how wonderful his mouth felt, how delicious his taste was. "*Dio*!" she said fiercely. "How complicated this is! I hope Brie is not having this sort of trouble." She got to her feet with all the dignity she could muster. "You can sleep on the couch. I am going to bed. *Buono notte*."

"Good night," he murmured, watching the sway of her hips as she went down the hall. He wasn't entirely sure he would even manage to sleep with the way his body ached, but at least the couch looked uncomfortable enough to take his mind off things.

Brie awoke the following morning with a bit of a start. The

room was unfamiliar, and so was the bed. Memory returned as she listened to the birds chirping outside the window and didn't recognize their voices. She sighed and got out of bed. She was half-tempted to think she had dreamed everything, but a look in the mirror told her that she *still* looked as if she had been kissed senseless. Any man who could leave a visible impact even hours later was one to keep away from sane women.

After a bracing shower in the adjoined bathroom, she felt a little more human again. Well, as human as she could be, she thought impishly as she got dressed. Steeling herself for whatever assault she might come under from Roberto, she made her way downstairs for breakfast. When she reached the foyer, she was surprised by a man in a uniform walking up with a bouquet of water lilies. "For you, *signorina*," he said with a smile.

"Me?" She took the flowers in confusion. "Who sent me flowers?"

"I believe *Signor* Viani did."

"Oh." She hastily handed them back over. "Please put them in water, Marco." At least, she hoped he was Marco! He sure looked like he knew the place and was in charge of it as well.

"Of course." He winked as he took the flowers toward the kitchen.

Water lilies! She furrowed her brow as she headed for the dining room. Either Roberto somehow knew what she was, or he had made an eerily accurate guess. Both made equally unnerving thoughts.

The dining room was empty except for Tori. "Where are Papa and Rafael?" Brie asked.

"In the boardroom upstairs. They're working on a rush order. They stole a client from the Deases, and they're trying to hash out the best possible campaign." He shook his head in amusement. "I keep telling them they need to be in a business other than advertisement. They've got the mentality of pirates!"

She tried not to laugh as she served herself from the buffet that was set out. She definitely liked Tori. "I'm sorry Alex abandoned you," she offered as she sat down across from the bodyguard.

"It's alright. I just hope everything is okay. You know how he loves his sisters."

"Mmm."

They were halfway done with breakfast when Roberto walked into the dining room. He smiled slowly when he saw Brie. "*Ciao, cara.*" He walked over and bent to kiss her cheek softly. His lips curved further when he saw the blush climbing her delicate neck. Her pulse beat rapidly, an enticement to press his lips there. Instead, he looked at a very bemused Tori. "*Ciao,* Tori."

"Hi." He propped his chin on his hand and grinned. "I'm not used to seeing you two act all lovey-dovey. It's a nice change of pace, for sure." First chance, he would corner Rafael and find out what had happened to change the direction of the winds blowing. It seemed as if everything had done a complete switch ever since Isabelle had lost her temper.

Roberto leaned over and murmured softly in Brie's ear, "*Grazie* means thank you, if you want to thank me for the flowers."

"*Grazie,*" she said very softly, and it again came out surprisingly fluent. She had never used an accent as comfortably as she did Italian. Must have been her half-blood. "For the flowers." She would have said that she loved water lilies, but she had no idea if Isabelle did. This was so much more complicated than she had been thinking it would be!

Tori excused himself a few moments later, and she very nearly called him back. She absolutely didn't want to be alone with Roberto. "Do you always eat over here?" she asked him softly. "What about your family?"

"It is just me. My parents took off on a world tour a year ago when Papa retired." He smiled. "I have postcards from five different countries and counting. He and Mama are having a grand time. But since that means I am alone at home, I get lonely. Rafe and I have been friends for two decades. I am as at home here as he is at my home." He tugged her to her feet as he stood. "Let us go into the parlor." His smile came slow when she blushed. "Do not worry. I will not have my wicked way with you, *cara*."

"You had better not!" She reluctantly let him tuck her hand into the crook of his arm as they left the dining room. Her fingers flexed softly, automatically testing the resilience of the male flesh under her touch. He was much, *much* stronger than he seemed. Heated lavender eyes flicked a glance at her, and she knew he had felt her curious examination.

Inside the parlor, she escaped his grip and pointedly sat on a chair so that he couldn't sit beside her. He just smiled and sat across from her on the settee where he lounged with the grace of a large feline. "Did you sleep well, Gabrielle?"

"Brie!" She didn't like the way he turned her name into a caress in his velvet voice. "And I did, thank you."

"I did not." A corner of his mouth kicked up.

Her belly tightened with a flutter of raw heat. Her hands curled together in her lap as she fought for control. "You said we were going to get to know one another." She kept her voice steady with effort. "What do you want to know about me?"

"Well, you surely know the first question, *cara*. You said you were from 3rd District."

Her lashes lowered. "I am half water elf."

"A real elf?" He sat up, intrigued. "Are we meaning Santa or Legolas?"

She shot him a dirty look. "Neither, thank you. What, you also think all faeries are the sugar puffs that Disney makes them out be?"

He grinned and held up his hands. "Easy. It was a fair enough question. What does being a water elf mean?"

"It means a certain control over and creation of water." She hesitated and then pulled off her headband. She lifted her hair away from her ears and revealed their delicate points.

Enchanted, he moved closer. He softly reached out and traced the line of her ear, following the gentle lines to her cheek and back

to the tip. There was something sexy about her ears, but he couldn't quite determine what it was. Delight filled him as he saw the tiny holes around the tip. "You pierced your ears?"

"Who hasn't these days?"

"I would like to see you wear earrings. I think your ears are lovely." He trailed his fingers over her ear once last time, wistfully. Someday, hopefully soon, he intended to kiss every inch and work his way down.

As soon as he leaned back, she hastily put her headband back on. Her ears were actually tingling from his touch, and the tingles spread deep and wide. She had never guessed her ears would be that sensitive.

"Tell me about your family," he offered. "I assume you must be half Italian to be identical to Isabelle."

"Yes, my mother was. My father was the elf."

He paused. "Was?" He kept his voice as gentle as he could.

"Trade Center." It was all she said.

"*Cara.*" Hurting for her, he moved to be kneeling in front of her chair. "I am so sorry. No wonder you were so interested in switching with Bella. You wanted a family again, even for a little while." When she looked at him in surprise, he brought her hand to his lips. "I think I know you quite well even in such a short time, *cara mia.*"

"Alright," she said in exasperation. "Just what are you calling me?"

"Beloved," he said softly.

She snatched her hand back quickly. "I'm not."

"I must disagree." He retook his seat. "What do you wish to know about me?" She said nothing and he sat back comfortably. "I am twenty-five," he offered. "I am the CEO of Inkwell, a small but lucrative advertising company. My father and Antonio have toyed with the idea of a merge since Rafe and I were ten. It seemed very convenient to do so now, with me and Isabelle marrying to cement the deal. There is some strong competition in the market now that Two More Minutes has come under new management." She remained stubbornly silent and he just smiled. "I have two degrees, one in Business Management and the other in Advertising. What about you?"

"I don't have a degree. I didn't see a need for college. Anything I want to learn, I learn on my own. I take free classes when they come up, but I'm mostly self-taught." Reluctantly, she admitted, "I'm an artist. I work best in pencils and charcoals. My day job, what Isabelle is hopefully enjoying, is being a waitress."

It was an utter waste of talent in his book. Artists needed to be *creative*. His native land had been built on art for centuries. It was in his blood even though he lacked the ability to create with any sort of medium. He had always greatly respected those who could, and frequently turned to his artist employees for advice. "I would like to see your art," he murmured.

"Maybe someday."

The doors suddenly opened, and Rafael walked in with a sigh. "*Scusi*, Bella, Roberto. I do not mean to interrupt, but I could use you, Roberto. Papa and I are absolutely stumped at this point. We need some fresh input."

"Naturally." Roberto offered a hand to Brie. "Come with us, *cara*. See what your family does."

"If you can make her interested," Rafael noted dryly, "I will give you twenty dollars, Roberto."

Brie took Roberto's hand and stood. "Just for that," she said loftily, "I will go along."

Rafael stared at her and then started laughing. "Me and my big mouth." He hugged her tight when she was closer. "I should have known you would do that." He wiggled his brows teasingly. "I was half hoping I would walk in on a kiss."

She elbowed him sharply. "Behave yourself."

Chuckling, Rafael walked into the boardroom. "I brought Roberto, and by opening my big mouth, I seem to have gotten Bella as well. It is just as well. Would you mind taking notes, *cara*?"

The affectionate term sounded entirely different coming from

Rafael than it did coming from Roberto. She found a smile and picked up the pad of paper sitting on the table. "I can do my best." She took a seat and tried to ignore Roberto sitting next to her. She had the scary feeling that she might be falling in love, and that was even worse than falling in lust. He was *engaged*.

The men began firing ideas back and forth across the table, talking loudly and over the top of each other. She listened, writing down ideas as they were thrown out, but after a few moments, she started to sketch out the scene they were trying to decide. It was an advertising poster for a large food chain, but they couldn't decide on any one particular theme.

She didn't even realize what she was doing until she noticed it had gotten quiet. She looked up quickly to find Antonio and Rafael looking at her curiously. "I'm sorry," she apologized. "Did I miss something?"

"You looked a little distracted, Bella. What are you up to over there?" Antonio asked affectionately. It was just nice to have his daughter interested in the company for once.

"I was . . . uhm." She tried to hide the sketch but Roberto snatched it out of her hand. "Give that back!"

He dropped the paper on the table where the other two males could see it, and both took quick breaths. The sketched outline was not only precisely rendered, it was also very skilled.

"What the . . .?" Rafael looked at Brie sharply. "You are not Isabelle," he breathed. "You cannot be. My sister cannot draw to save her life. No wonder you seemed so . . . different somehow." And no wonder Roberto and Alex had reacted so strangely to her presence! "Who are you?" He made his voice gentle. "You know us, so obviously you and Isabelle met."

She leapt to her feet and fled from the room as fast as possible. "Go after her, boy," Antonio told Roberto quietly. As he also ran out of the room swiftly, Antonio took a deep breath. "I think I know who she is, Rafe." His son looked at him sharply, and he got to his feet. "I need to make a few phone calls. I want to confirm my suspicions."

# CHAPTER FOUR

Isabelle awoke in the morning to the smell of coffee and bacon. With a large yawn, she pulled on a robe and padded into the kitchen to see what was going on. She had kind of been looking forward to cooking for herself for once. She had never really gotten a chance to try it before. "Alex?" she asked as she walked over to the counter.

"Good morning," he told her gravely. "I couldn't sleep, and you're on the morning shift, so I thought I'd cook something for us. There wasn't much to choose from, but I thought bacon and eggs would work fine."

"Oh. *Grazie.*"

He tightened his grip on the spatula as he stared at her. She was flushed and rumpled, her eyes still sleepy and her cheeks still flushed. It took every ounce of his willpower to resist lifting her into his arms and carrying her down the hall to bed once more. "Bella."

At the rasp in his voice, she took a wary step back, her hand lifting to her throat. "I will just go catch a quick shower," she whispered, and she fled down the hall once more. The entire way, she kicked herself. Why was she so afraid of her own feelings?

Because she was engaged, that's why. Yet . . . she wasn't being *forced* to marry Roberto. She had agreed because she had, foolishly, thought that she would never have Alex. He was the only one she had ever loved, ever wanted. And he wanted her too, which was more than she had dared dream of having.

She thought critically about the situation while she dried her hair. The business marriage didn't *have* to occur to support the merger. It was just a formality to make the paperwork less messy. If she told Roberto that she was in love with Alex, he would certainly agree to let her go. After all, he loved her too; he just wasn't *in* love with her.

Her father and Rafael would be more than happy with the situation. They also wanted her happiness. Besides, they were Italian. They were supposed to do things big and passionately. She felt long overdue for some serious drama. Maybe switching with Brie would have a much bigger, longer reaching effect than alleviating their boredom.

The instant the switch was done, she would talk to Roberto, cancel the engagement, and turn her eye toward Alex. He would be hers come hell or high water. She couldn't be sure of the depth of his feelings, but she absolutely would not settle for just lust. Oh, she would enjoy it, of that she was sure, but she wanted much more. He was still in her father's employ, and that made it stickier, but if she told Antonio she wanted Alex fired so that she could seduce him, her father would probably be willing. Slightly flabbergasted, but willing.

Feeling in control of her life once more, she got dressed in the black slacks and white shirt that made up 'her' work uniform. She would have to get some pants for herself. They were amazingly comfortable. Perhaps Brie would lend her a pair of jeans or two until she could get her own.

She headed back to the kitchen and sat at the counter. The size of the apartment did not lend to a dining room table, and Brie had turned the counter into the eating space. It was cozy and delightful. Isabelle was also pleasantly surprised when Alex handed her a plate with food. "I did not know you could cook."

He smiled. "Well, it's not part of casual conversation usually, and it isn't like I had a need to, living with your family as I have."

"You know," she said thoughtfully, "I do not think I really know as much about you as I thought I did. At least, I do not know the unimportant things. I know *you* but not the extra little details about your life. You are ten years older than I. You have got to have some interesting things to tell me."

He slowly lifted a brow. "This sounds rather like a date, Bella."

She arched a brow in return. "I suppose it does. But that is silly, is it not? After all, I am an engaged woman." She sipped her coffee calmly. "For now."

His hands curled into the edge of the counter. Roughly, he said, "Isabelle, if this is a game you're playing because you feel you need revenge, I don't appreciate it." She looked up at him, her blue eyes clear as the sky, and he felt his muscles knot with ferocious need. "Don't look at me like that."

"How am I looking at you, Alex?" she asked softly.

"Like you want me to touch you."

"That would be silly, no? I am as yet an engaged woman." She delicately finished her breakfast. He was truly quite good in a kitchen, even with something that simple. "Alex, do you remember the day we met?" He nodded slowly and she handed him her plate to put it in the sink. "Until that day, I had been fairly sure that I had skipped the hormonal phase of puberty. Then you walked in." She shook her head. "I had no more worries on that front."

He closed his eyes and counted to ten. "I wanted you the minute I laid eyes on you. But it was so hard to even be your friend that I knew I didn't dare tell you."

She smiled. "Alex, when I am feeling threatened or insecure, how do I react?"

"You get aloof and haughty," he responded promptly. The minute the words left his mouth, he found himself smiling. "You'd think I'd have realized sooner." He went around the counter and cupped her cheek tenderly. She might not love him yet, but she wanted him. She wanted a relationship. He could build from that. "It's good for Roberto that you're dumping him."

"Oh?"

"I've been close to breaking his nose for months," he admitted. "I'm afraid I'm a jealous man."

She suddenly grinned. "You are Irish and Italian. You are the type who would break his nose and *then* yell at him. I still cannot believe how even-tempered you are! The minute I heard about your heritage, I was all set for some good shouting fights in the house, but nothing seems to bother you at all. Such a disappointment, Alexander."

He tugged her up into his arms and enjoyed feeling her body along his. She fit perfectly, as if they had been made to be one. She smelled as wonderful as the rich wine of her taste. "There's only so much room in the house for bad tempers now that yours has been proven."

She went on her toes and linked her hands behind his neck. "So, tell me again. How *did* you know that Brie was not me? Was it her ears?"

He paused, wondering why her ears would have anything to do with it, then pushed it aside. He would ask later. "Actually, it was because I was not attracted to her," he admitted candidly. "She looked like you, sounded like you . . . but I knew she was not you. And she didn't smell right."

"Smell?" She blinked.

"I can't describe it, Bella. I just didn't think she smelled right. But you . . ." He nuzzled her neck softly and breathed in deeply. "You are perfection. Like red wine on a summer evening. Like grapes ripening in the sun."

Her knees went weak. "Alex."

The husky sound of her voice flicked along his nerves. "I would kiss you," he said roughly, "but I fear I might not stop. I will not shame you, Bella. You are still engaged." He slowly released her and his hands slid warmly over her body. "You have work. I will come with you and see if I can be of any use."

"You will distract me," she grumbled, but inside she was delighted. She didn't want to be away from him. She wanted to savor how he wanted her. It would only be better if he loved her as well. Ah, well. She had time to work on that later.

When they arrived at the restaurant, Mr. Prost was more than happy to see them. "Good morning, Isabelle! And who is your friend?"

She smiled. "Alex. He does not have anywhere to go today since he is visiting with me. Could he help in any way?"

"Certainly!" Mr. Prost smiled at Alex, liking the calm man's demeanor. "How do you feel about working a cash register?"

"I haven't done it in fifteen years, but I think I can manage."

"When you were sixteen, I was six," Isabelle murmured.

"Does that bother you?"

"Not at all. It mostly fascinates me." She started to walk away and then glanced over her shoulder with a smile that could only be called sultry. "Try not to distract the patrons."

Mr. Prost chuckled at the look on Alex's face. "I think I ought to worry she will distract you. And I thought Brie had a devastating impact on the male clientele. Like the moon and sun, aren't they?"

"Or water and fire," Alex murmured, unknowingly apt.

Perhaps a bit ironically, noticed by all, was the fact that he wasn't the one who had trouble keeping his mind on his work. It was Isabelle. She didn't miss her tables, didn't drop anything, but she was clearly distracted by the cashier. When she would take him receipts, and he would smile at her, her thoughts would clearly scatter. She very nearly started to serve the wrong things to the wrong tables, catching herself just in time if someone else didn't catch her.

The patrons were highly amused. Mr. Prost was, too. After the third near mishap, he finally shook his head and pulled her aside. "Isabelle, why don't you take the day and visit with your 'friend'? I won't hold it against you or Brie, I promise. You're no good to me like this."

She winced wryly. "I am truly sorry." With a sigh, she took off her apron. "I knew better than to tease him. I was just setting myself up." She walked over to where Alex stood and waited patiently until he finished ringing up the last tab in front of him. "We are being kicked out," she said in amusement.

He just grinned. "Somehow I thought that might happen." With much relief, he turned the last receipts over to another waiter. "And not a moment too soon. I was reminded just how much I hated working in fast food." He held the door for her and followed her out into the morning sunshine.

"Was that your first job?" she asked curiously.

"It was, but I bailed ship as soon as possible."

"Exactly how did you get into the bodyguard business? I saw your resume. It is very impressive."

"It was an accident, actually. I had always been interested in learning self-defense, and I took to it quite well. When I was twenty-four, a friend of my father's was going to be traveling somewhere a bit more hostile and asked if I would go along as a deterrent to would-be assailants."

"Would-be turned into attempted, I presume."

"Correct. I did such a good job that someone else asked to hire me." He shook his head wryly. "I enjoyed it enough that I decided to actually do it as a career. I met Tori about three years ago on another job. He scared the shit out of me. This guy, half my size, had me on the floor in seconds. I still don't know how he does it."

She laughed richly. "He is so unassuming! I suppose that is why he is so effective at his work." She unlocked the apartment door and headed inside. "Oh well," she sighed. "I suppose I ought to get in touch with Brie and see if she wants to call things off early."

She went to the fridge and pulled out the jar of tea she had spotted before. She had barely poured one glass when the front door opened and Brie rushed in. "Brie!" She started to smile but it faded as she saw the look on her friend's face. "Brie?"

"Your fiancé is driving me nuts!" Brie nearly shouted. "And he *kissed* me!"

Alex, somehow, found that entirely unsurprising. Being a wise man, he said nothing and sat down on the couch. It was both fascinating and slightly disturbing to see the two identical women beside each other. Curiously, even at a distance, he knew he would always know which was which. Now seeing them together, he could spot nearly elemental differences in the way they moved.

Isabelle cleared her throat, a bit bemused and lot curious. "Would you like to explain how that happened?"

"He knew I wasn't you. He said it was because he was attracted to me and he'd never been attracted to you." Brie took a deep breath. "And he kissed me." She groaned and covered her face with her hands. "And Vesuvius was just a little volcano seepage."

Isabelle bit her lower lip to hide the smile that wanted to spread. Were things really going to work out that wonderfully well? If Roberto and Brie got together, then it solved so many troubles all at the same time! "Why are you here? Was he that, hmm, intimidating?"

"I goofed." She sighed. "Your dumb brother bet Roberto twenty bucks that *you* wouldn't sit in a meeting. I went just to make him lose. They were talking about a poster, and I just sort of started sketching."

Alex winced. "Isabelle can't draw to save her life."

"Unfortunate, but true." Isabelle lifted a brow. "They caught you." At the nod, she sighed. "Well, that does it. We are going to be in a great deal of trouble. Oh well. It was fun while it lasted, no?"

Brie didn't get a chance to answer. The door opened behind her, and Roberto walked in as if he had a homing signal for her. "*Scusi*," he said to Isabelle and Alex. He caught Brie around the waist and tossed her over his shoulder casually. "Bella, *cara*, I hope you understand when I say I want to cancel our engagement."

She did her best to hide a smile. "Yes. Yes I do."

Brie managed to untangle her tongue and nearly yelped, "Put me down, you bastard! Ooh! What's Italian for bastard? I don't think he's listening to English!"

"*Bastardo*," Isabelle murmured, desperately trying not to laugh.

"Well, *that's* easy to remember. Bastardo! Put me down, Roberto!"

"Eventually."

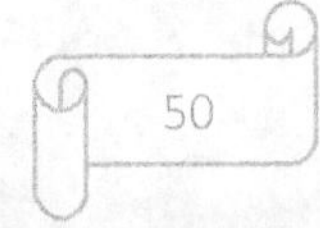

The door shut behind them and left a thoughtful silence. Isabelle looked at Alex, and he at her. "Well," she finally said. "I would appear to have been 'dumped,' as they say. Oddly, I am not that crushed over it. I suppose I should throw a tantrum and wail and curse his family, but I do not feel quite that dramatic. Do you mind?"

"Not at all." His brows lifted as she walked over and sat down on his lap. Desire tore through his body with the force of a storm as wild as his lover's blood. "Isabelle."

"I am single now," she said softly, linking her hands behind his neck. She teasingly brushed her lips across his. "But I do not want to be, Alex. I know you are still in my papa's employ, but I just don't care anymore."

His hands tangled into her hair and his eyes searched hers. There was something there, something he was terrified of naming for the chance he might be wrong. "Why, Isabelle?" he asked softly, huskily. "What do you want from me?"

"Passion and romance." Her soft hands framed his face. "And love." Her voice trembled softly. "I want that most of all." Softer, against his lips, she said, "*Ti amo,* Alexander." When his hands tightened, her lips curved. "I presume it does not need a translation. You do not need to love me yet," she added simply. "I can wait. But be warned now that I will do whatever it takes to have your heart for mine."

He brought one of her hands down to rest over his heart. It beat as wildly as hers. "It's yours," he said simply. "It always has been. I love you, Bella." He stood with her in his arms and turned determinedly toward the bedroom. "Your papa won't hire hitmen if I seduce his baby girl, will he?"

"Only if you abandon me," she warned gravely. "And in that scenario, you should be more worried about what *I* might do."

His lips curved. "I'll live in fear of your temper for the rest of my days."

She laughed. "As you should."

Roberto didn't put Brie down until they reached where he had parked his car. Unfortunately for her, that location happened to be a block away. Even dangling upside down over his shoulder, she could see the many people they passed. Every single one of them started grinning. "Mercy!" she wailed. "Put me down!"

"Not until I am certain you will not escape again, *cara*." He did put her down to open the passenger door, but only so that he could nudge her inside.

She knew better than to jump out again. She simply crossed her arms and stared out the windshield as he got in the driver's side. "I can't believe you dumped Isabelle!"

"You know she will not be hurt. And she has Alex in any case. I have often wondered over the last two years if there were true sparks between them. I am glad to see it confirmed. I love her a great deal, but only as a brother would. I wish her to be happy."

"And if you don't marry her, what happens to your precious merger?"

"We will have to see, will we not? It should not fall apart simply because I am no longer marrying Antonio's daughter." He glanced at her from the corner of his eye. She looked wild and untamed, as if he had somehow caught a creature of magic and confined it. She also looked frightened and miserable, two emotions he never wanted to see on her face again. "*Cara*," he said tenderly, "do not look so scared of me. You will break my heart."

"I'm more worried about you breaking *my* heart!" she fiercely retorted. "I don't want to fall in love with you, Roberto, because it would only destroy me when I couldn't stay with you!" She blinked as she realized he was parking the car in the driveway to a villa no less impressive than the Lucino one. "Where are we?"

"My home."

She scrambled out of the car and tried to run away down the driveway. He caught her in two long strides and once more flipped her over his shoulder. She began to beat on his back. "Don't you dare!" He walked into the villa, and she felt her cheeks heat as an older housekeeper came hurrying forward. "Oh god," she moaned, covering her face with her hands.

"*Signor* Viani." The woman put her hands on her hips. "What are you doing, young man? Is that . . . *Signorina* Lucino?"

"Actually, no. Bella and I canceled our engagement. This is Gabrielle. It is quite a long story, and I am not entirely in the mood to tell it right now. I will explain later, Maria." He went purposefully up the stairs without truly stopping once.

Maria gave a happy sigh as she hurried toward the kitchen. "Get out a bottle of wine!" she ordered. "We are celebrating."

Roberto walked into his suite and shut and locked the door before putting Brie down once more. She immediately backed away from him with her cheeks brilliantly pink. "Now then," he said softly. "Why are you so certain that you cannot stay with me, Gabrielle?"

"Are you nuts?" she shouted. "I don't know anything about your world! I don't belong in it, Roberto! Friggin' hell, don't you think I've been paying attention this weekend? You and the Lucinos come from the same background; you keep the chlorine in the gene pool and put lifeguards at every turn. I don't think my gene pool even *has* a lifeguard!"

"Clearly, *cara*, you were not paying enough attention." He began to unbutton his shirt as he stalked slowly toward her. "I am not dallying with you." His hands closed around her arms and he jerked her up against his hot body. "I am in love with you!"

"You don't even know me!"

Temper and frustration flared in his twilight colored eyes. "I see words are not doing any good. Let us see if actions can break through your stubbornness, Gabrielle."

Any protest she might have made was stolen by his hungry mouth taking hers. As the heat blasted into her body like a drug, a low whimper tangled in her throat. She wanted him so badly. Loved him so stupidly. Her legs lost their strength, and his hands curled into her hips to keep her standing. He drew her tight against his aching body.

He stole more than her breath. He stole her soul. There was an edge to his hunger, a desperation, as if he was fighting to hold onto her before she escaped. She tried to draw back, but his hand tangled in her hair and pulled her in again.

Her last resistance crumbled. She went on her toes against him, and her hands fisted into his open shirt to keep him closer. Her mouth went wild under his, her tongue tangling with his hotly as she strained to deepen the embrace.

He jerked back and stared down at her. "Mine." It was little more than a rasp. He jerked her shirt free of her skirt and rushed open the buttons, popping several in the process. He neither noticed nor cared. "I will know everything about you, *cara*," he vowed roughly. "And you will know me."

Dazed, she had no will left to resist as her shirt landed on the floor. Her skirt went next. His hands swept slowly, caressingly, over her skin until she shuddered with pleasure. "Touch me." He dropped stinging kisses along the slender line of her neck. "Know me."

The temptation could not be resisted. She pushed the shirt off his shoulders and hungrily took in the sight of his half-naked beauty. He was much more powerful than she had been guessing, every line corded with strong muscle. His golden skin seemed nearly bronzed, and the dark hair that lightly covered it was as soft as a pelt. She spread her hands slowly across his chest, savored his heat and strength, and watched his eyes darken to a violent, stormy color.

He caught her hands in his and brought her palms to his lips. He held her there for a moment, struggling for control before he took her on the floor.

As she sensed it, any lingering doubt swept away. Whether she could keep him or not, she believed that he loved her. She could see it churning in his eyes and feel it in the wild race of his heart. For all his hunger, he was trying not to rush her. He wanted to give her the chance to meet him halfway. How had she *ever* been unsure of him before? He was everything she needed.

She tugged her hands free and pointedly unfastened her bra. She dropped it on the floor and then hooked a finger in his belt loop to tug him closer. "You think you can catch someone like me?" Her voice was husky as she rose on her toes to tease his pulse with the tip of her tongue. "I'm not even human."

A shudder ripped through his body. "I do not care." His arms banded around her waist to lift her off her feet. He tumbled her down onto the top of his bed and savored how it felt to have her pressed against his aching flesh. His hands framed her face, his eyes memorizing her. "Do I need to protect you, Gabrielle?" It was little more than a rasp.

Her name sounded exotic. Foreign. In his voice, it became a caress. "Preferably—for now." Her fingers kneaded at his chest. "Touch me." It was little more than a breathless plea.

Nothing could have stopped him. He tore off the headband she wore and found the edge of her delicate ear with his teeth. She even tasted like magic, wild and unstoppable. He had a vision of a tiny dark haired girl with pointed ears sleeping in her arms, and his hands shook. "*Cara. Ti amo.*"

Some things needed no translation. As his mouth slid hotly across her skin, she buried her fingers in his hair possessively. Hers. Even if only a little while, this beautiful creature was hers.

He nuzzled between her breasts, his hands cupping her soft flesh as gently as he could. The nipples tightened and flushed, begging for his mouth, and his low laugh rippled over her skin as he studied her. "You know," he said thickly, "I think you are slightly better built than Isabelle."

She gave a laugh that turned into a moan as his lips closed over her nipple and tugged. "Don't tell her that!" The moan became a soft cry as he tugged again, his fingers kneading her flesh compulsively. Each tug pulled at something deeper and spread the pleasure into a demanding ache until she twisted under him wildly in a bid for relief.

He slid further down her body, teased her navel and the intriguing little hole near her bellybutton that might mean another sexy piercing. He then moved even lower, to the brown curls, damp with her desire.

Her hips arched desperately at the first teasing touch of his tongue on her most sensitive flesh. His fingers danced over the hot flesh of her thigh and somehow found nerves she hadn't imagined existing. He drove her up ruthlessly and savored her cries as she twisted beneath him.

The ache grew and coiled and tightened until every muscle quivered. She reached for him desperately and tugged at his hair in a bid to make him stop. His mouth closed over a secret bundle of nerves and everything seemed to shatter at once, shocking ecstasy ripping through her body without course. She would have cried out, but she had no voice any longer. He had taken it along with everything else.

With a near violent curse, he rolled to his feet and tore off the rest of his clothes before grabbing protection from the nightstand. As he slid onto the bed beside her once more, he saw steam curling up from her damp flesh. The sight of it clawed at his insides. He had never seen anything that outrageously erotic before. He took her mouth with his for a ravenous kiss as his hands stroked over her body fiercely.

She caught her breath as desire roared to life once more and gave her no room to recover, no room to breathe. Her body throbbed wildly for release in mere moments as if he hadn't just thoroughly satisfied her already. "I'm going to get you for this!" It was almost a sob.

His laugh sounded rich and sultry. "I look forward to it, *cara*." He slid over her, caught her legs over his arms, and slowly began to ease his throbbing arousal inside her. She was wet, more than ready for him, but petite enough that he struggled for control before he hurt her. "*Cara*?"

"If you stop," she gasped, "I'll kill you!" Her arms curled around his shoulders, and her fingers dug into his back demandingly. How could anything ever hurt when he touched her? Maddened by his slow pace, she arched beneath him and drove him deep into her body. Her eyes flew wide with shock and then darkened with hunger.

It was more than he could take. He kissed her wildly as he began to thrust, his tongue mimicking the motion of his hips. He stole her soft cries with his mouth and savored the feel of her silken body. His teeth grit together as he fought for control. Only when she arched and cried out against his mouth did he let go and give in to the need riding him so hard. He buried himself to the hilt and stayed there as ecstasy shuddered through his body. He would *never* let her go.

As he collapsed against her, she buried her face against his neck. He smelled wonderfully sweaty and untamed, and he felt even better. Her whole body seemed to pulse softly as it acknowledged his claim over her. It felt a bit primitive and uncivilized, but so were they. "You Italians," she murmured huskily, "definitely embrace passion, don't you?"

He laughed softly as he slowly rose onto his elbows. "You are Italian as well, *cara*. It is a wonder we did not set the house on fire." He trailed his finger down her arm, thrilled by the tendrils of steam. "I did not expect that."

She opened one eye and closed it again. "And yet, I'm not shocked by it."

"Did I hurt you?"

Her eyes opened quickly. "How could you even think that?"

"I just wanted to be sure." He kissed her softly and lingered over her magic and pure water taste. "*Ti amo*, Gabrielle. I do not think I can live without you. The merger can go to hell as far as I am concerned." He searched her eyes. "Tell me," he urged softly.

Her lips curved into a trembling smile. "I love you."

"Then it will be fine. In the morning, we will call Alex and Isabelle and have them meet us at the Lucino home."

"In the morning?"

He smiled slowly. "I am not done with you yet, *cara*. I may never be."

"Oh." It was little more than a contented sigh. "I suppose I can handle that."

# CHAPTER FIVE

As the morning sun began to creep in, Brie was curled in Roberto's arms and sleeping contentedly. He stayed awake and softly smoothed his fingers through her hair and down her arm. He had given up on the hope of ever finding true love, and then she had walked into his life and turned it upside down.

He had never really resented the thought of marrying Isabelle. He loved her, after all, and had thought that perhaps being married might make them erase their brother-sister relationship and allow them to possibly fall in love. And, even if not, he had known they could at least be happy. He had been uncertain of whether or not they would ever be lovers, or have children, but he had accepted that as well in exchange for the merger both companies needed so badly.

But Brie . . . she was so different from Isabelle! They were alike only in appearance, and he was still fascinated at how he could want Brie so badly but only have passing admiration for Isabelle. His Gabrielle was wild, passionate, and sultry in not just her face and body, but in her heart and soul. His lips curved. She was more Italian than she thought.

From the moment he had seen her in the dining room of the Lucino home, he had known in his heart that this moment would be inevitable. He had never been the kind to deny his heart, and he was certainly unafraid to claim what he wanted—especially when she had wanted it just as badly. It had not been easy, but the rewards had been worth every agonizing moment.

She fit into his arms perfectly. Her soft breaths comforted him on a nearly cellular level. To imagine her not in his life was to imagine hell. Yet, he knew she would run away again if she thought that she had destroyed the merger. He did not worry about it himself. He felt confident in himself and in the Lucinos, Rafael in particular. They would make this work. Mergers happened all the time without business marriages. He admitted to some old-fashioned ideals, but that one he could happily abandon.

She stirred sleepily and tucked her face more firmly against his shoulder. "Are you awake?" she asked drowsily. "It's dawn. Go to sleep."

"It is a bit after dawn, Gabrielle." He bent his head to kiss her softly and tenderly coax her awake. "You look quite at home in my bed, *cara*. You will have to stay here more often."

"That's one heck of a commute to my job," she retorted dryly. She trailed her fingers over his face and traced his beloved features. "3$^{rd}$ District isn't exactly around the corner from this part of Brooklyn."

"Mmm. We will figure something out." He had every intention of marrying her, but he knew better than to speak of it just yet. He had her soft and warm in his arms, sleepy and content, and he wasn't about to stir up her temper. "Do you want a hot shower?" he asked. "We can take one before we get breakfast."

"Well, yes, but . . ." A smile began to curve her lips. "Roberto, I have nothing to wear. You tore the buttons off my shirt. And it wasn't even my shirt!"

He just smiled. "I will have Maria get you one of my mother's shirts. They should fit you well enough. She is only a little bigger than you are." He tossed aside the covers and openly admired her naked body. "If I could have you always naked, I would be a happy man." He trailed his fingers over her bellybutton. "Pierced?"

"Yup."

"I would like to see it sometime."

"You have a fetish for jewelry." Her lashes fluttered closed as his lips teasingly nibbled at her ear. She had never known she was

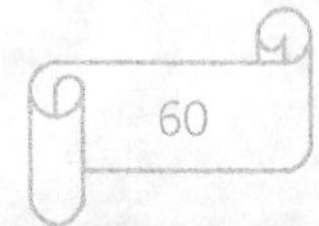

sensitive there.

"I have a fetish for you, *cara*. Up with you before I have my wicked way with you again."

She scooted out of bed quickly to go into the adjoined bath. Much to her bemusement, his inclination to not have his wicked way with her only applied to the bed. He took full and deliberate advantage of the close confines of the shower. By the time she stepped out again, she was clean, but her legs barely held her up. "Don't touch me, you fiend," she warned when he stepped closer. "I can barely walk!"

He just laughed and dropped a towel over her head. "I cannot resist you, Gabrielle." When no immediate retort came back, he lifted a brow. "You have stopped objecting to me calling you by your full name?"

"I sort of like it how you say it," she admitted. "And after last night, I don't really imagine you could get closer!"

The sound of the bedroom door opening was clearly heard in the bathroom. "Good morning, *Signor* Viani," Maria called cheerfully. "Good morning, *Signorina* Wisteria. I have brought some clothes from *Signora* Viani's closet for you, *signorina*. I will take yours to be, er, mended. There is a tray of food out here for you two. Please enjoy!"

Roberto chuckled as Brie's cheeks turned red. "She is happy that I have been thoroughly caught by a woman she likes," he offered. "She has known me many years. She chooses to retain the formality of titles, but that does not mean she ever hesitated to box my ears!"

"Did she do it often?" she asked dryly.

"I was an angel, *cara*."

"What's 'malarkey' in Italian?"

He laughed and tugged her into his arms for a fierce hug. "You suit me so well, Gabrielle. No other would do." He lifted her chin for a lingering kiss and then slowly released her. "We will eat breakfast and then I will call Alex. There are many things to do today."

In the 3<sup>rd</sup> District, Isabelle was the first to wake. She woke slightly disoriented as well for there was a heavy weight across her stomach and she couldn't move. When she turned her head and saw her lover, she began to smile. He was sprawled on his stomach with his arm thrown haphazardly across her waist as if to keep her from escaping. She had no intentions of anything like it.

Content, she admired him as he slept. There was a certain satisfaction in knowing she had worn him out. He had certainly worn her out as well. Her well-loved body still ached in places and reminded her of his thorough possession. If she had realized how wonderful claiming him would be, she wouldn't have wasted the last two years. The only unease she felt was only the very slightest of feelings in regards to her father's reaction. Still, Antonio was much his father's son; he would be thrilled at seeing her throw aside everything for love.

"Alex." She trailed her fingers down his arm and savored his strong muscles. He was incredibly strong and beautiful to her eyes. She had seen him shirtless before; it was hard to avoid when he liked to go swimming in the pool at the villa. She had also seen him working out with Tori, and unlike his partner, Alex stripped to the waist to do so. Even knowing all that, it was still entirely thrilling to have all that mouth-watering male landscape under her hands.

"Five minutes," he muttered into the pillow.

Enchanted with him all over again, she scooted closer until she was next to his ear. "Alexander," she said softly, nibbling at his ear, "it is morning and your lover is famished."

One brown eye opened and peered at her. "She ought to be after yesterday. There I was, all intent on being considerate because it was your first time, and every time I turned around, you were seducing me." He sighed deeply and tugged her ever closer. "I am a happy man."

With a laugh, she nipped at his ear. "Freedom, Alexander. Give it to me or I will have my wicked way with you again."

"Is that supposed to make me let go?" He lifted his arm and rolled onto his side with a smile. He propped himself up on his elbow and studied her contentedly. She was unbelievably beautiful. Giving and generous. And passionate. He had known she was capable of great depth, but she had still surprised him. She wanted him as thoroughly as he wanted her and reveled in their mutual emotions. "I am such a fool," he murmured. "To have wasted two years."

"I was thinking the same of myself." She slid out of bed and stretched languidly, sending sunshine rippling over her golden skin. "I believe I want a shower before food," she decided. She smiled over her shoulder, her blue eyes shielded by her thick lashes. "Do you suppose there is room for two in there?"

"I think we can try." He got out of bed and crossed the room to lift her into his arms. "Should we toss the sheets in the washing machine for Brie?" He carried her into the bathroom and set her delicately on her feet.

"Certainly, but I do not think she will be spending much time here." She laughed as she turned on the shower. "Roberto will not let her go, Alex. You can be sure of that. And I am glad for it," she added softly. "I want them both to be very happy. Meeting Brie was like finding a sister. And she needs *famiglia*."

The shower proved to be only barely big enough to hold them both. There wasn't room for fooling around, though much laughing was done as elbows bumped and hands slipped. As she briskly toweled her hair dry, she said warmly, "My shower is *much* bigger. You will have to sneak in sometime."

He reached out and combed his fingers through her hair. "I don't know how long this threat against you will last," he murmured, "but even if it should end tomorrow, I won't be going anywhere."

"You had better not." She gave him a lofty look. "I would hire kidnappers."

He laughed. "Or send Tori."

"True. He would get the job done quite efficiently."

They had only just finished breakfast when his cell phone began to ring. He snagged it from the counter and smiled wryly when he saw the number. He answered it with, "Are you sane this morning, Roberto, or should we be wary of your hot blooded temper?" He winked when Isabelle grinned at him.

"My temper is just fine." Roberto smiled as he said it. He was watching Brie get dressed, and the look on her face as she fought with the clasp on the back of the dress was adorable. "In fact, I do not think I have ever felt better. How about you?"

"Better than I've been in two years." He tugged Isabelle's hand to his lips and nibbled at the tips of her fingers. "I take it we're going to go back to the Lucino household to explain the goings-on."

"Naturally. I will bring Gabrielle if you bring Isabelle. I am sure Antonio and Rafael are very puzzled, and there is much we all need to discuss, in particular the merger." He tugged Brie closer and fastened the clasp for her. The slim gray silk suited her perfectly, though he rather thought she would prefer jeans. She was simply that type of person, and he loved her for it. "We will see you there."

She crossed her arms as he hung up the phone. "Are you sure?" she asked fretfully. "Not that I *want* you to marry Bella, but I don't want to see the companies struggle because of this."

"The merger will go through," he said confidently. He tipped up her chin and kissed her lingeringly. "Do not worry, *cara mia*. It will all work out." He tucked her under his arm protectively as they left the bedroom to go downstairs. "Do you drive?" he asked curiously as he helped her into the car.

"I have a license, but no vehicle. I usually ride my bike or a bus. Like I said, the commute will suck."

"I will drive you."

The tone was firm enough that she knew he wouldn't take no for an answer, and she had no desire to disagree anyway. With a wry sigh, she settled back in her seat. She wasn't entirely sure what the

future held yet. They were in love, and they were lovers. Logic said that someone really ought to mention cohabitation, but she hadn't been thinking logical all weekend. She was playing it by ear at that point.

She would have balked at walking into the Lucino villa, but his hand rested on the small of her back to prevent escape. It was with much relief that she saw Alex and Isabelle arriving in Alex's car. "Bella!" She ran to her friend and they clasped hands. "I'm sorry," she said dryly. "Maria is mending your shirt. Roberto ripped off the buttons!"

Isabelle laughed. "*Sì*, and you both look much happier for it!" She hugged her tightly. "I am so glad," she admitted softly, "that he found you, and you found him. *Sorella mia*." She kissed Brie's cheek softly. At the puzzled look, she smiled. "My sister. I see I must teach you the language of your birth."

"The language of my birth is American. But I might want to learn some things. Mostly so I can yell at Roberto." Brie grinned.

"Those are the easiest words to learn." Hands linked with her friend, Isabelle walked with Brie back over to where their men waited. "Shall we?"

Roberto gestured for them to go first, and they walked into the house before him and Alex. In the foyer, Rafael was leaning against a wall and waiting rather impatiently. Tori stood next to him. As the blond saw the girls enter, his brows went up. "Holy stigmatism, Batman. I'm seeing double."

Rafael walked over and bent slightly to peer into both faces. Curiously, now that they were next to each other, he could see easily which was which. It was something rather elemental, though he couldn't put his finger on it. There were minute differences as well, like Brie's hair being an inch shorter, and Isabelle's eyes being fractionally more olive shaped. "*Dio*," he said wryly as he straightened. "Bad enough there was one beauty, but now two. Your poor brother will never sleep."

"I'm not your sister," Brie pointed out.

"You are now, *cara*." He gestured toward Antonio's office. "Papa is waiting for us." He let the women go on ahead and lingered until they had entered the office. Then, as the males passed him, he murmured, "I suppose I need not ask what occurred over the last day. I will be happy for both of you, and my little sisters, once this mess is straightened out."

Inside the office, Antonio was staring a little blindly at the information before him. The grief staggered him. He had hoped, prayed, and wished with all his might, but he was far too late. All he had left was the beautiful daughter that Sophia had given the world. When he heard the door, he looked up. And despite his grief, he smiled. "Well, this will take much getting used to."

"Are you mad, Papa?" Isabelle asked hesitantly.

"No, Bella. I suppose I am relieved in some ways. You were long overdue for a good tantrum, and in doing so, you have brought home someone I have spent many long years looking for." Every pair of eyebrows lifted, and he sighed. "Please, sit down everyone." His experienced eye didn't miss the way Alex gently helped Isabelle into her seat or the way Roberto stood behind Brie's chair in a way more possessive than polite. He wholeheartedly approved of the entire thing.

"What do you mean you have been searching?" Roberto asked.

"First things first." He smiled at Brie. "Your name, *cara*?"

These people were sure casual with endearments, but she still preferred Roberto's way of saying it. "Gabrielle Wisteria. Most everyone calls me Brie."

"*Cara*, what was your mother's name?"

"Sophia."

"Maiden name?"

"I don't know. She never talked about her family." Her heart began to beat faster and her hands clenched together in her lap. "Why do you ask?" she managed to whisper.

"Twenty-two years ago," he said softly, "my little sister was disowned by our father for choosing to marry a man of 'questionable'

lineage. He was from the 3^rd District, and back then the stigma was much worse than it is today. Her name was Sophia Lucino. I kept watch on her from a distance for many years, but she somehow slipped out from under my radar. I have been looking for her, or you, ever since."

"Well." It was all Tori could think to say.

"So then Brie is our cousin?" Rafael asked softly. "No wonder she and Isabelle are identical! It is just another mystery that life likes to trip people with." He smiled at Brie. "You have got family in us now."

There was nothing she could say to that. She felt more than a little shell-shocked. She even jumped slightly when Roberto put a hand lightly on her shoulder. "Antonio," he said calmly, "Isabelle and I have called off our engagement. Our affections have turned elsewhere. I would ask that the merger continue solely on the basis of our companies' needs."

"Well, you know," Tori had to point out, "isn't Brie technically a Lucino as well? Marrying her would be the same as marrying Isabelle, right?"

"Hang on!" Brie said quickly. "I didn't agree to any of this!"

"Tori has a good point," Antonio told Roberto, ignoring her outburst. "Would you marry Gabrielle instead, Roberto, to cement the deal?"

"Of course."

Brie leapt to her feet sharply. "That's enough!" she shouted. "You can't just decide who I will and won't marry just because I might be part of this lunatic family!" She pointed at Antonio. "I'm not your sister! Don't think you'll dictate my life just because you're feeling guilty!" She whirled and smacked Roberto's hand aside when he would reach for her. "And you! *If* I marry you, it will be because you're on your knees asking, you got that?"

She whirled on her heel and stalked out of the office with enough force that the door slammed behind her. Isabelle hastily leapt to her feet and followed. All Rafael could say dryly was, "*Sì,*

Papa. She is a Lucino."

Brie was partway down the driveway when Isabelle caught up with her. "Don't talk to me," she warned.

Isabelle caught her arm and pulled her to a stop. "Brie." She was smiling as she turned her cousin to face her. "That was brilliant, *cara*!" She hugged her tightly. "I was so proud of you! It took me years to find my temper, and you found yours in minutes! You are a true Lucino after all."

The absurdity of the entire weekend caught up and Brie started laughing. She dropped her head on Isabelle's shoulder. "Oh god. I did not just say all that to your father and Roberto, did I?"

"You did, and it was *wonderful*." She sighed wistfully. "I wish I had done that when I was told they wanted me to marry Roberto. But then, perhaps we might not have met you." She laced their fingers together as they reached the sidewalk. "And I am very happy to have met you, Brie."

"I guess I'm happy I met you too, Bella." The sound of tires screeching reached her ears, and she looked down the street curiously. "I thought this was private property."

"It is." Isabelle began to get a bad feeling in her stomach. "We should go back in."

A long black limo skidded to a stop in front of them before they could get away. And though they backed up quickly, they were forced to stop as two men holding guns got out of the car. "Which one do we want?" one asked someone inside the car.

"Get them both." The voice sounded as careless as it did icy, and both cousins felt a chill run down their backs.

In the office, Alex walked over to Antonio's desk and held out a hand. "I want my contract back," he said calmly. "I'm quitting."

Antonio idly handed it over. "Yet, I presume, you will still defend Bella, no?"

"With my life." He tucked the contract into his back pocket. "But I can't have her for my wife as long as I work for her father. I should have quit before being her lover, but how was I to resist her after two years?"

"Around here," Tori said dryly, "I think they totally understand about passion, Alex." A piercing scream ripped through the air, and he leapt to his feet. "Son of a bitch! Alex!"

Alex was already rushing out of the office. Tori stayed right on his heels, and so did Roberto and Rafael. As one, they ran out of the villa and down the driveway. Brie and Isabelle were struggling with two men trying to shove them into the car. Two other men stood watching the tableau, and both held guns fitted with silencers.

"Let go of my sisters!" Rafael shouted as he lunged down the driveway.

One of the men turned and lifted his gun. Without hesitation, Tori threw himself in front of Rafael and knocked him to the ground. The bullet slammed into Tori's unprotected chest, and blood flew as he staggered back a step. His knees buckled and he fell to the asphalt. Blood began to pool under him.

"Tori!" Isabelle screamed, but there was nothing she could do. She and Brie were both shoved into the limo so hard that they sprawled across the seats painfully. The men got in behind them, and the one who had shot Tori put away his gun as if nothing had happened.

Rafael scrambled to where his bodyguard had fallen. "Tori! *Dio*!" He turned him over and blanched as he saw the gaping hole in his chest. But he was breathing still. It was faint and labored, but he was breathing. "Tori!"

Tori's lashes fluttered slightly. "You . . . okay?" His voice broke on a sharp lance of pain.

Alex ripped off his jacket and folded it up. "Press this to the wound," he told Rafael urgently. He looked at the villa where the servants and Antonio had gathered. "Call 911!" he ordered Marco. "Hurry!" He looked at Roberto and knew his face had to be just as pale, just as stricken. "Isabelle's necklace has a homing signal in it. We can find them."

"I'll drive."

As the two males rushed to where Roberto had parked, Rafael pressed the jacket harder against the wound, praying for it to stop bleeding. Tears welled in his blue eyes as he lowered his head. "Damn you, Tori. You can*not* die on me."

It was only minutes until the ambulance arrived, but it felt like hours. Paramedics rushed to take Rafael's place, and he was pushed back enough that he could not see what they did. "Is he going to live?" he demanded.

One paused, glanced at her colleagues, and then looked at him. "We will do our best. Does, er, he have family?"

"He is part of my family! I will go with you to the hospital." He moved closer once Tori had been put on a stretcher, and took Tori's hand in his. To lose Bella and Brie was bad enough, but to lose Tori as well would devastate him. Closing his eyes, he prayed in a way he had never prayed before.

# CHAPTER SIX

"Well, ladies." The voice was both cold and almost mocking. "How kind of you to join us. Please, have a seat."

Brie scrambled up to her knees and helped Isabelle up as well. They both edged back to sit on the nearest bench seat, hands tightly clasped as they tried to avoid being anywhere near the men with guns. It was all Isabelle could do to keep from lunging at the man who had shot Tori.

"I admit," the leader said, looking between them, "I was not expecting this. Which of you is Isabelle Lucino? The other may go free."

Brie squeezed Isabelle's hand tightly. Like *hell* she would abandon her cousin. Isabelle wanted to set Brie free, but she was more terrified to be alone. She clung to Brie's hand as a lifeline. They were in this together.

When it became clear that neither would answer, he settled back in his seat. His handsome face seemed to be carved in stone, and his black eyes looked unnervingly quiet. "The boss can decide what to do with you, then. Whichever of you isn't a Lucino is going to regret she kept her mouth shut." He reached over and cupped Isabelle's chin. "Maybe I will get to enjoy the imposter. You're both very beautiful."

The glass of water sitting on a sideboard suddenly seemed to explode and the water spewed into the air all over him. He jerked back hastily. "Very subtle of you, whichever of you did that."

"Where are we going?" Brie asked softly.

He looked up from wiping the water off his jacket. "It matters little to you. No one will be able to find you."

Isabelle softly touched the necklace she wore. It had been a gift from Alex for her twentieth birthday. She knew full well that it had been chipped just in case anything happened. It had been an amusement before. Now it was a salvation. Careful to mimic Brie's way of speaking, she asked, "Then why can't you tell us where we're going? If we're not going to be rescued . . ."

"Just shut up or we'll gag you both."

They shut up. The windows were tinted enough that looking out was just as hard as looking in. Two of the men sat against each door, completely eliminating the chance of jumping out when the limo stopped. It also didn't seem to stop often. Either they were on a freeway, or they were hitting every green light.

Eventually the limo rolled to a stop and the men got out. They dragged Brie and Isabelle out with them, and both blinked in the harsh sunlight after having been in the dim car for too long. They were nowhere that looked familiar. It was a nice villa of some kind sitting in the middle of its own acreage. It seemed vaguely reminiscent of the Lucino home, but a menace clung to this building.

There was no one around. Neither cousin said a word as they were escorted into the villa. Since neither resisted, the men let them walk under their own power. In the foyer, the leader said to the men, "Take them to a room upstairs and lock them in. I'll go talk to the boss."

The men did as they were told without question. They took the two women upstairs, shoved them into a ridiculously decadent bedroom, and then shut the door. The sound of the lock turning echoed loudly and eerily.

Brie ran over to the window, but it was shut and sealed as well. The window in the attached bathroom was far too small to climb out, especially from the second story. "This is just great," she muttered. "Just great!"

Isabelle sat on the side of the bed and crossed her arms around herself. She couldn't stop shivering. "What are we going to do, Brie?" Her voice broke and she buried her face in her hands. "They shot Tori. *Dio*, what if he dies? I could not bear it! He is part of the family."

Brie sat down next to her. "What the heck is going on, Bella? Why's there a death threat against you? What's up with the bodyguards and house arrest?"

"Two years ago, Papa and Rafael helped catch someone who was involved in a great deal of embezzlement. The man lost out on millions of dollars because of it. He found out that the Lucinos were involved and made some serious threats against us. The cops were not able to catch him, so he has been loose all this time. It was simply safer to hire bodyguards than to wait and hope the police caught the criminal. And he is nuts, Brie. They could give him an insanity defense and it would stick."

"What sort of insane are we talking?" Brie looked around the room as she spoke.

"Well, other than the part where he is trying to kill us, and the part where he set up a pyramid scheme that even Ponzi would shake his head at, he has been heard many times talking to himself. And I do not mean in a normal way. He would hold actual conversations with absolutely no one, and never pleasant ones."

"Great. So we've been kidnapped by a nutso. We have got to get out of here."

"How?"

"I say we knock a guard out and make a break for the door. We're dead either way, right? We can't expect them to simply put us here with three full meals and amenities while this guy nicely asks your dad for an apology." Brie looked at the door sharply as she heard footsteps and then glanced around. She spotted a heavy statuette and hefted it. She was completely playing by ear and praying that it worked. She swiftly darted over to the side of the door where she wouldn't be seen by anyone entering.

The door opened and one of the guards walked in. With much savage satisfaction, she recognized the bastard who had shot Tori.

She cracked the statuette over his head with all her strength. He dropped like a stone to the floor and did not move.

"I hope you killed him!" Isabelle said fiercely as she hurried to Brie's side. "We need to get out of here before the others come running!"

A peek into the hall showed it was clear. The foyer downstairs looked empty. Isabelle led the way toward the stairs and hurried down them, listening intently for any sign that someone had heard them and was coming after them. As Brie reached her side, she spotted movement. Instinctively, she shoved her friend into the hall beside them and removed her from sight.

"Well, well, well." The older gentleman who had spoken looked like an executive on his day off. He was cleaned up, well-shaven, and wore an air of authority. Casual khakis and a polo shirt seemed to indicate he might as well be heading to a golf game, but something not quite sane glimmered across his pale eyes. He crossed from the office doorway slowly toward Isabelle. "So you're Antonio's little bitch of a daughter."

"I do not think we have been introduced." She lifted her chin.

"How rude of me, dear. I am Martin Johns." He bowed mockingly. "I believe your father ruined my life."

"Interesting. I heard he helped to catch a thief and a liar. I would say he saved other lives, no?"

His face tightened with fury. "You're going to regret your sassy mouth, Miss Lucino. I intend to break you down until you're begging for your life." Something moved across his eyes. "It told me that you would escape, but I do not think so. My men would never betray me."

On pure gut hunch, Brie stepped forward from the hall to be directly beside Isabelle. As Martin paled, she asked, "How can you be sure you have the right girl? Do you know what Isabelle looks like? She does not have a twin, yet here I stand."

"No . . . no I told them specifically to go after Isabelle! They wouldn't have failed me!"

Isabelle smiled serenely as she laced her hand with Brie's. "And yet here there stand two of us. Which is which, Mr. Johns? Can you tell? Perhaps one of us is an illusion."

"How can you be sure you haven't been drugged, Mr. Johns?" Brie made her voice as gentle as she could. "Maybe we aren't even real. But then, I feel real. Do you feel real?" she asked Isabelle.

"Certainly I feel real. Maybe we are imagining *him*."

"What a silly thought! I would not imagine some like him."

"Oh, so true. What was I thinking?"

Their voices began to take on an identical cadence as they bantered back and forth. And though they wore different clothing, Martin began to lose the ability to distinguish between them. One of them was real. The other was illusion. But what if they were both real? That meant he had the wrong woman, and someone *else* would be after him.

"No, no!" He shook his head sharply as he backed up a step. "I'm just tired," he said fiercely, and it was hard to tell whom he tried to convince. "There's only one of you. You're trying to trick me."

"What trick?" both asked at the same time. The echoing voices sounded unearthly. "We are both real."

The other men suddenly rushed into the area with weapons drawn. "Mr. Johns! What's going on?" one demanded. "Why are they out of their room?"

"You see them? You see both of them?" Martin demanded.

"Well . . . yes sir." The man looked to where the women stood, and he was startled when he realized only one remained there. "Er. Uhm." He looked around quickly but there was no sign of the other female. "Wait."

The other men were just as puzzled for they only saw one woman as well. And yet, when Martin stared, he was sure he still saw two. One was smiling. The other waved. With a screech like nails on a chalkboard, he whirled on his men. "You!" he snapped out. "You did this to me! I knew you would betray me!"

The men, as one, began to edge back. All three faces began to reflect wariness as they saw just how far off the deep end their boss had started to dive. When Martin lunged for one of them, the man was forced to dodge quickly.

Isabelle and Brie carefully edged to the front door. It was locked. Brie, currently holding a watery mirror over herself to keep all but Martin from seeing her, glanced over to see him still attacking his men. Either they didn't want to hurt him or they weren't sure what to do, since all they did was try to stay out of his reach.

"How do we open the door?" Isabelle whispered.

"Do you trust me?"

"Of course!"

Brie wrapped her arms around her and concentrated fiercely. She had never attempted this before, but desperate times called for desperate measures. As her power rose, both began to dissolve. In moments they were nothing but a tendril of water. They flowed out through the open window over the door and then splashed onto the porch where they promptly turned back.

"Ouch!" Isabelle rubbed her sore hip. "The landing lacks something to be desired, Gabrielle."

"I'd never done it before, okay?" She scrambled to her feet and caught Isabelle's hand to tug her up. "Let's get out of Dodge!" Hands clasped, they ran down the sidewalk toward the curving driveway to the street.

Just as they reached the bottom, a familiar green car skidded to a stop. Even before it fully parked, Alex and Roberto leapt out. Isabelle forgot all thoughts of dignity and leapt into Alex's arms. "Alex!" she sobbed against his neck.

Roberto could barely breathe as Brie sprang into his arms. She wrapped her arms and legs around him like a vine, shaking so violently that it was a wonder her delicate bones weren't rattled. "Gabrielle. *Cara*." He buried his face in her hair. "You scared ten years off my life, *cara*."

"I've lost twenty!" Alex said shakily as he held Isabelle. He wanted to yell at her for even leaving the house, but she had merely gone after Brie. And naturally Brie wouldn't have known the danger.

The thought of what might have happened if Brie had been alone was as terrifying as what had nearly happened to her and Isabelle both.

"Tori." It was a broken sob against his neck. "Is Tori alive?"

"We don't know." He smoothed her hair back with trembling fingers. Fear made his stomach churn violently. "We came right after you two." He gently touched the necklace she wore. "You gave me hell, but you never took it off."

"I knew you would save me if it was ever needed."

Roberto somehow found a laugh. It was easier now that he had Brie warm and safe in his arms again. "Bella, the two of you saved yourselves. We are simply driving the getaway car. The cops are right behind us, so we can leave." He slowly put Brie on her feet and kissed her hard. "We will go to the hospital to see Tori. He is strong. He will be just fine."

Rafael and Antonio were sitting in the emergency waiting room when they arrived. Antonio looked like he had aged ten years in a matter of hours. Rafael was pale and terrified. When he saw his sisters running into the room, he leapt to his feet. *"Dio!"* He rushed forward and caught them both in his arms. "Bella. Brie. *Grazie a Dio.*" He kissed Isabelle's forehead and then Brie's. He could have loved his cousin no more if she had actually been his sister.

"Tori." Brie's voice shook as she clung onto him. "What about Tori?"

"He is in surgery." His voice broke but steadied again. "The paramedics think we were in time." He looked up sharply as he saw movement, and he held his sisters tighter as he saw the familiar form of a doctor in the doorway. He held his breath.

"You are the family of Tori Li?" At the nods, the doctor let out a soft breath. "Tori will be fine. He lost a lot of blood, and the bullet tore up his shoulder, but it missed his lungs. It missed everything vital. He'll need to stay in the hospital for at least two weeks, and he will need extensive care at home. He will also need physical therapy." He smiled suddenly. "But, knowing him, he'll be working out within months as if nothing had happened."

"You sound like you know him," Alex observed.

"I've known Tori for years. Now go home and rest. He will be in intensive care for a few hours, and he is sleeping. You may see him tomorrow."

"I will see him now." Rafael's tone booked no argument. "He took that bullet to save my life. He is my closest friend. Please."

The doctor stared at him for several moments before a tiny smile touched his lips. "Very well. Come with me, Mr. Lucino."

They left the room and Antonio got to his feet carefully. He felt every one of his fifty years in that moment. He made his way to his daughter and niece and pulled them both into his arms. "Never scare your poor papa like that again!" he said into Isabelle's hair. He kissed Brie's forehead. "And you, *cara*, are going to be kept under wraps with Bella until the threat has passed." He looked at Alex and Roberto. "The detectives called me while you were on your way here."

Roberto's stomach clenched. "They did not catch the man."

"They arrived moments after you left, but he had gone out the back. They want statements from the girls, but I told them they would have to wait until their family had been reassured." He looked at both Roberto and Alex evenly. "I believe you have things to discuss with my daughters."

"You have been adopted," Isabelle whispered to Brie. "You might as well accept it."

"Gabrielle," Roberto said softly, "I would like to talk to you."

She sniffed at him. With the danger past, her anger with him had returned. Never mind the fact that she really wouldn't have minded jumping on him again. Never mind the fact that when he had seen her, there had been so much emotion in his eyes that it had broken her heart. "I have nothing to say to you."

He sighed. "One day, *cara*, you will learn not to push me." He caught her around the waist and tossed her over his shoulder to carry her out.

"A match made in heaven," Isabelle murmured. She smiled at Alex. "Well, I suppose you have reason to stay on as my bodyguard now."

"I quit, Bella."

"You . . ." Her eyes widened. "You *what*?" She was so astonished that she did not notice her smiling father sneak away to give them privacy. "You quit? *Dio*, Alex! But why?" Her lower lip trembled. "Was this . . . was this incident too much?"

"No." He pulled her into his arms and kissed her tenderly, letting his emotions well in the embrace until she went limp in his arms. Only then did he lift his head. "I love you, Bella. I quit so that I could ask you to be my wife. I can't marry my boss' daughter, after all." He cupped her cheek. "Say yes."

Tears welled in her eyes as she wound her arms around his neck. "*Sì*. Yes. Any way you say it, my answer is yes. *Ti amo*, Alex. Always." Happier than she had ever been in her life, she pressed her face to his shoulder. She should have run away and met Brie sooner. Everything had worked out in the end.

Brie was not nearly in such a good mood. She crossed her arms sullenly, eyes narrowed, as she was carried out over Roberto's shoulder past many giggling nurses and several startled, yet amused, people in the emergency room. "Roberto, I think Mr. Johns wasn't the only who had lost his mind. You need help. You're certifiable. You can't keep running off with me like this!"

"As a matter of fact, Gabrielle, I can. I am much stronger than you are. And do not dare to turn into water to get away. I will find a sponge and absorb you up again."

"I wasn't thinking of it," she muttered. When she was finally put on her feet in the parking lot, she edged away from him a step. "I'm not going anywhere with you. Hear me? I'm not even going to talk to you!"

"You do not have to talk. But you will get in the car or I will put you there."

She made a little sound of frustration and got into the car. He just smiled and went around to the driver's side. He could see many long, happy years fighting with her in his future, and he could not wait. He would have been bored with Isabelle; he knew that now. Fiery as she had revealed herself to be, she was tame compared to her cousin.

Brie remained stubbornly quiet and watched the roads curiously. She had no idea where he was taking her, yet she found herself unsurprised when she recognized that they returned to his home. As the car stopped, she said fiercely, "If you think I'll let you touch me when I'm this pissed off, you have another think coming!"

"You are not talking to me, Gabrielle. Remember? Just come with me. You may be mad at me later if you so wish. For now, I have something I wish to show you." He opened her car door and held out a hand. Triumph flared as she slowly put her hand in his. He should have done this that morning when he had awakened to find her warm and beautiful and perfect in his arms.

To her surprise, he did not take her into the house. He instead led her around the side and to the backgrounds where an extensive garden resided. Statuaries lined stone walkways, and trellises dripped with brilliant flowers. A particularly stunning fountain made her fingers itch for pencil and paper. She knew she could spend hours in these amazing gardens and never be bored. "Wow."

"My grandfather's father built this," he admitted, "when he was younger than I. He met his wife while he was in the middle of building the house." He drew her into a gazebo made of warm toned stone that reflected across her ashy hair and golden skin and made her beauty magically deepen. "He brought her here and turned her to look at the shell of the home he was making. And he told her 'if you will be mine, I will share this with you.'"

"Very sweet," she managed to say, her heart tripping madly. "May I leave now?"

"Every generation since," he went on without pause, "the one who would inherit has brought the one they love to this very spot to make that same promise." He brought her chilled fingers to his lips and then went down on one knee. "*Ti amo*, Gabrielle. Be mine. Be my wife."

"I'm not human," she whispered.

"I do not care. I do not care about the merger either." When her eyes widened, he brought her fingers to his lips and breathed softly on them to warm them. "If Antonio had said that he would not accept a merger without my marriage to Isabelle, I would have walked out. Your Lucino blood is irrelevant. You are my choice, *cara*. You were my choice from the moment I saw you. Be mine."

She looked at him and then at the garden around them. It seemed to speak of promises. Of wishes she had never dared speak aloud. A home. A family. Someone to love her. She looked down into his lavender eyes and saw everything she had ever wanted. "Yes," she said softly. "A million times yes."

"Promise?"

She rolled her eyes. "No, I'm lying."

"Too late." His grin spread. "I have witnesses."

She looked over his head at the villa where many faces were pressed against the windows. She wanted to be embarrassed, she really did, but she found herself laughing instead. She tugged him up to his feet and wound her arms around his neck. "What did your great-grandfather do when his lover said yes?"

"He kissed her."

"Well?" She arched a brow. "I'm waiting."

His rich laugh was still echoing in the garden as he kissed her with all the love in his heart.

# CHAPTER SEVEN

*"Both Isabelle Lucino and Gabrielle Wisteria are reported to be fine and well. Tori Li, who was shot in the defense of Rafael Lucino, is listed in stable condition and expected to make a full recovery. Anyone with knowledge of the whereabouts of Martin Johns is encouraged to contact the police. A reward has been posted for tips leading to a successful arrest."*

Rhianna Taber lifted the remote control and turned off the rest of the news report. She knew everything that had been said and would be said. As co-owner of Enforcers, she had contacts in all places, including the news and police. If it affected a member of 3rd District, she was notified first.

Her partner was sitting on the side of her desk. They had been watching the news together, and Eric Mason's handsome face now looked very grim. "How much control do we have this time, Rhi?"

"Not as much as I want," she admitted. "Tori should never have been wounded, but we can as yet turn it to our advantage and get a happy ending for the entire Lucino family." She picked up the contract the two cousins had signed and watched the word 'Complete' appear. She added her notes to the bottom and then slipped the contract into a folder. It also signed as being completed, and she slipped it into a drawer labeled 'Lucino.'

"You moved very quickly to have Gwyn get them under contract," he noted softly. "Did you know this would happen?"

"No. And that's the entire reason I was worried. When I can't see the outcome," her hands clenched together for a moment, "then

I know that evil is on the move." And whenever she felt it, her guilt knew no bounds.

Her partner said nothing for several moments. Then, softly, he asked, "So what do we do next?"

"What else?" She smiled wryly. "We play it by ear."

*Status: File Begun*
*Analysis: Be she princess or pauper, every woman is richer when she is loved.*

Folder Two
RAFAEL

# CHAPTER EIGHT

The hospital room was quiet. Machines beeped steadily. Rafael had been sitting by Tori's side for the last hour or two. It had been almost a week since the incident. In that time, Rafael had spent more time at the hospital than at home. He simply couldn't bear to leave his friend's side. Tori had been nearly *killed*.

The door opened, and the doctor walked in. "Rafael," he said kindly, "go get some coffee. You look like you haven't been sleeping."

"Seeing someone be shot in my defense will do that to someone," Rafael shot back softly. He still got to his feet. "I can take a hint. I will come back shortly."

When the door shut had behind him, the doctor walked over to look down at Tori. "You, young lady," he said quietly, "are damned lucky that someone didn't try to remove your shirt to get to your wound at the scene."

Tori opened her eyes and stared up at the ceiling. It was about all she had the strength for, though she grew stronger with every day. She would be going home tomorrow. Her blood levels had been brought back to normal, and she could actually get out of bed for short bursts. "I know," she sighed quietly.

He sat down beside her and began to check her pulse. "When I first saw you, I was rather surprised," he admitted. "But I went along with things. I've never corrected anyone's assumptions, as you asked. Do you suppose you ought to tell me precisely why you've chosen this sort of life?"

A tiny, self-mocking, smile tugged at her lips. "No one wanted me around when I was a girl."

*(Nine years ago)*
The girls were whispering again. Tori kept her chin up as she walked down the hall. Her books were clutched to her chest, and she kept her eyes fixed straight ahead. At sixteen, she was too tall, too gangly, and too late for puberty. She stood eight inches over five feet tall, her legs and arms were thin, and she had absolutely no figure. In a school full of teenage girls becoming young women, she had a triple whammy.

As she tried to open her locker, her fingers slid off the lock. She looked in disgust at the greasy hair gel that had been smeared over her locker and now her fingers. Didn't they ever think of anything new?

"Having trouble there, Victoria?" one girl asked snidely as she walked past. "Since you never do anything with that mop you call hair, maybe the gel will be useful!"

Tori ignored the sound of the entire hall laughing. She wiped her fingers on her jeans and opened her locker to switch her books. Her reflection in the built-in mirror on her door sneered at her. Her hair was shorter than half the boys in the school, and her face hovered in a strange middle ground between feminine and masculine. Androgyny wouldn't be that bad if she *felt* androgynous. She just felt too much like a girl to be comfortable with what nature had chosen for her.

"Don't you have gym with her?" a girl said in a loud whisper as she went past.

Her companion laughed rudely. "Yeah, but she should be in the boys' locker room. She has no boobs at all. She doesn't even wear a bra to phys ed!"

People in the hall started laughing again. Tori slammed her locker door and slung her backpack over her shoulder. "If wearing a bra means cutting off the circulation to my brain and making me as stupid as you, then I'll be glad to go without one," she retorted.

"You want to say that again?" The girl went on her toes in an effort to get into Tori's face. "You think you're so tough?"

"Dude." The other girl with her tugged on her arm. "Dude, that's a really bad idea."

"Oh yeah? What's she going to do? She's nothing but a flat-chested beanpole whose mother dumped her in the garbage."

Tori's fist cracked across her jaw so hard that she was knocked flat on her ass. She began to sob with more drama than sincerity, and people rushed to her side with coos of sympathy. Not one spared Tori a single look even though she had been the one provoked. Arms crossed, she went directly to the main office. "I hit Paula Crothers. You might want to suspend me."

Astonished, the secretary stared at her. "Pardon?"

"Suspend me." She sat down in a chair. "I'd welcome it."

By the time her foster parents arrived to pick her up, the principal had decided to not only suspend her, but also recommend that she switch schools entirely. This event was the latest in a long line of them, and the principal didn't feel right punishing her when she was the one being tormented. He just couldn't seem to make anything change at the school for her; the bullies' parents were honestly no better in many ways.

Tori said nothing as the car rolled down the freeway. Her foster parents weren't really quite sure what to say. She was a very giving, very loving person. She had an infectious sense of humor, a sharp wit, and a brilliant mind. She was also an exceptionally talented martial artist with two black belts and several trophies to her record. At sixteen, she was only just starting to shine.

But for her two high school years and prior two junior high years, she had never once come home from school smiling. She talked little about the things that happened, but teachers were more than happy to fill in the details. Today was just another day for Tori.

"I just don't understand," her mother said softly. "How can the entire school dislike you? In our years of fostering, you're by far the most amazing girl we've ever known."

"It's not the entire school." Tori rested her elbow against the car door, her eyes watching billboards rush past. "Just the girls. I get along with the boys just fine. I'm not feminine enough for the girls to want to be seen with me. On the other hand, the boys feel comfortable with me because they don't have to worry about their hormones. I'm just one of the guys. And that's another reason the girls hate me. The hot guys hang out with me."

"You're a late bloomer, Victoria," her father promised softly. "You'll be beautiful one day soon. In the meantime, we should consider home study. Take off the peer pressure a little. Your mind is too good to be wasted."

"Yeah. Whatever. As long as I don't go back to that hellhole, I don't really care."

*(Present)*

Doctor Singh studied Tori for long moments. "When did you decide to start disguising yourself as a boy?"

"When I graduated high school. I moved to NYC to go to college and decided to forestall any issues with my peers. I decided to let them figure out what they thought I was, and since everyone assumed I was male, I let them. It stung, but at least I could survive, and I could make friends. I never lie about it, and I tell the truth if someone thinks to ask, but for all intents and purposes, Tori Li is a man as far as the world is concerned." She took a long breath. She felt weak and tired again. Just talking wore her out quickly, and it was becoming more and more vexing. "It solved all my problems. Girls aren't offended by me and guys still feel comfortable."

"Yet, somewhere inside, *Victoria* is hiding and wishing she could be free," Doctor Singh murmured.

"I keep her as quiet as I can. Saves my sanity."

The door opened suddenly, and Rafael walked in. A smile lit his face as he saw that she was awake. "Tori." He walked to her side and leaned over the rail to take her hand in his. "You are awake. How do you feel?"

"Tired. Bored."

Doctor Singh chuckled. "The second is a good sign." He got to his feet. "I will leave you two. Do not stay too long, Rafael. Tori needs his sleep."

Rafael kept a firm grip on Tori's hand while he tugged the chair closer. As the door shut, he said teasingly, "As if he thinks that I do not spend time here even when you are sleeping." He searched Tori's face, hating the pallor to his skin and the still dull color of his eyes. "Tell me honestly, Tori. How are you feeling?"

She found a smile for him. "I'm fine, Rafe. I will be fine. I just learned the hard way that I'm not bulletproof. I mean, I always knew I might someday have to make that decision to step in front of someone, so I'm not resenting my job, if that's what you're thinking. I really didn't even think about what I was doing, to be honest. It was pure instinct. I saw the gun aimed at you and . . ."

"And scared me to death," he finished in a low voice. "*Dio*, Tori. If you had died, it would have destroyed me. You may have come into my life as my bodyguard, but you know you are my best friend. Should all the trouble end tomorrow, I would still insist on you being in my life. No one knows me as well as you do."

Something painful that had nothing to do with her injury ripped at her heart. She had become a victim of her own circumstances. For two years, she had been desperately, maddeningly, trying to keep her emotions for her friend under wraps. From the moment she had walked into Antonio's office, she had been ridiculously attracted to Rafael. Over two years those flames had been fanned into something much more elemental and much more dangerous.

The real reason she had thrown herself over him had nothing to do with her contract. She could have been Isabelle's bodyguard and would have done the same thing. She had been in love with Rafael for almost these entire last two years. She would never stop loving him, but he not only thought her a male, but he loved her only as a friend. She genuinely did not think revealing her gender would make any difference in that.

Oh, she knew he wouldn't be mad over it. He and his family were humorously easy-going in some ways. They would realize they had made the mistake by not asking—and, in fact, Antonio *did* know—and they would accept her reasons and all would move on. She just feared losing her closeness with Rafael if he knew, so she kept quiet still. It would be her secret to her grave, whenever that happened. "It's funny," she said softly. "I never really had a close friend."

Rafael looked up in surprise. Tori very rarely ever talked about himself. He had briefly mentioned being in foster homes, and that he had been home schooled, but he had never said more than that. For all his outgoing, personable charm, he was frustratingly secretive. "You have *never* had one? I find that hard to believe, Tori."

"Believe it." She sighed deeply, her lashes drooping. "Sorry."

"No, it is fine." He smiled. "Sleep, Tori. I will be here to protect you."

A little smile touched her lips. "And who is the bodyguard, huh?"

That was his Tori. Rafael kept Tori's hand in his as he watched him slip asleep again. Only when he was sure that Tori was asleep did he bring his hand to his lips and press a kiss to his palm. He had a *big* problem. He had fallen in love with someone he suspected he might never be able to have. How did a supposedly heterosexual man tell his male best friend that he wanted him more than air?

He had honestly wanted Tori from the beginning, and his instant response to him had made him doubt his eyes saying Tori was male. Yet Tori had not corrected anyone, so Rafael had been left to assume Tori's fascinating blend of feminine to masculine had been enough to interest him anyway. After they had begun spending great deals of time together, Rafael had stopped caring entirely what gender his bodyguard may or may not be. Whenever Tori shot him one of those laughing, teasing grins, Rafael was forced to choke a desire to kiss those smiling lips.

He *burned*. Every day made his desire for Tori grow worse. And now . . . now, with Tori wounded, he had been forced to confront his deepest feelings. He was in love with his bodyguard. But, how could he *not* love Tori? His soul burned so brightly that it lit the area around him. In some light, he looked like a particularly attractive man. In other light, he looked like a particularly attractive woman. It was an enchanting sort of magic that Rafael had watched for two years and still didn't understand.

It was unrequited. He accepted that. Tori might never love him the way he loved Tori. But he would be Tori's friend. He would give Tori the family he had always seemed so hungry for. In a way, he almost hoped the man threatening the family would not be caught for a while yet. He wanted Tori close. The question remained, however, how long he would be able to resist the urge to kiss those ridiculously sexy lips that his bodyguard had. That, more than anything, would drive Tori away, and he could not bear even the idea of it happening.

Tori was released from the hospital the following afternoon. She was more than happy to see the last of her room. She was tired of being in bed, tired of constantly being poked and prodded by nurses, and tired of really crappy meals.

Getting dressed proved to be an interesting exercise, but she adamantly refused to wear that stupid hospital gown any longer. Since she could not use her left arm at the moment because it was excruciatingly painful *and* in a sling to put a straightjacket to shame, she was forced to yank on her jeans one handed. Her shirt proved even trickier, and she was scowling at it when a nurse came around the curtain.

"Oh for god's sake, Tori!" The nurse was more exasperated than surprised. "Let me help before you ruin all our hard work!"

She sighed and stopped wrestling with the shirt. She let her arm be limp so that the shirt could be worked over it. Even still, her wound throbbed in annoyance as her arm was put back in its sling. She grimaced and ignored it. She wasn't taking pain pills anymore. She absolutely wanted to get herself back into fighting form as soon as she could. Rafael was still in danger.

"You know," the nurse said casually, "you say you're not beautiful as a woman, but we were all talking about how lovely we think you are."

"You're kind, but you're also lying." She plucked at her shirt with her good hand. "I'm not wearing a bra, and you can't even tell that I'm a woman. I *might* be an AAA cup size, but really, why bother counting that?"

"Being a woman isn't all about your breasts, you know. It's something inside. Something deeper. Something you feel that comes into the air around you. You've probably been driving several men nuts because they're attracted to you but their eyes say you're a male." She smiled when she got a distinctly skeptical look. "Have you tried to be a woman on purpose, Tori? You might be surprised."

"Ha."

"Let's try this." She knelt to help Tori wiggle into her sneakers. "What would it take to change your mind?"

"Hmm. A bust size that can't be hidden by decent cotton and a guy who wants me regardless."

She arched a brow slowly and then hid a smile. She and every other nurse and doctor in the hospital felt nearly entirely certain that Rafael Lucino had a *very* personal emotional investment in his bodyguard. His reaction to Tori's injury and subsequent weakness had crossed the line from a good friend into the realm normally reserved for lovers. "You're just a late bloomer," she contented herself with saying.

"I'm twenty-five!" Tori snorted rudely. "If I haven't bloomed by now, I never will."

Another nurse called, "Are you ready to go?"

"Yes! Get me out of here before I climb the walls one-handed

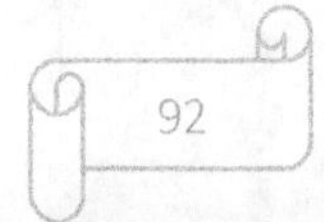

like Spiderman!"

Laughing, the nurse pulled back the curtain to reveal she had brought a wheelchair. She and the first nurse very carefully helped Tori sit down in the chair and firmly covered her with a blanket to combat the chill outside. "Stop pouting," she ordered. "You know the deal was that you could get out of jail early, but only if you were wheeled and not walking."

"Hrmph."

Tori's sour mood lasted until she was wheeled out of the hospital. The sight of Rafael standing next to his car waiting for her lifted her spirits as nothing else could. Just seeing him alive and healthy made every pain, every weakness, worth it.

He slowly smiled when he saw her, and it sent her heart into riotous pounding. He had the most lethal smile she had ever countered, and it constantly served to remind her that as much as puberty had skipped her physically, it had *not* skipped her hormonally. "Get me out of here," she told him dryly to cover her reaction. "They're threatening to tie me to the bed!"

"Well, do not think you will be doing anything except resting at home, either." He walked over and lifted Tori with casual ease out of the wheelchair. When Tori clutched his shoulders, he belatedly realized what he had just done. For a moment, he had entirely forgotten Tori was a male, and a strong one with it. "I am sorry. I did not think."

Knowing damned well she would be breathless if she tried to talk, she managed to simply smile and roll her eyes. It worked. He grinned and put her gingerly into the car. As soon as the door shut, she blew out a hard breath. She was only five inches shorter than he, and she weighed much more than she looked. He had still handled her as if she was Isabelle or Brie's size.

He got into the driver's side and shook his head. "If I offended you, I am sorry, Tori. I did not think for some reason. I did not want you to tire yourself out." He grinned quickly. "If you wish to get back at me when you are strong again, you may hit me if you are inclined."

She slid a glance at him. "It's my left arm injured. I could hit you with my right hand. But since I guess you saved me some strength, I can let you get by."

He laughed. "It has been so lonely without you at home! I have no one to talk to. Brie is living with Roberto, and Isabelle and Alex spend their time together. Even when we all have dinner together, it feels as if there is something missing. You are not there to tease me, or to talk with after dinner. I have not slept this week, Tori. I did not have you to talk with until I was tired."

His problems with insomnia were known only to her, and she only knew because she had caught him awake one night. Most nights since, they had stayed up together, talking or playing billiards, until they both felt tired enough to sleep.

She frowned. "You need to rest, Rafe. I can't protect you well enough if you are sick. Not right now." She put a hand on his arm. "I nearly gave my life for yours. You can't be wasting that, got it? Else I really will hit you!"

He smiled and covered her hand with his for a moment. "With you home, I will be fine. I will simply have to take care of you."

She laughed. "There you go again! Just who is being paid anyway?" She scowled suddenly. "And Antonio had better not still be talking about giving me that bonus!"

His brows lifted. "You heard that? I thought you were asleep."

"I was half in, half out. You Lucinos are loud." She rolled her eyes.

"*Sì*, but we are fun and we look after *famiglia*. You are family."

She couldn't argue that point. Just glad to be out of the hospital, she closed her eyes and settled in for a light nap. It was easy to let down her guard around Rafael. He made her feel loved, even if just a little.

Rafael glanced at Tori from the corner of his eye and then gently brushed the back of his knuckles down Tori's cheek. Tori muttered something wordless and grumpy, and it made his heart ache with tenderness. He loved him so.

A few minutes later, they pulled into the driveway of the Lucino villa. He smiled as he saw the crowd on the porch. "Tori."

She opened her eyes and yawned. "Are we there?" Her words stopped as she saw what waited for her. Her eyes slowly widened. "Wha?"

Every last member of the Lucino household, including the servants, stood on the porch of the villa. Alex and Roberto were helping Antonio hold up a giant sign that said 'Welcome home!'. Isabelle and Brie held flowers. The servants all had balloons or streamers.

Rafael parked the car with a smile. "You were missed."

"I see that!" She waited for him to come help her and let him support her weight as she carefully walked toward the entrance. She could walk on her own, but it would take all her strength. She felt no shame in letting Rafael support her as long as he didn't carry her again. It really was not her style, and it was sexier than she could handle.

"Tori!" The identical cousins rushed down the walkway toward her. "You're home!"

"Hey, no grabbing!" She grinned. "Unless you want to see me cry. My shoulder is killing me." With her free hand, she tugged on Isabelle's braid and then ruffled Brie's hair. The half-elf had cropped her hair to a point just below her shoulders to help tell her and her cousin apart more. "Nice look, Brie. How much fuss did Roberto give you?"

"Just a little, but he warmed up quickly." Brie smiled. "It's not the same without you here."

"Geez." It was all she could say.

When they reached Antonio, the older man let out a long breath. "*Grazie*, Tori. You do not know how much what you did means to me. That being said, do not ever scare us like that again. You are *famiglia*."

Under her breath, she muttered at Alex, "As if I wouldn't do it again. Is he nuts?"

Alex smiled wryly, understanding perfectly. "Can you manage the stairs?" he asked. "Or do you need someone to carry you?" When he was shot a scathing look, he held up his hands with a grin. "You can't kick my ass yet, so you'll just have to suffer if we decide to carry you against your wishes. You don't weigh that much, kid."

She just sighed and then laughed. No matter how much they teased her, no matter how embarrassing it was to be dependent on others, it was still good to be home.

# CHAPTER NINE

In slightly less than a month, Tori started using her left arm again. If it hurt, she grit her back teeth and ignored it. The mark had faded into a pink scar that felt tender, but it was not in danger of being reopened. As far as she was concerned, that meant she could start working on getting strength back. She started small and began to move her way upward. Alex, unable to stop her, finally sighed, threw his hands in the air, and agreed to help.

Going on two months after the incident, however, Tori had an entirely different problem on her hands. Because of the shock to her system, she had missed two periods in a row. She didn't complain over that, frankly, because it had always annoyed her to endure the annoyance of having a uterus without having any real need for it to be there. Two months in, her body went back to normal . . . and then some.

She didn't even notice at first until she went to get dressed one morning. She pulled on her shirt, tried to button it, and discovered that it didn't fit. Puzzled, she tugged at the edges of the shirt, but they wouldn't come together. She walked over to look in the mirror, turned to see her profile . . . and got the shock of her life.

She had breasts. They weren't *Playboy* material by any imagination, but her bust had to have increased at least two sizes. *She looked like a woman.*

She jerked on a t-shirt hastily and let out a quick breath as she saw that the folds still hid her chest. She would need to buy a sports bra or two, just to flatten the slight curves so she could skate by without awkward questions. What the hell was going on?

After locking the door so no one could walk in, she grabbed her cell phone and called the hospital. Doctor Singh had given her his direct line in case there was a problem because he knew full well she would not follow his orders. So, when he answered, she said bluntly, "My breasts grew. What did you do to me during surgery?"

There was a startled silence. Finally he said, laughter in his voice, "You have to be the only woman I can think of who would complain. Tori, we did nothing to you."

"Then what's going on? You told me that missing my period was perfectly normal after the severe shock to my system, but you didn't mention that this might happen! I'd swear I've grown two sizes or so. I'm probably an A or something. I'm too afraid to get a tape measure to find out."

"Hmm." He fell silent for several moments as he thought about things. "We had said you were a late bloomer," he said slowly after a minute, "but it could be possible that it was more literal than we thought. Physical and emotional trauma has been proven to be *extremely* hard on a mind and body alike. The shock of being shot might have, well, kick-started a process you were, for whatever reason, stunted from starting earlier. Remember, many women enter their final growth spurt roughly around your age."

She said nothing. Then, softly, she asked, "Would a physical and emotional shock from when I was newly born have been enough to 'stunt my growth' as you put it?"

"That is very likely," he agreed. "In fact, it is probably precisely what could have done it. As a newborn, you are developing and growing every second. It would not have taken much. Did you suffer a trauma, Tori?"

"Yeah." Her eyes closed. "My birth mother threw me in a garbage can."

The silence on the other end of the line was shocked and appalled. "Dear god, Tori," he finally managed to say. "Dear god, I am so sorry. How did you survive?"

"The garbage pickup came by within minutes, I guess. My foster mother told me that the guy who found me saved my life because he wrapped me up in his jacket and rushed me to a hospital." She found a smile suddenly. "I actually got to meet him when I was ten. He cried when he saw me, when I thanked him for saving me."

"I see." And, indeed, he did. It seemed to explain a lot about her personality and hard choices. "Well, I suggest, at this point, that you keep track of changes you notice to your body. If anything happens that is not normal, call me immediately."

"And going through puberty at twenty-five is *normal* to begin with?"

He laughed. "For you, Tori? It would seem so."

She hung up the phone with a huff of annoyance. On one hand, she was sort of tickled at the idea of finally having a figure. On the other hand, she was ready to beat her head against a wall. Why *now*? If she got too much of a figure, then she would have to get really creative to hide it. Her excuse for being allergic to chlorine so she could avoid going swimming only covered so much ground. Things couldn't possibly get worse.

Downstairs, Rafael sat in Antonio's office. He had been arbitrarily summoned by his father almost as soon as breakfast had been over. He was also fairly sure he knew what he was about to hear. The nudges and prods had been going on for five, almost six, years. Over the last two years, they had gotten less subtle, particularly when Antonio had noticed he had stopped dating.

He had no idea how he was supposed to explain things to his father. What was he supposed to say? That the person he loved and wished to marry could not have his children? That the family bloodline would continue only through Isabelle and Brie, but not with the Lucino name?

He didn't question that his father wanted him to be happy. Antonio would stand behind him completely. The rest of the family beyond this branch, including the head of the family in Italy, might not be nearly so accepting or understanding, however.

"Rafael," Antonio suddenly spoke up, "you are causing your papa a great deal of worry. I have not seen you go out with anyone since the trouble started two years ago. Are you so worried of bringing danger to a girlfriend or lover?"

Unsure whether or not he was glad Antonio hadn't guessed the real issue, he hedged, "You must admit, Papa, that in light of recent events, it would certainly be a better idea for me to be discreet."

"You can be discreet without being unhappy." Rafael stared at him, and he arched a brow. "You think I do not know my *bambini*? You are unhappy, Rafe. I do not like it. It has been especially bad since Tori was shot. You are guilty needlessly, and Tori would be the first to say so. His job is to protect you, and it was understood to be a risky task. He has survived and is nearly as good as new. Your guilt will only upset him."

Rafael just sighed. "*Sì*, Papa."

"Now, just so I can tell your *nonno* that you are looking to provide me with an heir, would you please go on a date with one of those nice young women you are always ignoring at work? Any one of them might be true love in disguise, Rafe."

"I suppose I will never hear the end of it if I do not."

"We have the gala opening for a client tomorrow night," Antonio urged. "Ask Theresa to go with you. She is lovely, and friendly. The entire family likes her a great deal, and she would fit in so beautifully with us. You may just not have noticed it yourself."

Rafael had in fact noticed such a thing, but not in a romantic sense. Meeting Theresa had been like meeting a lost sister. Certainly she was very lovely, and possessed a delightful humor, but he had never once been attracted to her. She would make someone very happy as their partner, just not him. Still, he wanted to keep peace in the house. And . . . who knew? Maybe going out with an eligible female might cure him of his obsession with Tori.

And pigs would fly.

"Very well, Papa," he sighed. "I will call Theresa. If you will excuse me?" When Antonio waved him off, he left the office as quickly as he could. Before he could convince himself not to, he went to the nearest phone and flipped through the contacts in the book beside it. Theresa was in charge of the publications desk at the main office, and her phone number was one of the first listed in their contact book. If they needed to pull an old job for reference, she was the one they called. It was Monday; she would be there.

The phone rang once before it picked up. "Just In Time, Publications Desk. This is Theresa."

"*Ciao*, Theresa." He found himself grinning. She always sounded so prim on the phone that he couldn't believe she was his age. "It is Rafael. How are you?"

"Busy." A smile filled her voice. "My bosses are always throwing things at me."

"That is because you are a fine catcher. I, in fact, have another thing to throw at you. I would appear to need a date." At the silence, he could all but imagine her staring at her phone as if it had grown legs. "There is no pressure, Theresa," he said gently. "It is mostly business, a little pleasure. I enjoy spending time with you."

"I'm sorry, you must have dialed the wrong number. You have me mistaken for the busty blonde in the legal department."

He laughed. "You know I do not. Please?"

"I can't believe I'm agreeing to this, but sure. It's not a date, right?"

"We will have to see, won't we? I will pick you up at six." He hung up on her sputter, still smiling. As he stood there contemplating what he had done, his smile began to fade. It felt, a little, as if he was cheating on Tori, but that was ridiculous. Tori, above any, would want him to be happy and find someone special. Never mind that *Tori* was his someone special.

Needing to see him, and to vent, he quickly headed for the gym located in the basement. He knew damned well that Tori would be there pushing himself much harder than he should be for someone who had been shot two months prior.

Tori was lifting weights cautiously with her left arm when she heard steps on the stairs. She hastily put down the dumbbell and dropped on the ground as if doing sit-ups. She hated to get scolded, and everyone seemed inclined to do it if they saw her overworking her arm. She saw Rafael in the doorway, and she sat up again with a smile. "Well, what did Antonio want? He went very 'Don Lucino' on you."

"What else would he want?" he asked ruefully as he offered a hand to help her to her feet. "He is lamenting my being a bachelor at such an old age of twenty-five."

She picked up her towel to hide a grin. "Uh oh. Did you get the 'heir to carry on the family' talk?"

"*Sì*, it was something to that effect." He sighed and sat on the side of a bench to watch as Tori began to put up equipment. There was something about the way he moved that was just so . . . unthinkingly sexy. It had been baffling him for years. "He convinced me to go on a date tomorrow night."

"Well, don't sound so thrilled about it. You'll scare someone." She told her jealous heart to shut up and walked over to sit beside him. She lightly bumped her shoulder against his. "You know that you guys are the modern equivalent of a kingdom. You're the heir apparent, so you need to produce another heir to pass along the throne to. Geez, and I thought this was the 21$^{st}$ century."

"One of these days," he noted ruefully, "you will have to meet *Nonno*. It will all make sense."

"So who's the lucky chick?"

"Theresa Adams."

She pursed her lips thoughtfully. "About five-five, thick and *ridiculously* long brown hair, brown eyes, and roughly one hundred sixty pounds. Works the Publications desk. Wears glasses and could be a model for your classic nerdy bookworm. Pretty and smart. Shy until she warms up."

He had to laugh. "You have an encyclopedia for a brain, Tori!"

"Hey, it's what I do. Where are you taking her?"

"To the gala tomorrow night. I told her it was mostly business and we'd see if it turned into a date. I am hoping that if sparks do not fly, which I doubt they will, at the least I will buy some time with Papa."

"Well, why don't you date anymore anyway? You were quite the playboy before I and Alex got hired. You were always going out. Then . . . nothing. I've heard of people quitting addictions cold turkey, but I didn't think you could do that to dating as well."

His lips twitched. Lacking the freedom to tell the truth, he said only, "It seemed safer for all involved. Ah, well." He got to his feet. "Thank you for listening to me, Tori."

"Anytime," she murmured. She watched him walk out and then raked her hands through her hair. She liked Theresa. That didn't mean she liked seeing her go out with Rafael. She had never considered herself a jealous woman, but she honestly loathed this scenario entirely.

She knew she really should go with Rafael and Theresa to the gala just as a deterrent to any would-be kidnappers, but she couldn't bear the idea of seeing them together. She would have to ask Alex to go in her place. She could just use the excuse that she was worried she wouldn't be up to dealing with trouble if it happened.

And what would she do if Rafael *did* find someone to love? She wasn't sure she could convincingly hide her emotions if that occurred. She wanted him happy, but she didn't want him to be with anyone else. "Friggin' hell," she muttered, dropping her face into her hands. "Now what am I going to do?"

Alex was fine with serving as a one-time guard for Rafael. On the other hand, Rafael felt very disappointed that he wouldn't get to have Tori there. He knew Theresa was his date, but he had been hoping to at least enjoy Tori's company as well.

Upon seeing Rafael's distinct unhappiness, Isabelle followed Alex into their room when he went to get changed. "Do you know what is wrong with Rafe?" she asked her fiancé. "I have never seen him as he has been since the incident."

He hesitated for a moment before sighing and buttoning his dress shirt. "I only have suspicions," he said carefully. "The one who would know best would be Tori, but I suspect Tori is at the heart of the problem." He sought for a way to say what he thought. "If it had been me shot in your defense," he finally said, "how would you have reacted?"

"I suppose I would have acted much as Rafe did. But I am in love with you." When he arched a brow, she grew thoughtful. "Hmm. Indeed, that would make sense of quite a lot. But I did not think Rafael liked men. Perhaps it is just Tori."

He kept the rest of his suspicions to himself and just smiled wryly. "Perhaps so." He lifted her chin and kissed her softly. "Will you wait up for me tonight?" he asked huskily.

Her lips curved. "Perhaps so."

When Alex got to the garage to meet up with Rafael, he was entirely unsurprised to find the younger man quietly staring out across the landscape. Tori was walking with Brie through one of the gardens, and they could be easily seen from the garage. "Rafe?"

Rafael sighed. "*Sì,* Alex."

"I didn't ask anything."

"You were intending to. The answer is still yes. Get in. I will drive tonight. You do not mind riding in the back?" He opened his car door and forced himself to tear his eyes away from the sight of Tori laughing with Brie.

"Of course not. I'm just decoration; you can't make your date ride in the back." Alex got in as well, turning over the possible things he could say to his friend and future brother-in-law. The situation was

complicated, frustrating, and potentially futile. "We don't pick who we love," he finally said. "Sometimes it gets picked for us. Brie told me that recently. I blamed her 3rd District upbringing, but I admit, she does seem to be right."

Rafael was still thinking about that when they reached Theresa's house. It was a small place in Brooklyn and not very far from the company headquarters. It looked curiously depressing somehow, even though it was kept in good condition and the garden bloomed happily despite some weeds. In truth, there was nothing at all displeasing about its appearance, but he *felt* depressed looking at it. He couldn't even be sure why.

He rang the doorbell, and Theresa opened the door moments later. She was a curvy and lovely woman with hair so long that it actually brushed the floor when she took it down. It was up now, and she had somehow braided and pinned it into an elegant chignon. The old-fashioned style suited her as much as the demure black dress she wore. "Hello, Rafe," she said with a smile. "All day I kept expecting this to be a joke."

"I would never do that to you." He offered his arm. "You look lovely, Theresa." He spotted movement and glanced up to see an old woman watching them from further in the house. Distrust and disgust mingled in her eyes. "I will bring her home before midnight," he promised.

"See that you do." The door slammed behind them.

Theresa's fingers bit into his arm for a moment, her brown eyes darkening behind her glasses. "My grandmother," she said softly. "She is . . . possessive. She does not like men."

"I will do my best not to give her reason to hate me." He escorted her to the car and opened the passenger door for her. "I believe you know Alex. He is chaperoning me tonight because Tori is still recovering."

Theresa shyly smiled toward Alex. "Hi."

"Hello. Don't mind me. I'm part of the furniture."

Determined to enjoy himself, Rafael forced away thoughts of

Tori and the trouble in their lives and focused instead on his date and the gala. It was a big, elaborate party for the company's newest product, and since Just In Time had launched the advertising that promoted it, they were VIP guests. Antonio was not much of a partygoer anymore, blaming his 'advanced' years, and that meant Rafael was in the spotlight to attend. He was more inclined to think his father just wanted an excuse to have a quiet night at home.

With Alex shadowing them discreetly, Rafael and Theresa made their way around the lobby where the product and others in its line were on display. "Technology eludes me," Theresa admitted to Rafael. "I can use a computer well enough, but I am much happier when you give me books. I still carry a CD player," she laughed. "I can't figure out how to work an MP3 one."

"Is that why you applied for our library?"

"That and it was the best paying job I was qualified for. I haven't gone to college. Grandmother doesn't believe in it."

Sensing a touchy subject, he diverted the conversation. "How many books do you read a week?"

"For fun or for work?" She smiled. "More than you probably can contemplate. I read through the archives just for kicks. If I could go to school, I would study English. I love words. I love seeing how words evolve. For example, I saw an ad from the sixties in the archives for the same product we did an ad for last year. They were *completely* different. Not just in style, but in language."

It didn't take long for him to realize there would simply be no sparks with Theresa. She was lovely and fun, but she was simply too even-tempered to suit him as a lover. He had hot blood. He liked to shout and argue and laugh and love. She needed someone with a bit of calm intensity who would protect her gentle nature. They just did not match as more than siblings. If *anything* got confirmed that night, it was that Rafael felt surer than ever that he and Theresa could probably have been twins in another life. He loved her quite intensely, but in the way he loved Isabelle and Brie.

Proving a surprising astuteness as he walked her to her door a

few hours later, she said softly, "Don't kick yourself that we didn't click, Rafe. Come on. Did you really think we might? We've been working together for a year. If there were going to be sparks, we'd have seen it by now. You are like . . . like a brother to me, and I think you already knew that."

He smiled wryly. "Was I so obvious?"

"I think it was just instinct." She smiled suddenly. "Love is love, Rafael. It can't be labeled. It can't be made comfortable. It can only be accepted."

He contemplated that as he went back to the car. He knew he had not mistaken her meaning. As he was driving home, he asked Alex, "Tell me something. Am I so transparent to everyone?"

"I only noticed recently," Alex admitted amiably. He wasn't going to pretend to misunderstand the conversation he had heard. "You did an admirable job of pretending, but you went to pieces when Tori was shot. Your reaction was a bit . . . strong."

"Do you have any advice for me? Please, Alexander. I just do not know what to do." He parked the car in the garage at the darkened villa and got out. Only two windows shone with light. One was waiting for Alex in Isabelle's room. The other was in Tori's room.

Alex got out of the car and draped his jacket over his shoulder. "You just need to decide if you want to fight for the one you love. Do you want to live with regret, Rafe, or move forward toward true happiness? It's your call."

Rafael watched him walk toward the villa before turning his gaze toward the second lamp lit window. A night wind ruffled his hair as he took off his jacket and walked with purpose toward the villa. No Lucino worth their salt would ever not fight for love. It was time he fought as well.

Tori's evening did not go much better than his. She played cards with Isabelle and Brie and beat Roberto at billiards. Dinner was lively as always, even with two empty chairs. It was all she could do to keep her eyes from straying to the seat where Rafael always sat. Thinking of some nameless woman someday sitting beside him instead of her was enough to bring her mood down over and over.

Claiming exhaustion, she retreated to her room almost right after dinner. Truly, she was not that tired. She was so acclimated to staying up talking with Rafael that it had become hard to sleep without having seen him.

As she shrugged into her pajama top, she discovered to her chagrin that it too would no longer button. The bottoms could be pulled up to her hips but went no further. Frustrated, she grabbed the tape measure she had reluctantly obtained. Naked but for her underwear, she walked over to her mirror and stared at her reflection—something she very rarely ever did. She was *definitely* getting a figure.

Her hips had grown three inches. Her bust had grown by five. She was staring in consternation at the tape measure when her door suddenly opened and Rafael stepped in. Shocked, she stared at him. She hadn't even realized she had left the door unlocked in the universal Lucino 'come on in' gesture.

He stopped dead in his tracks as he stared at her and slowly ran his eyes down her body. Though slim and slender, there was absolutely no doubt that he stared at a woman. Her hips curved just enough to entice, and her breasts seemed to be the right size to fill his hands.

As his gaze slid back up her body, he saw the vivid scar on her chest near her left breast. His breath wedged in his lungs. The mark was still more red than pink, but it healed rapidly. It was a stark reminder of what she had done and what had been done to save her life.

He raked his gaze over her face. Now that he knew, he felt foolish for not trusting his first instincts. Why hadn't she corrected them? He would have to find out, and find out what *she* wanted to be. For the first time, however, her deceptive androgyny seemed to have evaporated. She appeared to be all woman right then, not even a hint of masculinity in her stricken face and tousled blonde hair. She was, in fact, the sexiest thing he had ever seen, and he had honestly already thought she tipped pretty high on the sexy chart anyway.

He stepped back without a word and shut the door. Heart pounding, she dropped the tape measure and grabbed her t-shirt. She jerked it on and ran to open the door. "Rafe," she said as loudly as she dared in the sleeping house. "Are you . . . are you mad?"

He stopped in front of his door and looked at her. "No, Tori," he said gently. "I am, in fact, unsurprised. I will speak with you tomorrow. *Buono notte, cara.*"

His door shut softly behind him and she went back into her room. She felt confused and a little wary. Why was he suddenly calling her *cara*? Was it just because he now knew she was a woman? On a sigh, she sank down onto the side of her bed. How much more complicated would this get, anyway?

# CHAPTER TEN

Rafael didn't sleep at all that night. Even if he hadn't been struggling with insomnia for years, he would have still been awake. Both his body and his mind had tangled up in knots. Frustrated hunger burned in his body, stirred violently by the sight of Tori's beauty. Dozens of questions and guessed answers churned in his head.

Why the hell did she let everyone think she was a man? He could guess that one easily enough; the simple fact that so many people automatically made assumptions about her being male was a strong indicator that she hadn't been (or felt she was) feminine enough as a woman. He called bullshit. He had wanted her for two years. Clearly, whatever signal she put out was strong enough to reach his body and soul even though his eyes had been deceived. He wanted to kick himself for not being polite enough to just *ask* in the first place.

The tape measure was a curious thing. He would definitely ask about that. In fact, there were a ton of things he intended to ask, and he was damned well going to get every single answer. The most important thing he wanted to ask, however, required some . . . parental assistance.

A tiny smile touched his lips. He would try to get some revenge on his father for pulling the 'Don Lucino' act and then he would go find Tori and clear the air. If she wasn't in love with him yet, then he would make sure she was eventually. There was no other he wanted. No other he had ever wanted.

Once full sunshine came in the window, he got out of bed and caught a shower. Breakfast was in an hour, and he wanted his conversation with his father done before then. He felt fairly sure Tori would avoid breakfast with everyone, and that was perfectly fine. He didn't want any observers for their discussion either.

Refreshed and alert, he got dressed and headed downstairs to his father's office. Antonio was a naturally early riser, especially since he and Rafe worked mostly from home. The light was already on and clearly seen under the door. Rafael knocked lightly. "Papa?"

"Come in, Rafe."

A little smile playing with his lips, he went into the office and shut the door. Casually, he walked over and sat down in one of the chairs. "The gala went well," he began. "Theresa was a lovely companion to have along, but I am afraid that she and I will never be more than friends. Perhaps we should consider just adopting her into the *famiglia* instead." He thought about her grandmother. "Something tells me she could use some family love."

"That was my feeling, too. And you at least tried," Antonio commiserated. "That is all I wanted, Rafael."

"Yes, well, seeing her allowed me to open my eyes to something else entirely. Papa, I need you to fire Tori."

Antonio paused as he was lifting his coffee. He slowly put the mug down, a combination of confusion and suspicion in his eyes. "Why would you want Tori fired, Rafael? Are you truly that worried for his safety? He is your bodyguard. It is his duty to put his life on the line. I do not like it either for I care for him a great deal as well, but it must be accepted."

"As a matter of fact, that has little to do with it. I wish to marry Tori."

Antonio looked at his son a bit more critically. "I do not judge, Rafael, but I did not think you were interested in other men."

"I had wondered if I was," he admitted. "But it would seem I am not." He looked at his father a second time and then sighed. So much for his hoped for revenge. "You already knew that Tori is a woman."

"*Sì.*" Antonio smiled. "I ran a full background check on both Tori and Alex when I hired them, and I knew when she came for an interview that she was a woman—only to be surprised when I met her. She told me she would be whatever you and Bella assumed her to be, as that was how she had always done it, so I respected her wishes." He lifted a brow. "How did you come to know?"

Rafael smiled. "When I came home last night, I went to her intending to confess my feelings for her, even thinking she was a man. I walked into her room without knocking, since she had left the door unlocked. She was naked."

"I imagine that was quite awkward."

"I am surprised she did not hit me. Do I have your blessings, Papa? Will you fire her so I may ask her to be my wife?" He smiled a little wryly, a little wistfully. "I have loved her for two years, nearly since she was hired. When she was shot, it shocked me into realizing it. I would have had her for my own even if she had not been a woman. I had accepted that last night. Things are simply less complicated now where the extended *famiglia* is concerned."

"*Sì,*" Antonio agreed dryly, "as I will not have to deal with *mio papa*—though I would have for you if it had been needed." He took a long breath and dug in his desk. He pulled out Tori's contract and handed it to Rafael. It felt a little bittersweet to have his eldest finally be in love, no matter how much he had wished for such a thing. "She is no longer under my employ as of this moment. I admit that I am glad for it. I was trying to find a way to keep her with us even when the danger passed. She has become an important part of our family, just as Alex has." He suddenly laughed. "*Dio,* those personality quizzes! I should have known she was setting me up."

"She?" Rafael's brows lifted.

"Rhianna Taber of Enforcers. We have worked with them before, and when I mentioned offhand what I was going to do, she gave me the quizzes to be certain all went well. I should have known what might happen."

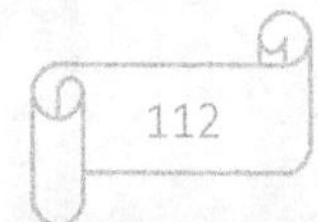

"All is well that ends well." Rafael got to his feet. "I am going to go have it out with Tori. I do not think she will be happy, nor will she believe me. But I will win." He looked as confident as he sounded. "Lucinos fight for love, no?"

The first thing he did was go to the kitchen to speak with the cook. "Peggy?" he asked as he walked into the bright kitchen. He stopped to take an appreciative sniff of the air. Everything smelled like cinnamon and pastry. "You are making cinnamon rolls."

"Of course." She shot him a smiling look over her shoulder. She had been with the family since he was ten, and he still loved her cinnamon rolls best. "If you are hungry, breakfast will be ready soon, Rafael."

"That is good, but I was going to ask if Tori had come by."

"He did indeed. Poor thing looked exhausted as if he hadn't slept. He let me know he would not be joining the family for breakfast, so I was preparing a tray for him." Up to her elbows in dough, she inclined her head to where a covered tray sat on the island counter. "Marco was going to take it up in a few minutes."

"I will do so." He peeked under the tray lid. "Is there enough for two?"

"Naturally." She fluttered her lashes at him as if she was as young on the outside as she was on the inside. "I know my kids. I knew you would want to keep him company." Her eyes twinkled merrily. One of the maids had overheard the parental conversation and quickly spread word. "Or, should I say, keep *her* company."

He stared at her. "How did you know?"

"Well, Betsy ratted you out on your conversation with *Signor* Lucino, but we staff have actually known all along. She had to tell us since we would not let her do her own laundry, and we do shopping for her like we do for everyone else. There are things that many women need that many men do not." She began to shape the dough into loaves for the oven. "We have enjoyed watching you fall in love, Rafael, particularly when you did not know the truth of who you loved. You merely *loved*, as you should." She nodded firmly. "She will make a fine *Signora* Lucino."

Rafael just smiled as he shook his head. "'You staff,' you say, but you are all family. I am not that surprised that you knew." He lifted the tray and then put it down again. "Peggy . . ."

She didn't look up, but she smiled. "Marco cut some flowers this morning. They are in the vase in the fridge."

"*Dio*, you frighten me sometimes." He opened the fridge and retrieved the vase of flowers. They were a mix of buds and blooms, caught in the transition between growth and full beauty. They were perfect for his Tori.

Vase on the tray, he carted the entire thing upstairs toward her room. He could not open the door with his hands full, so he called, "Tori? Open the door, please."

"Open it yourself," came the retort. "You're good at that."

He grinned briefly. "*Sì*, but my hands are full, *cara*."

The door jerked open. "Don't call me that!" Her words halted as she saw what he carried. "What is that?"

"Breakfast. Now let me in and I will share it with you. Peggy made cinnamon rolls." He stepped forward, forcing her to fall back or run right into him. She backed up and he carried the tray over to the table near the fireplace. All suites in the villa had their own bathrooms and small sitting area beside either a fireplace or a balcony.

He put the tray down and turned to study her. She wore sweatpants and a very baggy t-shirt, both of which concealed any sign of femininity of her body. Her hair, which had not been cut in three months, skimmed the back of her neck. It had not been brushed yet, and it was mussed and unruly from being slept on.

The morning light tried desperately to emphasize the fascinating hints of masculinity that she had often shown, but it did not seem to be as successful this time. He did not think it was just his eyes that had changed. *She* was changing, and she was blossoming like the buds in the vase. "You are beautiful," he said softly.

"Oh please!" She covered her face with a hand. "You find out

I'm a woman and suddenly you're calling me '*cara*' and telling me I am beautiful. What is wrong with you, Rafe? Did you hit your head yesterday?"

"I suppose you could say I was hit," he agreed amiably, "but it was not in the head." He lifted the lid off the tray of food. "You need your strength. Come eat, *cara*."

The intimacy of the way he addressed her had her watching him very warily. When Brie had laughingly said how it was so funny that the same word could sound entirely different from Roberto, Tori had been amused but not entirely understanding of what she meant. She definitely understood now. Rafael turned the endearment into nearly a physical caress when he used it toward her.

She sighed and sat down at the table to take her plate. She was too hungry to argue. "I guess you want to talk."

"Indeed." He sat down across from her and took his plate from the tray. "I have many questions. We will begin with something I should have asked much sooner: do you want to be addressed as male or female, neither, or both? I apologize for not doing this the first day."

"Very few people ever ask me that," she consoled him. She sighed. "Female is my preference. I am cisgender, as far as that goes. I was assigned female at birth, and I identify female, but Mother Nature is a bitch and decided not to give me three for three with my looks and body. I've always made an ugly girl but a passable boy, so it became easier to just let people think I was male instead of constantly being reminded by other people that I was a subpar woman. High school was hell, Rafe. I was tall and I skipped most of puberty. When I went to college, I effectively built a new life from the ground up. It wasn't hard. I didn't have a family to distance myself from."

"And people are so quick to judge that they have never assumed anything other than what you present," he murmured. "And those who know the truth because of legal reasons, such as Papa, keep quiet because you ask them to."

She shrugged. "Being a male allowed people to get to know me. I've never had trouble making friends since. People are more comfortable with a less masculine man than a less feminine woman. As much as it hurts to deny myself, at least I'm not *alone*. Also, Tori is a nickname, so you know. So, depending on what I'm signing, I use either version of my name, both of which are also legal. I tried to make things simple for myself."

"Yet they have grown complicated. You were measuring your breasts last night," he noted calmly. "Is there something wrong?"

A hint of pink touched her cheekbones. "According to the doctor," she muttered, "the physical trauma of being shot kick-started the parts of puberty I missed. My entire body is changing. I'm actually developing a figure, but it's happening so quickly that I can't keep up. None of my clothes fit anymore." She sighed deeply and pushed away her empty plate. "I had intended to tell you," she admitted softly. "I knew my days were limited until it became obvious. I didn't intend you to find out as you did."

"I am not complaining." His blue eyes seemed to smolder as he looked at her. "The view was amazing. You are lovely, Tori. But," he continued even softer, "I have thought so for two years. Be you man or woman, I wanted you. When I came to you last night, I had decided to tell you how I felt."

She stared at him in shock. "You're not funny, Rafael."

"I am not saying it to be amusing. Now, when I went to my father this morning, I admit I intended to have some amusement at his expense."

Humor lit her eyes. "You wanted to use me to get revenge for his 'Don Lucino' act, didn't you?" When he grinned, she just shook her head. "I can't even be offended. It would have been hilarious if he had not already known. Sorry about denying you that." She lifted a brow. "I imagine nothing is going to change, right, now that everything is out in the open? I mean, my identity has not affected my work over the last two years. You all know I am capable."

"Indeed you are." He pulled out the contract and held it up.

Deliberately, he tore it in two. "But you have been fired regardless."

"What!" She leapt to her feet, her baby blue eyes firing up with sheer fury. "Because I'm a woman? For god's sake, Rafael, I thought we were friends!"

"We are." He stood and began to stalk around the table toward her. "I just happen to want more than friendship, Tori. And as long as you were employed by my father, you could not be mine." His hands closed around her arms to jerk her soft body against his. Subtle though her curves were, they molded to his frame perfectly, tormenting him with thoughts of how she would feel under his hands. "I cannot marry my bodyguard. But you are no longer that, are you?"

"Are you out of your mind?" she shouted. She slapped her hands on his shoulders and pushed as hard as she could. He stumbled back but still managed to keep his grip on her. He swung around and pinned her against the poster of her bed. Shocked, her eyes flew wide as she felt him from head to toe and assuredly every inch in between.

His lips curved into a devastatingly sensual smile. "You look surprised, *cara*." He pressed closer so that she could not mistake his desire for her. He *ached* for her. "Were you not listening?" He skimmed his lips along the strong line of her jaw. He loved her height. It put everything within such delightful reach. "For two years I have wanted you. In fact, I do not think I have ever *stopped* wanting you. It just seems to vary in intensity between desperation and obsession."

Head spinning, she grabbed his arms for balance. She shook her head hard, trying to compute what he was telling her. "That's impossible."

"*Sì*, but it is true." He gave her a small shake. "Tell me you do not want me, Tori, and I will let you go."

Her lips trembled. She could not tell him that. She could not bring herself to lie to him over something so important.

"Kiss me, Tori." His lips hovered over hers, his breath flavored with cinnamon and rich coffee. "You gave me my life. I will show you how to live." Something stirred in her eyes that was longing and desperate and afraid, and it ripped at his heart. He needed her so terribly to save his soul.

When his lips took hers, the shocking delight of it sent a shiver through her entire body. That simmering need inside that she had fought so hard to control seemed to boil over wildly. Her arms were pinned and all she could do was feel. He devoured her hungrily, stealing her breath and her will and making her body ache fiercely. Her breasts, sensitive in their growth, throbbed where they pressed against his strong chest.

A low moan vibrated in her throat. His feelings or hers. She couldn't separate them, couldn't find the will to try. She pressed upward to deepen the kiss and shuddered with pleasure as his tongue eagerly curled around hers. He tasted of secret dreams, untamed passion, and of all the things she had thought she would never have.

His hands lifted from her arms and buried in her hair to drag her closer. Quivering with violent hunger, he broke the kiss and buried his mouth hotly against her neck. There was a birthmark there that had always tempted him, and he nipped at it teasingly before soothing the sting with his tongue. "I have wanted this for two years," he said again roughly, his accent thickening. The sound of it made her entire body tremble. "You cannot tell me that I do not want you."

He lifted his head when there was no retort and his stomach knotted hard. Her blue eyes looked dazed and her cheeks flushed. She pressed her lips together for a moment as if she didn't entirely understand why they were swollen. She was the most beautiful creature he had ever seen. "You are beautiful, *cara*." He skimmed his lips over her ear. "*Ti amo*," he breathed. "*Dio*, Tori. I have loved you for years."

She didn't get a chance to answer. Her unlocked bedroom door opened, and Isabelle and Brie walked in. "Tori," Isabelle was saying, "please come have breakfast with us! It is boring without you." She broke off in surprise at the sight of Tori in Rafael's arms. "*Dio!*"

"Ha!" Brie elbowed her cousin. "I told you Rafe wanted Tori!"

She eyed Rafael intently. "I still say he should have just admitted he liked guys, too."

Rafael reluctantly released Tori, but he was smiling. "In fact, Tori is a woman," he told his sisters. "There is nothing for me to admit except that I do not care one way or another."

"*Sì,* and that makes sense of everything." Isabelle shook her head in bemusement. "I had always wondered what was different about you, Tori! It is no wonder that I and Brie were always comfortable with you in a way we were not with other men." She frowned suddenly. "Why did you never correct our assumptions? Your choice of industry?"

Tori pushed Rafael firmly and forced him to release her. Her strength was nearly completely back and that meant she was as strong as he, something for which she felt grateful. "I'm not attractive as a woman," she said crossly. "It just seemed simpler. Magically, by being a boy, people stopped calling me ugly. It was nice to be accepted. You wouldn't have even given me the time of day if you'd met me when I was a girl."

"Bzzt," Brie said, "wrong answer! We like *you*, Tori. We don't care what you look like. And anyway, we've all said at least once that you were the kind of man who could rock being a hot guy *or* a hot chick, so, obviously, you're not as unfeminine or ugly as you think. Whatcha think, Bella? I bet we could take Tori out for new clothes and even make *her* think that she was sexy and gorgeous."

Isabelle's eyes twinkled. "*Sì,* Brie. It would be fun."

"Your entire family is nuts!" Tori told Rafael. "I'm glad I was fired; I can get out of here before I'm nuts too!"

"Fired!" Brie's brows shot up.

"Rafael wants to marry her," Isabelle decided. "Like Alex quit so that he could ask me to marry him. As long as Tori worked for Papa, she was off limits to Rafe."

"Quite." Rafael caught Tori around the waist and tugged her closer. "And I will not take no for an answer, *cara.*"

Alex knocked on the doorframe over Isabelle's head, and his

other hand lightly curled around her waist possessively. "You chose a bad time to fire her, Rafe," he said quietly. "You will need her more than ever to protect you. Another threat has arrived, but it was directed at you."

Isabelle clutched his shirt, her eyes darkening. "Alex, what threat?"

"It was a list of the places he has been to lately. Next to each, it was clearly noted when he had been either alone or away from Tori or I. At the bottom, it said 'I missed the last time, but I won't the next.' We have sent it to the police. They are going to check for fingerprints and do all those things that they do even though we know who sent it."

Tori's eyes darkened with dangerous fury. "Bastard." She glared at Rafael. "Un-fire me, damn it. Do you think I will stand by like some helpless heroine? I was *trained* to protect others, and I have protected you for two years. I was ready to die for you, Rafe. Like *hell* I am going to see all that wasted just because your hormones are out of control!"

"I have an idea!" Brie clapped her hands together. "Let's rehire Tori, but undercover! She can pose as Rafe's fiancée. Since his bodyguard is supposed to be a guy, then no one will look twice at Tori, especially if we call her something else. Is Tori a nickname for anything?"

"Victoria," she muttered.

Rafael loved it instantly. He had liked 'Tori' but somehow he liked her full name more. Perhaps because it represented the side of her that she wanted so badly but felt she could not have. "Let us go talk to Papa," he said. He grabbed Tori's wrist and pulled her along behind him firmly. "You are coming as well."

"Ouch!"

At the yelp, he released her quickly. "*Dio*! Was that your bad arm?"

"No." She smirked in his face. "Sucker." She crossed her arms and went past him firmly. "I can walk by myself. I've done it for a

quarter of a century."

Alex wisely hid a grin as he ushered Isabelle and Brie down the hall after Tori. Rafael just smiled and followed them. He loved Tori for everything she was, and he was very happy to know that it was only her gender she had hidden. It was clear that her personality was the same one he had known and loved all along. She would never hesitate to backtalk to him, or to get in his face if she felt he was out of line. She would still kick him under the dinner table or laugh at the way he could be as bossy as his father. She would still stay up at night with him, listening to anything he wanted to talk about. He had never realized it was possible to love one being that much.

Antonio looked up when they all walked in and then hastily sipped his coffee to cover a smile. Roberto, sitting in one of the chairs, arched a brow at Tori before looking at Brie. She nodded sagely. "We walked in on a serious embrace. I'd give it an eight for sheer heat factor. I was pretty impressed. Traumatized—we're talking about my brother here—but impressed.

Tori caught her in a headlock. "You be quiet, troublemaker." She looked at Antonio a bit shamefully. "Antonio, I am truly sorry that it all came out like this. I should have said something sooner to the others, but . . ."

"Say no more." He held up his hands with a smile. "No one is at all upset, for you are still our Tori. You are still a part of this family, and I will still always be grateful to you for saving Rafael's life. I will be glad to call you my daughter-in-law."

"I'm not marrying Rafael!" She released Brie and backed up. "I *might* be willing to go along with Brie's ridiculous charade because it will allow me to protect him, but I will not actually marry him! He's out of his mind."

"*Sì*, as I have been for two years. Put me out of my misery, Victoria."

She glared at him. "I don't like how you say my name. Cut it out."

"Good luck with that," Brie groused dryly. She looked at

Antonio. "I had an idea on how to make sure Rafael is safe without being obvious about it. We can't just sit around twiddling our thumbs forever. Isabelle and I are both having to postpone our marriages and honeymoons because of this, and now Rafe will be limited in what he can do for the company. So what if we set a trap?"

"What sort of trap?" Antonio asked with a thoughtful frown.

"We have Tori pose as Rafe's fiancée. He won't be without a bodyguard, but no one else will know that. If we can get Mr. Johns or one of his dumb thugs to lower their guard, maybe they can get caught. He grabbed me and Bella right from in front of this place, and you know he probably hates Rafe more than us. It won't be long until he tries to grab him too. Tori can handle things. We all know she can."

"I hear Detective Franklin in my head," Alex muttered, "and he's saying 'leave it to the cops.'"

"And what have they done so far?" Isabelle demanded. "Nothing! We have done all they told us to do so that we were safe, and Brie and I were still grabbed. Rafael was still nearly killed, and Tori still nearly died. I am tired of sitting and doing nothing! If not this, then I say we call *Nonno* and tell him to find those hitmen he keeps promising!"

Antonio looked at Tori. "It is your decision, Tori," he said quietly. "But know that I, too, have full confidence in you. There is no one else I would trust with Rafael's life. It will be risky, though."

"Please." She shook her head. "If I didn't want risk, I wouldn't even be in this business! But . . . this is not just business." She looked at Rafael. "It's personal, too. It's been personal all along." She blew out a breath. "I'm out of my mind. Fine, I will pose as his fiancée. But it's *just a cover*."

Antonio opened his desk to find a blank employment contract and instead discovered a neatly typed document. He pulled it out in confusion and read over it swiftly. A little smile began to tug at his lips. Entirely unsurprised, much as he had been unsurprised that morning, he placed the contract on the top of the desk and slid it across to Tori and Rafael. "There is no telling how long this may take," he warned Tori. "You could find yourself engaged to Rafael for a year or more."

"A long-term and then broken engagement won't ruin me," she said dryly. "Besides, no one wants me anyway." She signed the bottom of the contract before she could tell herself not to. Truly, there was no other option if she wanted to keep the man she loved safe.

Rafael signed as well and began to smile slowly. "I hope you realize that I will make this engagement very real, *cara mia*. After all, to be believable, people must believe I am madly in love with you. You have heard of method acting, *sì*? To act the part, you must become the part. I look forward to teaching you."

She backed up cautiously, her eyes widening as the sensual threat registered. "Don't you dare!"

"You cannot run from me, Victoria," he warned softly. "You are quite stuck now."

"*Sì*," Isabelle said happily as she grabbed Tori's right arm, "and Brie and I will take you out shopping! You cannot wear your old clothes if you are to be Rafael's wife. You are a woman of high class, and you should dress as such."

"I will begin plans for the engagement party," Antonio decided. "Rafael is my heir. We must have a grand party. Within a week, I believe. I will call Papa tonight and tell him of the good news. He and Mama will want to come out to attend. Let us say we will have it next Saturday. That will give Marco and Peggy plenty of time to prepare everything. It will be here at the villa."

A sort of panicked terror began to fill Tori's eyes as she realized just how deeply she was getting tangled into things. Brie leapt up from her seat and took her left arm firmly, ensuring she was caught and could not run. "Let's go, Tori! We're going to find you a dress that will make Rafe's eyes pop out of his head!"

"Oh god." It was little more than a despairing moan as she was dragged out of the office by her identical captors.

As the door shut behind them, Roberto said idly, "I did not

know that Don Lucino would come out to America for a farce engagement."

"Farce? What farce?" Antonio held out the contract.

The other three men moved in closer to read it, and all three began grinning, Rafael most of all. He hadn't even really read what he was signing, trusting his father knew what he was doing.

Clearly written were the words '*This contract is a binding document that can and will be Enforced to the highest degree. Victoria Li, hereafter Party One, and Rafael Lucino, hereafter Party Two, will commence a marital engagement to end in matrimony. During the term of engagement, Party One will serve as a secret bodyguard for Party Two until the threat of danger passes. When said danger has passed, the engagement will become formal and considered true and binding.*'

Rafael quirked a brow in amusement. "Is this contract from Enforcers? I recognize that standard language at the beginning. It is in all their contracts."

"*Sì*. It must have gotten mixed in with other paperwork that Ms. Tabor gave me recently for something else entirely." Antonio sighed fondly. "I will have to be certain to invite Ms. Tabor to the party, no? It seems she has a vested interest in the outcome."

# CHAPTER ELEVEN

Isabelle and Brie dragged Tori all the way to her room and shoved her inside. "Find something to wear for now," Brie ordered cheerfully. "We're going to go finish breakfast and then we'll meet you in the garage."

"I will make Alex go with us," Isabelle assured her, "so that we are twice as safe. It will also lend credence to your new persona!"

The door shut behind them, and Tori raked her hands through her hair. It seemed like every time she turned around, things just kept getting more out of hand. Frustrated mentally because she couldn't seem to keep up, and certainly frustrated physically thanks to Rafael, she all but stalked into the bathroom for a shower.

He hadn't just come out of left field; he hadn't even been in the park to begin with! Not once over the last two years had she so much as guessed that he was attracted to her. But then, she willingly admitted, she wouldn't have known what to look for. She had never had anyone of *any* orientation be attracted to her before. She didn't doubt that Rafael wanted her, but she couldn't quite determine what he saw when he looked at her. What did he see that she didn't?

She unexpectedly got her answer when she stepped out of the shower. She briskly toweled her hair dry and tossed it out of her eyes to see her reflection. As she saw her appearance, she was brought up short in sheer surprise. She was . . . kind of pretty. She had gotten so used to seeing herself as she had been years before that she hadn't noticed any changes, and her aversion to mirrors had not helped her case.

She wasn't gangly anymore. Her height had caught up to her arms and legs. Even with them being more muscular than the average woman, they still looked sort of appealing. Her breasts and hips, now more clearly curved, emphasized how naturally slender she was. With her hair a little longer, her face seemed . . . softer.

Curiously subdued, she wrapped herself in a towel and walked into her bedroom. What else wasn't she seeing clearly?

"There you are."

She stifled a yelp and whirled as she clutched her towel tighter. Rafael was sitting at the small table and waiting for her with a tiny smile teasing his lips. "Do you mind?" she demanded. "I've already had a near death experience; I don't need another!"

He got to his feet and walked toward her slowly. She looked damp and flushed and so desirable that he was highly tempted to pounce on her right there. She seemed to sense it because her body shifted fluidly, gracefully, into a slightly more defensive stance. He held up his hands. "I am not going to grab you, Victoria."

"Then what do you want?"

"That is a loaded question, *cara*." He leaned in before she could dodge and softly kissed her. He kept his hands in the air the entire time, even when her lashes lowered and a soft sound of desire slipped past her lips. The little longing whimper raked through his already tortured body. He stepped back and put his hands in his pockets as she looked at him in dazed bemusement. "You are beautiful, Victoria."

She shook her head quickly. "That was sneaky, Rafe!"

He grinned. "There is a saying about love and war."

"Just say whatever you're here to say, you fink." She crossed her arms firmly and then blinked. An odd look crossed her face. He lifted a brow at her, and she sighed. "Getting used to having boobs is not easy after almost twenty-six years of having none. They get in the way."

"But they are lovely," he said wistfully. "I envied your tape measure."

Her color rose slightly. "Why are we discussing my breasts?"

"You brought them up. I am quite a fan of art, so I was compelled to speak on the subject. I was never fond of busty women."

She burst into laughter. "Now you're outright lying! The last chick you dated before all the trouble started looked like she had come off the set of *Baywatch*! She bounced so much when she walked that it's a wonder she didn't give herself a black eye!"

He started laughing. "What an image!" Content, he skimmed his fingers across her cheek. "I am so glad we can still laugh like this," he admitted softly. He brushed his thumb over her cheekbone. "I like knowing that I can tell you anything and that you can say anything to me." His lips curved. "I get the best of all worlds in you, Victoria. A friend and a lover."

"I never said I'd be your lover!"

"It is inevitable," he said simply. "I will not settle for less than everything. I will take your heart for my own." Because guardedness was creeping back into her eyes, he eased back a step. He had time. "You are going shopping for clothes, correct?" When she nodded, he firmed his lips. "I will buy what you need."

"I'm not without money," she said in exasperation. "I've been paid well for keeping your ass out of trouble. I rarely buy anything anyway, so I am entitled to an indulgence or two."

"*Sì*, but since you are, technically, buying these things for your 'job', it only makes sense that I pay for them." He arched a brow, daring her to argue with him. "And I very much want to see you in the best because you by far deserve it. I have told Bella and Brie that you are not to pay for a thing."

She groaned and covered her face with her hands. "Next you will tell me that you told them to buy me lingerie!" She looked up sharply when there was no retort. "You did *not* tell them that."

"I merely said for them to outfit you from the skin out. How they interpret that is entirely their decision. But, *cara*, you *do* need lingerie. You may not be able to go without a bra for much longer unless you wish to give Jill a run for her bouncing money."

He said it so straight-faced that she couldn't help but laugh. "Get out of my room! I need to scare up something that I can wear in public. None of my shirts button anymore," she confessed dryly.

A little smile touched his lips. Holding her gaze with his, he slowly unbuttoned the shirt he wore. He shrugged out of it with a casual ripple of muscle and then wrapped it around her shoulders. He stepped closer and bent his head to skim his lips across her ear. "It will look better on you than me. It should only be just a bit too big." His hand skimmed down her side, heated even through the towel. "I love how tall you are. I do not have to reach to enjoy your beauty."

She wasn't breathing as he walked out of her room shirtless, as casual as if he had been fully dressed. When he had shrugged out of the soft silk, she'd had to fight an urge to run her hands over his powerful chest. She had seen him without a shirt before; he loved to swim and had always coaxed her into going along even if she didn't get in the pool as well. Things had changed now. It seemed as if she could no longer control her emotions or her hormones, and both were steadily going out of control. He had barely touched her and she felt restless and needy.

Unable to resist, she rubbed her cheek over the soft material of the shirt. It had absorbed the heat and scent of his body, and both were a seductive lure.

She dropped the shirt on the bed. She was *not* going to wear it. Unfortunately, she realized quickly that she had no choice. She had managed to find a pair of jeans that had once been too baggy in the hip and waist, but her shirts were out of commission. She could wear one of her t-shirts, but they all looked either like sleepwear or something she would work out in.

Resigned, she pulled on Rafael's shirt and buttoned it. She tied the ends at her waist since it was still long on her and then cuffed the sleeves twice to use her hands. There were a lot of technicalities in life. One technicality was that she stood only five inches shorter than

Rafael, and it was definitely a technicality because he was distinctly broader in the shoulder and overall bigger. She should have been able to forget being the stronger of them, but it did not work that way for her. Strangely enough, the bigger her client, the more protective she got. She had never been able to figure that one out.

Knowing that there was no escape, she headed downstairs. Marco was in the foyer sorting what looked like invitations. When he saw her, his smile came bright and delighted. "I am happy for you, *signorina*! *Signor* Rafael could not have chosen a better bride. We are all very happy that you will marry him. You do not need to worry about a thing! Peggy and I will handle the engagement party details!" He winked. "There is time enough for you to learn how to throw a gala."

Lacking anything better, she mumbled a thanks and hurried out the door toward the garage. To her reluctant amusement, Isabelle, Brie, and Alex stood next to the limo that rarely got used. The chauffeur was waiting as well, talking cheerfully with all three. As Tori got closer, he turned and beamed at her. "Congratulations! *Signor* Rafael was so happy when I saw him earlier."

"Isn't that the shirt Rafe was wearing?" Alex asked dryly.

"Mine didn't fit," Tori muttered.

The chauffeur was a wise man. He hid a chuckle as he opened the door for her. As soon as all four passengers had gotten inside, he whistled contentedly to himself as he went to the front of the car. He had won the betting pool that had been going for two years, ever since the staff had learned that Rafael was falling in love. All had known this was inevitable, but they had taken turns guessing how long it would take.

"What's up with the limo anyway?" Tori asked as she settled back in her seat.

"We're planning a slaughter of many stores." Brie pulled out her iPhone and began flipping through her notes. "We're completely going to need the room for bags. Isabelle called ahead to a couple places, and they are going to open early for us when we get there so that we can avoid some of the crowds. I've got a complete list of what we need to get for you. I've seen your closet; it's huge. It can hold everything."

"And so can the closet in the master suite," Isabelle added casually. "It is worth noting since Rafael will take charge of it upon his marriage to you. Papa was already rather gleefully beginning to box up his things. He wanted to turn it over to Rafael after Mama died, but there was tradition to uphold."

"I am *not* marrying Rafe," Tori repeated firmly. "This is just a cover, remember?"

"Why not?" Alex asked bluntly. "You want to tell us that you're not in love with him? I think we all know that already. In fact, Rafe may be the only one who does not know. You didn't take a bullet for him because of your job, Tori, and we both damned well know it."

"Will you give me some room to breathe?" she demanded. "None of you would know how this feels! You all have loving families. You've never doubted that someone wanted you there. You've never looked in a mirror and wondered why God hated you. You never questioned your own blood, afraid that there was something horrible in it!"

"There is nothing but good in you, Victoria," Isabelle said softly, covering her hands gently. "You are the ugly duckling, and we are the swans who welcome you home. We will help you see how beautiful you are inside and out. You were always meant to be part of our *famiglia*. You did not belong with those horrible ducks, ever."

After a long silence, she said softly, "It's hard, Bella. I can't change how I look at myself overnight. I already had a shock this morning after my shower. I looked in the mirror . . . and felt a little attractive. It was like having blinders taken off." She laughed wryly. "I think Rafael was shock therapy."

"It was a shock for us too," Brie agreed dryly. "If he'd been any closer to you, he'd have been on the other side!"

Tori glanced at Alex. "Cover your ears." When he did so with a wry smile, she lowered her voice and said, "You do *not* dare tell Rafe this, but that was my first kiss."

"*Dio*." Isabelle's eyes went wide. "You are joking."

"'Fraid not. Told you no one else wanted me."

"No, that's not how you say it," Brie argued with a grin. "You say that you were too picky to bother with lesser quality. You were holding out for the best." She lightly kicked Alex's ankle. "It's safe now. The icky girl conversation is done."

He just grinned. "I guess we're *all* lucky to have Tori. We men can talk to her as frankly as you women do."

"You are definitely the best of both worlds, Victoria," Isabelle agreed with a smile.

Tori just sighed wryly. She wasn't sure if she would enjoy this outing or not, but she knew she wouldn't be bored. "Just remember I know nothing about dressing like a girl," she warned. "I'm going to have to completely trust you."

"I'm an artist," Brie assured her. "I can add the trendy, stylish kick and Isabelle can make sure that you've got the classy look going on as well."

And thusly, Tori found herself escorted into one of the bigger and more expensive stores in the entire mall. The mall itself was fairly upscale, but this particular store catered to people like the Lucinos. She peeked at one price tag as they went by and then told herself never to look again else she chicken out. In a way, she was glad Rafael was paying; this would have wiped out even her savings.

Alex was a good sport, even when the first stop they went to was the women's lingerie section. He only paid half attention to the conversations and arguments; most of his focus remained on the area around them. They were the only ones in the store other than the clerks, for now, but that didn't mean he would let down his guard.

Tori felt grateful for his presence; Brie and Isabelle were hitting her with so much information that she had no way of being on alert herself. Come to find out, she was just shy of being a B cup, so that was the size bra they got just in case she grew any more. It was one of the stranger feelings she had ever experienced as she tried the first one on. It hit an interesting level between comfortable and uncomfortable, and when she pulled her shirt on over it, she could only gape at the mirror.

"How's it going?" Brie called over the dressing room door.

"I have cleavage. T'hell did that come from?"

"It's going good," she said to Isabelle. To Tori she added, "The manager says that you can go ahead and wear that one if you like; we've got the tag for it to be rung up when we're done. After all, you can't try on much anything else without it."

"Here you go, Victoria." Isabelle handed a hanger with a new article over the top of the door.

Tori took one look at what she was being offered and said quickly, "Initiate! I'm an initiate! I'm not ready for the mystery of the teddy yet!"

"Try it on." Isabelle's tone booked no argument.

"Jesus." She studied the strange blue silk contraption for a minute before figuring out how it was supposed to be put on. It wasn't made to go over a bra, so she had to take her new one off again. Her shoulder twinged in the process, reminding her again that she was still not one hundred percent better. "Ouch. Shit."

"What's wrong?"

"I can't unfasten this damn thing because of my shoulder."

"Pull your arms out of the straps and turn it around so the clasp is in front."

She blinked. She would never have thought of that, and much to her surprise, it worked perfectly. Freed from the device, she donned the teddy. As she looked in the mirror, she could feel the blush climbing from her neck to her forehead. There was a lot less to the garment than she had thought. It left little to nothing to the imagination.

The door cracked open, and Brie peeked in. "Wow!" she said. "Wow, you look great!" Rafael would go bonkers, and that was half the fun, but she kept that thought to herself. Tori was, as she had said, an initiate into the fun of having a lover. "You're pretty sexy,

Victoria. Seeing you like this, I totally can't believe we were all fooled."

"Alright, I'll get it too." She shoved Brie back out and shut the door again.

Ten minutes later, the teddy was in a cart along with a few other bras, matching panties, and an outrageously beautiful silk nightgown that Tori was reluctantly in love with. It was also blue, and it was close enough to the color of her eyes that it became extra flattering. Their next stop was the regular women's clothes area.

"Tell me something," Isabelle said suddenly. "Why do you keep your hair so short? Your face could handle longer hair very well."

"It doesn't grow very fast. It's taken three months to even get it to this point, and it's still only an inch or two longer than it used to be. I don't think I'd like long hair. I'd never know what to do with it." Tori eyed her warily. "Why?"

"I was simply thinking that you could get it styled. Something that is easy to manage, but something more flattering than simply chopping all of it off. You have such beautiful hair. I know many women who pay money to get that shade of golden hair, but you have it by nature. When Brie and I get our hair done for the party, you will come with us."

"Yes'm." Tori tucked her hands in her pocket. She knew better than to argue with Isabelle when she got bossy. And, anyway, she was at the reluctantly resigned stage. She was almost enjoying the excursion.

They left the store with two bags of items. Or rather, they obtained two bags. A cheerful clerk would actually take them to the limo so that they could hurry on to their next stop.

The tone for the entire day was set. With an amused Alex following and offering occasional commentary, Tori was taken through at least half the stores in the mall until her cheerful captors decided they had done enough damage. Sensing she was getting overloaded, they decided to make the shoe store their final stop. It was almost evening already.

Tori was not only overloaded but also overwhelmed. She hadn't recognized herself in the mirror once all day. Brie and Isabelle were ruthless in making sure that everything flattered her. Jeans clung to her hips and thighs. Skirts were long to emphasize her height. If a shirt buttoned, it was tailored to tuck in at the sides so it enhanced her bust. If a shirt pulled on, it was either in a baby-doll style, or simply snug. Slacks were tailored in a way not dissimilar from the buttoned shirts. Dresses had either no obvious waist or one cut slightly higher than average.

Tori was fairly sure she would remember nothing of what she had been told. Her consolation in that fact was that she knew everything she now owned could go together. If she pulled it out of her closet, it would work. Brie had stuck to cool tones, primarily blues and greens, and matched them with neutrals.

"Oh what about jewelry?" Isabelle suddenly remembered. "She will need some of that as well. She will wear some of Mama's jewelry to the party since she is Rafael's future wife, but she will need casual pieces."

Tori blinked. "Jewelry? What for?"

Brie pursed her lips as she sought an explanation. "Okay, it's like this. Say you have a room with really nice furniture. You put in accessories to emphasize certain colors and lines to really make the room look completed and awesome. Jewelry is like that for women."

Tori looked at Alex. "My life was so much less complicated as a man."

"I have been thinking the same thing all day," he countered wryly.

"Do you have pierced ears?" Isabelle asked her.

"No, why would I?" Her eyes widened. "Oh hell no. No one is sticking needles in me. I got enough of that in the hospital."

"It doesn't hurt," Brie said in exasperation. "Just a little pinch and a sort of dull punch. No pain. We'll do that after we get shoes. Your ears should be just healed enough for you to wear some fancy earrings at the party. You heal fast."

"Alex, save me," Tori pleaded.

"Sorry, you're on your own." He nudged her into the shoe store. "Stop being a chicken. I've seen you face down men three times your size and wipe the floor with them. You can handle a little body art."

"What size shoe do you wear?" Isabelle asked.

"Men's size seven. I don't know what I wear in women's."

She got her answer after she stuck her foot on a sizing device. She was a size nine and a half, borderline ten. She found herself parked on a padded bench while Brie, Isabelle, and an overly perky salesgirl ravaged the aisles for selections. "I don't know how to wear high heels," Tori muttered. "I'll break my neck!"

"They're not that high," Brie assured her as she brought over several boxes. "You're super tall, Victoria. You don't need high heels like Isabelle and I do. A subtle heel will work the same way on you that higher ones work on us. It's about making your legs look hot."

They settled on nothing higher than two inches. Luckily, Tori wore a pair of her new jeans, and they were able to see how effective the shoes worked at flattering her legs. After the first wobbly steps where she distinctly felt like an overgrown newborn colt, she got the rhythm and was able to walk more comfortably.

"You have incredible balance," Isabelle said happily. "I was certain you would be fine once you got used to it. And because we love you . . ." She held out a pair of chic sneakers. "These will go with any of your jeans."

"Sneakers!" Tori grabbed them and held them against her chest possessively. "My feet will take back some of the nasty things they've been saying about you."

Sandals in black, white, and tan were obtained along with a variety of casual and formal heels in primarily neutral colors so they would match anything. She opted to wear the sneakers out; they were as comfortable as they looked, and she couldn't help but like how they managed to be casual and chic at the same time.

She was so busy admiring them that she didn't realize they had reached the jewelry store until Brie suddenly intoned, "Dun dun *dun*."

She looked up and nearly did a double take. "This is real jewelry."

"You were expecting fake?" Isabelle arched a brow.

"I was expecting something that doesn't scream 'rob me.'"

"They have simple items here as well. We want elegance, not overdone." Isabelle smiled as the man behind the counter came around to greet her. "*Ciao*, Francis. It is good to see you again."

"And you as well." Francis smiled at Alex. "Hello again, Mr. LaGuardia."

"You've been here before?" Tori asked curiously.

"Alex got my engagement ring here." Isabelle held up her left hand where the fiery ruby winked merrily. "He said that he would not give me diamonds because I am too temperamental. I would turn them red. It was best to give me something red to begin with." She smiled at Alex in a way that had others in the store looking over enviously. "He knows me well."

Alex kissed her for that and then tucked her under his arm contentedly. "We're here for Victoria." He gestured to Tori. "She is marrying Isabelle's brother, Rafael. The notices will be out shortly."

"How delightful!" Francis beamed at Tori. "Congratulations! How did you manage to tie him down?"

"Duct tape."

"I think I am going to like you. Well, what exactly can I help you ladies find?"

With his help, they picked out a few discreet necklaces and matching bracelets, none of which got in Tori's way. She even liked the way the bracelets glittered around her wrist. Either her girly side had been asleep with the rest of her hormones, or she had just never felt safe to indulge in it. It could go either way.

Several pairs of earrings were chosen, and she found herself reluctantly sitting on a stool at the counter while Francis used a small pen to mark where the holes in her lobes would go. She looked in a mirror to be sure they were even and then squeezed her eyes shut. She didn't want to watch.

The first one was the shocking one. It definitely felt like a quick punch, but it wasn't entirely painless. It was more like a quick hit before turning into a faint throbbing. By the time she even recognized that it had hurt a little, her other ear had been pierced as well. Surprised, she opened her eyes.

"There," Francis said. "That wasn't so bad."

She looked in the mirror and turned her head to see the tiny silver studs. She actually liked them more than she had thought she would, so she smiled as she said, "I've experienced one of the worst pains known to mankind. I guess this definitely wasn't so bad."

"You have given birth?" he asked curiously as he began to ring up the purchases.

She could have bitten her tongue. "Uhm, no. I had to have shoulder surgery after an accident. I was happy to be drugged, I assure you."

"Nice save," Alex murmured.

By the time Tori dragged herself into her room, it was dark out. She was *exhausted*. They had dropped Brie off with Roberto and gotten burgers to eat since they had missed dinner. Once home, Alex and the chauffeur had grabbed Marco and the gardener to help haul in all of the spoils of the war on the economy.

The bags were all over Tori's room to the point there was really nowhere to walk. She didn't care. She fell face first onto her bed and contemplated not moving for a week. She heeled off her sneakers but that was all she had the energy left to do.

She couldn't even lift her head when she heard her door open. Into her pillow, she muttered, "Shoot me again, please. I'm already dead."

"I see that." Rafael's voice sounded warm with tender amusement. He picked his way gingerly across the room and sat beside her on the bed. Even though he only saw the back, he approved of the efforts. The jeans she wore made a spectacular showing of her lovely bottom. He barely kept from running a hand over it and down her leg. He thought she might be too tired to hit him, but he wasn't going to take the chance. "Tell me you at least had fun."

She propped herself up on her elbows with a wry smile. "I question my sanity, but I think I did. I think the fashion lessons are leaking out my newly pierced ears, but I did enjoy myself most of the time. Your sisters are shopping guerillas. Seriously."

"And that is why I do not go out with Isabelle," he admitted dryly. "I had suspicion that Brie might be just as bad, if not worse for her creative bend." He tugged on a belt loop lightly. "I approve. I am not certain my heart will withstand the sight of you in a dress, *cara*, but I look forward to that as well."

"I'm wearing a bra," she confessed in a mock whisper. "I feel like a grown-up now." When he laughed as she had hoped, she rolled over and sat up. "Are you plotting, Rafael? When I questioned if I needed to get something fancy for our 'engagement' party, I was informed by Isabelle that you were going to 'handle everything' once you knew what sizes I wore."

"That is because I have a surprise for you. You will see it soon enough." He leaned in to peer at her ears in the low light from the single lamp. "You got them pierced. I am glad. As the heir, my mother's jewelry came to me to be given to my future wife." She opened her mouth, and he continued calmly, "It is a Lucino tradition that the fiancée of the heir to the family wear the jewels at the engagement party. It would be questioned by many if you did not."

"Damn it." Sudden amusement made her grin. "Tell me, if Isabelle had been older and therefore the heir, how would that have worked? I don't think Alex would look good in diamonds."

"I am sure he could have managed. The earrings would quite

flatter him, but he might resent giving up his beloved Apple Watch for a bracelet." He said it with a straight face, but when she started laughing, he had to laugh as well. "I could not resist. Do not dare tell him I said that, Victoria."

"It's our secret. Now answer seriously."

"Seriously, Isabelle would have worn them herself. Old-fashioned *mia famiglia* may be, but both son and daughter have inherited in the past. Did you know that the Lucino family has been in America for over a hundred years, and has an even longer history in Italy?" When her brows lifted in surprise, he brought her hand to his lips. "I will take you to our land near Rome. We have a *castello*."

"I already get lost in this place," she complained. "You'll never see me again if you take me to a castle. Besides, I'm not the castle type. I don't go in for wine and cheese. I'm more like beer and pizza."

"There is a fifty-two inch television in the *castello* game room."

She blinked. "Wow."

"*Nonno* sneaks in beer when *Nonna* is not looking." He winked. "He claims it is his guilty pleasure."

"I still can't wrap my brain around the fact that eventually you will inherit a castle."

"It will be ours, *cara mia*." He pressed her hand to his heart and curled his free hand around the back of her neck to tug her closer. "I will chase you through the halls when no one is there and enjoy finding you when you are lost. I will show you my homeland. Italy will love you, Victoria, in a way that America never could. I will love you in a way no one else ever has, or ever will."

She could find no will to resist when his lips tenderly claimed hers. Her entire body went weak with a pleasure that was velvety and consuming. This was not the violent hunger of the morning. This was deeper. It seemed as if he kissed her from his very soul, and she couldn't help but surrender. Her heart demanded no less.

He slowly lowered her to the bed and eased back to look down at her. The light was doing its magic over her face again, making her features soft and sultry all at the same time. "It is a curious beauty," he said huskily, framing her face with one hand, "that can have so many facets. You are magic, Victoria. I look at you and see something new. I will spend a lifetime looking at you, and you will never look the same twice. I will lose my breath every time."

"You make me sound like a diamond," she somehow managed to tease. She felt breathless and needy, craving his closeness but equally afraid of it. He said he loved her, and he seemed to truly do so, but everything had changed so swiftly that she was terrified to trust her heart, or his. What if it was merely gratitude and friendship in disguise?

"I believe you are," he said after a moment. "Carbon is placed under extreme pressure and from it comes something beautiful. So, too, were you formed, *cara*. What you have endured has made you beautiful." He brushed her lips with his and slowly released her. "If I stay longer," he murmured huskily, "I may not leave at all."

She sat up and put her hand on his arm with a frown. "Will you sleep?"

"I will now that I have seen you. When I am with you . . . I feel safe. You will protect me. Knowing that, I do not fear my sleep so greatly. Someday soon, I will sleep with you in my arms, and I will rest better than I ever have before." He kissed her one last time. "*Ti amo*," he murmured against her lips. "Come to me, *cara*, anytime. I will love you for all the times no one else would."

She wasn't breathing as she watched him leave her room. A part of her wanted to go chasing after him. The rest of her was too afraid to take that jump. Something would happen soon, though. It had to. What was between them was too volatile to be contained much longer. She just didn't know if she had the courage. Fighting for her life was nothing. Getting shot had been minor. Nearly dying had been an inconvenience. Trusting her heart scared the hell out of her.

# CHAPTER TWELVE

The few days until the party proved a flurry of activity. Word spread like wildfire through the media, and Tori was highly unnerved to open a newspaper and see a picture of her and Rafael together. She was more unnerved if she walked past a mirror. Even if she just grabbed the first thing to come to hand out of her closet, she looked . . . good. Pretty. Feminine. It was surreal.

She had gotten smart and stopped thinking about it. She was rolling with the punches, so to speak, and just taking each day at a time. Rafael was either consciously trying to help or subconsciously aware of her unbalance. He didn't push her. He didn't act heavy-handed. He was simply . . . there. He held her hand. He would casually kiss her in passing. If they were together, he was always touching her. A hand on her shoulder or back. An arm around her waist. She had known the family was tactile, but having it focused toward her was both sweet and scary.

They still stayed up talking until they were tired. They still played billiards together. Once they were ready for bed, he would kiss her good night and offer her a place to sleep if she wanted. When she declined, he would simply smile and let it be. She had the unnerving feeling that his patience was the water dripping on the stone of her fear. It kept crumbling away.

The morning of the party, she was in her room, reluctantly flipping through a magazine of hairstyles that Brie had pointedly given her when she heard a large commotion from downstairs. Her brows lifted, and she headed down the hall to look into the foyer.

The commotion was the arrival of an older gentleman who looked like Antonio in twenty years or Rafael in fifty. He wore a pitch-black suit with the confidence of a man half his age, and he still stood tall and proud. He carried a cane, but it seemed more a prop than a necessity. Even at seventy, Vincent Lucino was attractive enough to turn heads. His hair was entirely white, and his sharp blue eyes looked nearly wicked with amusement.

Tori had a strong feeling that Rafael might be a chip off his *nonno's* block. Wary of going downstairs into the happy reunion, she hovered just out of sight. She sensed Brie come up beside her and murmured, "You too?"

"He disowned my mother," she countered just as softly. "He owns a *castle*, Tori. He has more zeroes in his bank account than the U.S. government."

"And where are *miei bambini*?" Vincent suddenly demanded in a booming voice that carried. "Why do they not come to greet their *nonno*, 'Tonio? Have you not been teaching them to respect a great man?"

Antonio laughed. "*Sì*, Papa, I have. That is why they do not come running."

His father laughed and gave him a hard hug. "You are growing old, 'Tonio. I will forgive you for being so rude."

Isabelle came running in from the kitchen, a brilliant smile on her face as she threw herself into her grandfather's arms. "*Nonno*! I am so happy to see you!"

"Ah, Bella!" He lifted her off her feet for a fierce hug. "You are more beautiful than ever! You will give me great-grandbabies, *sì*?"

"*Sì*. You will meet Alex shortly. He has stepped out to run an errand for Rafael." She kissed Vincent's cheeks. "You will love him. He is perfect for me. You will not be able to intimidate him at all."

"That is good."

"Where is Mama?" Antonio asked Vincent curiously. "She is not with you?"

"She could not come this time. She is recovering from

pneumonia." At the alarmed looks, he held up his hands. "She is fit and complaining, so I know she will be well. She has demanded that the wedding take place in *il castello*, as is tradition." In an aside, he added, "She is being lazy, 'Tonio, and she does not think I know. Pah! After fifty years of marriage, I know her mind better than she does."

"I wonder what it'll be like to be married for fifty years," Brie murmured to Tori. "You think I'll have gotten used to Roberto by then?"

Tori snorted softly. "You'll have learned all of the cuss words you need, that's for sure."

Rafael suddenly walked up behind them. "You are being cowards. He does not bite." He caught each by the shoulder and began urging them forward toward the stairs. "If you do not show yourselves now, then he will come find you. He has a nose like a bloodhound." As they reached the top of the stairs, he added, "*Nonno*, smile. You are scaring Gabrielle and Victoria."

Vincent's brows lifted. "I am not a scary man, Rafael. You must be mistaken. Your *nonna* is scary." His expression grew thoughtful as he looked at Brie. It was a little surprising to see that she appeared so perfectly identical to Isabelle, but he had seen many amazing things in his long life. "So you are Sophia's child."

It was Rafael's hand in the middle of her back that kept Brie from fleeing. "Yeah."

"'Yeah'? What is this 'yeah' that you Americans use? Why do you not use proper language?" He sighed heavily. "Roberto will bring you to Italy and you will learn culture. Now come greet your grandfather. I am old, and I am foolish, but I learn. If Sophia were alive, she and her husband would be welcomed home."

She hesitantly walked over to him and went on her toes to kiss his cheek. He hugged her tightly, and she carefully hugged him back, her breath unraveling. She had been half-afraid he would kick her out of the house!

"There." He kissed her cheeks and then lightly tweaked her nose. "You are very American, but we can fix that. Do you speak

Italian?" She shook her head, and he sighed. "*Sì*, and such a pity. You will learn."

"I am working on it," Roberto said calmly as he walked into the foyer from outside. "*Ciao, Don Lucino. Come sta?*"

"*Benissimo*, Roberto." Vincent smiled. "I suppose I shall have to like you now that you are marrying one of my *bambini*."

"I suppose you shall." Roberto tugged Brie into the circle of his arms with a smile.

"Now, Rafael!" Vincent beetled his brows at his heir. "Where is this woman that has stolen your heart?"

Rafael firmly pulled Tori the rest of the way down the stairs and gave her no option of escape. "This is Victoria Li. She saved my life, *Nonno*. I have since convinced her to live it with me." He brought Tori's hand to his lips and smiled as he looked into her wary eyes. "Do not overwhelm her too greatly. She has never had *famiglia* before."

"Li." Vincent arched a brow. "You are Chinese?" She shook her head. "Japanese?" At the next shake, he pursed his lips. "*Sì*, you do not look Asian. Where does your family come from, Victoria?"

"I don't know. I was raised in a foster home. My name was given to me by a doctor when I was taken to the hospital as a baby. I could be any ethnicity, sorry. I'm pretty sure it's mostly Caucasian since I'm naturally blonde and blue eyed, but I could be any number of European types too."

He studied her critically and nodded firmly. "Then you will do well for the mother of my great-grandbabies. It is good that the family has more new blood introduced. You and Rafael will have beautiful babies for me to spoil."

She could feel the blush climbing her face. "Thanks."

"*Scusi, Nonno*." Isabelle smiled. "I must steal Gabrielle and Victoria so we may go get our hair done. Alex will be meeting us there," she added when three sets of male eyes narrowed in concern. "You must get settled in." She kissed her grandfather's cheek. "We will make ourselves more beautiful so you may show us off."

"If you insist." Vincent smiled as the three women hurried

out—Brie and Isabelle mostly dragging Tori—and then turned to Rafael. His smile faded. "Tell me what you know of Victoria. I do not like that she does not know her own heritage. She does not hide well that it bothers her, this not knowing. We will fix it."

Tori was indeed dragging her heels, but only a little bit. Thankfully, they weren't taking the limo again. The chauffeur instead stood next to the regular Cadillac that the family used. It wasn't precisely as subtle as she might have preferred, but it was better than the limo. The windows were tinted in the back, and that helped her feel a little better as well.

As they headed to the salon, Brie asked, "Did you decide anything?"

"No." Tori tugged on a lock of her hair. "I really don't care, Brie, okay? Just as long as I don't have to fuss with it, I'm fine. And no extensions!" she added hastily. "That completely enters the realm of high maintenance. If you want to see me with long hair, you'll simply have to wait a year or two for my hair to grow naturally."

"Nothing curly," Isabelle told Brie. "She is not the curly type." Tori winced at the very idea, and she laughed. "Do not worry, Victoria. You are in good hands."

Alex was waiting for them at the salon, as promised, and looked much like a bull in a china shop. The salon was delicate and elegant, and he was too tall and too masculine to not stand out. He took it in good humor, though, and settled in the waiting room with a magazine where he could keep his eye on all three chairs the women would be in.

Tori found herself introduced to a stylist named Jon and then whisked into the washing station to have her hair fully scrubbed. While he was doing that, he talked cheerfully with Isabelle and Brie about what to do to her. She closed her eyes and tuned them out. They might as well have been speaking in Italian; nothing they said made any sense to her. What the hell was 'feathering'?

After wrapping her hair with a towel, he showed her to the cutting station. "Now," he said, "what I'm going to do is fancy up your hair specifically for tonight. After the party, you can wash out all of the product without any problems. Just blow dry your hair and it'll fall into its natural style." He winked. "Its new natural style. If you want to play with it, a little gel will do wonders. Just leave it to me."

"Do I have any other choice?" she muttered.

"You could go bald and wear a wig."

"Don't tempt me!"

He just grinned as he got to work on her hair. She didn't bother to look in the mirror at herself; she used the reflection to watch everyone and everything else instead. It felt as if someone was watching her, but she couldn't pinpoint anything overt. There were many people who would glance over at her curiously, but none of them seemed dangerous. And yet, she couldn't shake the feeling. When she glanced toward Alex, she could see him tapping a foot lightly on the floor. It was a telling gesture that meant he felt something too.

The hair dryer started whirring and she closed her eyes. The snipping had stopped and Jon was doing something with a strange round brush. "Did you bring the hairpieces?" he asked someone curiously.

"What hairpieces?" she asked warily.

"Keep your eyes closed," Isabelle ordered from somewhere to the side. There was a smile in her voice.

Tori muttered but kept her eyes closed, even when she felt Jon clipping something into her hair on either side of her head. Hair clips? Were they nuts? She was twenty-five, not fifteen.

"Now you can look." Satisfaction filled Jon's voice. "You're going to knock your fiancé on his butt."

Her eyes popped open and she stared at her reflection. He had cut her hair in a way that made it fall more toward her face and soften the lines and angles. It had been fluffed and tousled for more body, and looked . . . elegantly sexy. It was the only way she could think of describing it. She then saw what had been clipped into her hair and her breath caught.

The clips were slender diamond swans opening their wings. Set into her golden hair, they sparkled and shimmered with even the littlest light hitting them. They pulled her hair back away from her ears, and the final effect was so feminine that she could only gape. She very cautiously reached up to touch one of the clips. "Bella," she pleaded, "tell me they're not . . ."

"Oh, they are. They were made just for you."

She would kick Rafael's ass for this. How was she supposed to forget she had *real* diamonds in her hair? She would be terrified of turning her head too fast and accidentally losing one.

Brie's hair ended up being curled and pinned up in ringlets. Isabelle's hair was upswept into an elaborate coil of braids that looked like something out of a princess' guide to fashion. Brie had a sapphire circlet wrapped around her hair. Rubies on a delicate silver net covered Isabelle's coil.

With their hair finished, all three were free to have their nails done. Tori stared in fascinated horror at the little bottles of polish and the assorted nail tips. Brie blessedly came to her rescue. "Don't make her nails long," she told the lady cleaning Tori's nails. "She has a very physical job, and she would break them." She winked at Tori.

The stylist took the advice to heart and only extended Tori's nails enough that they went past her fingertips. "What color polish?" she asked Tori. "What does your dress look like?"

"Good question," Tori muttered.

Isabelle smiled. "She will be in white."

"I'll be in *what*?" Tori gaped at her. "I'll spill something on myself! That's like *asking* for karmic revenge!"

"*Taci*, Victoria." She admired her nails and the rich ruby color they were being painted. "It will all be revealed at home. Tonight you will be a swan."

Tori's nails ended up painted a soft gray color that she would never have imagined could look so pretty. The better part was that she could still make a decent fist without worrying about cutting her palm. The tips were nice and blunt, and not long enough to get in the way. "Thanks, Brie," she murmured as they headed on their way home.

"Don't thank me yet." Her grin turned wicked. "You've still got to put on makeup." Tori groaned, and she laughed. "Bella will hold your hand the entire time."

They snuck in the back through the kitchen with Alex serving as a decoy by entering the front door. Brie wouldn't have minded being seen by Roberto, but neither she nor Isabelle wanted Tori seen until they were completely done.

They ushered her into her room swiftly, and Isabelle instructed, "Put on the dress and we will return as soon as we have also changed. If you cannot fasten the dress, then you may wait for us."

Tori scowled as the door was shut behind her. She had once found Isabelle's bossiness amusing. It had become vexing now that she was the recipient of it. Muttering under her breath, she walked over to the bed where a garment bag had been laid out with two boxes beside it. One looked like a shoebox, and the other could have been anything.

She opened the strange box first and felt her cheeks heat. Neatly folded inside a bed of tissue were a strapless white bra, lace underwear, and sheer flesh-toned stockings. A note on the top from Brie read, *I convinced Isabelle that you weren't a garter type woman. They're normal silk stockings.*

"Thank you, Brie," she muttered.

The shoebox indeed held shoes, she discovered. They were a frothy confection of straps and beads that looked too ridiculously fragile to be worn on feet. A little more wary than before, she carefully opened the garment bag. As she saw what was inside, she stopped breathing.

The dress was definitely white, but the top portion to roughly her hip area was liberally covered with intricate beadwork that seemed to subtly hint at a pattern she couldn't quite decipher. From the hip to probably mid-thigh, the dress was made of white feathers. When she carefully ran her hand over them, she wasn't entirely surprised to discover they were real. Apparently Isabelle had been literal when she had said Tori would be a swan.

With a quick breath for courage, she pulled on her lingerie and then made an attempt to get into the dress. The zipper went up the back from her waist to that elusive place partway up her back that she would have to be a contortionist to reach. Designers were nuts, or they thought women had reverse bending elbows. It was debatable.

The entire thing was snug, even the feathered portion, but not so snug that she felt impaired in her movement. The end of the dress stopped an inch below her knees, more than long enough to go past her thigh-high stockings. The top of the dress had a straight line that just sort of teasingly hinted at the shadow of her cleavage. The straps were wide enough that they covered the tail end of her scar, something she had entirely forgotten about but was glad someone else had remembered. She was proud of the mark, but it would give her identity away.

The door opened and Isabelle peeked in. She sighed happily. "Oh, Victoria! You are lovely!"

"Wow!" Brie peeked around her shoulder. "You're hot, Tori. Totally." She hurried in, looking sleek and sultry in a long skirted dark blue silk dress covered in elaborate beading. She zipped up the back of Tori's dress for her before stepping back to study her critically. She nodded firmly. "Rafe definitely knew what he was doing."

Isabelle put down the case of makeup that she carried "Put on your robe," she told Tori, "so we do not risk your gown." In her red ball gown, she was as sultry as her twin, but she seemed to be more like the flame that smoldered than the flame that burned.

Once Tori was bundled in her robe, Brie got to work on her makeup. "Light," she assured her, "because your face doesn't need a lot. You've got perfect cheekbones."

"I do?"

Her lips thinned. "I'd like to kick all those people who made you feel ugly. You just didn't belong in their world. Different doesn't mean ugly. You absolutely need to look up all of those snotty little snits from high school and send them postcards from the *castello* after you and Rafe get married. Like a 'too bad you're not here' sort of thing. Make them green with envy."

"I'm not marrying Rafe."

Isabelle and Brie shared a smile but said nothing. Tori's protests had been steadily growing weaker, and it was clear that her resistance crumbled. She would tumble right into Rafael's arms if he pushed just a little bit harder. The two of them *belonged* together. It was a crime against love itself if they weren't.

Brie added a pale rose-colored lipstick for a finishing touch and leaned back. "Okay. Lose the robe and look in the mirror."

Tori took off the robe and cautiously walked over to her full-length mirror. The woman that stared back at her was a stranger. She was beautiful and sexy, strong, and yet feminine. She deserved to walk into a ballroom on the arm of a man like Rafael Lucino.

A light knock sounded on the door. "May I come in?" Rafael called.

Brie hurried over to open the door. Rafael walked in, a box in his hand, and stopped sharply as he saw Tori. His eyes slowly widened. He didn't even notice when his sister and cousin slipped out with smiles. His gaze was filled with the sight of the woman he loved.

She was . . . stunning. She looked a little shocked by her reflection and a lot vulnerable as she looked at him. Her hair begged to be mussed by his fingers. Her lips were soft and asking to be kissed. The dress he'd had made for her seemed to flatter everything he loved about her from her long legs to her gentle figure.

"*Dio*, Victoria," he whispered. "You are beautiful." He stepped closer and carefully touched her cheek with his fingers. "I cannot believe you are real."

She couldn't catch her breath. He looked exotic and gorgeous in his black tuxedo, and too handsome for her sanity. A white sash crossed his powerful chest, drawing emphasis to his strong shoulders. She somehow smiled as she tugged on it lightly. "Uh-oh.

Have you been marked as the future keeper to the keys of the kingdom?"

"*Sì*." He put the box on the bed and opened it. "And now you will be marked as my future queen."

Her mouth fell open as he lifted a silver and diamond necklace. "I'm not wearing that."

"Yes, you are. Turn around, *cara mia*." She reluctantly did and he slipped the necklace around her neck and fastened it into place. The nape of her neck was slender and delicate, and he could not resist the urge to press his lips there. She shivered softly and he ran his hands down her arms. "I cannot resist you."

Matching teardrop earrings were fastened to her ears, and he was deft enough to put them on her without bothering her still sensitive lobes. It did nothing good for her pulse, however, to have him standing that close. He smelled wonderful, felt hot and tempting.

"Now then." He picked up a smaller box that had been in the bigger. "It would not do for you to walk in without an engagement ring. And as I want you to keep it for your own, I had best do this properly." He went down on one knee as her eyes widened. "Marry me, Victoria. Marry me for real. Forget everything else. Love me. Be my salvation, my defender. Keep me safe in your arms."

Her stomach dipped with sheer terror, but as she looked into his eyes, she saw something she had never seen before. A trace of nerves, of pain and longing. He had always seemed confident before. So cocky and assured. Yet here . . . he was vulnerable. Wonder began to fill her softly. "You're in love with me."

"Have I not said it enough? I think I have loved you since I met you. Man, woman, neither, or both. It is *you* that I love. I have wanted you all along. You *belong* with me, Victoria. With my family. Please. Marry me."

She took a deep breath. It was real. It was scary and it was real. "I guess since I saved your life," she said huskily, "the least I can do is make sure it stays safe for the next seventy years or so. It was personal this time, Rafe. It should have been a job, but from the beginning it was personal. I didn't take a bullet for you just because it was my job. I wasn't even thinking in that moment. I just . . . loved you."

His breath came out hard and quick. "You scared me, *cara mia*." He stood and pulled her into his arms fiercely. "I would kiss you, but I would muss you up and Brie would yell at me. I will kiss you later when I am free to muss you up as much as I desire."

Someone banged on the door. "Let's go, you two," Alex called. "You're the guests of honor. You can't be late to your own party, and the natives are getting restless."

"We are on our way," Rafael called back. He opened the ring box and pulled out what was within. The delicate silver setting held a diamond just big enough to catch the light, but not big enough to be overwhelming. On the inside of the band, the words '*Ti amo*' had been engraved. "So you always remember you are loved," he said softly as he slid it over her finger.

"Don't make me cry," she pleaded. "I don't cry. I've never cried. I'm not going to be *that* much a girl. I like some of my boy self!"

He laughed and kissed her knuckle over her ring. "As do I. I shall endeavor to make sure you are always smiling, *cara*." He brushed a kiss across her forehead. "Let us go before Alex comes in and fetches us. Are you ready to face a room of wildly jealous people?"

"Jealous of me or you?"

"Me. I fear I might be in grave danger from many gentlemen, Victoria."

She shook her head in amusement, not entirely believing it herself. "I will protect you."

"*Sì, cara*. I have never doubted that for a moment."

# CHAPTER THIRTEEN

The layout of the Lucino villa allowed for an immense dining room and an equally immense ballroom. Tori had been in the dining room often enough and was always amused by the way the whole family gathered at one end of the large table. She had peeked into the ballroom once or twice out of curiosity, but she had never actually gone inside.

It was for that reason that she felt suitably impressed when she walked into the room and found it filled with people. The staff had gone overboard with decorations, and the entire place felt like it belonged in the infamous *castello*. She had to force herself to remember she was still in New York and had not been secretly teleported to Italy. It was overwhelming, especially when people began to clap and cheer as they saw her and Rafael. His arm tightened around her waist in support and made it easier to resist an urge to run away.

"Remember, *cara*," he murmured softly, "you are the queen here. There is no one who can compare, no one who would dare try." He skimmed his lips across her temple. He felt humbled by her bravery. He knew that this was exceptionally hard for her because she had never stood in the spotlight before.

"Don't leave my side," she pleaded softly, "or I really will run away."

"I am not going anywhere. Just think of this as your prom night."

"I never went to prom," was her mutter. "The boys didn't want me."

"Then you knew only fools. I would have claimed you for my own without a second thought." He walked further into the room, and his arm around her waist forced her to go with him. "I will introduce you to people, and you will be yourself. Everyone will love you."

She wasn't quite that confident but she was committed. There were a lot of big names in this crowd of people. Several politicians, other corporate owners, businesspeople that the Lucinos had worked with, and other high-class elite made up the majority of the crowd. The rest were the employees of Just In Time, Inc. To her immense relief, the crowd wasn't as big as it had initially appeared; only fifty or so people were in attendance.

She began to relax after the first hour of mingling. People were being genuinely friendly and welcoming. Even the politicians seemed to be truly happy for Rafael, but she took that with a grain of salt. She trusted no one who had to be elected for anything.

It didn't take long for those in the crowd to realize that Rafael was madly in love with his fiancée. He never once left her side and either kept his arm around her waist or held her hand with his. If he looked at her, there was something powerful in his blue eyes. His voice, when he would speak to her, always seemed more intimate.

And Tori? There was no question as to her feelings as well, though there was an obvious shyness or sense of wonder if she looked at her fiancé. Truly, that did not come as a surprise to anyone. Nearly no one in the crowd had ever heard of her before, so she obviously came from a different background entirely. To suddenly jump to the top of the totem pole would be disorienting for anyone. Reactions were a bit tepid to her at first, but she was so friendly, so personable, that even some of the snootier guests found themselves liking her a great deal.

There was, however, one person in the crowd who knew Tori and knew where she had come from. Tori herself did not realize she was there until Rafael escorted her over to meet one of the politicians. "Victoria, *cara*," he said with a smile, "meet Assemblyman Davis Harkin and his new wife, Paula."

Shocked, Tori stared at an equally startled Paula Harkin. The former Paula Crothers, the girl Tori had knocked on her ass so that she could be suspended to escape school.

At twenty-five, Paula was as beautiful as ever, but there were tiny lines already beginning to appear at the corner of her eyes and mouth, as if too much unhappiness had started dragging her down. Still busty and yet petite, she wore an emerald green dress that showed off nearly every one of her assets. It also showed that her formerly trim body looked much skinnier than might be healthy for her size. Her desperation to fit in had only done all the more damage to her internally and externally.

For the first time in her life, Tori realized she did not feel outclassed. Her entire body relaxed. She had always wondered how she would feel if she met someone from her past again, and now she knew. She felt . . . nothing. If she was a swan as her family said, then Paula had to be a duck. They just belonged in two different worlds, neither better nor worse than the other. "As a matter of fact," she said calmly, "Paula and I knew each other years ago. We went to high school together."

Rafael's arm tightened possessively and protectively though he kept his smile. "It is a small world, no?"

Harkin inclined his head with one of those polished 'good guy' smiles that Tori had always hated. "It's a pleasure to meet you, Victoria." He looked her over slowly in a way that made her hackles rise. "Rafael, you have spectacular taste as always. It's good to see a young man marrying for love. I had to wait for my chance." He smiled at Paula affectionately.

Somehow, Tori didn't think love had anything to do with their marriage. Harkin looked old enough to be Paula's father, and the look in his eyes felt more . . . covetous than loving. He may have been pleasant enough in appearance, perhaps, but there was simply something about him that felt disturbing.

Paula forced herself to smile at Tori though it did not reach her eyes. "I didn't expect to see that you were the Victoria Li I once knew."

"I imagine you didn't. Congratulations on your marriage. I'm sure you're very happy together." Tori unconsciously rubbed her cheek lightly against Rafael's shoulder. "I'm sure you're happy for me too."

Paula's back teeth audibly clicked together. Her eyes narrowed with visible jealousy as she stared at Tori. It wasn't fair! The tomboyish caterpillar had somehow turned into a beautiful butterfly, and she had also bagged one of the hottest and most eligible bachelors in the state. The *way* that Rafael looked at her . . . Paula had married Harkin for his power and money, and she hated every minute of her life. Tori was getting more position, far more money, and a gorgeous husband who doted on her to go with it.

Snidely, she said, "It's so odd, Victoria. You disappeared for years. You dropped out of high school and that was all we knew of you."

"Actually," Tori's voice cooled, "I went into home study. I graduated perfectly on time. I chose to come out here for college. I've been working a rather confidential job for the last few years. I met Rafe on the last one."

"Well, at least you've stopped being so ugly."

A startled hush fell on the room as people heard Paula. Her color rose, and her husband began to look uncomfortable. Tori knew that proper etiquette probably called for her to ignore the insult and move on. It was a big party, there were dozens of bigwigs in the crowd, and taking the bait would probably embarrass the Lucinos.

Proper etiquette could go to hell. She'd had enough. "You're right," she told Paula. "I did stop being ugly. Unfortunately for you, your ugliness is still to come. You're going to get old, Princess Paulie, and I'd bet you're not going to do it very graciously."

"Don't call me that!" Paula hissed.

Tori leaned in until they were eye-to-eye. "I still don't know why you hated me or why you went out of your way to make my life hell. In the end I'm the one who is marrying the man of my dreams. I'm the one who will never doubt that my husband will want me even if I get old and wrinkly. The minute your boobs start to sag, you're going to be tossed over for the latest model. You and I both know it. I'd start saving money for some high class plastic surgery if you want to keep your cushy home."

"You can't talk to me like that!"

"Actually, I can. And it feels damn good. Almost as good as the time I knocked you on your ass. Push me, Paulie, and I'll do it again. I'm nine years older, nine years stronger, and nine years meaner." She straightened and turned away. "Fill your flapping jaw with some appetizers. I'd stay away from the bread though; I hear it's bad for ducks."

Several people started laughing as they got the reference. Harkin grabbed Paula's elbow and hustled her away from the scene much faster than would be expected of a man his size. In a voice that carried, Vincent called, "*Sì*, Rafael! You have chosen well! She will give me fierce and fiery *bambini* to spoil!"

Tori's cheeks turned red. "Oh god," she said under her breath. "I did not just make a scene."

"*Sì, cara*, you did." Rafael swung her into his arms with a wide grin. "But Lucinos enjoy making scenes. You will make a fine Lucino. Perhaps you are Italian as well."

She wound her arms around his neck with a sudden smile. "I'm probably a mutt, Rafe, with a little of everything."

"But the Italian is the important part." When she laughed, he ushered her into the middle of the room. "We will dance now. I wish to have you in my arms."

"I don't dance," she blurted in horror. "Rafael, I'll humiliate us both."

"I will teach you." He pulled her into his arms and bent his head to brush her ear with his lips. "There are many things I will teach you. Do not drink too much wine, Victoria. If you are tipsy, then you will not enjoy my lessons nearly as much."

An entirely different sort of heat flushed her body and made her cheeks pink. Her legs went weak but she somehow stayed on her feet by clinging onto his arms. It was nearly impossible to quell an urge to turn her head and kiss his sinfully tempting lips. "Teach me to dance," she invited softly, her voice huskier. "Then teach me everything else later."

A thrilling mix of hunger, laughter, and love filled his eyes. "How you tempt me, *cara*."

On the other side of the room, Antonio was smiling at the sight of his son and future daughter-in-law dancing when a stunning redhead in a green dress walked up to him. The Grecian style to the piece suited her in a way that seemed purely elemental. "You look pleased," Rhianna told him.

"I am well pleased. Did you know all along that this would happen?" He lifted a brow at her.

"Now how would I know that, Antonio?" Her black eyes widened innocently. "It was a coincidence." Her gaze turned faraway as she glanced to where Theresa was looking very unnerved and flustered by the cluster of males standing near her. "There are more as yet to come," she murmured.

"*Scusi?*"

"Nothing." She smiled. "I must excuse myself, Antonio. It was lovely to see you." She offered a hand.

He smiled and bowed gracefully. "A delight as always, Rhianna. Do not be a stranger. You will attend the wedding in Italy, yes?"

"I will do my best to make some free time."

More than one pair of wistful eyes followed her as she walked away. Practicality said she had to be in her fifties, or more, considering how long she had been in charge at Enforcers, but she looked to be barely in her mid-twenties. She was as beautiful and vibrant as any woman half her age.

Antonio had always admired her, and he felt it a great shame that so fine a woman would have been single her whole life. She deserved to have someone to hold her when her work grew too hard. But then, it would take a singularly exceptional person to handle such a powerful female. He hoped he saw it happen in his lifetime.

Tori was ready to escape by the time midnight arrived. With a sympathetic Alex covering for her, she snuck out the back and took off her shoes. Her very happy-to-be-freed feet were silent as she tiptoed through the quiet villa toward her room. Maneuvering on tile in stockings was not easy, though. Thank goodness that her balance was above average.

She spotted a light under her door and her brows drew together. When she peeked the door open, her sigh came long and contented. She owed one of the maids a big hug. The bed had been turned down and there was a fire cheerfully crackling in the fireplace to combat the winter chill.

She put her shoes on the top of the table. She then peeled off her stockings and dropped them in the hamper. Just that alone felt wonderful. She went into the bathroom and gingerly removed her earrings. She put the simple studs back in so that the terrible two wouldn't yell at her for letting the holes close that soon after getting them pierced. She removed the necklace as well and put it and the earrings in the waiting velvet box. She felt . . . odd, for some reason. As if she was waiting for something.

Her answer came when movement in the mirror caught her attention as she was wiping off her makeup. Rafael stood in the bathroom doorway, leaning negligently against the door as he watched her with a soft smile on his lips. He had shed most of his tuxedo and wore only his black pants and open white shirt. "*Scusi*," he said softly. "I am looking for the most beautiful woman in the world. Have you seen her?"

She covered the sudden flutter of her heart with a wry smile. "Sorry, you've got the wrong address."

"Then you are not looking in that mirror, *cara*." He stepped up behind her and lifted her chin so she looked at their reflection. "If you could only see through my eyes," he murmured in her ear, "then you would see how beautiful you are." He nuzzled her neck and softly tasted her skin. "Do not tell me to go, Victoria. I do not have that strength."

She drew a long and trembling breath. "I don't want you to go. But . . ." She made a helpless gesture.

"But it is new for you, and you are nervous." He turned her in his arms and calmly began to remove the clips from her hair. "Do not look surprised, *cara*. Am I a fool? You believed you were ugly for many years and then lived as a male. Where in that time would you have tried to have a lover?" He combed his fingers through her hair and thoroughly demolished her styled coif. Golden locks tumbled in her eyes and others scattered in a million directions. She looked a little wild, a little untamed, and very unsure. "You break my heart when you look at me like that."

"I'm not afraid," she argued. "Just . . . understandably apprehensive."

He cocked his head. "Then you will not mind if I peel this dress off you."

Her lips curved. "I'd be grateful, actually. I can't reach the zipper. It really is beautiful, Rafe. I never thanked you properly." She rose slightly on her toes and softly pressed her lips to his. A soft sigh of pleasure was captured by his mouth when he lazily deepened the kiss, his tongue gliding over hers without hurry.

She didn't even notice that he had unzipped the dress until he tugged the straps down her shoulders. She freed her arms and he tugged lightly on the hem of the skirt. The entire dress came free and slid to the floor, leaving her in nothing but her bra and panties. She didn't even think to cover herself. He was still kissing her, still consuming her in that drugging delight, and it was the only important thing.

He lifted her off her feet and carried her into the bedroom. To feel her so soft and welcoming in his arms . . . He wanted nothing more than to take his time and savor everything about her. He did not want her to ever question again that she was loved and desired.

"I can't catch my breath," she whispered as he let her slip down his body to stand on her own feet. "I didn't expect this."

He framed her face with his hands. "It is not all about flash and frenzy." He teased her lips lightly with his and nibbled on her lower lip. "We can have that later." He slowly smiled. "I am sure we will have that many times. But not this time, *cara mia*."

She had no will to resist as he kissed her again. Every muscle went limp with pleasure until only his hands held her up. She couldn't breathe or think, but it no longer seemed important. He kissed her as if that alone was all he had ever wanted. Even when the kiss lazily deepened, he didn't overwhelm her. It was much easier to surrender when he was utterly gentle with her. She had no room for apprehension or nerves.

His lips glided along the line of her jaw. "Touch me," he murmured huskily. "I need to feel your touch."

Her hands lifted and spread across his chest slowly. Matching shivers rippled through their bodies. She felt her fingers tingling with a nearly electric charge as she softly traced the line of his muscles. The quivering in his body was a thrilling reminder that she had an entirely different strength over him as well.

She pushed at his shirt, and he shrugged out of it easily. "I'm amazed you even left it on," she said softly, a hint of amusement in her husky voice.

"I would not scare you." He slid his hands slowly up her sides and then around her back. He unhooked her bra and let it fall to the floor in a flutter of white. His breath lodged in his chest painfully as he looked at her. She was more beautiful than he remembered. "I do not want you to change more," he said, his voice thick. "You are perfection for me."

A soft moan was her only answer as his hot hands tenderly cupped her breasts. Somehow she was sure that her sensitivity had nothing to do with her growing figure and everything to do with him. It didn't seem to matter where he touched her. All that changed was the intensity of the pleasure. There was nothing that did not respond to him.

He pressed hot kisses along her strong shoulder and then down along her collar. His soul quivered with shocking emotion as he discovered the scar that sat starkly against her nearly flawless skin. His tongue traced the length of the mark before soothing it with kisses. He wanted to remove every memory of pain, every memory of fear, for the both of them. No matter how long he lived, he would never forget what she had done.

All she could manage was a whimper when his lips found one stiffened nipple. It tightened further as her breast swelled. The sensation was foreign and thrilling all at once. The ache spread like ripples in water until her body began to quiver with the need for release. How could anything that shockingly tender be so incredibly powerful?

She was barely conscious of him slowly stripping away her underwear so that she stood naked in his arms. Her eyes opened slightly and she saw the look of utter absorption on his face, the wonder in his eyes as he looked at her. He made her feel as beautiful as the diamond he had called her. "Rafe."

A shudder went through his body. He stood and lifted her into his arms to gently put her on top of the bed. With unashamed delight, she watched as he removed the last of his clothes. He was ridiculously male, unbelievably gentle. The contrast was thrilling, and even more so when she saw how aroused he was.

He eased onto the bed beside her and tangled his fingers in her hair to bring her up for another drugging kiss. When he assuaged the hunger for her lips, he began a slow exploration of her body. There was no inch that did not feel his lips or fingers, no curve or line that went unloved. Only when she was quivering wildly, her voice breathless, and her hands desperately tugging at his shoulders did he slowly make his way back up her body. His entire body was knotted and pained with violent hunger, but he leashed it desperately. He had waited too long for this moment to rush it.

"Look at me," he said thickly. Her lashes lifted to reveal

darkened blue eyes swirling with need and desire and love. "Hold me. *Dio*, hold me, Victoria."

The plea shook her to her soul. She fiercely wrapped her arms around his shoulders as her legs instinctively curled around his hips. Nothing was more important than protecting this man. This incredible person who had loved her at her worst and helped her to find the best inside and out. "I love you," she whispered softly.

His control crumbled. A low sound of mingled need and elation rumbled in his chest. His kiss held both as he took her lips, and he clung to whatever will he had left as he slowly pressed into her welcoming heat. Her breath hitched but her darkening eyes told him it was not pain. Wonder slowly filled her gaze as he settled in completely. There were no words she could find to explain the sheer beauty of that moment.

There were no words for either of them. In a silence that held more promises than a single voice, he slowly took her, again and again, until she was clinging onto him with a strength that soothed him to the deepest level, bringing a sense of safety as thrilling as the feel of her body, soft and welcoming beneath him.

The shattering ecstasy that claimed them both was velvety and deep, as emotional as it was physical, and it swelled on and on until it erased every sense of self, every memory of being separate and alone. In that final moment of fusion, his lips found hers one last time as her hands framed his face. Neither was alone any longer. They never would be again.

By the time she noticed the room was getting a little chilly because the fireplace had dimmed, she was sprawled across Rafael's chest. He had rolled onto his back and tugged her on top of him, and even though he seemed to be lightly dozing, his arm still curled possessively around her waist.

She carefully disentangled herself and slid out of bed. Assorted aches made their presence known, and a tiny thrill went through her body. She looked at Rafael lying in her bed and could only marvel that someone that beautiful belonged to her. She knew that night, no matter how many others followed, would be permanently burned in her memory.

She knelt to stoke the fire and make it kick out more heat. The villa had central air and heating, but everyone kept costs down by using fireplaces for heat. She had always been warmed by the knowledge that the one family who had money to spare would be careful with it. It made them more real, more approachable.

"You left me."

The drowsy rasp of Rafael's voice teased along her nerve endings. She smiled and straightened to see him propped up in bed. "You're the insomniac," she teased as she walked over to him. "I thought you'd appreciate being left to get some rest."

"I am not capable of resting without you, *cara*." He buried his fingers in her rumpled hair and tugged her down for a lingering kiss. "Are you hungry?" he asked against her lips. "You did not eat much at the party. I believe you were quite nervous."

"I was wearing diamonds worth more than this villa in a crowd of elite sharks." She pulled a face. "I was entitled to be nervous." Her stomach rumbled lightly, and she had to grin when he arched a brow. "But I'm definitely starving. I burned a lot of energy tonight."

"*Sì*, and you will burn more as yet." He rolled out of bed as lithely as a large feline. "You start the shower and I will ring Peggy to bring us some food."

"Don't disturb her!" She crossed her arms. "It's two in the morning!"

"And the party has no doubt only just ended. She will be awake, and she will be very happy."

Red climbed her face. "You mean we snuck out way before the party ended."

He grinned. "*Sì*." He skimmed a finger down her nose. "And I am sure that everyone there found it greatly amusing. *Nonno* will be especially happy. You made a beautiful scene, we danced as if we were already lovers, and then we snuck out together to be alone and indulge in passion." He sighed gustily. "My life is in danger, but I am a happy man."

She found herself laughing. "You are horrible, Rafe." When he tugged her into his arms, she went willingly. Her head rested on his shoulder. She liked his height as much as he liked hers. "I'm happy," she said softly. "It's a strange feeling. I'm not sure I've ever been truly happy like this before."

"That is because you are as happy with yourself as you are with your world." He tipped her chin up for another kiss. "Go start the shower and I will help you wash the 'gunk,' as you called it, from your hair."

Smiling wryly, she went into the bathroom and turned on the shower in the immense stall. She had always loved her bathroom for how ridiculously large it was, but now it had a practicality as well. Then again, maybe she wouldn't need it that long. Would she move in Rafael's room, and then they move into the master when they married? That was silly. She refused to pack up twice.

"That is a curious look," he noted as he joined her. "You look to be annoyed and yet puzzled."

"I think that sums it up." She arched a brow at him. "Our room arrangement."

The wonderful thing about how long they had known each other, and how good of friends they were, was that she did not need to say anything else. He knew exactly what she asked and why. "I would love to have you in my room, *cara*, but I would not trouble you to pack twice. We will simply alternate between rooms until we are wed. When we return from our honeymoon, we will take over the master."

"I can handle that. I hate packing." The shower was the right temperature, and she climbed in and sighed happily at the feel of the hot water. He joined her, and she could only be bemused that she felt so comfortable with him. Then again, she thought as she looked him over wistfully, he was even more gorgeous when naked *and* wet. She had many frustrated memories of him getting out of the pool like a god rising from the sea while rivulets of water streamed down his body.

"I must know what you are thinking," he murmured. "Such a curiously feminine look in your eyes, Victoria."

"Just thinking about how frustrating it was that you made me go to the pool with you. How you didn't notice me staring at you lustfully every time . . ."

His chuckle sounded low and masculine. "I was distracted by ignoring my emotions for you." Realization made his brows lift. "It suddenly comes clear to me. You are not allergic to chlorine. It was another cover."

"Yeah. I miss swimming. I liked it even when I hated how looked in a bathing suit."

"You will need a suit," he said decisively. "I will take you swimming with me here and at the *castello*. How much would I need to beg to see you in a bikini?" he asked wistfully.

"A bikini?! Me?" She sputtered as he ducked her head under the shower. "Hey!"

"Do not argue with the man who knows every inch of your body. You will be beautiful in a bikini." He skimmed his finger down the scar on her chest. As always, he felt his heart quiver at the sight of it. He didn't think he would ever get over how it felt to see it there. "This is a badge of honor."

She wouldn't argue over that one. Deciding to ignore the entire bikini conversation, she firmly scrubbed and washed away all of the gel and hairspray. It felt good to have it out of her hair, and she was oddly curious to see what her 'natural style' was once her hair had dried.

Finding out got a little delayed. Rafael insisted on helping her wash the rest of her body, and he was too sensual a man to not take advantage of her obvious weakness to his touch. "I told you," he said huskily against her neck, "you will need your strength."

"Yeah." Pinned between him and the shower wall, she couldn't help but marvel at his own strength. If things kept getting better between them as they seemed to be inclined, then she could see many happy years together in their future.

They got out of the shower and toweled off, and with tender amusement, he showed her how to use the hair dryer to dry her hair. She had always just toweled off the excess and left the rest to the air. She couldn't be displeased with the new effort, though. Her hair, once dry, fell naturally around her face in a very appealing way. "I don't think I'd ever pass as a guy again," she decided. "But I'm not unhappy about it. That time served its purpose."

"*Sì*. It led you to me." A towel knotted around his hips, he walked into the bedroom and smiled as he saw the covered tray sitting on the table. "Come eat something, Victoria, before your stomach makes another impersonation of a lioness."

"And yours is any quieter!" She swathed herself in a towel and went over to join him. A part of her wanted to be embarrassed that Peggy would have walked into the room and seen haphazardly discarded pieces of clothing and heard the shower running, but she was too bemused by the entire situation to bother.

After demolishing the food, she felt much more human again. She couldn't believe it was three in the morning and she was sitting naked in her bedroom with a lover. Her *fiancé*. And not just any lover, but potentially one who was the most amazing man in the world. Even when her 'job' ended, she knew she would always protect him.

He suddenly walked over to her and lifted her into his arms. He carried her over to the bed and dropped her down onto it. "Are you refueled, *cara*?"

"Quite." She skimmed her fingers up his arms with a smile. "But I'm not sure I could sleep right now."

Loving her all the more, his lips curved slowly. "I am sure I can help you become tired."

# CHAPTER FOURTEEN

Tori didn't wake in the morning feeling as if birds were singing and the world was sunshine and roses, but she certainly woke content. She was cuddled against Rafael's side and had an arm flung across his chest possessively. While she had never been happier than knowing she was truly loved, her internal alarms now warbled very loudly. She could actually *feel* the danger hovering around Rafael.

"You are supposed to be smiling, *cara*," he murmured huskily. She looked up at him and he skimmed his fingers down her cheek. She looked rumpled, flushed, and very, very sexy. "I have you in my arms, and you are not smiling. I must not be trying hard enough to please you."

"If you tried any harder, I wouldn't be able to walk," she protested. She started laughing as she hastily rolled out of bed before he could grab her. "Don't you dare, Rafe!" She grabbed her robe and held it like a shield in front of her naked body. "As it is, we've likely missed breakfast and they'll wonder what we're up to up here."

The corner of his lips kicked up into a wicked smile. "I am sure they know, Victoria." He got out of bed and tugged her into his arms. "I will not have my wicked way with you right now." He nibbled on her chin and then her lower lip. Her ridiculously kissable mouth had tormented him for two years. It was exhilarating to finally know she was his. "I will kidnap you for lunch and have my wicked way with you then."

Her knees went weak as she held onto his arms for balance. "If you insist," she managed to say.

"I do, I assure you." He ran his thumb over her lip and cupped her cheek. "Now then," he said softly, "tell me what is wrong. There is something bothering you."

"The fact that your life is as yet in danger bothers me a lot," she shot at him. She pulled away and crossed her arms as she stalked toward the bathroom. "I woke feeling as if I could actually *see* the danger around you. Forgive me for not being all smiles."

He winced good-naturedly as she shut the door firmly. His bodyguard had a bit of a temper, which he often forgot until he provoked it on accident. Her biggest button had always been his safety, and he honestly didn't see that changing even when the danger was gone. He would have her no other way. She kept more than his physical self safe. She protected his very heart and soul.

He knocked lightly on the bathroom door and called, "Put on something pretty. We will go have breakfast in the city. I do not feel like sharing you with my family for a little bit longer."

She sighed. She wanted to tell him no, she really did, but the whole reason she had gotten that deep was because she was supposed to be his undercover bodyguard. They couldn't catch a crook without bait. That didn't mean she couldn't take extra precautions, though. "Alright."

With a grin, he grabbed his clothes from the night before so he could go back to his own room. He made a mental note to have some of his things put in her room, and vice-versa. It would be much more convenient until they married.

He caught a very quick shower and got dressed. When he went back to Tori's room, he wasn't entirely surprised to discover she was still getting ready. He could hear the muttering coming from the closet. "*Cara*," he said warmly, "anything you wear will be fine. I was merely teasing you." He stepped into the doorway and was promptly silenced as he stared at his lover in shock.

She continued to very competently assemble a small gun. "Don't look surprised," she told him. "Alex and I have both been armed more than once over the last two years. You can't handle everything with your hands. Antonio is fully aware that we're armed, and he even has copies of our licenses and permits."

He felt a little flustered. "Neither Isabelle nor I knew."

"Well, of course not." She lifted her brows at him. "Having a bodyguard was enough of a reminder of the danger you were in. Antonio decided it was best you not know all the details." She put the gun to the side and grabbed a pair of slacks. "I would have told you later if you hadn't found out now."

"*Sì*," he agreed dryly, "as I would have no doubt discovered it when I next had you naked." He felt less unnerved by the realization that his lover was armed than he might have expected to be. In a way, it made him feel better. For her safety, if not his own. He had seen firsthand just how much damage a bullet could do to someone.

The fact that she was moving and using her left arm as if she hadn't been that someone barely months before was a testament to her strength. Unable to stand it, he moved forward and tugged her into his arms. He buried his face in her hair for a moment. "Hold me, Victoria. Do not let go."

She wrapped her arms around him and held on fiercely. Too many emotions to name closed her throat. It seemed impossible to love one person that much. "I'm here, Rafe," she soothed softly. "I'm not going anywhere." She lightly framed his face with her hands when he reluctantly released her. "What brought that on?"

He lightly touched the pink scar. "I see this and I am afraid again," he admitted. "I will have nightmares forever of watching you take that bullet for me."

"At the risk of making it worse," she warned gently, "I will do it again if needed, Rafael. You know that. Tear up as many contracts as you want, but it will not change who and what I am and how I feel for you." She kissed him tenderly and then let go. "Now quit acting so emotional. Who's the girl around here?"

He found himself smiling. That was his Tori. "I believe it is you." He sighed contentedly. "And you are a very beautiful woman, Victoria."

"I'm almost starting to believe it myself," she admitted.

In less than half an hour, they headed on their way to a favored café of his. They served breakfast, and the place was quiet and intimate. Tori had been there more than once herself, though not in her 'new persona.' It felt very odd to be talking to the baristas and realize that they didn't notice she was the same person. Well, some of them didn't. A few of the people who worked there winked at her merrily; they had obviously caught on.

Coffee and breakfast in hand, Rafael and Tori caught a table near a window. She felt wired already, and she had barely touched her coffee. Her eyes moved restlessly over the entire café. It felt the same as it had the day before when she had sensed someone watching her while she was getting her hair done. There were a few other people in the café, but no one looked remarkable.

One of the baristas suddenly walked up to the table, her face pale. "How's everything?" she asked with a false cheer. She held out a note. "I was asked to give this to you."

Rafael frowned and opened the note as she hurried away. His mouth instantly went dry and he felt a chill run down his back. Tori snatched the note out of his hand and felt sick. Very clearly, it read, *Two men stand outside each door. Unless you walk out quietly, they're walking in shooting.*

Tori bore the personal evidence of their willingness to commit murder. She was not happy with this scenario. They had been planning on luring out one idiot, not an entire squadron of homicidal maniacs. She took a little breath, her mind running through every possible scenario. "Do you trust me?" she asked softly.

"With my life," he said simply.

"Let's go. And just play along with whatever I do." Hoping like hell she could act convincingly like a frightened woman when she had spent years living as a male bodyguard who was capable in most any situation, she clung onto his arm as they walked out of the café. A false sense of security. She desperately needed to build it in the enemy.

Two men stepped forward from near the door. Both wore heavy jackets with familiar bumps underneath. Tori and Alex had long before decided that holsters were far too damned obvious and had opted for other means. At that moment, her gun was in an ankle holster. As long as no one strip-searched her, they wouldn't find it.

"Come with us," one of the men said.

Rafael hesitated but went with his instincts. They had never failed him before. "Let my fiancée go," he said softly. "She is not a part of this."

The other man scoffed. "If we let her go, then our boss will have our heads. He said to grab you both, so we are." He glanced at the curb as a limo rolled up. He opened one of the doors. "Get in."

They got in, and Tori scooted all the way over into the other corner. Rafael joined her, crowding her back so that it looked as if he was protecting her. The two men got in followed by two others, the door shut, and the limo rolled off down the street. "Where's your bodyguard?" one of the men asked Rafael curtly. "I was surprised I didn't see him dogging your heels as always."

"As he was shot only months ago," Rafael retorted in a clipped voice, "you can imagine why he was not at my side. Victoria and I wished to have breakfast without *mia famiglia*. If I had realized you were such fools as to come to a public café, I would have suffered my sister and brother-in-law flirting over the breakfast table."

"Well, can't blame you for that," one of the other men admitted. "Your fiancée is hot."

Tori somehow kept her jaw from dropping. As she had thought, the men were certifiably nuts, and she wasn't entirely sure they weren't high on something with it. She kept her lips closed and burrowed closer against Rafael's back. Under the cover of hiding behind him, she had already turned on her cell phone and dialed Alex. He would be able to hear everything, and since the phone hid nicely in her bra, they wouldn't find it. Wearing a bra had *far* more practical uses than she had ever imagined, honestly.

It seemed like forever before the limo stopped. The men

ushered Rafael and Tori out of the vehicle, then, to Tori's horror, separated them. Rafael was taken one way while she was escorted another. She struggled against the male holding her arm, but not yet with her full strength. "Let me go!" she snapped. "Rafe! No, let me be with him!" The one holding her was the one who had called her 'hot' so she tried to give him a pleading look. "Please!"

He paused and then cursed. "Sorry, no dice." He looked up in relief as he heard a light step. "Here she is, like you ordered."

She glanced up and felt her heart freeze. The man looking at her was handsome, but there was a coolness inside his eyes that she recognized. He would put a bullet in a man without flinching, of that she felt sure. And yet . . . something seemed slightly off about him, though she could not put her finger on it. "Don't touch me!" she snapped when he reached for her arm.

He ignored her and grabbed her much more firmly than the other man had. She knew that even her full strength would not break her free. She dug in her heels as hard as she could, but she was still dragged down a hall. The building looked like an abandoned factory of some sort, and she couldn't orient herself as to where they were located.

He swung her into a room and shut the door before releasing her. He watched her move several steps away. Calmly, he asked, "How is that bullet wound doing?"

Her eyes narrowed sharply. She didn't know how he knew, but she refused to play the bluff game. "Perfectly fine, no thanks to your buddy. If you know who I am, then why the hell did you specifically tell them to grab me?"

He reached into his jacket and emerged with a paper. He handed it to her without a word. She skimmed over it and then had to read it twice more to be sure. There was no mistake. The signature at the bottom of the document was Vincent Lucino's. The letter read, simply, that the elder Lucino was looking for a hired gun to remove the threat to his family. The utter incongruity of the years of threats of finding a hitman colliding with the fact that he had, in fact, done so, left her reeling. "Wait, you're one of the *good guys*?"

He shrugged. "I wouldn't necessarily call myself that."

"Then why haven't you shot the bastard yet?" she snapped. "If something had happened to Isabelle, or if I hadn't thrown myself over Rafael, then you can be sure *you'd* have been next on Don Lucino's list!"

"If I hadn't been here," was the retort, "then Isabelle Lucino and Gabrielle Wisteria wouldn't have found it that easy to escape. My 'men' were of the opinion that roughing them up would put pressure on Antonio Lucino. I convinced them to back off by making them think I would handle things."

Her head was still reeling, but her gut told her that he could be trusted. It was the same hunch that had told her there was more to him than met the eye. Oh, she fully believed he could still kill someone in cold blood, but why else would Vincent have hired him? You didn't get rid of crazed madmen with sunshine and lollipops. She yanked her phone out of her bra and said sharply, "Did you hear?"

"Yes," Alex responded instantly. "And Vincent has confirmed it. We have the GPS location and we're on our way, Tori! Just get Rafe out of there!"

She hung up the phone and looked at her unexpected ally. "Where is Rafe? And what's your name?"

"The top floor," he answered immediately. "And my name is Van D'Angelo."

A hired gun who was named 'the angel.' She knew she would eventually find it funny in fifty years, providing she managed to save her fiancé and actually make it to the altar with him. It was looking more and more debatable with every minute, and her nerves kept stretching more and more. "Let's end this madness. Take me to the top floor, Van."

Rafael found himself dragged upstairs and handcuffed to a steel pole that helped hold up the ceiling. The entire floor had been gutted pending a remodel, and it was an eerie collection of partially built walls and steel poles. Only a handful of windows were uncovered, and the sunlight coming in only added to the gloom. Some electric lights were on, but the bulbs were bare. He had a feeling he would never look at a horror movie the same way ever again.

He was terrified. Not only for himself, but also for Tori. Was she okay? He trusted she could defend herself, but he couldn't stop thinking of all the possible scenarios where she might end up at the mercy of those bastards. This plan was the most asinine thing he had ever agreed to do, but he couldn't be mad at Brie for thinking of it. He had thought it was a good idea at the time, too.

The crack of a whip caught his attention, and he turned as much as he could to see Martin approaching. The hair on the back of his neck stood straight up. There was something odd about the way Martin walked. The older man was weaving back and forth as if drunk, and there was a glassy sheen to his too bright eyes. The whip was in his hand, and there were assorted other alarming items tucked into the belt he wore. "You do realize," Rafael said as coolly as he could, "that murder and torture are much more severely looked upon than embezzlement, *sì*?"

Martin's response to that was to snap the whip at him. The leather strip at the end cut through cloth and skin alike as it wrapped around his arm. "I look forward to breaking you apart," Martin sneered. "A mighty Lucino, begging for his life!" He jerked on the whip and savored Rafael's flinch. A snap of his wrist made the whip let go, but he promptly attacked again, this time opening a cut along Rafael's cheek. "I'm very good with one of these," he said loftily. "Practiced by taking the heads off chickens back home."

"For a man who concocted a featherbrained scheme, the fact that you once played with chickens is not a surprise." The whip snapped across his other cheek, but he ignored the pain. "Where is Victoria?"

Martin scoffed. "Probably having some 'fun' with my bodyguard. He was insistent that he have access to the bitch." He smirked when Rafael snarled at him. "Oh, does that bother you? Too bad." He stopped abruptly and looked to the side at absolutely no one. "You lie!" he shouted at the air. "He wouldn't betray me! You said my men would, but they didn't! It was just a trick by that little 3rd District freak!" He recoiled violently and dropped to his knees with a terrified sob. "I'm sorry! I won't mention that place again!"

Rafael had known of Martin's instability, but it was many times worse to see it firsthand. Somehow, seeing this was far more frightening than the whip he carried. His skin crawled as something inside him urged him to get away. He was in the presence of evil. He just knew it inside.

Martin's head snapped up, his glazed eyes manic. He leapt to his feet and sent the whip flying for Rafael's neck.

It didn't reach him. Tori stepped in front of him and interceded the whip. The end coiled around her arm and bit into her skin. Before Martin recovered, she yanked the whip out of his hand and let it drop to the ground. "Sorry, but Rafe isn't into the kinky stuff," she said icily. Martin scrambled for the knife he wore, and she calmly lifted the gun in her other hand. "Not a chance, dipshit."

Martin stared at her in horror as he finally recognized her. He didn't doubt her aim, her skill, or willingness to shoot him. What he *did* doubt was how she had managed to get away from Vick. "You! How did you get up here?!"

"A little thing called 'stairs.' Try them sometime."

"That isn't what I meant!" he screamed. He whirled around sharply. "Vick! Vick!" He spotted movement and saw Van stepping around from behind another pillar. "There you are!" he roared. "Shoot her! Kill her! Kill them both!" He covered his head with his hands and moaned in pain. "Kill them before they kill me!" He heard the sound of a gun cocking and looked up to see Van aiming not at Tori, but at him. "No." It was a thready whisper. "You would never betray me!"

"I never worked for you," Van said quietly. "Therefore you can't say I'm betraying you."

Martin yanked what looked like a remote control out of his

belt. "I have explosives!" he shouted. "I'll blow up the whole fucking building!" He began to emit a high-pitched laugh. "You won't win! It was wrong! You won't win!"

His finger started to depress a button and both Tori and Van fired. Both shots hit the center of Martin's chest. He lost his grip on the remote and toppled over. Tori leapt forward and grabbed the remote before it hit the ground. It was better safe than sorry. A putrid scent suddenly stung her nose, and she looked down to see a disgusting slime seeping out of Martin's body.

"Get back!" Van ordered sharply.

She scrambled back and put herself in front of Rafael as the slime slowly crept across the floor. It began to rise up into the air with a stench so strong and rancid that even Van's stomach churned. A malevolent face seemed to form from the slime, and it bared broken, razor edged teeth in a mockery of a smile.

The cavernous mouth opened and Van fired two more shots. They did nothing as they were absorbed by the slime. In fact, it barely spared him a glance as it began to lunge toward Tori and Rafael. Tori turned and threw her arms around Rafael to make him less of a target.

Blinding white light lit the entire area as a pure beam of it streaked through the air and slammed into the slime. It screamed with the voice of the damned and recoiled back. With a guttural roar in a language no one recognized, it changed targets and began to rush across the floor.

Tori lifted her head and instantly spotted a familiar redhead standing only feet away. "What the hell?" she said in shock. "Move!" she shouted.

Rhianna held her ground. The slime lunged forward and engulfed her entirely, and Van dropped his gun as he ran toward her to help. He was only a few steps toward her when bright white light burst through the slime and blew it away. Remnants of it splattered against the ceiling and floor and dissolved. Rhianna looked relatively unscathed, though she had taken some nasty cuts to her arms.

On shaky legs, Tori went to Martin and grabbed the key that had fallen on the ground. She freed Rafael from the cuffs, and her stomach rebelled as she saw the bloody mess of his wrists. The cuffs had been so tight that his every movement had made them cut into his skin. "Oh god, Rafe." She dropped her head onto his shoulder.

Van picked up his fallen gun and put it away. "Eric will not be happy with you," he told Rhianna.

"Naturally not, but there was no time to be wasted." She looked at Martin's body with cool satisfaction in her eyes. "Tori, your gun repeat fires, correct?"

"Yes . . ."

"Good. Van, you were not here."

"No, ma'am." He tipped an imaginary hat and disappeared into the shadows around the room.

"I am very confused," Rafael said softly.

"You and me both!" Tori muttered.

Rhianna glanced at them. "I will handle things. Tori shot Martin twice in defense of Rafael's life. Rafael's current state is evidence enough as to why."

Tori refrained from mentioning ballistics. Rhianna's company had more power than the federal government. If she said both bullets came from Tori's gun, then sure as hell no one would question it. Just like Tori wasn't going to question the horror movie sequence she had just experienced, or Rhianna's incredible display of power.

Rhianna seemed to disappear as mysteriously as she had arrived, and only moments later, a full SWAT team of cops burst into the top floor. Alex was with them. He ran over to Tori and Rafael immediately. "Are you two okay?" he demanded sharply. He saw the state Rafael was in and began to curse softly.

"I will be fine," Rafael assured him. He cupped Tori's cheek. "Yet again, Victoria saved my life." He pressed a kiss to her forehead and pulled her into his arms, uncaring that his wounds protested the movement.

She clung onto him for a moment before forcing herself to let

go. She scooped up her gun and held it out to a cop. "This is mine. My name is Tori Li. I'm Rafael's bodyguard. I can provide any documentation you need me to, including permits. Martin was threatening to blow up the building. I couldn't take any chances."

It didn't take long for the cops to find the explosives. There was enough C-4 scattered around the top floor to take out the building as well as anything else close by. Rafael was taken immediately to a hospital to be treated, but most of the wounds turned out to be minor. Doctor Singh patched both him and Tori up, and he scolded them both for being reckless.

It took even longer for statements, and neither Tori nor Rafael was very surprised to see someone from Enforcers at the station. With her presence there, it was actually not very long before they were free to go home with Alex. It was already late afternoon, and it felt like a week since that same morning.

Alex drove while Rafael rode with Tori in the backseat. Rafael couldn't bring himself to let her go just yet. She had scared him far too much lately for him to recover easily. First she had taken a bullet for him. Now she had faced a madman and some sort of manifestation of evil. He had stopped breathing when she had thrown herself over him. "No more, *cara*," he said in a quiet voice that shook slightly. "No more. You will not be in danger again. You are going to quit your job."

"And do what with my time?" she asked politely. "Sew? Knit? Please!"

"You may do whatever you like so long as you are not in danger," her fiancé retorted. "You once lamented not going to a university for a graduate degree. You may do so. It will be safe there. You will study something tame and boring like fire walking so that I do not die young of a broken heart or heart failure."

She was silent for a moment. Humor began to well, and she started laughing. "Rafe, I think you just pulled your own 'Don Lucino' act. Do you have *any* idea how you just sounded?" She lightly framed his face, careful of the bandages covering his wounds, and kissed him hard. "Fine. I'll find something safe and boring. What about trapeze acts? Can I study that?"

"Only if you wear a skimpy leotard and let me catch you." He rubbed his thumb over her cheek with a smile. "You are one-of-a-kind, Victoria. My beautiful diamond swan." His grin began to widen. "And I am sure we are embarrassing Alexander."

"Don't mind me. I'm just trying not to cry."

Tori snorted at that as they pulled into the driveway of the Lucino villa. She spotted Roberto's car, which was not a surprise, and then spotted an unfamiliar car as well. "Ugh." She sighed as she got out of Alex's car. "More visitors? I so don't want to deal with that. Can we sneak in the back?"

"Now, you know we cannot." Rafael slid an arm around her waist to keep her close as they headed for the door. "We will reassure everyone that we are fine, and then we will escape to my room and hide away for a week. Perhaps two. Then we will begin making plans for the wedding in *Italia*." He nipped at her ear teasingly. "And we will honeymoon in the *castello*."

"Can we kick everyone else out when we do? If you say yes, I might consider wearing a bikini."

"Deal," he agreed instantly with a grin. He knew a good bargain when it presented itself. Besides, he very much wanted her all to himself. Perhaps by their fiftieth anniversary, he might have recovered from the whole ordeal.

Brie and Isabelle gave glad cries when they saw them and rushed to hug both Tori and Rafael fiercely. They were mindful of Rafael's injuries but not willing to let him go for long moments. He held them just as tightly. "It is all done," he promised. "We are safe now." He glanced up at the sound of footsteps and saw Vincent and Antonio, both of whom looked older than they had the night before. "I am sorry for worrying you."

"You!" Tori aimed a finger at Vincent.

He held up his hands. "It can be discussed later, Victoria. Come into the parlor. There is someone that you need to speak with."

"Oh god," she groaned. "Now? Seriously?" She sighed as Roberto began to push her toward the parlor. "I'm going to kick your ass, Roberto."

"*Sì*, but you will need to wait until after I am wed so you may teach Gabrielle the proper etiquette for it."

Rafael glanced at his father and grandfather who both nodded. Understanding, he pulled Tori closer and began to escort her himself. "You will wish to meet this person," he told her softly. "And I hope it will finally bring you peace, *cara*."

Inside the parlor, there was a man roughly Antonio's age standing in the middle of the room. There was absolutely nothing familiar about him at all to Tori, though she felt she ought to know him. It was only when he turned and looked at her that her stomach clenched with nerves as she realized what might be happening.

He had baby blue eyes.

"Victoria," Antonio said softly, "I would like you to meet James Montgomery. He has been looking for you for many years, *cara*."

She would have run, but Rafael was still holding her. She grabbed onto his hand like a lifeline. She was barely aware of the Lucinos, Roberto, and Alex as they formed a protective shield behind her. "Is that so?" Try as she might to make her voice careless, it came out as barely a whisper.

James took a deep breath. "Your mother told me you were stillborn. I never believed her. I just . . . couldn't give up hope. Sit down, Tori," he urged. "Please at least listen to me. If after I've spoken, you want nothing to do with me, I will leave. But at least let me answer your questions."

"I am here," Rafael told Tori softly. "I will not leave you."

"Nor will we," Vincent said just as softly. "You are part of our *famiglia*."

She took a breath and slowly sat down on the settee. "Alright," she said. "Let's talk."

# CHAPTER FIFTEEN

It was very uncomfortable in the parlor. Peggy brought in tea for everyone and refrained from fussing over Rafael and Tori. She would fuss over her kids when there wasn't a stranger present. She did, however, shoot James a warning look. If he hurt Tori, all bets were off.

For James, it was very painful to sit across from his daughter and realize that she not only didn't like him, but that she had every right to feel as she did. "Ask me anything," he told her. "I will not lie."

"How did you find me?"

The corner of his lips kicked up. "Your future grandfather-in-law. He called me last night and informed me that he was willing to fly me out here to meet you. As to how he found *me*, I'm not sure I want to know."

"*Sì*, you do not," Vincent said. "However, I called in a favor or two. Tori was in the system because of her childhood. You were in the system because of some petty theft when you were young. It took little work to find the connecting threads between you two."

Tori rubbed her hands over her arms. The motion reminded her of her wounded arm and she hastily dropped her hand. Rafael's arm slid around her waist and held on firmly. It was only his presence and the presence of the rest of her family that gave her strength. She could not handle this alone. "You said my . . . my mother told you I was stillborn. She threw me in the garbage. Why?"

His lashes flinched. Vincent had told him, but hearing it said again was horrifying. "We met when we were in our early twenties and stupid. We weren't serious about each other. She was seeing other men, and I was eyeing a few other women. She came to me out of the blue and raged at me for getting her pregnant. It was certainly possible I had; as I said, we were stupid." He sighed. "And I knew she was sure it was mine because she had other prospects who would have paid her a lot of money to get rid of the baby. She knew I wouldn't."

"I'm glad you didn't, obviously, but why not? You were young and stupid."

"But I love kids," he said simply. "And while she wouldn't have been my first pick for the mother of any child of mine, once you were made, I wanted to keep you. I told her she could have an abortion if she wanted, but if she was willing to deliver you, then I would take you right after birth and she'd never have to be tied down by you. She decided to deliver you under those conditions, and I agreed to help support her." He sighed. "Unfortunately, she didn't try very hard to keep you unharmed while she was pregnant. She continued to smoke and drink and do reckless things. When she entered her third trimester, I nearly took her to court over it. Then, one day, she disappeared. I went out of my mind because she was so close to delivery."

Isabelle gently rested her hands on Tori's shoulder to remind her that she was not alone. "And when she came back to you, she claimed a false birth, *sì?*"

"Said that the doctor had tried, but the baby was born dead." His hands curled into fists. "I didn't believe her. I wouldn't have imagined she had done . . . what she had done. I thought at most she would have surrendered you to the hospital or the cops, just to get back at me. Maybe I did know the truth. I just couldn't stand looking at her ever again. I moved upstate, and she moved to the Midwest. I've kept tabs on her in the time since, just in case I ever found any evidence of what she'd done. She married a while ago but doesn't have any children."

Tori let out a long breath. "The guy who picked up garbage

found me right after I was dumped. Rushed me to the hospital; literally saved my life. I was in a foster home until I was eighteen and got my independence to move out here and start over. My foster parents were wonderful, but I never fit into society."

"Society," Brie disagreed fiercely, "just didn't know how to handle someone as amazing as you!"

"Vincent and Antonio told me . . . told me what has been happening. I wish saying I am sorry for not being there would make it magically better, but I know it won't." He sighed anew. "I married a while back. I have a daughter around the age of fifteen. I told my wife but did not tell my daughter what I was coming out here for. She wants a big sister, and I refused to get her hopes up. If you have no desire to know her, or me, then I will leave and not tell her. But if you'd like to have a chance to extend your family . . . then I know she and my wife will love you. *I* love you, and I'm proud of you, Tori."

"It is your decision, *cara*," Antonio told Tori. "We are your family, but if you wish to know your *papa*, then we stand by you."

Tori slowly nodded. "I guess it can't hurt. I mean, I can't hold my mother's actions against you. You didn't have any choice in the matter. And I guess it might be kind of cool to be a big sister." She snorted. "Though I think I'd be better at being a big brother, frankly. Whatever, same difference. Yeah, I'd like to know you guys. And you can come to the wedding."

Vincent nodded firmly. "I will make the arrangements for your wife and *bambina* to be flown out here soon. The wedding will be in *il castello* in Italy."

"Thank you." James got to his feet, sensing a dismissal. "I will see you soon, Tori. And thank you for giving me a chance."

"We all have our stupid moments. At least yours gave me life, so I can't be mad about it." It was also curiously reassuring to finally have answers. Someone *had* wanted her. It was something. Even still, the tension did not leave her shoulders until he had left. The door shut behind him, and she doubled over with her face in her hands. "That sucked!" She shot to her feet and rounded on Vincent. "You ever go behind my back like that again, and I'm going to find your 'hitman' and sic him on you!"

Vincent hid a grin. He was *well* pleased with Rafael's choice. He admired anyone with the nerve to yell at him. He had no doubt Tori would get along just fine with his Natalia. They were very much alike. But then, Lucinos had fabulous taste. "You were unhappy, *cara*," he said gently. "And that is not acceptable to me."

"What is this about a hitman?" Isabelle demanded. "*Nonno*, what have you not told us?"

He arched a brow. "There was danger to *mia famiglia*. It was unacceptable. I contacted a few people here in New York who put me in contact with a few others. I discovered Van D'Angelo and told him of the situation. He was aware of it because of Gabrielle's involvement as he has worked for Enforcers off and on for a few years."

"Oh god," Brie groaned as she covered her face. "Rhianna and Eric employ *hitmen*? As if they weren't scary enough!"

"He is a hired gun," he corrected, "which does involve death, *sì*. But he is an honorable man, with much integrity. He works with the police as well, though I know not his contacts there. Sometimes there are simply things that justice cannot touch, *cara*. This was one of those things."

"Does that mean things are finally done?" Rafael asked.

"I would certainly hope so," Vincent agreed. His phone began to ring, and he pulled it out. "Ah. Speaking of whom." He answered the phone and said, "*Ciao,* Van. *Grazie* for protecting *miei bambini*. I will have your payment forwarded to you."

"Don't pay me yet," Van said quietly. "I was just calling to tell you that I got my hands on Martin's files. He wasn't working alone. I don't know who his partner is, but I'm looking for him. He may be merely corrupt rather than evil, but I wish to confirm that before I call this job done. If he is a true danger, I will handle it. If he is simply corrupt, I will turn him over to the police."

"Is my family safe?"

"Best I can determine, yes, the physical danger should be past. Focus on the weddings, Don Lucino. I will handle the rest." He hung up the phone.

Vincent slowly closed his phone as well, aware that everyone watched him warily. "Van suspects there is another involved, but he does not believe there is any physical danger. Perhaps professionally you should be cautious, but the need for bodyguards has passed. I trust his instincts. Ms. Tabor told me that they are as good as fact."

"She does seem to be involved a lot, no?" Roberto murmured.

"Sorry," Brie grumbled. "Enforcers take the District and its people pretty seriously."

He lightly kissed her. "As they should, *cara mia*."

Rafael got to his feet and tugged Tori up with him. "If that is all," he said firmly, "then I am taking Victoria to my room so that we may wash away the events of the day. In fact, you may not see us again for a few days. Please ask Peggy or Marco to bring food else we waste away."

The others let them go without protest. Careful of Tori's wounded arm, he instead held her elbow to escort her up the stairs. He went directly to his room and ushered her inside. The door had barely closed behind them before he yanked her into his arms and kissed her wildly. He yanked fiercely at her clothes, desperate to have her naked so he could see she was unharmed. "*Dio*!" he said roughly. "I will never recover from these events!"

"I'm not the one who was hurt this time!" she managed to say. Something hot and wild rose inside, and she rushed open his shirt. So close. She had come so close to losing him. She didn't want to think Van's shot might have been the one to kill Martin. She wanted that satisfaction for herself. If she hadn't been there . . . a shudder ripped through her body.

She stifled a startled yelp and grabbed his shoulders for balance as he lifted her off her feet. "Your wrists!"

"I do not care!" The bed was too far away. He instead bore her down onto the floor. Only when her arms were around him, only when he was inside her once more, did the panic finally start to fade.

They did eventually make it to the bed, and she re-bandaged his wrists and arm. He insisted on tending to her injury as well, but it was already healing quickly. It didn't surprise him. Once he had made sure the tape was back in place, he lifted her left hand to his lips and kissed her engagement ring. "*Ti amo*," he said softly. "I am sorry for rushing you as I did. I should have given you more time."

"Yeah, you're just a paragon of patience," she retorted dryly. She sighed and tugged his hand to her heart. "Rafe, I'm not sorry about anything. I'm not. It was scary and it was horrible at times. But you were there. I loved you all along. I needed you to push me, to shake me up and make me see what I could be. And . . . I'm happy now. Isn't that the important part?"

He looked at her and how the evening light made her soft and sultry and so beautiful she took his breath. "You will not fly away?" he asked huskily.

She smiled. "No. I finally know where I belong." When he kissed her, she slid her arms around his neck and held on, savoring how it felt to be wanted for who she was. "I need postcards," she murmured when he lifted his head.

He arched a brow, intrigued by the very feminine smile on her lips. "What for?"

"No reason." A twinkle appeared in the corner of her eyes. "No reason at all." She laughed as he tumbled her down onto the bed once more. If this was how he intended to end all their conversations, then their future looked very bright indeed.

A cheerful Peggy brought them dinner, and they watched a movie on the television in his room. And when they were ready to sleep, Rafael, for the first time in his life, did not struggle with insomnia. With Tori in his arms, there was nothing left for him to fear. He knew she would keep him safe.

When Antonio went into his office the next morning, the contract for Rafael and Tori was sitting on his desk. Across the middle, the word 'Complete' was very clear. He left it where it was while he went to get his coffee, and it was nowhere in sight when he returned. Unsurprised, and pleased with the events, he settled into his chair. He had a wedding guest list to write for Marco, but it wasn't hard to get started. There was one name already on it.

He knew she would be pleased with the events too.

# CHAPTER SIXTEEN

Eric was not a happy camper as he watched Gwyn patch up Rhianna's wounds. "You went in there by yourself," he said in a low voice. "You knew what you were up against and you didn't even tell me." Try as he might, there was a hint of pain in his voice. He and Rhianna had been best friends for two thousand years and were more like twins than mere friends.

"I've been hunting that thing my entire life," she countered softly. "It hates me more than I hate it. I know it would do anything to destroy those I love. I wasn't letting you or anyone else near it, Riku. I won't apologize for that."

Gwyn's husband, Taylor, was leaning against the wall of the office to observe. He was relatively normal, all things considered in the District, but he possessed strong gifts of his own. Among them was an ability to sense danger to those he loved. It manifested as a burning in his hands, and the fact that he was currently staring at them told Eric that he still sensed danger around Rhianna.

Rayna Mason ducked into the office and put the completed contract onto Rhianna's desk. Her hand slipped into Eric's as she leaned against his arm. She and Gwyn were a few years apart in age, but looked and acted enough alike to be twins. "There's one more, isn't there?" she asked Rhianna.

"Indeed." Freed from Gwyn, her arms now bandaged, Rhianna slipped the contract into a folder which also reflected 'Complete.' She slid the folder into a drawer labeled 'Lucino' and shut it. "Another long overdue to be done."

"Do you have more control over this scenario than you've had so far?" Taylor asked.

Her lips twisted into a half smile. "I sure hope so, Taylor."

It made none of her friends feel better to see Rayna frowning. She was Truth and had the ability to hear the truth over lies. Rhianna was telling the truth; she didn't know if she had control. It seemed more and more as evil grew in strength, her grip on events loosened. It didn't bode well.

Just what hadn't she told them yet?

*Status: File In Progress*
*Analysis: What may be ugly to some can be beautiful to another if the one looking is looking with the eyes of love.*

Folder Three
THERESA

# CHAPTER SEVENTEEN

"Theresa!!"

The echoing bellow through the house made Theresa cringe as she tried to brush out a particularly nasty tangle from her hair. In a way, the yell did not come as a surprise; her hair always managed to knot itself just before her grandmother went on a rampage. She wrangled the snarl out and put down her brush. Somehow her fingers were steady.

She calmly left her room and headed downstairs to the den. Her grandmother waited inside. "You called?" she asked. She very nearly asked if she had bellowed, but she bit it back. She knew better.

Ruby Collins narrowed her eyes warningly. "Someone saw you having lunch with Rafael Lucino."

"And his fiancée," Theresa noted. "I work for Rafael. We were discussing a project soon to be underway that will heavily involve me."

"Fah! I care not if he is engaged! Men cannot be trusted."

She barely stifled a sigh. It wasn't the first time she had heard this tirade in the two months since she had reluctantly let Rafael take her as his date to a gala. Truthfully, she still felt surprised that Ruby had even allowed it at all. "Yes, Grandmother."

Ruby glared at her for a long moment. "You will cease wearing slacks to work!" she snapped. "Pick out long skirts and oversized sweaters. I do not want you to tempt those lascivious males in your office!"

The only 'lascivious male' in her office was one she wouldn't give the time of day. The rest were happily married or far too old. Still, she didn't argue. She had never bothered. It did no good. She had no control over her life. She could not pick her friends—she had none other than Rafael—she could not pick her clothes. She could not go to college for a higher education. She only had a GED because she hadn't been allowed to attend high school. "Very well. Is that all?"

"Don't take an attitude with me! Go to your room!"

She promptly turned on her heel and walked out. Going to her room was her only escape. She had hundreds of books crammed into her bookcases, and they allowed her to get away from her reality. A line from a favored Disney movie echoed in her mind. *When will my life begin?* At twenty-five years old, it was a good question.

The other nice thing about her room was that some strange quirk of architecture allowed her to have a perfect view of the Enforcers' building within the 3$^{rd}$ District some distance away. It had always been a comforting sight. She wanted to go to the District and see the magic that people whispered about. She had seen it come into the Lucinos' lives. She could use some magic of her own.

On the other side of Brooklyn, the sound of a cell phone loudly playing Celine Dion had many people staring at Van with combinations of fascination and shock. He ignored them as he moved around a corner out of sight. He sighed and answered. "Hi, Mom."

"Van!" The tone was as scolding as it was warm. "When are you coming home for a visit?"

"I told you I was in the middle of a job." He pinched the bridge of his nose. "Please don't mail me plane tickets. I can't get to my P.O. box right now. It would be a waste."

His mother sighed heavily. "Oh, come on! I don't care how busy being a private bodyguard is! You can spare a few days to come home and celebrate your father's promotion."

"I can spare a few days when I've finished this job. You want me to just abandon my client?"

"Well . . . no. I guess not. But we miss you."

He just sighed. The conversation was not a new one. His parents had no idea what he did for a living, and he took great pains to keep it that way. It meant fewer visits than they would like, and fewer than he liked as well. There were times where it was just easier to stay away. He did not regret what he did, but he sure as hell had moments where he couldn't stand to be around anyone. Not even his parents. "Look. Let me finish this, and I'll come home for a while. Okay?"

"When?"

"*Soon*." He hung up before she could do more than sputter. The phone immediately began ringing again, but this time he had been expecting the call. He hit the receive button. "D'Angelo. How is she, Officer Marks?"

Marks' sigh was audible. "Alive and recovering. A bit traumatized, of course. She thought you were going to shoot her too."

"I don't involve innocents. She didn't belong there." Van's black eyes moved sharply around the area to ensure that no one had come up while he wasn't looking. "I assume that she knows that I wasn't there?"

"Someone from Enforcers came through to make sure of it. You have very, uhm, interesting associates."

"Useful ones, anyway. Let me know when she goes home. I want to send flowers."

"Yeah, you're a real gentleman, Van."

A hint of a smile touched his lips. "Hey, just look at my record. I'm a shiny, squeaky-clean pillar of society. I even vote every time."

"You also pay your taxes, you don't litter or speed, and you freaking abide by parking laws. It'd be so much more fun keeping your record clean if you didn't make it so easy. Can't you just try to bend a normal law a bit? Make it harder for me, c'mon."

"Okay, fine." He rummaged in his pocket and found an old receipt. "Here, I just dropped a piece of trash. Find me and ticket me."

"Asshole."

Van smirked and hung up the phone. He abided by all the laws he could simply because he had to break others frequently. There were things that only he could do. Things that justice could not touch. He had a contact in every police department in the city. He had contacts in other cities as well. All knew he worked with Enforcers directly. All turned to him when there was something that needed his particular skills.

His latest job had turned into a mess of Gordian knot proportions. He didn't even know much about the man he pursued. The mysterious figure had worked with Martin Johns on the scheme, but whether he had been involved with the attempted murders of Rafael and Tori, and the kidnapping of Isabelle and Brie, Van just didn't know yet. His first step was to establish if his target was evil or merely corrupt. The latter meant going to the police. The former . . . not as much. Evil did not belong in the world. It took too many innocent lives. He just balanced the scales, as Gwyn always said.

*(Two days later)*

It was madness inside the Publications Office at Just In Time, Inc. Theresa had her hands full with far too many things happening at once. She stared in dismay at the shiny computer being set up on her desk and complained, "Why do I need this thing?"

The technician rummaging underneath the counter said, "Sorry, Theresa. The whole company is going digital. That means even you need to use a computer now. You've *had* email. You just weren't being forced to use it."

She heard a familiar footstep and turned to see Rafael sauntering toward her. "You know I hate these things."

"*Sì.*" His voice held amusement. "But I also know that you are a quick learner and a smart woman." He tucked her hand into his elbow and firmly escorted her down an aisle of massive bookcases holding the entire history of the company. "Theresa, we are not heartless. We are asking you to do something that is quite uncomfortable, and we are asking you to go above your normal duties to begin the problematic process of scanning every file that exists here."

"Why me?" she sighed. "Rafe, really."

"Who else but you knows this place best?" he asked gently. He sighed gustily. "Perhaps I should not be appealing to your heart. Would you prefer a raise?"

"I really don't want one!" she blurted hastily.

"No? Well, too late. It was effective as of this morning." He grinned when she glared at him. If she had been anyone else, he would have expected a few curse words. He truly pitied anyone who finally managed to make her mad. The slow burners always burned the brightest. "Why would you not want a raise, Theresa?" She did not answer, but he had his suspicions. He knew who cashed her paycheck every month. "If it will ease your mind, our system is having some difficulties. It is not accepting the increase properly."

She stared at him. "You mean we're going electronic and we've already broken something."

"*Sì*. Who knew? As it stands, you will have to receive two checks." He spread his hands. "I am sorry, Theresa. But at least no one will know of your promotion should you not wish it. I know you are shy, *cara*." He flicked her in the nose lightly before tucking his hands in his pockets and walking away.

She realized her jaw was hanging open and hastily closed her mouth. A flutter of nerves in her stomach told her that he might know more about her home life than she had thought. It seemed suspect that the system would conveniently have issues with her new pay. She didn't even believe in coincidences.

She wouldn't have to give Ruby her extra pay. She could start saving money to get away. If she could just afford to get herself another place to live! Freedom. How tempting it sounded. For a chance at it, she would be willing to put up with those silly boxes of useless machinery. Well, if she didn't break one anyway.

The technician was nice enough to stay and show her how to turn on the computer, and he even left a huge book of instructions. They would be letting her learn things in pieces, thankfully. First the computer, then the scanner, then the electronic file system itself. She might even manage to get through things unscathed if they kept feeding her instructional books.

Her eyes widened as she opened her email client and saw the literally thousands of emails she had ignored by not having a computer. She groaned and dropped her head on the desk. What was *wrong* with people, anyway? Technology was making people dumber. She felt sure of it.

She did manage to get other work done, thankfully. The system threw a hissy fit when she tried to delete all the emails, and she had to make Carl come back downstairs to take care of it. While he muttered swear words at Microsoft Office, she got to work on the job she had been asked to pull for duplication. It was an old ad for a company they worked with, and they wanted some nostalgic posters for an anniversary.

She had half loaded her cart when her scalp tingled warningly. She glanced up sharply and found one of her coworkers standing in the aisle. Her shoulders tensed. "Did you need something, George?" As subtly as she could, she put the cart between them.

"When're you going to go out with me?"

"Never."

The conversation had been repeated a hundred times, but he refused to give up. She just didn't know what she was missing. Chick didn't date, and she sure as hell didn't have a man in her life. She didn't even have a woman. She was fair game. "C'mon, Theresa! I'm harmless. I'm totally healthy and I'm cute. How can you do better?"

"How about someone willing to listen when I say 'no'?" Her fingers tightened around the cart handle. "I appreciate the attention, but I'm not interested. Please leave me alone or I'll file a harassment suit."

He looked around nervously and yanked at his collar. He knew the Lucinos liked Theresa a lot. So did Tori and Alex. If they thought he was hassling her, someone would break his nose. "Okay, fine. I'll stop pestering you at work."

"At all!" she insisted as he walked away, but he didn't answer. Not that she really *wanted* to complain to Rafael or Antonio, of course. It was just a last resort. Maybe he would finally take the hint and leave her alone now. She couldn't imagine how much clearer she could make herself.

She managed to make it through the day without blowing up the computer—Carl gave her a B+ for her first day—and she gratefully left the building to head for home. She made it barely a block before her hair seemed to again warn her that trouble approached. A hand closed around her arm, and she barely bit back a yelp.

She whipped around and swung her purse at her assaulter's head, and George ducked on a shout. "Holy shit, don't kill me!"

Heart pounding, she stared at him. "You scared me!"

"I called your name but you ignored me!" He kept his hand on her arm and huffed out a breath. "Let's go get dinner."

She yanked at her arm. "I don't want to." He gave her a quick shake, and her eyes went wide. Real fear began to flutter inside her heart. Her hand tightened on her purse strap. Could she hit him hard enough to make him let go? She couldn't be sure.

"I don't know what you're such a chicken about," he shot at her, "but I'm really sick of how you think you're too good for any man. You let Rafael Lucino take you out, but you won't let me take you to even lunch? Hey, newsflash, babe, he's taken. You want a prince to rescue you or some shit?"

"Excuse me."

The chilly male voice had George slowly looking up to see a stranger standing behind Theresa. The newcomer looked handsome enough, but the hardness to his face kept him from being actually beautiful. His eyes looked as cold as his voice sounded. Inexplicably, without reason, George felt himself beginning to sweat. His skin crawled warningly. "Uh. Are we in your way?"

"Take your hand off her." The instant Theresa was freed, Van pulled her back and firmly stepped in front of her for added protection. "I believe she told you no. Would you like me to enforce the point? I would be glad to oblige."

George back-stepped so fast that he tripped over his own feet. "No! I, er, I'm good. I get it, I get it. Hands off. I won't bug her again." Hard black eyes stared at him, and he waved his hands in the air. "I'm going, I'm going!" He swung around, smacked into a store wall, and staggered back to fall on his ass. A mocking snort of derision had his color flaring red, and he scrambled up and ran away. Theresa was *crazy* if she thought she was safe with that guy!

Inexplicably, she actually did feel safe. She didn't doubt her rescuer's ability for violence, but she also didn't doubt that he would not harm her. Her hair didn't itch, and it always told her of trouble. "Thank you . . . ?" Her voice trailed off as he turned around, and she tried to keep her jaw from dropping again. Every pulse in her body began to flutter wildly as an unfamiliar yet strangely known longing rose inside. If this was the prince out to rescue her, then she was *happy* to be rescued!

"Van." A hint of a smile softened his face and warmed his eyes. "Van D'Angelo. May I escort you home?"

"Uhm. Yes. For a little ways." She fought to make her heart stop tripping over itself as she fell into step beside him. A fairly gleeful heat skipped merrily through her veins as she desperately searched for something to say that didn't involve something along the lines of 'I'm single; date me!' "Ah, thank you. For rescuing me."

"Yeah. No problem." He rubbed the back of his neck and looked for something intelligent to say. He hadn't intended to get involved, but he just hadn't been able to stand seeing her get manhandled like that. "You know that guy?"

"Work with him," she admitted.

"You should file a harassment charge."

"Yeah."

Another awkward silence fell. He finally glanced at her to see what she was thinking, and he found her smiling. "Something funny?"

She looked up at him, and her brown eyes had turned to warm whiskey from her humor. "He ran into a wall."

He felt his shoulders relax, and he had to smile in return. "I can't imagine why. I have such a comforting presence."

"You're a paragon." Her shoulders relaxed as well, and she quickly tucked her hair back when she saw strands clinging to his shirt and jeans. "My name is Theresa Adams. I really am grateful for the rescue. It was pretty scary," she admitted. She looked at her arm and saw the red marks were fading quickly. At least George hadn't bruised her.

On pure impulse, Van asked, "Can I buy you some coffee?" She looked up at him in surprise, and he felt his ears turn red. "If you say no, I'll listen. I promise."

Her gaze lowered almost shyly. "Actually . . . I wouldn't mind coffee. I'll probably be up late reading. I'll need the caffeine."

He changed direction and lightly cupped her elbow to escort her along. He realized what he had done and immediately released her to stuff his hands in his pockets. She looked at him for several moments and then lightly curled her hand around his elbow. A hint of shy pink to her cheeks made him damn tempted to lean down and kiss her. There was an honest sweetness inside her that drew him like a lodestone.

They got cups of coffee from a shop and grabbed a table in a corner. He put his back to the wall without thinking, but she didn't seem to notice anything unusual. He felt something tickle his arm and looked down to see a thick lock of her hair had wrapped around his wrist. He couldn't bring himself to free it. Somehow . . . it felt sensual. "You like to read?" he asked.

"Love it. I'll read anything and everything you give me. I probably have a million useless trivia facts inside my head. In this case, I have to learn to use a computer, and I have a book on using it. At least I'll enjoy learning. Do you read, or are you more of a movie type?"

"Books," he said fervently. "I like movies now and then, but I really love reading. I used to stuff suitcases with more books than clothes until I gave in and bought a Kindle. Instant library on the go."

She sighed wistfully. "I've thought about getting one, but technology scares me." He grinned a bit, and she stuck her tongue out at him briefly. "Don't make fun of me. I grew up in an old-fashioned household. We don't own computers. I don't even have an MP3 player. I'd break it."

"I dropped my Kindle from a ladder. If it can handle that, it can handle a technophobe. But I don't recommend any iThings. They're delicate." His heart clenched when she laughed, and he fought to ignore the needy hunger inside his body. He couldn't even tell if it was more physical or more emotional. He felt starved for her presence. He wanted to see her more. Needed to have her near. "Theresa?"

She suddenly went white and grabbed his wrist to look at his watch. "I have to get home!" She leapt to her feet. "My grandmother will be furious with me!"

He stood as well and frowned. "I'll go with you and explain."

"No!" she blurted. She shook her head hard. "Thank you, Van, but that would make it worse." She made a helpless gesture. "She hates men. *Please* don't follow me." She hesitated and then rose on her toes to briefly kiss his cheek. She tried to hurry away and was brought up short by her hair gripping his wrist. "Oh, don't do this now!" She yanked, and it finally let go.

He watched her run out and gave her a minute before he pointedly followed her. He stayed back enough that she didn't know he was there, but he wasn't sure it was necessary. She seemed blind to everything except getting home by a certain time. What the hell was going on?

The sight of the two-story house she lived in made him oddly depressed, and he didn't know why. He lingered just out of sight but could clearly hear her rattling the doorknob. "Grandmother!" she shouted. "Please, let me in!"

The retort came back, "Oh, look who finally decided to come home! Obviously you don't need a roof over your head since you don't care how much time you spend loitering at work. Go sleep in your precious lobby!"

"It won't happen again!" She struggled back tears. "Just let me in!" The door blessedly opened, and she rushed inside without looking at her grandmother. She didn't breathe again until she was safely in her bedroom.

From the outside, Van frowned darkly as he slowly walked away down the street. Something didn't feel right in the entire scenario. Maybe it was his exposure to the $3^{rd}$ District, but he just could feel 'something' in the air around that melancholy house. He glanced back toward the second floor balcony, and he thought he saw a glimpse of Theresa silhouetted against the curtains. Her long hair rippled as if alive.

His job was to hunt down Martin Johns' absent partner, and the last thing he ought to be doing was getting himself tangled up in whatever problems Theresa's family had. And yet . . . maybe spending time with her might actually benefit his job as well. If *he* was going to strike at the Lucinos, he would want information. Who would be a better target than the woman who had access to all the files? He could spend a little more time with her, get to know her more, and hopefully take care of two problems at once.

What could possibly go wrong?

# CHAPTER EIGHTEEN

Theresa's knees shook as she shut her bedroom door and locked it. She slowly sank down to sit on the ground and stared blindly at the opposing wall. She had no doubt that she could very well have been forced to sleep outside or at her desk. The threat had been there ever since she had become a legal adult. Just a little reminder that she was beholden to Ruby for a roof over her head.

Looking back, she knew that her grandmother's possessiveness had not changed as she grew up. It had always been over-the-top; she just hadn't thought much of it. Her parents had been murdered when she was a baby. She had always assumed that Ruby feared losing her too. But as an adult . . . strange how adults could see things differently from children. She didn't feel protected. She felt trapped.

She got to her feet and forced herself to put it aside. She would not let anything mar the one bright spot in the day: Van. She knew she didn't dare see him again, didn't dare mention him to anyone. It was enough to have met him. Perhaps meeting him was what had opened her eyes to her situation. He *did* make her feel safe. He also made her feel a laundry list of other things that were both fascinating and alarming. Maybe she could look him up when she got free, and she could ask him out.

Yeah, right. She snorted at herself as she changed into more comfortable clothes. While she could claim plenty of knowledge of the world, it came from books. Practical application had always eluded her. But . . . then again . . . maybe Van wouldn't mind being her practice buddy. He had seemed to like her well enough. She didn't know what he had intended to ask before she had noticed the time, but, maybe . . .

"Stop thinking about it!" she muttered at herself as she grabbed her brush. She started to yank it through her hair, and she felt her scalp burn briefly. She groaned as she recognized the sign. She let go of her hair, and sure enough, it now pooled on the floor. Another five inches had grown in. She snatched up the scissors she kept on her dresser and carefully trimmed it above her ankles again. She didn't dare go any higher. She chucked the hair into a basket and threw herself into her reading chair. She knew a sign when she found it.

There were times she honestly felt as if her hair was alive. It did things on its own that just couldn't be explained as an accident. It grew far too fast and far too long to keep it shorter than ankle length. She had once tried to cut it to her shoulders. It had retaliated by growing over everything like a vine. Ruby'd had to cut her free because she had ended up trussed from the ceiling. After that, they had worked to keep it at the floor. Theresa normally gave the cut hair to Ruby, but after that evening, she didn't feel right doing so. She would burn it first opportunity.

She half expected to be forbidden from going to work, but Ruby didn't say anything to her at all. She quickly hurried to the office, and she reluctantly booted up the Beast that now lived on her desk. Her eyes moved around the area quickly yet she did not see any sign of George anywhere.

"Theresa?"

She almost jumped out of her skin and swung around sharply to discover Rafael stood behind her desk. To her further astonishment, Van stood beside him. She shot to her feet. "Uhm, sorry. I'm just a bit jittery."

"*Sì*, I imagine so!" her boss scolded. "You have not been honest with me or Papa, Theresa. Why did you not tell us that you were being bothered by George?"

Her color rose as she shot a look at Van. His expression didn't change other than the slight lifting of a brow. "It wasn't a big deal until last night." She rubbed her hands over her arms. "I don't want to file a report."

Rafael wasn't surprised; Van had told him that would likely be the case. "It does not matter. George has been relieved of his duties and moved to another area. He knows he is not to speak with you again. In the meanwhile," he clapped Van lightly on the shoulder, "I would like for you to meet Van D'Angelo. He is a friend of the *famiglia*. He heard we were short on a guard for the library and Publications area and has offered his services. You may count on him, Theresa. He is an honorable man."

"We've met," she admitted softly. "I know I'm safe with him. Thank you, Rafe."

"It is my pleasure." He tapped her lightly on the nose and ambled out of the area. Only when he was in the hall did he start to whistle merrily. The moment Van had told him and Antonio that he wanted to be hired as a guard—in that particular area—both Lucinos had wondered if he had his eye on Theresa. It suited Rafael just fine. They just seemed . . . right together. It would be interesting to see how things went.

A bit awkward, Theresa linked her hands together. "You have a big mouth."

Van sighed. "You wouldn't have told either Rafael or Antonio, and we both know that something needed to be said. I think he needed more than to just be scared off or transferred, but I respect your desire to be low-profile." He leaned on the counter beside her. "If you don't want me around, I can always ask for another area."

He found himself holding his breath as she stared at him. Then, finally, a hint of a blush touched her cheeks. "No, I don't mind," she admitted softly. "And I'm sorry for rushing off last night. My grandmother is a hard woman."

He bit the tip of his tongue before he said what he really thought. "I was more worried than offended." He glanced at her desk, and his eyes warmed. "Forcing you to use a computer, huh?"

"I've only broken it once. I'm impressed with myself." She turned to sit down and unexpectedly got brought up short by her hair snagging on something. When she turned back, she realized the something happened to be Van. There were long locks wrapped around his forearms and legs alike. Bright red flooded her face as he slowly arched a brow. "I don't . . . I can't . . . oh god." She buried her face in her hands.

He studied the hair clinging onto him. As it had before, it felt sensual against his skin. He tugged gently on the confining strands, and they stubbornly held firm. They actually wound even more around him before his very eyes. Suspicions began to churn inside. He lifted his arm and looked at the hair. "Let go." His voice was soft and firm. "I am not going anywhere."

After a pause, the hair slowly unraveled and released him. It dropped back into place and pooled on the floor as if to prove it had lengthened right then and there. At least a foot of hair now sat docilely on the tile. He looked at it for a moment before reaching out and gently tugging Theresa's hands off her face. "You want to talk about this?"

"My whole life." She couldn't meet his eyes. "My hair just . . . grows. I have no control over it. We can't keep it short. I've tried. It gets mad at me." She tried to smile. "I think it's possessed."

The suspicions began to turn into alarms. He had spent far too much time in the 3$^{rd}$ District and worked with Enforcers for too long to dismiss something as merely a fluke. "If it does grab me again, I don't mind. I promise. I'm think I'm flattered. Hey." He lifted her chin to force her gaze up to his. "I wouldn't lie to you."

She searched his eyes and unexpectedly smiled. "I believe you." Her breath caught as his thumb rubbed over her skin softly and sent flutters of heat flickering through her nerves. Something softened in his face, and it made him unbearably beautiful as if a mask had melted away.

Both heard voices approaching, and he swiftly released her. She dropped into her seat and he walked several paces away. By the time the other employees reached them, everything looked normal. He inclined his head slightly when the two female clerks looked at him warily. "I'm the new guard."

"Uhm, okay." The blonde edged back carefully. "I'm just going to go to my desk now. Er, good morning, Theresa!" She whirled and hurried off around a large set of bookcases.

The brunette actually stood her ground though she held her purse almost like a shield. "I'm Sally. You are . . . ?"

"Van." He propped a shoulder against a bookcase. "I'm an *unarmed* security guard, if that will put your mind at ease."

Sticking a gun on a guy that mean and scary seemed entirely overkill! There didn't seem to be anything comforting about him at all. Forget protecting the library; who in their right mind would even enter the *building* with him there? "Sure, that's, ah, great." Her eyes darted around quickly. "Er, well, I'm on the clock. Later!" She dashed off hastily.

Van looked at Theresa. "I can't imagine what their problem is."

She laughed out loud and quickly slapped a hand over her mouth. Her whiskey eyes were wide over her palm and they danced with humor. She shooed him away with her other hand, and he very nearly smiled as he obligingly walked away. He had no idea why she didn't see him the way others did, and he didn't actually care. The idea of scaring her made him feel slightly ill.

He took the time to duck out of sight and sound, and he yanked out his cell phone. He hit a quick call button and waited. He watched the window as the other side rang; he had a perfectly reflected view of the open area where Theresa sat.

The other side clicked. "Enforcers."

"Theresa Adams," he said bluntly.

Rhianna hesitated audibly. "What about her?"

"Don't try that bullshit, Rhianna. I've spent too much time out there."

"Mmm. I suppose that's fair." She sighed. "Yes, I know her, Van. What's the problem?"

"Her hair. Do I need to elaborate?"

"No, of course not. But do I need to remind you that certain things leave my control once they enter the ether beyond my District?" She smiled when that was met with silence. "You really have spent too much time out here. I will be frank: yes, I know Theresa, and yes, it has to do with more than from the Lucinos and yet it also has everything to do with them. Yes, I know about the difficulties of her hair, and yes, I know exactly what's wrong. Anything beyond that, I'm simply not at liberty to tell you."

"Is she under contract?" He bit back a sigh as no answer was given. When it came to Rhianna, he couldn't assume it was an agreement. Theresa might or might not be 3$^{rd}$ District born. She might or might not be under an Enforcers' contract. His gut said yes to both, but he could be wrong. "Damn it, Rhianna."

"Just do what you're doing. I still don't have as much control over events as I want, Van." She gently hung up the phone.

He slowly put his phone away. He had been counting on having Enforcers at his back in case things went to hell. Being told they were effectively on their own was *not* comfortable after what he had witnessed around Martin Johns. If his partner was consumed by the same thing, and it came right for Theresa, it would get ugly. How the hell would he protect her from something that he couldn't shoot?

It did nothing to improve his mood to realize that something also felt off about the library portion of the Publications office. There were locked racks that held personnel and personal files, and he eyed them more than once as he wandered through the surprisingly cavernous area. When he found himself in front of them for the fifth time, he stopped and looked closer. What was tripping his alarms?

"Only I, Rafael, and Antonio know what's in these racks."

The sound of Theresa's voice didn't surprise him even though he hadn't heard or sensed her approach. He could normally detect anyone within a twenty-foot radius, but she slipped easily under his radar because he knew she was of no danger to him. No danger to him physically, anyway. She was Danger with a capital D to his heart and soul. He turned around and studied her. "What's in them?"

She smiled. "Things." Her gaze lowered and a hint of pink climbed her cheeks. "Uhm. I was wondering if you'd like to have lunch with me."

"Yes." As he realized how quickly he had agreed, he cleared his throat. "I would be very happy to have lunch with you."

"I'll meet you at the elevator at noon. There's a café next door that has good food." She touched his hand without any fear though she kept her touch her brief. She hurried away before anyone spotted her with him.

Not that he would knock his luck, but something had him wondering just what was going through her mind. Maybe she thought she would be safe at work where her grandmother couldn't see them. He pinched the bridge of his nose as he sighed. Yeah, she was probably under contract. This just smacked of Enforcer influence. He might have to kill someone in order to protect others, and he was falling in *love*. Incongruity. Its name was Rhianna.

Right at noon, he waited by the elevators for his 'date.' She came down the hall toward him after a moment, and he wistfully watched her hair move around her body. Will of its own or not, he liked the way it framed her full figure. He really wouldn't want to see it cut short; it just suited her. In fact, he liked everything about her exactly as it was. She had a beautifully curved shape all over, as if Nature had forgotten to use any straight lines in her figure. She looked soft and appealing and perfect. He had an inexplicable urge to cuddle, and he was assuredly *not* a cuddler.

"Van?" She tilted her head as she stopped in front of him. "You're staring."

"You seem surprised by that." He punched the elevator button.

"I suppose I am." She winced wryly. "Don't ask Rafael about his engagement party."

He made a mental note to ask at the first opportunity. "What happened?"

"It was strange. These men kept trying to ask me to dance."

"Ah." He coughed. "I assume you realize you're lovely, Theresa. Of course they would be interested." The way she eyed him assured him that he did, indeed, need to ask about the party. The idea of her not knowing what to say or do with unexpected admirers amused him more than it triggered any jealousy. Odd how that worked.

The café was not quite busy yet. They both got sandwiches and moved toward the rear of the place. He automatically put his back to the wall once more, and this time he saw her study him briefly. She smiled and shrugged it off, and his shoulders relaxed slightly. Compelled to explain, he said, "When you live putting yourself in danger, you pick up habits. I never have my back to a door."

"I can't say I blame you." She let out a quick breath. "I assume you're confused about why I asked you to lunch."

Disappointment, not a lack of surprise, made him stifle a sigh. "I will assume by your phrasing that it isn't a personal interest in getting to know me."

"Maybe a little bit," she confessed. "But mostly, really, there's something at work that I've noticed, and that I wanted to tell you. If anyone can figure it out, it's you."

His brows lifted. "You have my attention."

"Those confidential files that you kept eyeing. Something felt odd to you? It felt odd to me as well. I think someone is messing with them somehow. When I was examining them recently, I noticed that the one lock looked a bit . . . ragged."

"Like someone had tried to break it." It wasn't a question.

"Or something. I want to tell myself my imagination is overactive, but I saw you. I think you're sensitive like I am. You felt something off. You know about the problems the Lucinos have had lately. I mean, I can't imagine Rafe or Antonio hiring you without warning you about the recent trouble."

He sighed. "I did, and yes, they did." He sat back for a moment. "I'll watch the place tonight. See if we're both just overreacting. In the meantime, try not to worry about it." He felt something move and flicked a glance under the table to see that her hair had grabbed his ankle. Never one to ignore a sign, he asked, "So . . . a little bit of a personal interest?"

Her color rose. "I think we both know I'd be lying if I denied it. And you seemed to have one in me."

"Slightly more than a 'little' interest." He rubbed his thumb over the back of her hand. "I'm not exactly an expert on dating or courting or whatever the hell people call it, but I wouldn't mind playing it by ear with you. I know you're scared of your grandmother. I can be discrete."

"I've seen the way you can blend in. I believe it." She took a deep breath. "I'm kind of out of my depth." She glanced up but he didn't look surprised. "Maybe we could play it low key, and once I save enough to move, we could see what happens?"

"How about we see what happens and play it low key at the same time? Let's get to know each other. Ask me anything. I'll try to answer if I can. There are things I can't say," he warned.

"I don't mind. How about starting with the obvious?" She smiled. "Age, origins, and so on?"

"I'm twenty-nine, almost thirty, I was born in Texas where my parents still live, and as if my name wasn't a clue, yes, I have Italian blood as well. It's jumbled up with a lot of other things, though. I've been at my job for, hmm, about five years now. There was a need for my skills," he said simply. He didn't intend to keep it a secret forever, but it was assuredly not a conversation to be had in the middle of a busy café. "You?"

"I turned twenty-five a few months ago, and I'm not sure of my whole origins." She slowly stirred the lemon in her tea. "My grandmother is my mother's mother. My parents were killed when I was a baby. Grandmother has raised me since then. I don't really remember either my mom or my dad. I have some photos of them, though. I've never asked about them."

He kept his silence on his suspicions. Instead, he slowly slid his hand over hers and held on. She turned her hand over, and their fingers laced together. "I'm sorry," he told her softly. "My parents have never really understood me, but I've never doubted they loved me." He thought he had a better understanding then of why the Lucinos were drawn to Theresa; family was everything to them, and they somehow knew she needed one terribly.

They both knew it was getting to be the end of lunch, and they slowly and reluctantly pulled their hands back. They dumped their trays and stepped out into the afternoon sun. Impulsively, he grabbed her hand and held onto it as they walked. She looked up with a surprised expression that quickly turned to a smile. She rested her head against his arm on an unconsciously contented sigh.

Her scalp unexpectedly began to itch. As soon as she noticed it, she felt the tension in Van's body. She took a quick breath of fear and quickly swallowed a gasp when he swung her around the corner of the café and into an alley. He pressed her back against the side of the building. "Say nothing." His voice was nearly soundless.

She pressed her face to his shoulder and tried fight the shivers running through her body. She couldn't get warm. The itching had become a burning. She knew what it meant: her grandmother was somewhere nearby watching for her. She had completely forgotten that Ruby liked to occasionally spy on her at work. The first stirring of anger began to swell inside her heart. Why was she a prisoner?

Van's free hand gently curled around her arm, and he bent his head to say in her ear, "Breathe. Relax. Trust me. She's almost gone."

She took a long breath and was almost immediately distracted as the scent of his skin reached her. Something dangerous clung to even his scent, yet it still didn't scare her. She had been watching him all day. She could logically see why people were afraid of him. She could even see that he did nothing at all to reassure them—and she didn't blame him for it. Perhaps what drew her to him, drew them together, was more elemental than just desire. She wasn't the only one trapped in a tower; in a way, he had been just as isolated from the world.

His shoulders relaxed finally, and he eased back a bit. "It's safe." He smiled a bit wryly. "I'm sorry if I was flattening you against the wall. I didn't trust you to stay put. Frightened animals who aren't sure of their claws will always run from a threat. It was safer to stay here." His breath hitched as he saw how she looked at him. "Theresa . . . don't." Her hand came up to tenderly frame his face, and he closed his eyes. Her touch felt like heaven. "You're making it impossible to let go."

"Then don't." Her eyes searched his face. The mask had melted away again. She knew she saw the real him, and what she saw was everything she had ever wanted without knowing she wanted it. She didn't want a prince; this undercover cop was perfect. Oh, she had no proof that was his real job, but she couldn't shake her gut feeling. "Van?"

He cupped her chin and bent his head to kiss her. The whiskey colored eyes watching him widened slightly, and his body tightened greedily as he saw the color darken with a matching hunger. Her free hand settled lightly over his heart in an indelible claim. He felt something soft yet strong move against his skin and knew her hair had captured him again. It seemed superfluous to him. He had been captured the moment he saw her.

The kiss slowly deepened, and he slid his arms around her waist to bring her body close. She felt perfect. When they finally parted for air, he murmured huskily, "If I promise not to grope, can I keep holding you? I love how you feel."

"I'm a bit pudgy." It was said a bit breathlessly. "Everyone says I should lose weight."

"Don't do it on my behalf." He freed a hand to smooth her hair out of her face. At least a foot of the locks had coiled around his wrist again. "Please tell me that wasn't your first kiss. I won't be able to let you go without kissing you again."

She bit her lip and winced sheepishly. "Uhm." She sighed and rose up on her toes to kiss him again. His hands tightened, and the signal of his shaky control was wildly thrilling. It seemed oddly empowering to know she could affect this man that deeply. A gasp caught in her throat when he stole the kiss and aggressively parted her lips. If her first kiss had been a beautiful and tender thing, her second one was nothing but flash, fire, and wicked delight.

The strains of a familiar song broke the mood, and she pulled back enough to say huskily, "Your phone is playing Celine Dion."

"My mother is calling." His voice sounded rough, and his black eyes churned with emotion barely held in check. "Also, I think we might be late back to the office by now."

"I work for Italians. They understand passion. Rafael seduces Tori in his office."

He unexpectedly laughed. Though the sound came out a bit rusty from lack of use, it was still very genuine. "Does he know you know that? And does she?"

Her lips curved. "They do. They also know I'm discrete." She took a long breath and reluctantly released him. She tugged on her hair and it just as slowly let him go. Her breath wedged in her lungs as she saw his eyes flare with hunger at the feel of her hair sliding over his skin. She slowly backed up a step. His hand lifted as if to stop her, and she hurried away before she did something stupid like ask him to take her to wherever he lived. She was in way too far over her head. They needed to back up a step for a bit before they did something stupid. Why couldn't she shake the feeling that he was in danger by being involved with her?

He blew out a hard breath and grabbed his phone. "What?" he demanded.

A pause hung for a moment until his mother said drolly, "Well, that answers that. I was going to ask if you intended to bring anyone home with you on your next visit. We need to clean out the guesthouse if so. You sound . . . a bit *strained*, honey."

"Stop laughing at me." He hung up the phone with a scowl, but it shortly turned to a wry smile. His parents were going to *love* Theresa. Bringing her home wasn't exactly an option anymore. He would be damned if he let her escape from his life now. He knew he had a fight on his hands to get her to trust him to protect her, but he also had plenty of patience. He had no worries about the job taking him away, either. Everything was connected *somewhere*. He just didn't know where yet.

At the least, he finally had a good feeling of what story they were 'tangled' inside. He should have guessed. Rhianna wasn't very subtle sometimes.

# CHAPTER NINETEEN

They were indeed back to work a bit late, but no one said anything about it. Most were too afraid of Van to try, and the rest liked Theresa too much to question her taste. She did encounter Roberto in the halls, though, and he winked at her saucily. The merger moved forward quickly, and she was used to seeing him as much as she saw Rafael. In fact, the merger was another thing adding to her work stress. Just In Time had more square footage for storage, and Roberto's company slowly brought over things for filing.

As she stood staring in dismay at the stacks of boxes, Sally materialized at her side. "You need to buy some jeans, girlfriend."

Theresa winced wryly. She didn't deny the charge, yet she knew her grandmother would never allow it. Maybe she could buy some and hide them at work. "I must concur. We'll need more shelving, though. That old corner where we used to stuff old supplies needs to be cleaned up and used for more storage. Antonio told me that if we need to expand into other offices on this floor or commandeer space on another floor, to just let him know. So far so good, but I'm thinking about the future. Even going electronic, we can't just destroy this stuff. It's original art."

"Agreed." Sally made notes on the iPad she held. Seeing Theresa's look, she grinned. "Technophobe."

"It's not a crime. And, hey, I haven't broken the computer more than once. Pluses for me." She scooped up a box. "One down, a million to go."

"Pebbles and road, bygones." Sally eyed her as they headed

back toward the front. "You be careful, okay?"

She didn't pretend to misunderstand. "He's a good man. I feel safer with him than I do in my own house. He makes me feel happy. It's an odd feeling."

Considering they had all noticed the lingering melancholy that clung to Theresa—and the fact that she never accepted invitations to barbeques or birthday parties—it was a welcome sign that she might finally have found someone that made her happy. "You going to ask him to go with you to Italy for the wedding? You were the only one invited by the Lucinos, you know."

"I know, and I'm still not sure I can attend myself. It's complicated. But if Van wanted to go, I wouldn't mind taking him as my date." She winced wryly. "I wouldn't have minded having him as a date at the engagement party."

Sally grinned. "Hey, you looked hot, hon. You can't be that surprised. And didn't I rescue you from that tipsy guy?"

"You did, and I still owe you cookies." She put the box down on her desk and sat down with a sigh. "Back to the grindstone." A funny noise had her looking at her computer, and she groaned when she saw the infamous blue screen of death. "I didn't even touch it!"

Carl obligingly came down to fix it while she put things away. The shiny new scanner had arrived and needed to be assembled still, but the technician helpfully gave her the manual early. It seemed fascinating how fast things could change.

The rest of the day went by fairly quickly. Van very nearly offered to escort Theresa home, but he knew better. Frustration gnawed at him as he watched her walk away down the sidewalk. He very badly wanted to grab her up and steal her away to someplace he could keep her safe and secure from the rest of the world. He was driven in his life, and choice of career, by an urge to protect. This was more personal than it had ever been before.

"It is hard," Roberto murmured sympathetically from behind him. "To take that fall and know that the one you love is fragile."

Van glanced at him as he stepped forward. "Brie didn't strike me as fragile when she threw water in my face or smashed Cauly over the head before I could deal with him myself."

"She is brave, *sì*, but she is fragile. In many ways, can it not be said that the ones who are the most fragile can be the most brave? They have the most to lose." He looked the direction Theresa had gone and could just see her figure as she disappeared around a corner. "Theresa has more bravery than she knows. Yet, perhaps, she is more fragile than she knows. She has been tempered by her life. I do not know much of it, but it does not take direct knowledge to recognize the signs of mental or emotional abuse."

"Your instincts are not wrong," Van admitted. "I don't know the details yet either, but you didn't tell me anything new." Under his breath, he muttered, "Locked in a tower."

Roberto very nearly smiled. He had been wondering about that. "I have always felt there was an answer in the story that was obvious from the beginning yet never used. In every version, I have seen it." He clapped Van on the shoulder. "You are a good man, Van. And you are smart. You and Theresa can save each other. If you have need, you only have to ask and we will help. Rafe and Antonio love Theresa a great deal. She is part of their family in their hearts. Why do you think Antonio wanted Rafe to try to date her? Free her from her tower, and they will adopt her in a minute."

Van watched him walk away and smiled to himself. He could see what Rhianna had meant about things having both nothing and yet everything to do with the Lucinos. It was no coincidence that Theresa had ended up working for them. Perhaps the connection between everything was Theresa herself. It might well be that it was her story that had started it all. He would need to do some digging to be sure, but in the meantime, he had a library to babysit. Just who was tripping his internal alarms, and what were they after?

Theresa thought the entire way home about ways to play off things if Ruby noticed there was anything different. She certainly *felt* different though a look in a mirror had told her there were few lingering effects.

To her surprise, the house was blessedly empty. She hurried through to her room and took a quick shower in the attached bath. She actually enjoyed bathing despite her hair; it never retained water unless needed. By the time she got out and toweled off, her hair had already mostly dried. It was fully dry when she got dressed and went to the kitchen for food.

The door opened and closed as she stirred a pot of soup. "Welcome home, Grandma," she called. She hurried to pour a cup of hot tea and put it on the table as Ruby entered the tiny kitchen. "I made dinner."

Ruby sat down heavily at the table. "I'm not hungry." She took the tea and sipped it gingerly. "How was work?"

"Relatively normal, all things considered." Where normally she had told everything before, she found herself editing the events for once. "One of the employees got a transfer for hassling others. The scanner has been installed, and I've got the instructions to read. I had lunch with a coworker today to discuss the issues."

Ruby grunted lightly. "When do you get paid?"

"Friday, same as normal." She held onto her smile until Ruby walked out and then slowly released the breath she had been holding. She dished up a small amount of soup for herself but she didn't much feel like eating either. Lately, her grandmother had been acting . . . unusual. More tired. Sometimes in more pain as if she had been injured somehow. Something smelled rotten, and Theresa didn't know what it was or why she felt it. Maybe it would be answered by whatever Van found.

Van had been on more than one stakeout in his career. He found the ideal place to watch the restricted area from and settled in to wait. He kept one ear alert to the sounds of the quiet building, and he kept his eyes on the locked bookcases. Despite his best efforts, his mind began to wander. Was Theresa okay? Had her grandmother seen them? What was it about Ruby that he just did not trust? There were just too many loose threads in the entire scenario for him to be comfortable with anything.

A faint noise diverted his thoughts, and his eyes narrowed as he watched a small flashlight beam move across the floor. He didn't move until the figure holding the light came into view. His night vision had always been exceptional. There was nothing familiar about either male that started fiddling with the case, and they looked pitifully young. He straightened and began to move forward.

The lock wouldn't open, and the thief cursed softly as he tried to wrangle it. They had been trying for days to get in, but the stupid thing was old and rusty. The situation was not aided at all by the chills going down his back. Something dangerous lurked nearby. "Joe, you got the pliers?"

"Urk!"

It was the way he made the noise as much as the noise itself that made him whip around. Joe had been laid out flat on the ground, and another man stood with a foot on his back. Erwin almost went for the knife he wore when he saw that the newcomer held a gun very calmly and wore a guard's badge. His hands shot into the air. "Oh shit."

"Indeed." Van applied pressure to Joe's back to keep him down. "Why don't you two be the upstanding citizens I know you can be and tell me just what you're doing back here?"

Erwin tried to keep his knees from knocking. His sweaty palms felt clammy and cold. He would have tried to grab the flashlight to see the guard better, but what little he could see was *not* comforting. "We got lost."

"Very cute." Van pointedly checked the clip in the gun.

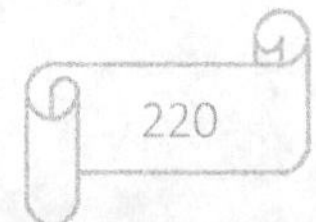

"We wanted the files on the Lucinos!" Joe blurted. "That's all! They're in these cases, and we were just going to nip them for some chick. No harm, no foul. Please don't shoot us!"

Something smelled rotten to Van. If Theresa and the Lucinos were the only ones who knew what these files were, then *she* sounded guilty. He would sooner believe in the Easter Bunny or non-partisan politics than the idea that she had any reason to steal files she could access without suspicion in the course of her normal job. She was being used. "Sit," he told Erwin.

The shorter male sat down fast enough that he almost fell on his ass. Van didn't take his eyes off the burglars or move the gun as he pulled out his cell phone and lifted it. "Officer Marks?"

"I heard. We'll be there in two minutes."

Van tucked the phone into a pocket. "Your new friends will be here shortly, kids. And I recommend a change of career. You're lucky I'm such a nice guy. My contract says I can shoot first and ask later."

Marks and two other cops arrived shortly thereafter and put both males under arrest. Van had warned Marks ahead of time that something might happen, and the veteran cop had trusted his instincts enough to be standing by. While the thugs were read their rights, Marks stepped aside with Van. "What the hell was that? They trying to frame your, ah, *friend*?"

Van ignored the subtle dig. "Sure as hell sounds like it. Do you need me, or am I free? I need to talk to her quickly and find out if my gut is right."

"Get moving. You can give a statement later." He watched Van walk out of the area and smirked as both Erwin and Joe visibly relaxed. "Aw, he was making friends again. So glad he didn't shoot them this time. It's always such a mess."

The males went glassy, and Marks' partner murmured, "You're such a dick sometimes."

"Y'take your perks where you get 'em."

Van made his way as fast as he could to where Theresa lived with Ruby. The tiny house was even more depressing in the midnight gloom than during the day. It looked completely dark and shut down for the night, but there was a very dim light coming from the room that he knew was Theresa's. She had again stayed up late to read.

She had a balcony, thankfully. He jumped up to grab the edge and hauled himself up and over the railing. He knocked very lightly on the glass doors and called softly, "Theresa? It's Van." Silence met him, but it felt deliberate. "Theresa. Please. Open the doors. I'll be quick."

The curtains parted a tiny bit, and she peeked around the edge. "You shouldn't be here," she urged just as softly. "She'll kill you!"

"I'm hard to kill. Believe me, people have *tried*." He pressed his hands to the glass. "Let me in." Let me hold you. Though the words did not come to his lips, they seemed to echo in the air around him.

She slowly reached out and unlocked the triple bolts on the doors. She tugged them open and stepped back to let him step inside. As he stared at her, she looked down quickly. She had on her normal camisole for sleeping though she had thrown on the pants as well at his knock. "What?"

"If I tell you that you're sexy, will you believe me?" he asked huskily.

She hastily grabbed her robe and pulled it on. "Unfortunately, yes, and don't you *dare* kiss me!" She struggled to free her hair from under the robe and ended up with her hands stuck. Even in the dim lamplight, her cheeks were bright as Van moved closer and helped free her. "It's worse," she admitted miserably.

He released her hair and watched almost two feet of length pool on the ground. "Without provocation?"

"It rarely needs any." She grabbed the scissors. "You want to see how bad it is?" She twisted her hair around her wrist and quickly lopped the strands off at her waist. The cut hair immediately dissolved into dust, and the shortened strands sparked at the edges before abruptly surging outward and returning to floor length. "It's not normal."

"No." He blew out a quick breath. "Theresa . . . I think you are

3<sup>rd</sup> District born." He sat down on the side of the bed and tugged her down beside him. "It would have to be your father. I couldn't get any information out of Rhianna Taber, but she admitted she knows you beyond your connection to the Lucinos. There's only one reason she would. I have other suspicions, but I can't confirm them. All I know is that we're on our own, and you've got a shitload of danger breathing down on you."

In a way, it was reassuring knowledge. "What kind of danger?"

"You were right. Someone was trying to get into the files. Two idiots trying to get the personal files on the Lucinos themselves. They said they were doing it for a 'chick', and it sure as hell makes you look guilty. On the other hand, I'm not an idiot. Have you told your grandmother about those files, or about work?"

Her mouth went dry and her heart began to beat harder. "Yes," she whispered. Her hands clenched together in her lap, and his hands covered them soothingly. "I have to tell her everything else she won't even let me keep the job at all." She leaned forward and dropped her head on his shoulder. "She's framing me. I had started to think lately that . . . that maybe she didn't love me after all, but this . . . this is not what I expected."

He pulled her onto his lap and wrapped his arms around her tightly. Little shivers rippled through her entire body and he tried to absorb them. "There may be more that we don't know. I'm going to start looking into her history. My gut tells me that she might be connected to Martin Johns somehow. I don't believe in coincidences. Brie said that it might be her fault Enforcers got involved, but I wonder if it might not be you instead."

"I started working for the Lucinos after Johns started causing trouble."

"Was it your idea or your grandmother's?"

A violent shiver ripped through her body. "Hers," she barely whispered. "It was the only job I was qualified for without going to college or having a high school degree. I never . . . I never understood why she suddenly was willing to let me work." She wrapped her arms around his neck and clung onto him with all her strength. "Why, Van?"

"I don't know, baby. I swear I'll find out." He pressed his face to her neck for a moment. He very, very badly wanted to carry her out of there and go stash her away safely at the Lucino villa or at the Viani place. He could have Tori and Alex guard her until he figured out what the hell was going on! "At least you know more of your origins," he tried to tease.

"3rd District." Longing filled her voice. "There might be somewhere I belong?"

He couldn't stand it anymore. He eased her back and smoothed her hair out of her face. "You belong with me," he urged softly. "Trust me. Let me protect you. Grab some things and leave here with me. If you can't trust me, then I'll take you to Rafael. Tori and Alex are the best I've seen at what they do."

She took a long breath and met his eyes evenly. "Who are you?"

He closed his eyes briefly and then opened them again. "It depends on how generous you want to be. The kindest term, I think, is a mercenary. Hired gun and hitman have been applied as well. I take care of things that the system can't. Vincent Lucino hired me to remove Johns; I helped kidnap Brie and Isabelle and then worked to keep them safe. I got Tori free so she could get to Rafael before it was too late. There's no knowing which of us killed Johns; I hope, for her sake, it was her. She deserved the honor." He searched her eyes and saw no condemnation. "You don't look overly surprised."

"I don't think I am. I had guessed you were an undercover cop, so I suppose I wasn't far off. Does knowing the truth change how I feel? Of course not. It just explains why others react to you the way they do." Softer, she added, "And why I feel safe with you. It's hard to not feel safe with a man who would, literally, kill to protect you." She smoothed her hand over his beloved features. "Alright. I trust you."

A heavy fist suddenly slammed on the door. "Open this door!"

Ruby shouted. "I swear, you had better open this door, Theresa! I know there's someone in there with you! Unlock the damned door!" The banging grew in force.

Theresa leapt to her feet. "Get out!" she urged Van. "Hurry! She won't hurt me, but she might kill you! *Please*. Trust *me* on this."

He stood and tried to reach for her, but her hair rose up and shoved him back. He stared into her eyes for long moments before cursing under his breath. He ran out onto the balcony and swung over the side to drop down underneath where he could not be seen. He quickly made his way across the darkened landscape until he was out of sight and sound. He needed to get that research done *fast*. She could not stay there any longer.

Theresa stifled a yelp as something heavy smashed the lock and the door suddenly swung open. "Are you mad?" she demanded of her grandmother.

Ruby rushed into the room and looked around wildly. There didn't seem to be any sign of anything, and certainly Theresa was more than dressed. Overdressed, to some extent. Yet Ruby rounded on her and screamed, "Who was in here with you?"

Disdaining to lie, Theresa didn't answer the question. "I'm twenty-five, not five. Whether you like it or not, I'm a legal adult." She walked over to her closet and felt strangely calm over things. "I'm done, Grandmother. I'm leaving."

Ruby grabbed her arm and her fingers bit in painfully as she swung her around. "I will not let you waste yourself on any man! Do you think he loves you? Men don't love! They *use*! They lie and cheat and abuse the ones they profess to love! He'll tear you up and throw you aside and then you'll come crawling back to me! I won't let it happen, Theresa! I tried to teach you, but you just won't listen!"

"How do you intend to stop me?" She nearly stopped breathing as she saw the gun in her grandmother's hand. "You wouldn't shoot me."

"No, of course not." Ruby pressed the muzzle against her own head. "But you think I won't kill myself right here?"

Nausea rose and Theresa's hair seethed violently around her body. Truthfully . . . she couldn't be sure it was a bluff. It seemed like the kind of thing Ruby would do, and Theresa would never be able to live with the guilt if she was wrong. She couldn't help loving her grandmother. "You win."

"Pack." The order was curt. "I'm taking you somewhere that bastard won't find you." She whirled and stormed out.

Theresa dragged out her single suitcase and threw things inside it a bit blindly. She knew Van would find her wherever she went. She trusted him to rescue her from whatever new tower she entered, be it literal or metaphorical. She would do whatever it took to help him when he did. She was getting sick of being the meek and helpless mouse she had been for years. If she was from 3$^{rd}$ District, then she had the chance at a happy ending. She would damned well fight for it!

# CHAPTER TWENTY

The benefit to having cultivated contacts over the years was that Van had associates in some of the strangest and yet also useful places. He had picked up people from all walks of life, and he even knew people within relatively similar fields. In this case, if he wanted to investigate Ruby's background, he needed someone experienced with digging into histories and unashamedly willing to break into a few computers as needed.

It was nearly one in the morning, but the situation was too dangerous to wait until later. He flipped through his contacts in his phone and punched one in. It took quite a few rings until the other side was finally answered, and before the other person could speak, he said, "It's Van, and I have an emergency that has put the life of an innocent young woman on the line."

Silence, then, "Shit. Let me get dressed and grab some coffee. I'll meet you at my office in fifteen." An annoyed cry from a baby had him muttering, "And you owe me for waking Jayden."

"Tell Aenya that I'll pay for the next upgrade she wants for her club."

A woman's voice groused in the background, "I'm holding you to that."

Van almost smiled as he hung up the phone and tucked it away. He had gotten to know Hiro Michaels through the Enforcers, and by far the other man was one of the best private investigators that he had known. He had been quite glad to have Hiro as an ally; it was entirely likely that Hiro might be the only one who could successfully track him even if he didn't want to be tracked.

Fifteen minutes later, he stood outside the small office that Hiro operated from. He spotted the slightly disheveled investigator approaching and asked, "Teething problems?"

"No, thankfully. Brian Matthews made a blanket that keeps that at bay." Hiro unlocked the door on a sigh and walked inside. He flicked on lights and dropped into his chair behind the desk. "Let's hear it. This ought to be good, at the least."

Van kept it as concise as he could, but he had to start at the top with the Lucinos. He finished with, "I need to act fast if I want to get Theresa out of her tower."

"No shit." Hiro was already working on the computer. "Nice to see another worthy man take the fall. The minute you mentioned you worked with Enforcers, I had a feeling you'd eventually get to this point."

"I'm not from the District."

"You didn't have to be. Did you feel at home there?" At the nod, he shrugged. "There you go. Maddie told me once that sometimes it just takes a while to find your way home. I've sure as hell seen it myself many times. I'd bet Rhianna had her eye on you from the get-go. Did she contact you the first time?"

Van winced. "Now that you mention it . . ." He blew out a breath. "It would explain a lot, that's for damned sure." He sat on the edge of the desk and watched over Hiro's head. "What are you looking for?"

"Ruby's bank deposits. Seems odd that she didn't let Theresa work until last year and doesn't work herself. Where's she getting money? I'm sure Social Security covers a bit, but it ain't going to help raise a kid and it sure as hell wouldn't have bought that house they live in. She owns it outright. No loan. Paid cash."

"Now you know why I called you at one am."

"You're still an ass." After a few more minutes, he said, "Here we go. She banks somewhere that I've accessed records before." He grinned briefly when Van lifted a brow. "You're not the only one with contacts." He ran a finger down the screen. "Check deposits of one thousand dollars every other week for the last several months. I'd bet it goes back even further. Let's see . . . Ah. Here we are."

Van leaned closer to see the scanned copy of the check. "Orson Collins. Same last name; I wonder what relation he is to her. Hang on." He grabbed his phone and began flipping through notes. "I have the info I pulled from Martin Johns' files in here."

"Gotta love modern technology. Let's see what Google says . . ." Hiro plugged the new name into the search engine and wasn't disappointed. The very first link took him to public records. "The plot thickens. Forty-five years ago, Ruby and Orson Collins got a divorce. Records are sealed but I see some old paper clippings from a library archive that imply it wasn't precisely amicable. Looks like there was a bitter custody battle, and I see that there are reports of physical abuse."

"One of the notes I got from the file had the initials 'O.C.' in it." Van flipped pages. "OC popped up a lot. My gut said he might be the absentee partner. If we assume OC is Orson Collins, and he's obviously still in contact with his ex, then that means Ruby is using Theresa as a spy on the Lucinos for him. Johns was ruined when the scheme fell apart. Collins must have had some sort of backup."

"Something doesn't compute here for me." Hiro sat back. "Let's assume that Johns and Collins are partners and want revenge on the Lucinos for ruining them. A year in, Collins goes to his ex-wife and pays her to put their granddaughter into the company as an unwitting spy. I can't imagine any amount of money making her willing to cooperate. I would assume he's the reason she hates men, and her obsessive protection of Theresa seems to imply that she wouldn't let her out of the house willingly."

"When I went to work for Johns less than a year ago," Van said slowly, "I could only earn so much of his trust. I never knew where he got his information. I could only act quickly to keep things in line. He was a paranoid evil-possessed psychopath. Maybe he wasn't the one behind everything."

Hiro looked up sharply. "You think Collins is the root of the evil."

"There's something about what Rhianna said that's constantly bugging me." He tapped a finger on the top of the desk. "Theresa is at the heart of this. If she's under contract, it's been in place since she was a child. Who signed on her behalf? It would have to have been her grandmother; her parents were killed when she was a baby." He broke off. "Son-of-a-bitch."

Hiro closed his eyes. "Collins killed his own daughter and son-in-law, and because the son-in-law was 3rd District born, Enforcers was involved. They moved fast to protect Theresa, but it wasn't enough for Ruby, who has gone overboard in the time since. Collins showed back up, and I'd lay money on him threatening our slightly sheltered Rapunzel in order to force Ruby's compliance. You said that the evil eating Johns seemed slightly omniscient?"

"More than slightly." His voice sounded as grim as he looked. "I think it's worth noting that it couldn't stand hearing mention of the 3rd District, and it went right after Rhianna directly. If Collins was already possessed, that would be a good reason to hate his son-in-law and, by proxy, his granddaughter. Fast forward two decades and you have two possessed nutcases that Antonio and Rafael Lucino helped ruin. Rhianna set up Brie and Roberto, Alex and Bella, and Tori and Rafael—possibly to protect them from the evil itself. Say the evil knew that. It's a whole new reason to hate them."

"Throw Theresa in to unintentionally spy on them, and all of Collins and Johns' most hated people are now together. Except for the problem that they utterly failed to do anything to the Lucinos other than some surface damage to Rafael and a bullet wound to Tori that turned out to be advantageous." Hiro's stomach churned uneasily. "You didn't think the Lucinos were in any more danger physically. Of course they aren't. They have completed contracts; they're under direct protection and can't be touched. Theresa isn't. Her contract is obviously still open. And how better to strike at the Lucinos than to target her directly, when she is so close to the family that Rafael has actually referred to her as his sister to more than one person?"

Van said something explicitly rude and whirled toward the door. "No wonder Ruby is getting worse! She knows her granddaughter is right in the middle of a warzone! Theresa's been developing her courage and is at her breaking point; she can't be controlled anymore. I've got to talk to her before Collins goes after her personally!"

"Don't do anything stupid!" Hiro shouted after him. Under his breath, he added, "Things just get worse as time passes. What the hell would cause such a grudge against the District?"

Van had to cool his heels until later in the morning when he could get into the office. He knew he didn't dare return to the melancholy house so soon. He bided his time as patiently as he could, but Theresa did not show up at her normal time. He immediately left the building and called Antonio directly. "Where is Theresa?" he demanded.

Antonio blew out a breath. "I had been hoping you would know that, Van. I have not talked to her this morning, but her *nonna* called me and very politely informed me that Theresa would not be returning to work. What has been happening? You sound very strained, and it is very unlike what I have seen of you until now. You love Theresa, *sì*?"

"As if you didn't guess already." Van's eyes moved sharply over the landscape. "I think I know what's going on, and Theresa is right in the middle."

"You will handle it." Antonio's voice remained calm. "You are a good man, Van. Papa put his faith in you, and so shall I. When you have saved Theresa, you will accept your pay and use it to take her on a vacation; a cruise, I think. You will bring her home soon thereafter, however. Our library would fall apart without her, and we will need to have a party to welcome her into our family officially."

Van stared at the phone as it was hung up on the other side. Unexpected humor stirred. Vincent was the only *actual* Don Lucino, but Antonio and Rafael could both pull it off convincingly. He sure as hell wasn't going to try to disagree. If they came out of this intact, he would be more than glad to kidnap Theresa himself and hold onto her until the fear went away again. He didn't like fear very much, and like everything else, she had brought a lot of it into his life.

He knew it would be empty, but he made his way back to the maudlin house surrounded by flowers. No lights were on inside, and it just *felt* abandoned. The doors had been locked, and he broke the one on the back to get inside. The windows illuminated the structure with gloomy light, and it disturbed him to think of all the years Theresa had lived there. His eyes told him it was a perfectly lovely home, but his heart could see it for the prison had become.

He found Ruby's room on the first floor and went over it briefly. There was nothing of interest to be found; the only documents he located were ones that Hiro had already pulled from online.

Partway up the stairs, his skin crawled in a familiar way. He drew his gun and moved silently down the second floor hallway toward Theresa's room. Dead silence—unnatural silence—seemed to echo through the area. He reached for the doorknob and then quickly turned it and shoved the door open without moving into the opening. Nothing happened. He knew he wasn't alone, but his guest did not wait in the room.

He stepped inside and looked around. It definitely showed the signs of someone packing in a hurry. The balcony doors stood open and he moved over to them. A shimmer of something caught his eye and he crouched down. Long strands of brown hair glimmered in the sunlight. His breath hitched as he realized they spelled out the words 'find me'.

His head jerked up sharply and he hit the ground fast. The bullet mostly missed him but it did graze along his arm close enough to draw blood. He looked at the doorway and found Ruby watching him with eyes too wide and too glassy. She stood on a precarious point. "Interesting introduction," he told her calmly.

Her grip on her gun was steady if white-knuckled. "You think

you're any better than the people you kill?" she raged at him. "I know who you are, Van D'Angelo! Nothing but a cold-blooded murderer! I won't let my granddaughter waste herself on a man who kills for a living!"

He didn't bother to deny the charge or defend himself. It would be a waste of breath. He rolled to his feet and put his gun away. "Your ex tell you that, Mrs. Collins? Bit of a hypocrite, wouldn't you say? Where's Theresa?"

"You won't find her!" Her glassy eyes almost looked a bit mad. "She will stay there safely until Orson gets what he wants and goes away again!"

There were flaws in that logic big enough to drive a truck through, but he again didn't argue. She could not be reasoned with. He let his eyes flicker over her shoulder, and she instinctively swung around. He immediately turned and jumped over the side of the balcony. He landed relatively softly on the muddy ground and ran around the side of the building swiftly. He would have to thank Marks' teenage son for teaching him some parkour tricks; they could prove useful in the damnedest places.

He grimaced and peeled his torn shirt away from the wound. He'd had worse before, but it still hurt like hell. He kept first aid supplies in his car for just such an emergency and gingerly wrapped the graze as best he could. That done, he stared out the windshield toward the tall city buildings in the near distance. There were millions of places that Theresa could have been stashed. It would be literally like finding a needle in a haystack.

Something glimmered in the wind, and his eyes narrowed. He looked again, and he knew he couldn't be mistaken. There were very long strands of hair drifting through the air. As soon as he noticed one, he began to notice more. No one along the sidewalks had noticed them. Only his eyes could see them. It was a trail. "Better than breadcrumbs," he muttered as he started the car.

The strands in the wind eventually led him to a cluster of high-rise urban living complexes. They were the latest and greatest, and they were made of reflective glass from top to bottom. Each reached ten to twenty stories tall. The only entry points were through front doors accessible by key card or by an external glass elevator. Trying to break into one of these places would be damned impossible. Anyone and everything would see you. Hell, just using the elevator would be putting yourself on display; the elevators were not made of the same reflective glass as the buildings.

A patient man by nature, Van found it difficult to cool his heels until nighttime finally arrived. Night was never truly dark in the city, and the urban area was designed for the nightlife so it had a lot of lights and clubs nearby. He didn't even know which 'tower' Theresa was being held inside, and he carefully crept around the base of all of them. Something tickled his arm, and he looked up sharply to see strands of hair falling to the ground.

He grabbed a few from the air and saw something move in a window near the top of the ten-story building. He held his breath as he watched a thick rope of hair lower slowly toward him. It looked like an actual rope, yet he knew it was Theresa's hair. It coiled around his waist and legs tightly, and he held on as it began to swiftly bring him up the side of the building. While heights were not his favorite thing in the world, he had absolutely no fear of falling. He trusted that rope of hair more than he trusted cables or the infamous duct tape.

The window stood open, and he climbed inside it as the rope released him. He had thought that nothing more could surprise him, but he discovered very quickly that he had been wrong. He stopped short, and his eyes widened slowly as he stared at the scene in the main area of the condo.

Theresa sat in the middle of the living room floor, and her hair literally covered and climbed every surface in the area. She had been partially tied up herself, and the thick brown locks resembled vines as they engulfed the entire place. She had her face buried in her hands, but she sensed him and looked up sharply. Tears streaked her face and continued to well in her eyes. "Van?" she managed to whisper.

He knelt in front of her and reached out to cup her cheek. "I'm here," he said softly. He ignored the coils of hair that wrapped around his arms and legs. "I'm not going anywhere." He tugged her closer and kissed her deeply. A shudder ripped through his body as her arms went around his neck and clung onto him wildly. Her hair wrapped around them both, and he eased back enough to say huskily, "I think we're getting kinky now."

Her lips trembled. "I can't walk anywhere. It weighs too much. My neck is killing me. I haven't eaten since lunch."

He managed to free one hand enough to get out his pocketknife, and he flipped open the largest blade. He grabbed a handful of her hair near her waist and quickly sliced through the mass. A few more cuts freed her entirely. The cut vines immediately began to dissolve into glittering dust that disappeared from the air around them.

The ends of her cut hair sparkled but they didn't grow more than an inch. She tried to smile. "Maybe it was just going overboard for you to get up here." His arms closed around her, and her breath caught. A bit desperately, she held on in return. She couldn't tell which of them was shaking harder. "I knew you'd find me," she whispered against his neck. "I should have gone with you last night!"

"Everything happens for a reason, I think." He took a long breath. "Let's get some food into you, and I'll tell you what I've learned today." He saw her staring at his bandaged arm and glanced down to see a hint of a bloodstain through his shirt. "It's just a graze."

"Someone shot you?!" Temper started to move in her eyes. "Who would shoot at you?"

"More people than you think, actually. In this case, it was your grandmother." He got to his feet and tugged her up as well. Her hands rested passively in his, and the temper in her eyes had turned to horror. "Did she say anything when she put you in here?"

"Only that she'd be back tomorrow afternoon." She slowly reached out to touch the stain, and her lower lip quivered. "She really tried to kill you." She burrowed against his chest and curled her fingers into his shirt. Only the feel of his arms soothed her anymore. "I'm so sorry, Van! I've made things so complicated for you."

"Technically, I guess that's true." He lifted her chin and brushed a tender kiss over her lips. "Now ask me if I regret it."

She searched his eyes intently. "Do you?"

"No." His thumb rubbed over her cheekbone. "It's hard to regret finding love." He smiled when her eyes widened. "You can't be surprised." He kissed her again. "I love you very much, Theresa Adams. If you're under a contract, and I'm the one picked for you, then I'm both humbled and elated. I couldn't have asked for more."

Joy slowly turned her eyes incandescent, and her smile seemed both shy and hopeful and also utterly beautiful. "When did you realize?"

"From roughly the luncheon," he admitted. "Earlier, probably, to be honest. I knew you were going to be trouble from the moment you smiled at me the first time. I never really could keep you at a distance. I didn't even bother to try. I need you to hold me." He rubbed the back of his neck. "I sound ridiculous saying these things."

"I think you sound wonderful," she countered simply. She slid her arms around his waist. "I'm very happy to keep holding you if you'll hold me. I love you very much, Van D'Angelo, and I don't care about a contract or anything like that. I'm just happy that I have you now. *You're* my happy ending."

He lifted her off her feet for a moment and buried his face against her neck. "If we want that happy ending, we're going to have to fight for it," he warned softly. He slowly and reluctantly let her go as she eased back. "Food."

"And information," she agreed. She took a deep breath. "Just how bad is this mess?"

The explanation didn't make her feel better, and sandwich she had just eaten seemed to uneasily move in her stomach. He lifted her from where she was sitting at the counter and carried her to the loveseat. He sat down beside her and kept her curled safely in his arms. "Is there anything you can tell me?" he asked.

"Other than the 'you have good instincts' thing?" She pressed her face to his shoulder. "Even the police suspected that my grandfather murdered my parents. They called it revenge for the divorce, but there was no evidence. Why would he wait twenty years to go after my mother? I think you might have the answer: my father." A shudder ripped through her body. "And now he hates me too."

"He hated you all along, baby." His arms tightened, but he reluctantly let go as she pulled away and got to her feet. "The answer is obvious. We get out of here and stash you with the Lucinos until I can remove Collins." He studied the line of her back and tensed shoulders. "Unless it bothers you that I would."

She made a quick gesture. "If he's done everything we think he has, then I'm *glad* you have the will to do what you do." She swung around and her whiskey eyes were bright with mingled frustration and temper. "I am just getting tired of doing nothing for myself. Do I want to run and hide? Yes, I do. But I can't. I just can't, Van. I need to face this monster with you. Unknowingly, he has controlled my entire life. I have to take it back!"

He got slowly to his feet. "You do know that that goes against the grain of everything I am and do, right? I don't involve innocent parties in these situations. I could very easily call any number of people and have this tower stormed." He pulled out his cell phone. "I have Don Lucino on speed dial. He makes things happen faster than a force of nature. You'd be packed in cotton, and Alex and Tori would happily sit on you."

She lifted her chin. "Then do it. I wouldn't even be mad at you over it. I know what kind of man you are, Van. I'm asking you to let me get involved even though I'm an 'innocent party' and you love me. If you choose to take away my freedom and put me away safely, I won't fight. I respect what you are." She added softer, "I'm asking only for the same respect. I won't ever be free of the tower unless I confront the reason why I'm in it."

He held her gaze for long moments and slowly opened his hand to let the phone fall on the carpet with a thump. "I have only two conditions. One, when I think of a plan, you will follow it to the letter. You'll be looking evil in the eye, and we don't know whether it'll trigger a fight or flight in you."

"Done," she agreed immediately. She cocked her head. "What's the other condition?"

He hesitated for a moment. "I want to hold you tonight," he finally admitted softly." Just to sleep. You said I make you feel safe. You make me feel . . . loved. Peaceful." He shrugged uncomfortably. "I don't wholly have the words. I just . . . want to hold you."

"That's all you want?"

His lips twisted wryly. "I'd be lying if I said I don't want you more than I want air. But that's *your* decision to be made. I'm not going to take your free will. That sort of decision needs to be *yours* and yours alone." He reached out and skimmed the back of his fingers down her cheek. "We have a lifetime to become lovers."

When he started to pull his hand back, her fingers stopped him and held his palm against her face. Her eyes had softened and swirled with an enchanting blend of shyness and welcome. "We've been lovers from the day we met. It's just never been consummated. I'm not afraid at all. Not if it's you." She huffed out a little breath. "You can hold me tonight, but I want to hold you. And . . . I want to make love with you." She suddenly smiled. "I never realized what a beautiful phrase that is." She gave a breathless laugh when he caught her around the waist and swung up off her feet. "Oh, wow. A romantic," she teased. "Are there romances in that Kindle of yours?"

"I live with thrills and horrors. A man needs to escape somehow. Before I ruin it by not knowing where I am, point at the bedroom." He nipped teasingly at her lower lip and enjoyed hearing her breath break. "We can try out a floor when we're in my place."

She gestured down the hall. "Rug burns."

"Only on your knees."

"That sounds intriguing." She bit back a laugh as he swung her into the bedroom. "Don't drop me on the bed! It's not very bouncy."

"Remind me to invest in a better spring mattress for home." His mouth captured hers as he lowered her down to her feet once more. The playful, lighthearted desire felt perfect for that moment. His knees went weak with delight when she teasingly took control of the kiss, her hands settling feather light on his face to tug him closer. Hunger rode hard inside his body, but he ruthlessly held onto his control. He wanted a lot more than just physical release. He eased back from the kiss and smiled. "Can I undress you?"

"I'll trade you clothing for clothing."

"That's not a fair trade when you wear a bra."

"It can count with my underwear." She ignored her trembling fingers and got to work on unbuttoning his shirt. The only nerves she had were of pure need. She still did not feel embarrassed or afraid. It was hard to feel uncertain when he looked at her with desire burning in his normally cold black eyes.

He gingerly shrugged out of the shirt, mindful of his wound, and she sighed contentedly as she studied him. "Another new understanding of a phrase for me." She lightly trailed a finger down the sculpted line of his chest. "Six pack." Tempting dark hair covered his skin, and she could see silvery white lines that marked prior wounds. An oddly shaped one along his waist implied he had, indeed, been shot before. "Fast healer?"

"Depends on the injury. Bullets are easy. Paper cuts take forever." The corner of his lips curved wickedly. "Are you going to stare, or are you going to touch?" He stopped breathing as her hands slowly slid sensually up his chest and her fingertips teased over his nipples. "I think I like a well-read woman."

"I read *everything*." Her lashes lowered as he began to unbutton her blouse. "I'm afraid you won't find anything scandalous under my clothes. Not only did I not have any means of obtaining it, but it's often hard to find in my size."

Practical white silk and cotton contentedly cupped her lush breasts, and he trailed a finger down the edge where it touched her body. A flush rose along her skin temptingly. "My blood pressure couldn't handle anything scandalous," he admitted thickly. "And don't you dare lose those pounds. Wherever they're being carried is exactly where they should be. Are you healthy?"

"Ridiculously, according to my doctor."

"Then stay just like this." He curled his hands around her waist and flexed his fingers. "More for me to hold."

Solemnly, she told him, "They say that men in their thirties like softer women. It's the instinct to breed."

"I'm an early bloomer." He lifted her off her feet effortlessly and buried his face between her breasts. Her hair teased along his sensitive skin, and a coil wrapped around his wrist just tight enough to keep him from escaping. He couldn't imagine why it thought he would. He could not escape if he wanted, and he sure as hell had no desire to try. "Speaking of breeding," he muttered against her skin, "I can protect you."

"Can we try for kids later?" she asked hopefully. Her heart clenched when he looked up in surprise. He looked . . . shocked, as if he hadn't thought she would want a family with him. "You have so much love inside you, Van." She unexpectedly laughed. "But we better hope for a boy. I think you'd go to pieces over a little girl!"

"We'll bribe Tori to teach her how to defend herself." He tumbled her down onto the covers of the bed and swiftly stripped her skirt away. "Kids. Later." His mouth moved voraciously over her skin until her fingers dug into his shoulders. "It's only us right now." The mental image of her rounded with child made his hands shake with longing and delight. She would be incredibly beautiful. "Maybe tomorrow."

Her laugh turned into a moan when he tugged aside her bra and his mouth hotly captured a tight nipple. "Our deal!" she managed to gasp. She tried to catch a breath as he released her and stripped away the rest of his clothes. He took care of hers as well, and when he joined her again, naked skin pressed to naked skin. It felt incredible. He burned with a heat that melted the cold inside her heart. They weren't alone anymore.

They tumbled breathlessly over the covers, and her hair tangled around them both. Hands moved everywhere, and lips found hidden secrets. Aching, desperate, he caught her underneath his body protectively. Her arms and legs alike coiled around him, and the knots in his heart eased. When he took her, he did so slowly, savoring every perfect second. Her eyes darkened erotically and her little gasp was taken by his hungry kiss as he settled in wholly. His lips moved over her face hungrily, memorizing every beloved feature. His beautiful secret princess.

Hearts had to give way to bodies at last, and they came together again and again until ecstasy finally broke free and claimed them both. They couldn't know what would happen the next day, but both knew that if this was all they would get, then it would be enough. They were together. It was all that mattered.

Sometime around midnight, Van found himself awake and thinking about everything. He went over every scenario in his mind, and he began to finally piece together a plan. Theresa stirred beside him and sleepily cuddled closer, and his arm tightened around her. She tilted her head back and looked up at him. "You should be asleep," she murmured.

"So should you." He caught a handful of her hair and watched it slip through his fingers. "Floor length again."

"I don't mind it touching the floor. Anything else is annoying. It doesn't get heavy until it pools. I think it defies gravity." She studied his face curiously. "What are you thinking?"

"I'm thinking I might just have an idea on what to do tomorrow. Does your hair always dissolve when it gets cut?"

"Actually, no." She propped herself up on an elbow. "It just does that when I cut it too fast. If I cut it carefully, it retains its form. I used to give it to Grandmother to burn, but lately I was doing it myself." Finally, belatedly, it dawned on her. "The answer was there all along," she murmured. "I was never actually trapped. I just had to see the way out."

"Roberto alluded to it yesterday, and I admit that it had been swirling in my mind." He tugged her down for a lingering kiss, and he saw her eyes darken with the same need churning inside him. "If just a kiss is going to get us going," he said huskily, "I see a happy future together looming." He kissed her again a little deeper and savored the little sound of pleasure she made. "It's tomorrow."

"Let's wait until tonight when we're in your reputedly softer bed," she countered just as huskily. "We'll celebrate breaking out of the tower." She smoothed his hair back from his eyes. She loved the way they watched her, loved the way he never wore a mask around her. "What's the plan? I can do anything."

He outlined everything, and she drew a long breath. Risky, yes, but it had a good chance of working. She knew she could handle anything if he was there with her. It was time to break out for good.

# CHAPTER TWENTY-ONE

When Theresa heard a key scraping in the lock the next day, the clock read as one in the afternoon. She didn't move from where she sat on the loveseat and attempted to braid her hair. She heard the door open and said without turning, "I don't want to talk to you."

"Well, aren't you the spunky one? You're a lot like your grandmother in her youth," a man countered merrily.

She turned around quickly and discovered that Ruby stood inside the entrance with an older man beside her. He looked roughly the same age though he did not carry it nearly as well. He smiled with friendly enough attitude, but his blue eyes looked dead. A chill raced down Theresa's back. "Who are you?" she demanded.

"My name is Orson Collins, m'dear." He walked into the condo and looked around with mild curiosity. "I'm your grandfather, though Ruby would just love to pretend I don't exist." His eyes landed on her, and something unnatural and ugly moved through his gaze. "You look like your father."

"Do I? How nice since I never knew him." She got to her feet and laced her hands together tightly. It took all of her strength to stay in one place. Her entire body had tensed against her will. She looked at Ruby and found her cowering back meekly. An ugly bruise mottled her face with dark colors. She didn't bother to ask where it had come from. "What do you want, Mr. Collins?"

The smile faded from his face. "Revenge. Get me the files on the Lucinos, Theresa."

"Seeing as my grandmother had me quit, I can't imagine how

I'll be allowed to get in the building."

"You can call Antonio Lucino and tell him that there was a misunderstanding and you want your job back. You will then get me all the files like a good girl and start sabotaging their precious new system."

"No."

For just a moment, his jaw actually dropped open. "Excuse me?"

"I said no. It's a word defining a denial. As in 'I will not help you ruin the Lucinos.'"

He stared at her for a moment and then calmly drew a gun from inside his jacket. He aimed it not at her, but at Ruby who went white with terror. "Do not think I will hesitate to put a bullet in her, dear." Though friendly enough, there was a bite to the tone. "I will kill her if you do not do as I tell you."

"Feel free." She shrugged lightly. "I'd be better off without her controlling my life. In fact, I'd actually *have* a life without her. I could make my own decisions, go wherever I want. Do whatever you like, *Grandfather*. I just can't care."

"You think to call my bluff?" He clicked his tongue. "I'll raise the bet, sweetheart." He cocked the gun and calmly began to depress the trigger. "I don't need her anyway."

A gun barrel suddenly pressed against his temple. Calmly, Van said, "How about I see that bet and raise it myself, Orson?"

Orson gave a bitter cackle that seared the air. "I wondered if our paths might cross! Please, D'Angelo. You think I believe you'll prove yourself a murderer right in front of Theresa? You can't kill a man in cold blood right in front of your precious little lover!"

"As a matter of fact, I can. She knows I can kill to protect her, and she is perfectly fine with that. I'm fairly sure my reflexes are faster than yours, old man. I'll shoot you before you shoot Ruby, though I can't argue that Theresa is right about being better off without either of you."

Orson abruptly threw himself backward and removed the gun

from the side of his head. He swung his own weapon around toward Van, and his finger again tightened on the trigger. He spotted movement from the corner of his eye and tried to turn around again, but he was too late. The frying pan in Theresa's hands smashed into the side of his head and something crunched audibly. He dropped like a stone to the ground.

Van stared at the scene and then at Theresa. "I can't believe you did that."

"I can't believe it worked!" she retorted shakily. "I mean, it's *Disney*. When is it ever real?" A sound had her looking down sharply, and she saw an ugly ooze seeping out of Orson's pores. She stifled a yelp as Van yanked her backward, and she nearly shrieked when her hair burst out of its braid and shot forward to consume Orson. It cocooned him entirely, and the ooze could not break through the strands.

Van moved quickly though he took the care to cut her hair slowly. The ends dropped back around her waist where they sparkled, and the rest remained trussed around Orson. He had a feeling that nothing would free the old man unless the hair wanted him to be free. At a sound, his head jerked around, and he saw Ruby had picked up the fallen gun. Her hands looked steady though her body shook. The end of the barrel aimed right for his heart.

Calmly, without fear, Theresa stepped in front of him. She said nothing. Ruby's hands began to shake wildly, and she fought to keep her aim steady. Then, finally, she dropped the gun on the ground once more. Sobs wracked her body as she fell to her knees. "I just wanted you to be safe!"

The sound of sirens ripped through the building through the open window. Van glanced outside and saw several police cars and a team of SWAT members entering the building. Hiro had impeccable timing. "Cavalry."

"Get out of here." Ruby took a steadying breath. "Both of you get out of here. Let me take whatever punishment may come." She looked at Theresa and her lips trembled. "You look like your mother, too. Have the happiness we never did."

Theresa slowly nodded and ran over to the window where Van waited. He dragged out the ladder of hair they had made the night before, and he threw it out the window to create an escape. He went down first just in case she lost her balance, but she didn't have any trouble climbing down. It was quite a descent, and both winced wryly when more than one resident inside the complex stared at them in shock as they went past windows.

When they reached the ground safely, Van quickly hacked through the bottom of the ladder. The hair swiftly dissolved into shimmering dust and faded away. He turned sharply at a footstep and pulled Theresa back safely. His shoulders only relaxed when Rhianna calmly stepped forward out of the shadows. "Rhianna."

"Let's get out of here," she countered calmly. "We can talk back at Enforcers' headquarters."

"What about Orson?" Theresa whispered.

"He will be handled by other Enforcers." She gestured toward the street where a rather non-descript sedan with tinted windows sat patiently. "I know you have many questions. Come with me, and I will give you the answers."

"All of them?" Van muttered as he urged Theresa toward the car.

Rhianna smiled. "All of them."

She rode in the front seat while Van and Theresa shared the back. Van kept Theresa's hands between his in support though he didn't say anything. His gaze stayed out the window, and the mask had settled over his face again. It didn't bother her at all. She leaned her head against his shoulder and thought of a future where maybe she could convince him to do something a little less dangerous. Maybe if she was pregnant; he would hate the idea of risking their child to losing a parent the way she had.

At Enforcers HQ, they followed Rhianna up to the top floor where her office was located. She ushered them inside and shut the door. "Have a seat." She sat down behind her desk and rummaged in a drawer. She emerged with a stack of papers and offered them to Theresa.

It felt only a little surprising to see her name at the top. "I *am* under contract," she said softly. "How is it possible? Who put me under contract? My grandmother?" She skimmed through the pages and felt her heart stop as she saw the signatures at the end. "My parents? But how?"

Rhianna linked her hands on top of the desk. "Most everything you have surmised is correct but for one thing. It wasn't Ruby Collins who came to us for your protection. It was your parents. The moment your mother realized she was pregnant—pregnant with a child who would be District born—she and your father knew that you were in danger. Orson had already made noises about his hate for your parents' union. They chose to put your safety into the hands of the Enforcers."

Van lightly rested a hand on Theresa's knee. "That's how she escaped the murder."

"The exact stipulations of the contract state that she cannot be harmed by evil if it looks her directly in the eye. She also has a very powerful gift to heal should she start seeking it. That life power directly opposes evil." Rhianna sighed. "Unfortunately, healers are not exactly *resilient*. We decided to take things a step further and give her hair sentient will."

"My hair really is alive?!"

"It is both a weapon and a tool." She smiled. "Once your contract completes, it will bend to your will. You will be able to use it the way you use your hands and feet. It will grow perfectly normally unless you want it to grow more or less. Until now, it has responded purely to even your subconscious needs."

"That is daunting and yet reassuring." Theresa took a long breath and tossed the contract onto the desk. "And I think that about sums up this entire situation. I feel . . . odd. It seems so strange that I'm free now. Yet, I always could have been free if I'd just tried." She looked at Van and smiled. "I guess I just needed someone to open the window of my tower." She glanced back to Rhianna. "You said my contract isn't complete yet. What do I need to do?"

"Van knows. He is quite familiar with Enforcer contracts."

He did, and he was. "On that note, we'll take our leave." He tugged Theresa to her feet and kept her tucked safely against his side as they walked out of the office. Neither said anything as they took the elevator downstairs. His car sat outside at the curb, and it didn't surprise them at all. He opened the door and sighed. "Well."

"Yeah." She blew out a breath that turned into a smile. "Can I go home with you? Also, I need to call Antonio and Rafael and ask if I can have my job back. I suppose they will be disappointed to lose you as a guard." She tilted her head. "Will we have to travel, or can you work here?"

He lightly cupped her cheek. "I've decided to retire." His eyes softened when hers widened. "I've decided that I'm going to ask Antonio if I can stay on as a guard. Steadier pay, safer lifestyle, and a new type of job security. Of course, I'll still need to do some outside work if needed. Rhianna and Eric have repeatedly said they want to more formally keep me as a consultant, and I'd rather deal with them than the police." He winced wryly. "We'll gloss over the fact that I think that was their intent the entire time they planned to set me up with you."

"I'm not going to lie," she admitted softly, "that I had hoped you would pick a safer job. I just found you, and I don't want to lose you. If you were a normal cop, I could handle it. It's a lot harder to love a gunslinger, though."

"Gunslinger." He contemplated that. "I think that is officially the nicest thing I've been called."

"It's much more accurate," she corrected gently. She smiled. "Home?"

"First things first." He pulled a small gift out of the car and offered it. "Happy belated. I, ah, sort of picked it up for you after we met. Been holding it until now."

She tore off the paper and started laughing when she

discovered herself holding a brand new Kindle. "Library on the go! Did you pre-load it with anything for me?" she teased. "You know me and technology."

"Turn it on and see it for yourself."

She pushed the button at the bottom and waited. The screen obediently lit up and went to the main menu. Her breath caught in her lungs and delight slowly spread through her heart as she saw the title of the only loaded book. *'Will you marry me?' By Van D'Angelo* She dropped the Kindle and leapt into his arms on a cry of joy. "Absolutely I will!" She held on with all her strength as he lifted her off her feet, and her hair immediately reached out to hold him as well. She kissed him with all the love in her heart, and she felt a strange heat run through her hair. It dropped free and fell into place, and she eased back in surprise. "What happened?"

He smiled and tugged her in for another kiss. "An Enforcers' contract," he murmured huskily against her lips, "is only complete when the subject's dreams come true."

"Oh." She tilted her head slightly and began to smile. Her hair lifted and tugged him closer. "Well, in that case, let's start our happy ending. Take me home, Van. We're both free of our towers now."

"How do you feel about trading a tower for a cruise ship?"

"I've always wanted to go on one," she admitted. "Why do you ask?"

He just smiled. "No reason."

# EPILOGUE

Rhianna had just poured herself a cup of coffee when she saw a glow from the contract. She walked over to look at it, and smiled as she saw 'Complete' appear in red. She added her notes to the bottom and slipped it into a folder that also marked as completed. She placed it inside the Lucino drawer, closed it, and locked it tight. The word 'Finished' appeared across the front and she sat back with a sigh. Another job well done despite the difficulties.

Eric walked into her office unannounced and said without preamble, "Collins has been judged and punished. The evil inside him no longer exists. Ruby Collins has entered into a women's shelter in hopes of taking back what remaining life she will live. Seems everything is taken care of now."

"I'm glad for her. She was a pawn as well."

He studied her for long moments. More than ever, he could feel there was something she had not told him. The stirring evil that encroached more and more lately was driving her further and further away from him. "Rhi." He knelt beside her chair. "You know I love you more than anyone except Rayna. Let me help you."

She tenderly touched his cheek. "I love you, Riku, but there is nothing you can do. Just let me be alone for a while. This was harder than usual; I still feel guilty over what Tori endured."

He slowly got to his feet. "Talk to me when you can." He went into his office and shut the door quietly behind him.

She closed her eyes for long moments and then slowly opened one of the desk drawers she rarely ever accessed. Inside, sitting on a

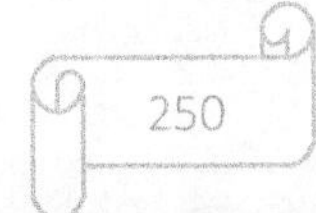

broken box, was an ancient scroll. She carefully pulled it out, treating it gingerly because of reverence and not fear for damage. It had endured for thousands of years. It would endure for thousands more.

The Ancient Greek language of the contract resembled Modern Greek in many ways but could still even confuse scholars. She read it clearly. Every word had been engraved inside her soul. Perhaps it was for that reason that the glaring red VOID across the front in English seemed harsh and cruel. She trailed a finger across the word and her lips trembled. "Eros." On a broken sound of pain, she buried her face in her arms.

When would she ever heal?

$\varphi$       $\varphi$       $\varphi$

*Status: File Complete*
*Analysis: There is no tower you cannot escape from if you are willing to take a risk and cut away the invisible chains of the past. Sometimes it just takes a loving hand to open a window so you can see the answer.*

*Just what has been happening in Mirage while evil churns outside the District? Only one person really knows, and he has his own secrets and story to be told . . .*

Bonus Folder
DAMIAN
Magic Spells

# CHAPTER ONE

Some things happened in yearly cycles on Mirage. Seasons were one. Rites of passage for princes were another. Cursed kingdoms were a third. Damian Lucksworth, prince of the Luckdom Kingdom, heard about the latest cycle while he was voluntarily mucking a stable. The stable master happened to be outside talking to a milkmaid, and the latter said, "Sounds like trouble in the northern kingdom."

The master sighed. "What else is new? And here I thought that the north would be having less trouble now that the one king returned from hiatus with a bride. What's his name? Nikolas something? Can't he help?"

"Nah, he's got his hands full already with a newborn daughter." She gestured lightly. "Anyway, the king whose kingdom just got cursed managed to get to safety. His daughter is trapped in a tower, though."

"Always with the towers."

"Why change tradition? He's calling for able-bodied princes to come try to break the curse and rescue his daughter. Whoever can do it can marry said princess and also have a chunk of the kingdom." She giggled. "I guess we don't need to worry about Prince Damian going. He's not exactly 'able-bodied' when it comes to princely duties!"

"I heard that!" Damian called. "Don't make me feed your cows herbs that'll turn them pink again!"

"Don't you dare!" she scolded. "I still haven't lived the last time down." She walked into the stables and hopped up to sit on the side of the stall. "Besides, you can't be mad at me when I'm telling the truth. We all love you, Prince Damian, but you're just not the normal princely type!"

He couldn't argue with her on that point. At twenty, he should have rescued at least *one* damsel in distress, but he just didn't really feel the need. He hated giving orders to people, even servants, and truthfully he often forgot he *had* servants—the servants, of course, loved him all the more because of it.

He couldn't ride horseback very well, but he was excellent at caring for them and raising them. He *enjoyed* working in the stables. He sucked with using a sword in combat, but he was really good with the more 'feminine' long bow. Every princess he had ever met had become one of his friends; he might make a superficial attempt at courting, but it always took less than three days to turn into friendship. To say he was vexing his parents would be to put it mildly.

As if she was following his thoughts, the milkmaid said, "Everybody's brother." She sighed gustily. "Damian, you're breaking hearts."

He grinned up at her. "I am not. You know that the princesses I know are very happy to have a male friend that they don't need to fear having designs on them or their kingdom." He hopped nimbly over the wall between stalls. "Maybe I got my prince genes crossed with a princess somewhere. I would be completely happy to have a woman sweep me off my feet and rescue me. Maybe there's a princess out there who doesn't want to be rescued."

"You're looking for love at first sight."

"Aren't we all?"

She couldn't argue with that either. "I just worry that you sitting around at home means you might miss out on something amazing." She got to her feet and winced as she heard a bellow from the direction of the castle. "The king calls for you."

"No, he *yells* for me." He sighed and put up the rake. "I guess I had best change clothes. Last time I tracked manure into the throne room, Mother almost had a heart attack. If you don't see me again, find someone to rescue me from the dungeon."

"No tower?"

"Nah, that's for women. Men get the dungeon treatment. Which is a pity since towers have a *view*." He crept around the back of the palace and quickly snuck inside and up toward his chambers. He wasted no time in stripping, bathing, and quickly putting on more acceptable clothing. Another bellow echoed, and he grimaced as he went downstairs toward the throne room. "Protect me," he muttered at a lady-in-waiting as he went past. She giggled at him, and he sighed. He opened the doors to the throne room and walked inside. "You yelled?" he asked dryly.

Predictably, his parents sat on their thrones at the other end of the room. They wore their full, heavy-duty, formal crowns. And not for the first time, he wondered why neither had neck problems from the weight. They also wore their formal robes and clothing, and he felt underdressed even in velvet. Why didn't they smother in those hundreds of layers?

"Damian." His father's brows pulled together. "What's that smell?" He groaned. "Damn it, boy, were you out doing peasant work again?"

"I, er, accidentally broke a valuable vase and that was my chosen punishment." He crossed his fingers behind his back. Really, it was always easier to make it sound like he had gotten in trouble rather than explain that he liked manual labor.

"Again with the vases. You are so clumsy," his mother scolded. She sighed. "Son, we love you dearly, but you're not living up to your potential."

"My potential, or the potential that you expect of me?"

"Don't sass me, young man!" She aimed a finger at him. "You need to get out into the world and start acting like the prince you are! You need to make a man of yourself, Damian. Go rescue a princess, slay a dragon, or *something*."

Because, of course, being a man meant being a chauvinistic

jerk. He refrained from rolling his eyes. Surely princesses were getting tired of always being rescued, and he couldn't imagine the dragons were entirely sunshine and lollipops over the whole slaying thing. "Are those my only options?"

His father beetled his brows. "We are getting tired of things, Damian. You just don't take your duty seriously!" He threw a scroll at his son and it bounced off his head. "You will depart at once for the Karmic Kingdom and get rid of the curse to rescue the princess! You cannot come back unless you come back with a bride!"

Damian rubbed his head where the scroll had hit. "Seriously?"

"Very seriously!"

He stared at his parents and then picked up the scroll to look at it. It was a map of where he needed to go. The journey seemed more annoying than long. He scowled and stalked out of the throne room. "If I have kids," he muttered, "they'll get to decide for themselves how to live their lives!"

In the very center of Mirage, not far from where the River Styx attached the world to the one known as Earth, was a place of concentrated magic and beauty known as the Faerie Realm. As the name implied, it was from within this forested land that Good Faeries came forth to aid heroes on their journeys. Good Faeries had to be trained in the ways of magic and conjuration before they could be assigned, and graduating school could be a trial all by itself. Some who graduated didn't become official Good Faeries for many further years if their grades hadn't been good enough.

Unfortunately for the Realm, the latest curse and the promise of land along with the princess had brought princes and heroes out of the woodwork. Even recent graduates were being assigned to go help these able-bodied people. Faeries who returned after completing one job would be immediately sent right back out.

Elder Thom found himself in a bit of a pickle when the magic cup suddenly spit out a rune stone with a new name on it. "Damian Lucksworth." He winced. "Bad enough that we're out of faeries, but that kid doesn't know anything about what he has to do!" He drummed his fingers on his desk for a moment. With a sigh, he got to his feet. He had no choice. He had to grab Teydra. "Teydra!" he bellowed as he walked out of the consulate and crossed toward the magic streams that surrounded the Realm.

The lovely faerie lounging along the side of the stream winced and ducked down behind the spell book she held. Her shimmering cream-colored hair turned a deep pink color that matched what climbed her neck and cheeks. She peered up at Thom and tried to look innocent. "I didn't do it?"

He sighed in exasperation. It was impossible to be annoyed with Teydra. She was beautiful and charming and sweet. She was also the worst student of her graduating class, and no matter how hard she tried, she always managed to screw up even the most basic of spells.

The entire Realm loved her, but they just couldn't figure her out. She had one of the most potent gifts of all Good Faeries—they called it Mood Magic—yet she had no control over it. It manifested in the changing of her hair color to show her moods (which showed on her face anyway), and if she ever learned how to use it right, it would make her the most sought after Good Faerie on Mirage.

"Get up, girl." He offered a hand and tugged her up to her feet. Most faeries were small, but Teydra stood at an unusually taller height of five-seven that had her towering over most of her race. Save the delicacy of her frame and the glowing cerulean colored wings on her back, she could have passed for human. "What are you doing out here?"

"Studying," she admitted. "I figure if I focus on one spell hard enough, I have to eventually get it right."

"Which spell?" he asked warily.

"Summoning an enchanted sword. I figure screwing it up won't,

you know, flood or burn down the Realm."

He couldn't hide his relief. "Thank you for the consideration. Now come along with me." He linked his hands behind his back as she walked beside him. "You know we're short-staffed right now."

"Yeah. It's the rescuing princesses equivalent of harvest season." She cocked her head, and one pointed ear tilted at an angle. Her long lineage was evidenced by the length and delicacy of her ears. "Do you need me to watch the Pot while you go out yourself?" It wouldn't be the first time.

"Actually, no." He handed her the stone. "You're going on a mission."

"What!" Her hair went bright red. "I can't even cast a fireball!" she yelped. "You told me I was the worst Good Faerie graduate of all time!"

"You are. But luckily for you, your charge is possibly the worst prince of all time. Perhaps your mutual ineptitude will result in some success!" He flicked a hand and a swirl of magic popped into appearance over her head. "Off with you, Teydra! You know the rules; you can't come back until he reaches the final leg of his journey."

"I'll get him killed!" she wailed, but it was too late. The magic had already sucked her up, and her lack of skill meant that she could not cast a locator to cushion the landing. She was in so much trouble!

She wasn't the only one in trouble. Damian had managed to make it a few miles away from his kingdom before he got beset by the first of what he knew would be many issues. In this case, it was a small horde of ugly demons. The natural antithesis to faeries, demons existed to *stop* heroes. Maybe it was a good sign; if they were attacking, he must have been doing something right.

He took care of the first demon relatively easily with his sword, but the other two were far bigger and far more powerful. His relatively amateurish use of the weapon could be easily countered, and one of the demons thunked him in the stomach hard enough to knock him onto his ass in the dirt.

He scrambled back up to his feet just as a strange shimmering magic appeared in the air. He and the demons looked up at the same time, and he stifled a yelp as a young woman unexpectedly flew out of the magic with a yelp of her own. She landed on his back and he once more found himself eating the dirt, though this time literally. He craned his neck enough to look back at her, and relief filled him. She had wings! "Are you a Good Faerie?"

Teydra shook her head hard to clear the spinning stars. "Uhm, yes."

"Great! Shoot the bad guys."

She blinked and focused. Her hair swiftly turned bright blue in alarm. "Uh-oh!" She grabbed her spell book out of midair and began quickly flipping pages. "It's in here somewhere! Why can't I *find* it?!"

He dropped his forehead on the ground in understanding. "Oh, god," he groaned. "They gave me the *apprentice!*" He looked up hastily when he heard movement. The demons were closing in. "Let me up!"

She scrambled off his back and fell into a flower bush. She turned pages as fast as she could in her book. "Fangs, Fauns, Figs— ah! Fireball!" She swallowed a yelp as a huge ball of fire shot from her hands. "Get down!"

He threw himself to the side and watched wide-eyed as the fireball swallowed a demon. "Okay, that could have hurt." He swung his sword at the other demon, and the blade bounced off its head. It glared at him indignantly, and he back-stepped quickly. "Anything in there for making my sword pierce armor?"

"Uhm." She flipped through the chapters. "Swords. Where are the swords?" She found a spell and aimed a hand at him. "Points right and left and up and down; make the blade sharp enough to pierce through sound!"

The sword in his hand got sharper all right. It also got bigger. It instantly multiplied in size and became so heavy that he lost his grip. The hilt hit the ground with a thud that shook the area, and the weapon wobbled precariously. He dove out of the way as the blade finally crashed over and landed on the demon. It squished flat and spewed bits of debris in all directions. He winced and swiped at the muck now on his pants. "Ugh. And I thought manure smelled!"

Teydra blew her hair out of her eyes and fell over on her back. "Darn it, Elder Thom!" A shadow moved over her face, and she opened her eyes to see Damian looking down at her. Her breath caught in her chest as she stared up at him. For just a moment, it seemed as all sound went away around her. She could see nothing except him in her sight. His shaggy green hair reminded her of her favorite meadows.

*Prince*, her mind reminded her pointedly. He was a *prince*. It was completely against the rules for her to be attracted to him, but, dang it, it wasn't *her* fault that he was gorgeous! Belatedly remembering her hair, she grabbed a handful and looked at it. Sure enough, it had turned purple. Not. A. Good. SIGN.

Damian had no idea why her hair kept changing color, but it fascinated him. Her cream hued eyes changed color, too. Magic rippled over her skin and lay across her cheekbones in a blend of glitter and sparkles. He had for some reason expected faeries to be fair, but she had a beautiful light chocolate color to her skin. She looked impossibly delicate, yet when he helped tug her to her feet, he discovered she stood only half a foot shorter. "I always thought faeries were smaller."

"I'm kind of tall, yes," she admitted. She rubbed the back of her neck and looked up at him shyly. "I'm Teydra. And I'm a Good Faerie but I'm kind of not officially one. I almost flunked school."

He winced. "It figures. Look, I appreciate the help, but I think I'd better handle this alone." He started to turn away and she grabbed his arm. Startled, he looked down at her. She was stronger than she looked, and she radiated a surprising heat that felt deeply alluring. He skimmed his eyes over her again, this time more wistfully. Too bad she wasn't a princess. He liked her one hell of a lot more than he had liked anyone else.

"I can't go home until I get you to your goal," she pleaded with him. "I always mess up, and Elder Thom wouldn't have sent me if he had a choice! I need to do this to prove I can be useful! I try so hard, but I always mess up! I just don't know how to be a Good Faerie, I guess. Damian, please let me help you!"

An odd sense of kinship moved through him. He knew painfully well how it felt to not fit into the expectations of other people. Maybe they weren't a bad pair; maybe they were a perfect one. And, well, it wouldn't be hardship to let her stay at his side. He totally didn't object to the very real possibility that his attraction to her might turn into love. Everything else smacked of love at first sight; it was Mirage, after all. That kind of stuff always happened. "Okay," he conceded. "You can go with me." He offered a hand. "Damian Lucksworth, prince of the Luckdom Kingdom, and heir apparent should I actually 'make a man of myself.'"

Her smile lit the area around them as she put her hand in his. "Teydra, sucky Good Faerie-in-training who can't memorize spells but can read *really* fast." Her eyes widened and she caught a breath as he brought her hand to his lips. A mottled purple and pink color swept through her hair. "I dunno, Damian. You have the princely arts down so far."

"Handshakes just don't cut it with most women; some things you learn by sheer self-defense." He walked over to his fallen sword and winced. "Dare I ask you to try to shrink it again?"

"Probably not. But canceling a spell is super easy. Even I can do that." She knelt and tapped on the sword and it glowed brightly before going back to normal. "See?" She scooped it up and offered it to him. She saw his wide-eyed look and bit back a giggle. "Magic," she told him solemnly. "I could probably lift you off the ground."

"I think I like you," he decided with a grin. He sheathed the sword again and offered her the map. "Can you read maps better

than you do spell books?"

"Sure!" She opened the scroll. "Okay, I know where we're going. Follow me."

He eyed her legs and hips wistfully as he trailed behind her. He didn't object to following her anywhere. The back view was as spectacular as the front. More, actually. Her beautifully glowing wings made his fingers itch to touch.

He sighed with more exasperation than annoyance. A faerie. It just figured, didn't it, that he *still* couldn't get anything right.

# CHAPTER TWO

As they walked together down the road, Damian studied his new partner curiously. Not that he knew everything about faeries in general, but he had always held a lot of beliefs that suddenly seemed wrong. "Hey, can I ask some questions?"

Teydra smiled at him. "Of course. I'll answer if I can. We don't have any secrets or stuff. I mean, even if I told you about our magic, you'd never be able to cast it. I'm not saying humans can't do it, but the elders always said it would require something dramatic for a human to cast faerie magic without having any faerie blood. I don't even know what it is."

"That's fair. How come you're this big? I don't mean your height, though. I thought faeries were much smaller."

Her hair and eyes turned a mischievous yellow color. "Like this?" Sparkles swirled around her, and she was suddenly only a foot tall. "Tada!" She flew around his head and landed light as a feather on his shoulder.

"That would be a useful skill!" he admitted wistfully. "Which is real?"

"Technically both." She sat down and braced her hands around her hips. "The big size is called our Monarch form. This size is called our Pixie form. We can use and control both from roughly about the same time that we learn to walk and fly. We're like humans in some ways, but we grow much slower."

"Let me guess. You don't walk or fly until you're five?"

"Thereabouts, yep. We grow one year for every five of yours, give or take a few." She grinned when his head swung around quickly, and she gave him a smacking kiss on his nose. "I'm technically eighty years older than you physically, but emotionally and mentally, we're the same age."

"How long do you live?" he demanded. The average for humans ranged between eighty and ninety years.

"Rarely more than five hundred, but if the magic is strong, it can be longer. We can also opt to grow older faster if we want to live among humans. Magic is awesome." She flew off his shoulder and the swirl of sparkles returned her to full size. She linked her hands behind her back as she fell once more into step beside him. Her hair shimmered and turned back to normal. "Of course, the person who sucks at magic would think so. I hope I can keep liking it even though I have trouble casting it."

"I still like women even though I'm being all but forced to marry," he offered helpfully.

She giggled. "Fair enough! Why are you, anyway?"

"Will you buy that I'm a hopeless romantic?"

"Aren't we *all* hopeless romantics at heart?"

"You haven't met my parents. I think they were in love when they got married, but their determination to foist me off on the first available princess makes me wonder." He winced wryly. "At this point, they might even be willing to settle for me marrying a servant so long as I *did* marry. I never seem to do anything right either, Teydra."

Her cream eyes darkened to gray in empathy. "The shoes they want you to wear are so small that they pinch your feet and give you no room to grow, and try as you might to walk in them, you just split the sides and end up worse than you started?"

His heart clenched in a combination of complex emotions that he couldn't wholly decipher. "Yeah," he said softly. He couldn't resist skimming his thumb across the shimmer of her cheeks. "Your shoes don't fit either, right?"

"Never have. I'm supposed to be really powerful, and I have a unique gift, but I just . . . am no good at things."

"Which gift?"

"My hair."

"The color thing? I was wondering why it did that."

A hint of pink climbed the stands. "It changes with my moods. I could be the greatest actress on Mirage—and I'm not—and my hair would give me away every time. Before you ask, yes, I know what most of the colors stand for. I even know what my gift could turn into, should I ever figure out how to control it."

He could make some guesses of his own based on their short acquaintance. The pink had to be embarrassment, and he thought the red might be shame or anger depending on the intensity. The yellow had to be playful. The purple, though, he had no idea yet. It seemed to crop up every time she looked at him for too long. It also turned gold now and then, too. "What can it become?"

"Mood influencing abilities. Like . . . I could make someone be not mad if they were really angry type stuff."

Wistfully, he asked, "Can I sneak you home in my pocket to keep my parents off my case?"

She grinned. "Only if you promise to feed me and not put me into a jar or something."

"And you'd look so cute on my dresser!" He grinned back and enjoyed watching her hair turn yellow with her lighthearted mood. A tempting thought curled through his mind before he could stop it: what color would her hair turn if he kissed her? Before he could stop himself, he reached out and tucked her hair behind her ear. Her eyes shot to his, and the silken strands turned a deep hue of purple laced with stripes of gold. His body clenched with greedy desire as he saw the look in her violet eyes and understood. Purple meant *passion*. "You're going to be trouble for me," he said softly, huskily, "aren't you?"

She took a breath that turned into a startled yelp as four bandits came lunging out of the shrubbery along the side of the road. Her eyes widened as Damian protectively yanked her closer, and her hair turned a wild combination of colors as it tried to keep up with her tumultuous emotions.

The leader of the bandits sneered at Damian. "Looks like we found ourselves another prince on his way to be a hero! It's like harvest season for us, too! Hand over your valuables, and you can be on your way."

"I'm not carrying any valuables," Damian told him in exasperation. "I only have money for food, sorry." Under his breath, he asked Teydra, "Can you turn my sword into a bow? I'm much better with one!"

"I can try," she whispered back. She took a deep breath, looked over the bandits' heads, and blurted, "Dragon!"

They whipped around instinctively, and Damian hastily shoved her to the side so he could draw his sword. He knocked one of the enemies down before the other three could turn, but things quickly turned bloody since they knew more about what they did. Teydra grabbed her spell book and flew through the pages as fast as she could. "Please work!" she blurted as she threw magic at the sword.

The blade turned into a handful of flowers. Damian couldn't pull the strike in time, and the blooms smacked a shocked bandit in the face. Angry red hives rose on his skin and he started sneezing violently. Damian blinked, realized the problem, and shoved the flowers more firmly in his face. The bandit reeled back only to trip over his own feet and face plant on the ground. "Bow!" Damian begged Teydra as he scrambled out of the way of the other two enemies.

"Oooh! Darn it!" She threw the book down and started grabbing whatever magic she could muster. "Eat a fireball, jerks!" Flames sparked along her skin and rippled down into her hands where it began to pool. The force grew hotter and hotter and bigger and bigger, and it began to drive her backwards through the dirt.

Damian quickly grabbed her around the waist to brace her, and he watched wide-eyed as the fireball grew bigger than both of them. The bandits belatedly realized they were up against something potentially painful and grabbed their fallen partners to run away. They only made it a few feet before Teydra loosed the fireball. It hit the four bandits with such force that they were sent sailing into the sky and off into the distance. Unfortunately, it had the reciprocal effect of sending her and Damian flying backwards into the bushes.

He landed first and grunted when she landed on top of him. He heard a cracking sound and opened his eyes to see broken branches about to fall. He hastily grabbed his faerie and rolled with her out of the way. The branches smashed into the ground where they had been, and dust billowed in the air. Eerie quiet finally descended.

He carefully lifted himself onto his elbows and winced as his wounds protested. He had more than a few slices from that fight. "Teydra?" He smoothed her hair out of her face, and she opened her eyes. Relief almost made him lightheaded. "Thank goodness. Are you okay?"

"Sore." She grimaced. "Very sore. And I burned my hands." She held them where he could see the ugly blisters forming across her palms. "I can heal it. One of the few spells I'm any good at is a healing one." She tried to smile. "Lucky for you." She sighed and closed her eyes again. "Goofed again. Almost killed you, too."

"You did not! Hey." He tugged a lock of her pink hair until she opened her eyes again. "You cast the fireball just fine. It was just too big. And, well, that sword had more use as a handful of posies than as itself. I can buy a bow in the next town, okay? I'm just glad we're both alive."

"People have wondered how I made it to my age," she admitted.

"Hey, I've been accused of deliberately trying to kill myself because I have no sense of self-preservation. We're even." The smile slowly faded as he stared down at her. His pulse began to pound hard and fast, an ache settling deep inside with the need to touch and caress the woman in his arms. She smelled like magic, and her lips tempted him to find out if she tasted the same. Her eyes widened suddenly and a combination of purple and pink swept through her hair. He coughed to hide a laugh. "Not that you didn't just notice, but I feel compelled to at least say out loud that, yes, I want you very badly."

"Believe me," she muttered a bit breathlessly, "I noticed!" It wouldn't have been so bad if she hadn't wanted him in return! He felt as good as he looked, and he gave off a wonderful body heat that made it darned tempting to just snuggle in and hold on. Also, if he didn't stop looking at her like that, she was going to kiss him and that would be a *really* bad idea.

His lips skimmed delicately over her forehead. "I'm beginning to read your moods," he murmured huskily. "Is the purple what I think it is?"

"Probably." She quickly pressed her fingers to his lips when his black eyes lit with greedy desire. "Okay, yes, I want you like the Styx on fire, but it's *not* an okay thing, Damian! I'm a Good Faerie-ish and you're a prince!"

"Ish."

"We're not compatible!"

"Evidence points to the contrary, Teydra." He skimmed his fingers down her arm and watched a trail of goosebumps follow behind on a delicate shiver. More purple than pink colored her hair, and the gold had come out again. "We seem very compatible. Faeries are mammals, right?"

"Well, yes, but," her breath hitched as he pressed his lips to her neck, "but that doesn't change that we're not *socially* compatible!" Her eyes went dark with distress as he lifted his head. "We need to ignore this and keep going as we are. We both have a duty to fill."

He stared at her for long moments before reluctantly releasing her and rolling to his feet. He reached down to lift her up as well and winced. "Okay. We'll pretend that nothing has changed. Let's get rid of our injuries and get back on track."

It didn't take long for her to remove the worst of the wounds on them both, and they were both very careful to keep their conversation light. Things felt a little strained initially, but eventually they fell back into easy companionship. Unfortunately for Damian, though, he got his first true test of self-control with the way her hair would turn purple and gold every time she looked at him. He still didn't know what the gold meant, and he had a feeling it might be a good thing. It was difficult enough knowing that she wanted him as badly as he wanted her!

For her part, Teydra couldn't put her finger on the color's origins either. She remembered it being important, yet she could not seem to bring up what her studies had mentioned about it. Her hair had never started turning that color until meeting Damian. What did it mean?

Perhaps miraculously, they made it the rest of the way to the city without any mishaps. It had started to become evening from afternoon, and there was still time to ask around about things. Merchants always had the latest gossip, and Damian stopped at one of the carts. "Hey, the Karmic Kingdom is cursed, right?"

"Yep. Been lots of princes and heroes through here lately." She eyed him. "You don't look like one of them."

Teydra bit her lip to hide a giggle, and he sighed. "So I've been told. What's the word on things?"

"Last I heard, it had to do with ogres or something. I think someone said the king had betrayed them in some sort of weird alliance thing."

"Ugh. Ogres. Great. They're big *and* smelly. Thanks for the information." He eyed Teydra as she turned into Pixie form and trailed along at his shoulder. "Are you trying to make me look more convincing?"

"Yup. Amazing what having a Good Faerie, even a bad one, can do for a prince's image." She landed lightly on his shoulder and poked his temple. "Ogres are better than demons, you know. They're big, but they're dumb. You'll have plenty of time to shoot them at a distance. And, really, if you beat them, then it won't matter what weapon you used, right?"

"I suppose that's true. Let's see what else people have to say."

The stories varied, of course, but the general consensus was that ogres were definitely involved. The reasons why were where people disagreed, and they ran the gamut from alliances to hunting to just random havoc. The only thing that bugged Teydra and Damian alike was that curses weren't normally an ogre's style. They tended to be more the style of wicked wizards, rogue faeries, and stuff like that. The other thing bothering them was the quantity of princes who had tried and yet apparently failed. Why hadn't they started home if they couldn't break the curse?

The Karmic Kingdom sat not far from their current destination, with only another city between where they were and where they needed to be. "Let's stay the night here," Damian offered. "We could both use the rest, and I'm not keen on camping when I seem to have an 'Accost Me' sign around my neck."

She wouldn't have minded accosting him herself, but for entirely different reasons. Even grubby and messy, he looked ridiculously gorgeous. "Fair enough. I'm hungry anyway. Casting magic can burn a lot of energy."

They got rooms at the inn and went to the dining room for dinner. He watched in bemusement as she piled her plate higher than his; apparently, she hadn't been kidding about burning energy. "So tell me about Good Faerie school," he offered as he dug into his food.

"We learn conjuration, casting, and the rules and regulations of being essentially bodyguards for people. Mostly princes and heroes, but we've been assigned to the occasional princess or bard. Depends on what they're doing and where they're doing it." She munched on a vegetable. "Once we graduate, the length of time to assignment depends on how well we did in school. A perfect student might immediately get sent out. Others like me have to wait a while."

"How old are you when you graduate?"

"Roughly eighty or so. Sixteen by your standards."

"You feel time passing the same as we do, right?"

Her gaze lowered and a hint of pink climbed her hair. "Yes."

He very badly wanted to grab her up and cuddle her tightly.

She had been on standby for as long as he had been alive. No wonder she didn't have any confidence! They had never given her a chance to prove herself. "What does an unassigned faerie do?"

"Study. Tend stuff. Watch over the Magic Pot that gives assignments when there's no one else around. It's not really that bad. I've learned some different things that others don't. I'm a great cook, for example. And I play a lot of instruments. I even know how to sew really nice things. Oh! I *did* get to help out another Good Faerie," she offered. "She had to give a princess some dresses that could fit inside a walnut but become full-sized when extracted. I got to make them. I must say they were *exquisite*. When she won her prince, I made her wedding gown, too."

"Delivered in a walnut?"

"Actually, we used a normal box for that one." She grinned. "I've always thought that if I completely flunked out on being a Good Faerie that I could just set myself up as a seamstress and help out princesses in a different way entirely."

He grinned back. "Come work in my kingdom. The upper class will keep you plenty busy."

She fluttered her lashes. "I'll make a wedding dress for that bride you need to find." The reminder of why they had met immediately brought her mood back down, and she pushed her plate away. "Well."

The reminder was even less pleasant for him. He didn't think any princess would ever make him as happy as he felt when he was near his beautiful faerie. He was falling more and more in love with every passing moment, and he knew it. Some things you just couldn't mistake.

They were contemplating dessert when a traveling merchant came up to their table. "You're a prince, right?" he asked.

"I am." Damian frowned. "Is something wrong?"

"That depends on your definition of wrong. I just thought I ought to warn you if you're on your way to the kingdom. Most of the princes who have tried to get past the ogres have gotten eaten."

Teydra's eyes widened. "*Eaten*?"

"Eaten. I know, it's unusual. Just thought I should give you a heads up." He tipped his hat. "Good luck, Your Highness."

Damian looked at Teydra. "Well."

She slowly shook her head. "I don't like the sound of that, Damian. I mean, one or two princes are usually lost to every curse, but never that many! I don't think you should keep going on. You're not really good in combat, you know?"

"I know, but it's too late for me to go back. I have to keep moving forward."

Distress began to turn her hair a pale bluish-gray color. "There are other ways of proving yourself a man. You could go slay a dragon or save another kingdom where there aren't any ogres. What about going to sea?"

He sat back and lifted a brow. "Aren't Good Faeries supposed to keep their assignments on track? If I divert, you won't get to go home either, right? Why is this bothering you so much, Teydra? You can't be that worried about the ogres. Like you said, I have an advantage with a bow. Where's this fear coming from?"

"I don't know." She shook her head a little. "Logically, I completely believe you can succeed where others didn't. I can't figure out why that suddenly bothers me." His hand lightly covered hers, and she looked up quickly to find his black eyes watching her warmly. Something tender moved through his gaze. The sudden vision of him smiling at anyone else like that had her hair turning bright green with ripe jealousy. She didn't want him to go because he would win, and if he won, he would get the princess as his bride. She would have to hand him over to another woman. Sudden misery and mingled grief turned her hair black.

He didn't know what was going through her head, but he had watched the cacophony of color changes through her hair. "Teydra." He brought her hand to his cheek. "Calm down. Everything will be okay. Hey. Look at me." He lifted her chin until her eyes met his. "I know you can do anything. We'll get there together, and you'll be what makes me into a real hero. I think you're amazing."

The black melted away into gold once more as she looked at him longingly. No one had ever believed in her before. It didn't seem fair that all of this was happening. By Eros, how was any of this fair?

Her heart gave a wild lurch. Eros. The God of Love. His token color was gold. If her hair turned gold whenever she looked at Damian . . .

She shot to her feet and almost knocked over her chair. "I need to go out!" she blurted. "I'll see you later!" Without waiting for an agreement, she flew as fast as she could out of the inn. She needed to get away from him, get somewhere she could think and breathe! She didn't want to be in love with him. An attraction was okay. She could handle that. Loving him would destroy her when she couldn't keep him!

Damian very nearly went after her but forced himself to let her go. He had entirely lost what remained of his appetite, and he retired to his room for the night. He stayed up a while to read a book, and each time he heard a noise, he would listen intently to see if it was Teydra coming back. None of the noise ever came from the room beside his.

He didn't sleep at all that night. Sleeping had always been difficult enough for him without being in a foreign location. If it wasn't insomnia, it was nightmares. He hated the dark. Or rather, he hated the things that hid in the dark. He just couldn't sleep when there was absolute darkness. He kept a small lamp on his bedside at home, and even that didn't wholly help.

By the time dawn arrived, he had gotten an hour of sleep at most. Frustrated and concerned, he got dressed and went next door to scold Teydra about worrying him. The worry only compounded when he discovered her room was still empty and looked entirely untouched. Where *was* she?

He paid for both rooms and rushed out of the town. Luckily for him, she had been fleeing in her Pixie form, and she left a trail of glitter in her wake from her wings. He could just barely see it lingering in the air. His stomach churned the further he got from the city. She had gone a long way. The trail veered off the road into the thick forests, and he glanced up at the cloudy skies. They would have to move fast to get to the next town before the storm arrived. Damn it, what was wrong with her?

He unexpectedly found her sitting in the middle of a patch of flowers, and she was in her larger Monarch form. She had her face buried in her knees, and her wings drooped from her back. Painful blackness clung to her hair, and it seemed to have lost its shine. Relief at seeing her unharmed mingled with his frustration at being left behind, and he almost shouted, "Teydra!"

She stifled a yelp as she swung around. "Don't scare me!" she snapped at him.

He yanked her up off her feet and gave her a shake. "You scared *me*!" he retorted hotly. "What's wrong with you, running off like that? Were you out here all night? You could have been attacked by bandits or something!" He gave her another little shake. "Just tell me what's wrong and I'll help, okay?"

"You're what's wrong!" she shouted at him. She shoved at his shoulders but he was much bigger and stronger. Her wings fluttered madly as she fought to free herself. "Leave me alone!" She beat at his shoulder with one of her hands as tears welled in her eyes and her hair began to cycle madly through every color in existence. "I don't want to do this anymore! I can't handle it! You're going to break my heart!"

He yanked her against his aching body and kissed her with all the frustrated hunger in his soul. A shudder rippled through her body and then her fingers locked in his hair and she surged upward to deepen the kiss even further. She wrapped her arms and legs around him and held on wildly. She met and matched the aggressive thrust of his tongue, and her hair turned a vibrant shade of purple before starting to glow brightly.

It had to be the most erotic thing he had ever seen. Uncaring for time, location, or really anything else, he tumbled her down into the flowers and rushed open the laces on her dress. Delight filled him as he saw the silky corset beneath. "Who knew faeries were so wonderfully old-fashioned? You're so delicate; why do you need this thing?"

"I actually," her breath hitched on a soft whimper as his lips teased along the curves of her breasts, "actually find them comfortable. Also, it—stop, tickling me!—it also covers me well enough that if I lose my dress somehow, I'll be still dressed." A low moan vibrated in her throat as he buried his nose between her breasts. He curled his hand hotly around her waist and seared her even through the layers of cloth. She knew she should stop him, but she couldn't find the willpower. She wanted him too much. Loved him too foolishly.

Nature itself took away the problem. Lightning flashed brightly and thunder rumbled right overhead. He looked up sharply and glanced around. Even through the knots of desperate lust, he could be amused. "Never the time and place." He looked down at his faerie and found her violet eyes seething with matching emotion and bands of gold running through her purple hair. "Teydra." He started to lower his head again, and this time lightning struck close enough to shake the ground. "Whoa!" He hastily scrambled up and yanked her up as well. "We need to get moving!"

She clung onto his hand and ran quickly at his side toward the road. She felt frustrated, miserable, aching, empty, and a little bit pissed off. She tugged her laces closed with her free hand as best she could. "No more of that, Damian," she warned him fiercely. "You're supposed to be pursuing the *princess* not the *faerie*! You can't touch me again, got it? Not like you just did!"

He couldn't make a promise he wouldn't keep and therefore kept his mouth shut entirely. He didn't *want* any princess; he wanted his faerie! He would never want anyone else now that he'd had a taste of her rich magic flavor. If things went on for much longer, he would be too in love with her to ever let her go again.

Just what the hell was he supposed to do now?

# CHAPTER THREE

They didn't beat the storm to the city and were forced to take shelter in an old hut along the road. They sat huddled under the roof to avoid the rain, and Teydra surprised both of them by successfully creating a small fire without blowing up anything. "I guess maybe I just needed more practice rather than more study," she murmured as she stared into the flames.

Damian couldn't help but wonder if perhaps it had more to do with whatever was between them. If he felt like he was maturing at a rapid rate by the events, he could only imagine what it was doing to her. Being an adult meant scary emotions and learning to fight for what you wanted. No matter how things ended, he would not be the same going home as he had been when he had left. "I doubt I can say the same about me and a sword. I've practiced for years. At best, I at least know the pointy end goes in the other guy."

She grinned briefly. "You're several steps ahead of some others, I'm sure." She looked at the bow and quiver of arrows he now sported. "How good are you with that anyway?"

He grabbed the bow and notched an arrow. "See for yourself." He took careful aim at a small flower in the distance. "I'll pick that flower without bruising the petals." He fired the arrow and smiled as the flower flipped into the air and landed safely on the ground. Even from a distance, it looked pristine. "See?"

"I do indeed. I can't imagine why anyone would object to you using one."

"It's a 'girl's' weapon, or so they say. Princes are supposed to be dashing and daring and swing shiny swords as they cut down dangerous villains preventing them from rescuing fair damsels in distress." He leaned back on his hands. "Weird, isn't it, that we expect that of princes, and yet kings can be completely different? I mean, presumably, a prince grows up to be a king, right?"

"Typically, yes." She smiled at him. "Speaking as a faerie who has seen a lot of princes and kings, you're not as in the minority as you think you are. Times have been changing lately, and for the better. Life happens in cycles. Every hundred years or so, things shuffle around. We're shuffling now. Did you know that a hundred years ago it was completely common for royal heirs of both genders to be banished for the silliest things? Now the boys get sent out on missions and the girls stay to be rescued. Maybe in another hundred years it'll switch."

"Can we have the towers? Dungeons are very boring."

"Well, they have no view."

He snorted softly. She really was too utterly perfect for him. And though he knew he should put it aside, he couldn't help but go over the logistics. His parents would adore her, and he knew his people would, too. The only thing he couldn't put his finger on was whether or not she would, well, be any good at being a queen. That kind of thing would really decide what outcome he worked toward. No matter how much he loved Teydra, if she would be uncomfortable or simply unsuitable as a queen, he could not put her on a throne.

That didn't mean he would walk away. Definitely not. If she couldn't rule, then he would abdicate to one of his cousins and settle into a peasant life with her. He would probably enjoy it a lot more than being a king! But if she *did* turn out to be as amazing as his gut said she might, then he would absolutely stick her on the throne beside him and they could learn together just how those heavy crowns managed to stay in place.

He sighed at his own thoughts. There were a lot of what/ifs in the scenario, and he didn't even really have the right to claim her as his own. She would fight him every inch of the way, and he couldn't blame her. They were shaking up a lot more than mere gender roles. He just didn't know what the hell to do about it.

The storm lessened within another hour and they were once more able to get on the road. It turned out to be an entirely unremarkable journey, and it put them both on the alert. Where were the bandits and the demons and the other sundry things that always plagued a prince's road?

The answer came in the form of a commotion from the small village they approached. Shouts and raucous laughter told them what they would find long before they ran into the town limits and moved toward the center. Sure enough, a pack of bandits ran amok. They tipped over some carts, uprooted gardens, grabbed purses, and generally caused a lot of low-key terror. The villagers had nothing they could say or do; it was only a farming town that served as a stopover point for the Karmic Kingdom.

Damian grabbed Teydra, and they crouched down behind the edge of a chapel. "I can pick off two of them before they get to me," he told her in a low voice. "Can you fireball at least one of the others?"

She nodded. "I think I can actually use a rooting spell to snare two of them before I use a fireball on the third." She winced. "At worst, I might accidentally make a couple trees grow under them."

"Which could be just as effective." He readied an arrow and smiled. "I know we can do this."

Strangely, she did too. She gave a little nod and moved to the side. As soon as he let the first arrow fly, she shot a blast of magic toward the two closest bandits. To her delight, roots quickly entangled them and dropped them cursing to the ground. One of the two remaining bandits rushed Damian only to be shot down, and she zipped off a fireball at the other. She winced when he evaporated into ashes. "Oops."

"I wouldn't spare him any pity," a woman said a bit shakily from behind her. "He was making some really nasty threats!"

The only two bandits who survived the ambush turned out to

be the ones that had been rooted. Damian was *damned* accurate with his bow. The local guard took charge of the prisoners, and the village began to get back to its business. Everyone felt very happy with Damian and Teydra alike, and they were more than happy to share what information they had. Again, it came down to ogres and no real idea of the *actual* issue, but supposedly an escapee of the kingdom would be arriving on the morrow with more information.

Since it would be worth waiting to find out, Damian and Teydra found themselves with an entire day to waste. They hit the surprisingly busy market to see what sorts of wares were on offer, and each managed to get a new change of clothes. Teydra, showing the lovely lack of modesty that marked her race, delighted many present by stripping off her ruined dress in the market and pulling on a new tunic over her corset. Damian even had to glare at several rivals to impress the point that the faerie was *his*.

Before he said or did something really stupid, he headed for the end of the market. An old peddler selling unusual shell jewelry caught his eye, and he moved closer to look. Mixed with the shells were pearls of all colors, and he picked up a lovely necklace whose multi-hued color reminded him of Teydra's mood changing hair.

The peddler suddenly asked, "What bothers you?"

The surprisingly youthful voice coming from such an elderly face startled Damian, and he looked up to find oddly young and yet ancient blue eyes watching him. "A lot," he admitted. He put the necklace down. "I doubt you want to hear my tale of woe."

"On the contrary, son. I am quite interested. I may even be able to help you."

After a brief pause, Damian sighed. "I'm a prince who supposedly sucks at being a prince, and I'm supposed to rescue a princess from a cursed castle in order to prove myself a man. Being a prince and on a quest, I have been given a Good Faerie to aid me. Said Good Faerie is no better at her job than I am at mine, and I'm tripping over my own feet in love with her."

"Have you kissed her?"

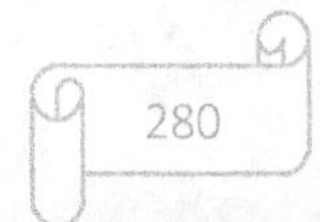

"Unfortunately."

"That good, eh?"

"Better." He trailed a finger over a lovely statue depicting some sort of goddess rising from a scalloped shell. "She wants me in return, and I'm going crazy because her hair shows her emotions and therefore I *know* she's just as frustrated as I am. I think she's the woman of my dreams, and that really isn't so surprising since I can't seem to get anything else right. I just don't know what I'm supposed to do next."

"Hmm." The peddler contemplated things for a moment before offering, "I think I can help you. How about we make something of a deal? If you will do a few tasks for me, I can guarantee by the end of them that you will have a much better understanding of what your heart wants."

"Alright, you have a deal. Should we shake on it?"

"Actually, let us do this just a bit more formally." He offered a scroll. "This is for your sake more than mine. This scroll will be the ticket to your happy ending, Damian."

Damian took the scroll and skimmed over it quickly. It was a contract, and it clearly stated that the peddler would issue three tasks that would lead to clarification in Damian's course of action. However . . . "This part near the end. I can't read it."

"You will be able to read it when it is necessary to be read."

He looked up quickly. "You use magic?"

"I have some gifts," was the modest response. "Do we have a deal?" He offered a pen.

"Deal." Damian signed his name across the bottom of the contract and then tucked it into the quiver where he carried his arrows. "I don't object to menial or manual labor," he admitted wryly. "I rather enjoy it. What do you need me to do first?"

"Nothing very complicated, in fact. First and foremost, I need some lumber hauled in from the edges of town. You may use the cart over there for it." He smiled when Damian looked at him oddly. "Trust me when I say that the simplest of tasks can often have the most far reaching effects, young prince."

Amiable, though a bit confused, Damian grabbed the cart and lugged it toward the edge of town. Stacks of wood sat waiting to be split into lumber, and he hefted an axe to get to work. As he made the first chop, he heard an unexpected burst of giggling from a bunch of kids. He looked over curiously and felt his heart flutter in tune with his pulse.

A handful of schoolchildren clustered around Teydra, and she was telling them something that had them wide-eyed with delight. Her quick fingers fashioned wreathes of flowers for the boys and girls alike. A very little girl tugged on her leg, and she scooped her up to spin her in the air. The sunlight glowed over her wings and skin, and she seemed to sparkle with magic and beauty as she put the girl down again. She popped into Pixie form and zipped off with a giggle, and the children gave happy chase.

Breathless with wonder, he barely dragged his eyes away to get back to splitting the lumber. She loved kids. Well, of course she did. She loved a lot of things. He was willing to bet a lot of her non-Good Faerie duties had involved watching little faeries. A bit wistfully, he couldn't help but wonder what kind of mother she might be. Could humans and faeries have children together? They could always adopt if not.

He scowled and put the thoughts out of his head. He was distracting himself when he had work to do. He got down to things and shortly had the lumber split and loaded. He brought it back to the peddler and huffed out a breath. "I'm not thinking clearly. I'm getting distracted."

"Happens to the best of us, my boy. Here you go." He handed over two large buckets. "Water from the well on the other side of town, please."

"Why can't you at least challenge me? Sheesh." He hefted the buckets and carried them easily through the town toward where the well was located. He had to wait his turn since someone else was there, and he looked around curiously at the area. There seemed to be quite a bit of construction going on. "What happened over here?" he asked.

The farmer in front of him explained, "We had some damage in the last big storm before the one this morning. Lost a couple houses. We've been trying to rebuild them before winter comes in for good." He started filling his second bucket. "That your partner over there?"

"Huh?" He looked over quickly and discovered Teydra had been abandoned by the kids. Instead, she hovered over a builder's shoulder and seemed to be having a lively discussion with him over something. She adamantly shook her head and turned into Monarch form to start pointing and issuing orders. Much to Damian's bemusement, people leapt to obey. "Yeah, that's my partner. I didn't know she could take charge like that."

"She certainly knows how to make people do what is needed." He chuckled. "And I'm glad for it! Maybe I'll have a roof over my head before the next rain." He lifted his buckets. "Your turn."

"Thanks." Damian started drawing water, and he kept an eye on the scene not far away. Teydra had indeed taken charge of things. She read plans and made suggestions, and she got everyone quickly organized. He had no idea how she did it; issuing orders was on the list of princely things he had never learned. He had always assumed it was a talent he just didn't have. Teydra certainly had it. He watched her wistfully. They complemented each other perfectly. They had strengths that the other didn't, and yet they were so much alike inside.

Beginning to think about things, he carried the buckets of water back to the peddler and handed them off. The peddler merely lifted a brow with a smile. "Last but not least, would you mind terribly hitting the inn and getting the fresh baked bread the innkeeper owes me? You might have to wait for it to be packaged."

"No problem at all." He tucked his hands into his pockets and headed for the inn. The building had gotten lively later in the day, and he realized that most people went there to eat if they weren't eating at home. He ducked through the crowd and made his way toward the back where the innkeeper stood. "Bread?" he asked over the din.

She smiled. "I'll get it for you. Give me a few minutes." She ducked through the doors into the kitchen.

He turned to watch the room, and he grinned when he noticed a lovely bard sitting at the bar counter. Perched on the bard's shoulder was a Pixie-sized Good Faerie. It made him feel better to know he wasn't the only one on a quest around there. He didn't know what she was doing, but he hoped she succeeded at it.

Speaking of Good Faeries, he spotted his swinging in the front door. She had her arms full of flowers, and there was a light flush across her chocolate skin. Her creamy hair had turned a silvery hue that he thought might be happiness. She dropped off the flowers with a waitress and started laughing when she got unexpectedly hugged by her fellow faerie. The sound of her voice lifted over the room, and she drew many smiling looks. She spotted Damian then and turned toward where he stood. The silver of her hair was replaced by the unknown gold color, and her eyes shimmered purple. She smiled almost shyly at him before she got pulled into a conversation with the bard as well.

He felt an emotional fist hit him hard and powerfully. It really was too late for him. It had been too late from that first moment he had met her. He had fooled himself into thinking there might be any other outcome. What was he supposed to do next? He was supposed to fight anything and everything in order to have her for his own! He had seen plenty of evidence to prove he was right about the brilliant queen she could be. They needed to sit down and have a serious talk about things. His parents wanted him to come with a bride; they had never specified it had to be a princess, now had they?

The innkeeper suddenly offered him the basket of bread, and he quickly made his way back to the peddler. "Here you go."

The peddler smiled. "Do I sense someone might have a better idea of what he needs to do?"

"You sense right, and you were right about those tasks forcing

me to think clearly. If I'd been working too hard, I would never have been able to watch Teydra as I have. I'm going to fight for her as hard as I can."

Something eternally sad moved through the gold eyes watching him. "Love is the one thing worth fighting for in life."

"Did you learn that lesson too late?" he asked softly.

"It was a bitter, painful, and perhaps a bit ironic lesson for me to learn." The peddler waved a hand. "Off with you, Damian. You have quite a fight ahead of you." To himself as Damian ran off, he murmured, "Love always waits."

Back at the inn, Damian made his way to the bar where Teydra was now sitting with the bard. The other Good Faerie was still in Pixie form and sitting on the bar top. He didn't need to ask why; the only open seat was the one they had saved for him. "Many thanks," he noted wryly as he sat down. He offered a hand to the bard. "Damian Lucksworth."

"Janaya Corgan." Her green eyes lit with humor. "I have trouble being formal with royal types. I hope you don't mind."

"I will take it as a personal favor if you aren't formal, actually, as I have trouble remembering how to be a 'royal type' to begin with." He smiled at the other faerie. "It's nice to meet you as well."

"Vriya." She slid a look at Teydra. "I've known Teydra since she was very little. I'm glad to see she's finally matured enough to actually serve in her proper role. You've been a, hmm, good influence on her."

Pink climbed Teydra's hair. Though she hadn't told Vriya everything, she knew her mentor had seen the gold from earlier. "What were you up to?" she asked Damian. "I saw you doing quite a bit of work."

"Just helping out a peddler in town." He leaned on the bar with a sigh. "It's been crazy the last few days. I need a drink."

"You and me both, friend," Janaya agreed with emphasis. She gestured lightly to the bartender. She took one of the drinks that slid her way and sighed. "Going on a quest for the one you love. Vexing, frustrating, and painful. Worse, I don't even know if I'm going to succeed. We've kind of got a station problem."

"Ah, you must love a member of the royalty." He shook his head and sniffed at his drink. "I would hope any parents just want their child to be happy."

"It's complicated," Vriya demurred. "Janaya has to fight a lot more than just station. That's why she has me to help."

He saluted with his glass. "Good luck to you."

Janaya saluted back. "Same to you." She smirked when he took a drink and then choked. "I have yet to see a member of any royal family who can keep up with a peasant in a drinking contest."

A bit challenged, he defiantly took another sip. It burned all the way down, but it wasn't that bad on the second pass. "I'm more like a peasant than a prince, thank you. I think I can hold my own."

"Uh-oh," Teydra muttered.

Vriya grinned at her. "Just let it happen. They need to unwind a bit."

Unwind they did. The challenge had been called, and the amused bartender kept track of what they consumed. It turned out that Damian *did* have the better constitution, but he didn't beat Janaya by much. They were both happily tipsy by their fourth beverages. Two more and they were wholly drunk. They sang songs together, told bad jokes, and commiserated over journeys of growth that involved bandits, demons, and sneezing flowers.

Damian squinted as he tried to focus on his new friend. "Sneezing flowers?"

"Sneezing." Janaya scowled into her nearly empty glass. "Kept hearing this little 'choo' noise. Finally figured out that it was the flowers. They were allergic to me. I shortly got covered in flower snot. I smelled like a perfume bottle for a day!"

He blinked owlishly at Teydra. "I like demons more."

She bit her lip to hide a smile. "I imagine so." She shook her head as she watched him woozily sway on his seat. "Okay, Damian. You two are done. I'm going to pour some water in you and put you to bed."

"Aww, Teydra." He grumbled as she tugged him up to his feet. The room tilted happily and he quickly grabbed her for balance. "Whee."

Now trying not to giggle, she moved him carefully toward the stairs. Such was the glamorous life of a good sidekick. She healed wounds, fireballed bandits, and kept him from drunkenly face planting on the ground or into a wall. She maneuvered him down the hall and unlocked the door to his room. She had secured it earlier while he was off doing his tasks. "In we go!" she told him cheerfully.

He sighed and leaned more heavily against her as he tried to put one foot in front of another. She dumped him on the side of the bed, and he watched her longingly as she poured him a glass of water from the pitcher. Not even being drunk made him want her less. "I love watching you move," he confessed.

A hint of pink climbed through her hair. "I walk like anyone else." She put the glass in his hand. "Drink. The last thing you need is a hangover."

He drank the water, but he kept watching her. "You sort of . . . float. And you sparkle. You taste like magic." He didn't argue when she tugged off his boots though he reached out to grab a handful of her hair. "I don't want to rescue the princess. I want to take you home. I'm so stupidly in love with you."

Gold overtook the pink in her hair and eyes alike as she looked up quickly. His eyes looked very serious despite not being sober. She could not doubt that he *believed* he meant every word. She fiercely fought to ignore the longing welling inside. She had lost track of the ways she wanted him. Emotionally and physically topped the list, but even her magic seemed to reach out hungrily for him. She struggled to ignore it to the best of her ability. "Shirt off and into bed."

He tried to take off his shirt but got tangled up partway. "Little help?"

Amused again, she helped him get free and then tossed his legs onto the bed. "Sleep, Damian." She turned to leave and his hand shot out to grab her wrist. Prepared for another test of her control, she glanced back at him. Perhaps surprisingly, there was a trace of genuine panic in his eyes. "Damian?"

"Don't go," he pleaded. "Please don't leave me. It's too dark. I can't sleep. I know you will keep away the nightmares. You protect me." He rolled onto his side and buried his face against her hip. "I don't wanna be alone."

She hadn't known he was afraid of the dark. Her lips trembled as she brushed his hair out of his eyes. How could she leave him alone? "Alright," she said softly. "I'll stay." She headed for the lamp and felt as much as heard him tense. "Trust me. You don't need the lamp if I'm here."

He bit back the protest that welled and said nothing. The light clicked off and his heart began to pound hard in rising terror. Then, suddenly, softly, he saw a soft blue glow beginning to emanate from her wings. It shrouded her in beautiful shadows and brought just enough light to the room that he could see. The soft blue hue could not disguise the gold of her hair as she returned to his side and slid onto the bed beside him. "What's the gold mean?"

"Nothing special," she lied. She tucked her legs up and had to smile as he wrapped his arms around her waist and snuggled close like a child. She couldn't quite stop herself from imagining what it would be like to have a little boy just like Damian running around. Faeries could have children with humans, and they had been crossbreeding for ages. Really, the only thing standing in front of her union with Damian was the sheer fact that she was a *Good* Faerie. It just wasn't right or fair.

He fell asleep easily in the sheltering light of her wings, and she stayed awake for a while longer. She knew it was already too late for her. He had said he was stupidly in love. A more appropriate phrase didn't exist. She was an idiot for wanting what she could not have. She would need to be Cleansed if she ever wanted to move on. Knowing it, her arms tightened around him. Could the Cleansing really even take away her memories of this most important person?

Damian woke slowly and a bit groggily as the first light of dawn began to slide in the window. He had a serious case of dry mouth but blessedly no hangover. He also felt more rested than he had in a long while. The feel of strong yet slender arms holding him had his eyes opening quickly, and he discovered himself tucked safely in Teydra's arms. His heart quivered painfully. She had held him all night. He hadn't dreamed any of that. Her wings still glowed softly, and glimmers of magic trailed through the air.

He carefully extricated himself from her grip and went to get some water to clear the taste in his mouth. He kept his back turned toward the bed, but he could see her reflection in the mirror. Her creamy hair still looked gold in color. It only turned that color for him. Striving for a distraction, he grabbed the contract from the quiver and looked at the bottom to see if he could read it yet. Surprisingly, he could.

*'Mood Magic possessed by Party A shall serve as the barometer for the status of the relationship between Party A and Party B. If the color of Party A's hair turns the color of gold that heralds the presence of the God of Love, then Party B shall be given all rights and privileges to claim Party A. This contract is a binding document that can and will be Enforced to the highest degree.'*

A sort of trembling began to spread from the heart outward. Her hair turned gold when she looked at him . . . because she was in love with him, too? He looked down at the contract again and finally saw the second place where her signature needed to go. If she signed, then there was nothing and no one that could stand in their way. Not even her faerie elders would be able to stop it. He didn't think she would sign it willingly, though. He would need to trick her.

He turned to put the scroll back, and his arm bumped into a statue on the dresser. The arrow held by the little cupid figurine jabbed into his skin, and he bit back a startled yelp. He looked quickly and saw only a tiny scratch. Gingerly, he moved the statue back before he did more damage. He turned around to go wake Teydra, and he came to a sharp stop as every bit of his hunger for her roared violently to life. There no longer seemed to be any way to control it.

*His*. This beautiful creature belonged to him. His hands slowly curled into fists at his side, then let go. He could not fight his heart anymore.

Teydra woke to drugging pleasure radiating from the hands tenderly caressing her body. Lips teased hers lightly until she whimpered and strained upward to deepen the embrace. "Wake up and look at me," Damian's husky voice coaxed. "I need to see your eyes, my faerie."

Her lashes lifted and she caught a breath as she realized she was naked in his arms, and he wore no more clothing than she did. The wonderful heat she felt came from his bare skin against hers. "Don't," she tried to say, and the word broke in half as his mouth claimed hers hungrily. Try as she might to resist, she just could not. She would already have to be Cleansed. Why not take that one moment to be truly happy?

Magic radiated from her skin and swelled in the air. It felt thick and drugging and sensual. He lifted his head enough to ask softly, "What did you do?"

"Shielded us from prying eyes of my kind." Her hands framed his face and her lips teased his. "This is just us." Her lips trembled. "I can't let you go just yet. I will have to later, but not right now." She tugged him down for another kiss, and she let the magic inside froth until it spilled from her mouth to his. The way his pupils expanded in shocked delight made something clench low in her body. She wanted to give him everything.

Hands caressed and lingered. She watched her darker hands move across the fair skin of his chest and felt enchanted herself. Her perfect opposite. Her perfect match. She gave a breathless laugh when he pulled her up to a sitting position and buried his face against her neck. The edge of his teeth scraped teasingly in an erotic threat. "No marks," she warned huskily.

"I know someone with amazing magic. She'll make them go away again." He tugged her onto his lap. Her wings curled around them both, and he eagerly reached out to touch. To his surprised delight, they were not at all what he had expected. He had thought they would be silky like her skin, but they felt as if they were covered in tiny down feathers. He trailed fingers across the surface and watched magic ripple in his wake. Her breath broke on a moan, and her hair and eyes turned to a beautiful blend of purple and gold. "Sensitive?"

"There's," she couldn't quite bite back another whimper, "no place more sensitive." He laid her down again, and she tugged him close; she needed to feel his weight and heat. His kiss stole her breath and her soul alike, and she felt his body greedily consuming her magic like a sponge soaking up water. It would eternally make him more sensitive to all kinds of magic. Even when they parted, he would carry her gift inside for the rest of his life. It would have to be enough.

They explored every inch, caressed every line and curve, and lingered over every new secret. When neither could bear it any longer, he finally rolled onto his back and held her braced over him. He watched her eyes as he slowly took her, and the gold grew stronger than the purple. His entire body quivered violently. "I won't stop loving you!" he told her fiercely. He buried himself to the hilt and watched her head fall back helplessly. Magic glowed over her skin and wings, and she was the most incredible thing he had ever seen.

There were no more words between them as they rushed desperately toward ecstasy. A sudden memory ripped through her mind as she felt the first wild pulses of release, and she reached desperately for her magic. It locked down sharply inside her body just as the greedy tension broke and sent wicked pleasure ripping through her senses. She couldn't do anything else but hold on and ride out the storm.

He shuddered wildly as he watched magic explode like fireworks in the air around her. He dragged her down and stayed buried deep inside her throbbing body as pleasure pounded through his entire body in a magical wave. She collapsed onto his chest, and he had only enough energy left to wrap his arms around her and keep her close. Little aftershocks rippled through both of them, and he had no words. He had expected nothing of what had happened. If that was what holding out for true love got you, then he was *very* glad he had waited!

When dawn gave way to morning sun, she finally stirred in his arms and tilted her head back to look at him. "It changes nothing," she told him softly. "We both have a duty, and my elders will never approve of our union."

"And if you get pregnant?" He lifted a brow.

"I won't. I used magic to cancel my fertility." The disappointment in his eyes tore at her heart and soul. She tenderly traced his lips and cupped his cheek. "You know it would have been a bad thing."

It would have given him grounds to demand her hand, that's what it would have been! A permanent bond between them. The longing to have a child with her had been planted the day before, and now he couldn't shake it off. They could have a *family*. "I don't want duty, Teydra. I want *you*. Why should I settle for duty when love is in front of me? In front of *us*?"

"Because the expectations and rules of being a Good Faerie vastly outclass whatever you grew up with. Attraction is okay. That's kind of expected in some cases. But being lovers, let alone being mates?" She slowly shook her head. "I asked Vriya. It's just not fair to you."

"How is it not fair?"

"Because you're dependent on me!" she shouted. She jerked out of his arms and rolled to the side. She curled into herself painfully. "What you feel might not be real! It's happened before. Heroes falling for a faerie only to discover it wasn't real once they reached their goal."

He jerked her over again. "Your hair turns gold when you look at me!" he challenged.

"Yes, it does." Tears shimmered across her now black eyes. "I'll love you eternally. But you may not love me the same."

He bit back the retorts and seething anger inside. He *knew* she

was wrong, damn it! And yet . . . maybe it might just be worth it to go along with things. She needed to believe in him. "Fine." He rolled out of bed and grabbed the contract. "I'll make you a deal. I'll continue this journey. I'll rescue the damned princess. But if I don't find myself in love with her, I'm coming after you. You won't be able to tell me I don't love you like I know I do!"

She hesitated. Maybe she could go without being Cleansed until she was sure. The elders wouldn't know what had happened. Only Vriya might guess, and she had vowed to keep quiet over everything. She was kinda helping Janaya on the down low, too. "Alright." Without looking or changing her mind, she flicked her fingers and her signature appeared on the bottom of the scroll. Only then realizing, she frowned at her hands. "I have control over my magic now."

He put the scroll away and knelt on the bed beside her. His fingers sank into her hair and he tugged her up for another hungry kiss. "You just needed to start using it more," he muttered against her lips. "That anti-fertility spell good for a while? I'm not letting you go yet, Teydra. Let me make memories of you. I'll never stop wanting you. You enchanted me."

She surrendered on a soft sigh and turned her face up for another kiss. She was the one who had been enchanted. They would part soon enough. One more memory would help her hold on until the end, no matter how it came.

Could he really love her?

# CHAPTER FOUR

It was noon by the time they checked out of the inn. Both were miserable for different reasons though they doggedly pushed everything aside and tried to go back to being friends. Unfortunately, it had become harder than ever to ignore the attraction between them. Becoming lovers had just made the hunger deeper and more powerful. Knowing what they had together made it impossible to resist having it again. It was not aided by the fact that Damian carried Teydra's magic inside his body now. It created an odd magnetism that she had not expected.

They stopped at the market to buy some food and were halfway through their lunch when a town guard hurried up to them. "Your Highness, the escapee from the Karmic Kingdom arrived this morning."

Damian cocked his head. "Okay. What did he or she have to say?"

"She, sire. And according to what she witnessed, the ogres came to the kingdom because the king initially tried to sell his daughter to them but then changed his mind." He winced in agreement as both groaned. "The rumor is that the princess was seeing someone he did not approve of and he first thought to just hoist her off onto an easy money-making opportunity. Her protests changed his mind."

Teydra muttered, "Yeah but now he's offering her hand to whoever can rescue her from the mess he made in the first place!"

Damian sighed. "At the least, I might be able to help her out.

You know. Rescue her and then get her to whomever she loves, providing he doesn't beat me there. I can completely sympathize with her." He smiled at the guard. "Thank you for the information."

"You are very welcome, sire." He bowed and took his leave.

Damian turned to Teydra. "Greed."

"It's always greed," she complained. "That explains why the ogres were so mad about things! It's still unusual for them to be chucking curses, but I almost can't blame them." She frowned. "Still, something just doesn't feel right. Just *how* did they get the power? Also, the eating princes thing isn't settling right with me, either."

"The only way we're going to know for sure is to just go there." He tugged her up to her feet. "We have only a short way to go. It'll all work out. I'll free the princess, prove that I'm yours alone, and even your elders will have to accept me."

She said nothing though she let him continue to hold her hand. It hurt too much to think about. Their time together was a lot shorter than he thought. She could not go with him into the kingdom itself. Her duty ended when he reached his destination. He would have to take everything she had taught him and do things on his own.

"Tell me about your family," he said unexpectedly, bringing her out of her thoughts. "Do you have one?"

"Uhm, kind of. My parents are both Good Faeries too, of course, and they're often on a lot of missions because they're so talented. I don't see them much though I'm sure they'll come home to celebrate me surviving my first assignment, grudging as it was for Elder Thom to send me. I've mastered my magic more, and I think I might actually be able to use my Mood Magic, too."

"You can't wait to try it out on someone."

She winced sheepishly. "I have a few classmates I wouldn't mind teaching a few lessons to, yes. They were always polite, but some of them were jerks." Apologetically, she added, "Sometimes Good Faeries forget the 'good' part of their name. They deserve a kick or two."

"Siblings?"

"Several, in fact. And, yes, same job. I kind of couldn't avoid going into things myself. I have a long lineage. I think I know why everyone enjoys their work. It's kind of thrilling to take care of someone and see them become what they are meant to be. The faeries who have lost their charges . . . I feel bad for them. I'm not sure I'd be able to handle losing you, even if—even if I didn't feel like I do."

He fought an urge to grab her into his arms. "You think you'll be sent out on more jobs now?"

"Probably." She found a smile. "It might be interesting to deal with a 'real' prince, though I think I'm fond of the 'ish' type. Maybe I can work with the non-traditional types. I'm not normal either."

"I disagree." He tugged on a lock of her hair. "Yeah, in the beginning, you definitely scared the hell out of me, but you seem to have everything down now. I think you're just a Good Faerie now. No 'ish' about it, Teydra."

"My real test is ahead, actually, so we'll see."

Silence fell between them again as they continued down the road. Even at a distance, the menacing darkness clinging to the Karmic Kingdom was very obvious. The ugly storm clouds and flickering lightning showed classic trademarks of a good old-fashioned curse. It was barely late afternoon by the time they finally reached the edges of the outlying farmlands. Damian started to go down the closest dirt road and realized that Teydra was not with him. He turned quickly. "Teydra?"

She slowly shook her head. Her hands clenched together in front of her body. "I can go no further, Damian."

"Do curses hurt faeries?"

"No." She tried to smile but couldn't manage it. "My duty has ended by successfully escorting you to your final destination. Everything from here on must be you alone. All I can do now is give you three enchanted items that may aid you in your final battles."

He grabbed her shoulders. "Why can't *you* aid me?"

"Because I can't. I've broken too many rules already. Don't

make this harder than it is. You just don't know what will happen." Her eyes closed and a tear slid down her cheek. Black had slowly crept in to overtake the cream of her hair and eyes alike. "If you get to that tower and fall in love, I don't want to be there."

"It won't happen!"

"You don't know!"

"She *has* someone she loves!"

"We don't know that for sure!" she shouted. "I've seen dozens of princes or princesses be in the middle of courting or even be engaged only to have it changed overnight by the arrival of true love!" She shoved him away. "You know I'm right!"

Right about what she had seen and yet wrong about it applying to him. He already had his true love! He seethed and bit back further arguments. He knew they would get him nowhere. Her stubbornness rivaled his. "Fine. What three items are you going to give me?"

She drew a ragged breath and held up her hands. The magic came willingly when she called it, and the spell swirled through her mind without any difficulties. It seemed strange how she could remember everything now. A shimmering new long bow appeared in her hands along with a quiver of golden arrows. "An enchanted bow, to begin with." She offered it to him. "Tradition dictates a sword, but it would be useless to you. These arrows can pierce even the toughest of hides."

It weighed next to nothing in his hand, and he dropped his old one on the ground. He drew back the string and found that it was even easier than before to hold onto. Yet when he fired a test arrow at a tree, it buried itself to the end of the nock; it had gained rather than lose power. The arrows themselves glowed softly with magic. "This is amazing!"

The black in her hair began to be replaced by silver and pink. She really was getting good at it, and his praise meant everything to her. "Next will be a tool that the ogres won't like." A swirl over her hands became a golden horn. "This should render them asleep and allow you safe passage through. Break the curse and they'll have to leave. It's just the way stuff works. It might not work on all of them, though, hence the bow."

He tucked the horn into his belt. "What's the third item? I can't imagine I need anything else."

"Not need, no," she said softly, "but it is something I want you to have." She plucked a strand of her hair and offered it. "It will protect you from magical attacks. It should counter what happened when we—when we made love. My magic is inside you, Damian. You will always be sensitive from now on. My hair should keep that sensitivity from being a danger."

He twirled the hair between his fingers for a moment to admire it. He then began to wrap it firmly around his left ring finger. It felt warm and soothing, and it pulsed softly against his skin. "Teydra." He curled his other hand around the back of her neck and drew her closer. "You act like this is goodbye. I *will* come back for you." He lifted her up to her toes and kissed her tenderly, trying to give her the endless generosity of his love. She was breaking his heart with her doubt. How could she think he would ever let her go?

She clung onto him for a desperate moment but finally forced herself to let go. She took a trembling step backward as tears shimmered across her eyes. Before he could say anything, she whirled and ran away. She simply dissolved into the sunlight in mid-step. It took only a moment until it seemed as if she had never been there. All he had to show for her presence was an enchanted bow and horn, a single strand of hair, and the aching pulse of magic inside his body. He determinedly turned toward the road and got marching. The sooner this was done, the sooner he could find a way to the Faerie Realm!

The road went in only one direction, and there was nothing to block his way. Everyone who hadn't been caught by the curse had fled for their lives. The low rumble on the air told him that the ogres were still present and still hungry. He crouched down outside the partially open castle gates and peered inside carefully.

Ten or twelve pasty ogres wandered in the courtyard. They

looked a strange washed out color rather than the normal green or gray that marked most others of the breed. A sort of menacing haze clung to their skin and seared the air with a disturbing scent that Damian could not place and yet felt sickened by.

He sensed movement and turned his head sharply. His jaw dropped as he saw who had joined him. "Janaya?" he whispered.

She winced. "The person I love is stuck in here. I figured the least I could do was make a go at things myself. Vriya gave me an enchanted sword, mirror, and a one-time use fireball."

He brightened. "You can use a sword?"

"Uhm, yes actually. Quite well, in fact." She looked at the bow he held out, and she began to grin. "Well, okay. This might work out perfectly. I won't tell anyone about the bow-using prince if you won't mention the sword-using bard. What else did Teydra give you?"

"A horn to put them to sleep. The other is . . . personal."

Sympathy filled her eyes. "Love is love. We can't make it comfortable. We can only be thankful to the gods that we were given the gift to begin with."

"I'm fine with it. She, on the other hand, needs to be convinced. I figure I'll break the curse and prove I'm not destined for the princess or something equally ridiculous and then help get said princess to whoever it is she *does* love so that I can then go after the one *I* want."

She blinked. "I think I followed you. Okay then. What's the plan? You put them to sleep with the horn and we rush in to kill everything else?"

"Depends on what that mirror is for."

"Vriya told me it would cancel out invisibility or morphing spells to make sure I wasn't ambushed by hidden enemies. It also reflects magic when struck."

He frowned. "If there's anything I've picked up, it's that we wouldn't have these items if they weren't needed. I'll use the horn to get everything I can and then we'll rush inside in the confusion. You have the mirror out just in case, and we'll see what is left to kill. And throw the fireball at anything that blinks funny."

"Deal." She drew her sword with one hand and held the mirror with her other. Her confidence with the weapon showed in the way she stood casually.

He lifted the horn and began to play it quickly. A haunting melody rose on the air, and the ground shook as heavy ogre bodies began to fall over. Janaya shoved the gates open and rushed inside with the mirror held like a shield. She looked around sharply and yet all of the ogres seemed to have been felled by the horn. "We're clear right now."

Damian ducked in beside her and kept an arrow notched and ready. He grimaced as he looked around the courtyard and saw the strewn bones that were all that remained of the former princes and heroes who had come through. "I don't want to be dinner."

"You'd be a bit gamey, to be sure."

Unexpectedly, the hair wrapped around his finger began to glow brightly. He felt the strange pulse of magic moving through his body, and his eyes widened as the glow expanded around him. "What's going on?"

"Uhm. Damian? Did you sleep with Teydra?" His wide-eyed look was an answer, and she winced. "There's an old legend that says that a human can learn faerie magic if it is given freely between lovers. If you got your hands on a spell book and learned the ropes, you'd be able to cast the same spells they do."

"She didn't know," he murmured mostly to himself. "The elders said it would take something dramatic for a human without faerie blood to cast faerie magic."

"I suspect I'd call what happened fairly dramatic, friend. And also useful. Hold still."

He frowned when she aimed the mirror at him. "What're you doing?"

"Nothing. I think."

He opened his mouth and then swallowed a yelp as the magic around him abruptly shot toward the mirror. It promptly ricocheted back out into the courtyard and began to bounce off every surface.

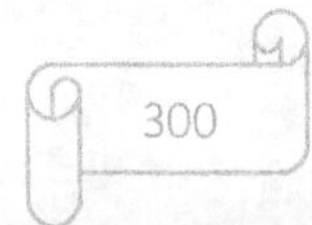

An unnatural shriek filled the air and made their skin crawl. Something moved in the darkness and began to bubble across the ground like a sickening, putrid mass of festering tar. Evil. There could be no other word for it. Neither Janaya nor Damian had ever seen evil before, but they knew it for what it was. "I think we know why the ogres were acting weird," she whispered.

Several ogres lumbered up to their feet and stood swaying in place like the undead. "You take care of them!" Damian told Janaya swiftly. "I can resist magic! Let me handle the blob thing! I think I can drive it out!"

"Done!" She went running toward the ogres on a shout, and her first strike sent one of their heads flying.

He whirled and dashed off the other way. He fired off the first arrow at the blob, and it screeched again as it began to pursue him. It tried to fire a blast of ugly power at him, and the attack seemed to splash harmlessly off his skin. Strangely, rather than go after another target, the blob only seemed to become more enraged at him. He used his apparently endless supply of arrows—he liked that enchanted quiver!—to keep it at bay while he kept the corner of his eye on Janaya. She had taken a few hits, but she was winning.

The blob realized magic didn't work and rushed forward in a berserk rage. A slimy fist thumped him in the chest and knocked him backwards through a wooden coop of some kind. Rather than try to get out again, he started shooting arrows as hard and as fast as he could. "Janaya!" he shouted.

"I'm kind of busy, Damian!"

"That fireball would be appreciated!"

She glanced over, saw the tableau, and winced. "Shit!" An ogre swatted her away hard enough that she stumbled, and she had an idea. She grabbed her mirror. "Hey, ugly!" She hurled it right at the ogre's head. It grabbed it reflexively and blinked at her. Fire swirled around her now free hand. "Hold still and this'll only hurt a little!" She chucked the fireball with all her might, and it bounced off the mirror and toward the blob. The mirror shattered, and the ogre holding it was torn to bits.

Just as another grabbed her and hoisted her as if to throw her, and the blob almost closed in on Damian, the fireball landed with the force of an inferno. A horrifying scream of agony rose viciously on the air and then abruptly cut out as the blob disappeared. The ogres instantly crumbled to dust, and Janaya landed unceremoniously on the dirt. "Ouch!"

The familiar waiting silence of a normal curse filled the air in the aftermath. Damian gingerly picked his way out of the debris and plucked at the splinters in his skin. Everything seemed to hurt, and blood trickled down his face and arms. Janaya looked little better than he did as he carefully limped over. "I think we know why there were so many princes getting eaten. I guess we just needed some non-traditional fighting to take care of the problem."

"Seems so." Something unreadable moved through her eyes. "Guess you get to rescue the princess now. Can I come watch?"

"Don't see why not. It won't be dramatic." He hooked his bow over his shoulder. "Let's hope I don't get lost trying to find which tower she's in."

"The north one." She fell into step beside him.

"Oh, yeah. You mentioned you were from here." He glanced at her. "You want to go find your lover? I'm good on my own."

"It won't do me any good with the curse still in place," she noted reasonably.

"Fair enough." He gingerly stepped over and around the people who had fallen in the halls and made his way toward the entrance to the north tower. It wasn't hard to find; most castles had been built all the same. He could have navigated them in his sleep. The only fun parts of a castle were the secret passages; they were the only thing varied from place to place. His had one that went into the gardens. It would be perfect for a faerie queen.

The tower stairs were narrow enough that he and Janaya had to go single-file, and he pushed open the door at the top. He then winced in wry amusement at the highly feminine and delicate décor.

"How would I ever guess a princess lived here?"

Janaya's hands clenched together. "She actually likes this stuff. It's not just because she's a princess. We all say how wonderful she will be as a queen because she loves so generously."

He paused as he reached for the bed curtain and slowly turned around. Suspicions began to churn inside. The look on Janaya's face looked one hell of a lot like the look on Teydra's face when she had let him go. "Janaya. You want to tell me what's going on? I get the feeling that you haven't told me the whole truth."

"Her name is Vanessa." Misery and longing mingled in her green eyes. "She likes to read stories to other people, and she hates sweets. Tarts are more her style. When she smiles at you, the world is perfect."

He sighed deeply. "What did her father object to more? Your station or your gender?"

"It was a bad combination of both. His bloodline would end, you see. He could have overlooked my station, but that he wouldn't get to keep his precious blue blood on the throne and maybe have to let some—gasp—adopted child into the family?" She slowly shook her head. "Ness wanted to elope with me. We thought that just getting married might make it too late for him to argue. But then he tried to sell her." Her hands clenched into fists. "She tore a strip off him, and he began to rethink."

"But it was too late."

"Yeah. I was so mad when I heard what he had offered, but then I thought maybe I could rescue her. I met Vriya on accident. She liked me. She said she has a fondness for the troublemakers of the world."

He had seen her affection for Teydra. He believed it. Delight slowly began to fill his heart. "This works out *perfectly!*"

She stared at him. "I'm beginning to think the blob hit you too hard."

He shoved the horn into her hands. "No, no! This is great! I wasn't here at all! I completely had nothing to do with this! You stormed the castle and killed the ogres and saved your love!" He grabbed her arm and shoved her toward the sleeping princess. "Kiss her awake. You're her true love, right? You can break the curse *easily*! I bet I wouldn't have even been able to wake her at all! This is *great!*"

It finally dawned on her, and she started to laugh. "You really are in love with your Good Faerie!"

"And only came here to prove that it's a real love and that I won't suddenly forget her by seeing a princess." He whirled toward the door. "Live happy and invite us to the wedding, okay? Send the invite to the Luckdom Kingdom. I have to find a way to get to my faerie!"

Helpfully, she said, "Vriya said she would wait outside the kingdom to see how I did. You might be able to find her." She smiled as she sat on the side of the bed beside Vanessa. "We'll invite you to our wedding if you invite us to yours." As he ran out, she looked down at her sleeping lover, and her eyes softened. "We all deserve a happy ending."

He had barely reached the farmlands before the storm clouds started dissipating. The gloom lifted entirely, and the people who had been lying in the fields began to stir. He spotted a familiar small figure starting to fly away and ran quickly after her. "Vriya!"

The faerie turned around in surprise. She recognized him and landed as she changed into her Monarch form. "Damian. You surprised me. You helped Janaya, I take it?"

"I did. Of course I did. I knew going in that I wouldn't miraculously fall in love with the princess just by rescuing her. I knew that even before I figured out why Janaya was there." He huffed out a breath. "The look in your eyes tells me that you suspect what I might tell you."

"Let's just say that any faerie you meet will assuredly notice." Her eyes narrowed slightly. "You want to explain?"

"I'm in love with Teydra." He shook his head quickly. "I have been from the moment I met her. We need each other, Vriya. You have to take me to her! I made her a promise that I would see if what

I felt was real and if it was, I would find her. It's *real*. I'm dying without her. Let me see her, please! Here, look." He held out the scroll. "This is a legal and binding contract. She signed it herself. Her hair turned gold!"

Vriya skimmed the contract and recognized the language. She had seen more than one of these sorts of documents in her long life as a Good Faerie. They cropped up whenever a set of destined lovers needed a gentle nudge from a stronger power in the right direction. That he held the contract at all was proof of his claims. "You really love her?" she asked wistfully. "Could you make her happy?"

"I want to spend the rest of my life trying. Vriya, please. Take me to the Faerie Realm. I think it's time I did some princely things right, like rushing in to rescue my true love from the tower of her own making."

She handed the scroll back over. "The elders won't be happy with us, but I want Teydra to be happy." She offered her hand, and when he clasped it, she saw the hair around his finger. She said nothing about it. He would learn soon enough just what it entailed. She reached out for her magic and opened the portal that would take them to the Faerie Realm. Things were bound to get interesting.

# CHAPTER FIVE

When Teydra walked out of her portal, the first thing she saw was a cluster of other faeries waiting. They exploded fireworks and threw streamers and confetti at her. "Congratulations, Teydra!" one of her former teachers said happily. "We always knew you could do it if you tried!" Her smile faded to a frown as she saw the black of Teydra's hair. "Honey, are you alright?"

Teydra forced the color away, and it returned to normal cream. "Just a bit sad that it's done, I guess." She linked arms with two of her friends and managed to smile. "Do we have cake to celebrate as well?"

Cake there was, along with copious other desserts and treats. Everyone felt very happy that she had so successfully done her job, and it didn't take long for them to get word that the curse had broken. Elder Thom walked into the party and announced, "Things should go back to normal. Janaya Corgan and Damian Lucksworth have gotten rid of the ogres and curse alike." He shook his head in amusement. "Lucksworth still didn't manage to act like a prince, though. Turns out Janaya is the true love of the princess."

"I'm happy to cheer on *any* type of true love!" one faerie decided merrily. He lifted his drink. "To love!"

They all happily bumped their glasses together, but Teydra was no longer smiling at all. Her heart beat wild and hard inside her chest. Damian hadn't fallen for the princess. Did that mean he would come for her? But *how*? Humans couldn't get to the Faerie Realm.

Thom looked at her for long moments. "Teydra, come walk

with me, please." It wasn't quite a request.

"Yes sir." She got to her feet and kept her head down as she followed him out of the hut. "Is something wrong?"

"I was hoping you'd tell me," he said mildly. "You're not the same Teydra that left us a few days ago. This Teydra looks a bit heartbroken." He gently cuffed her chin. "She isn't smiling, and we always count on her smile. Tell me what happened, my dear."

"I would rather not." She quickly stopped walking as two small faerie children ran into her legs while shouting at each other. "Hey, easy!" She pulled them apart and knelt to look at them equally. "What's going on here?"

"He called me names!" one accused.

"He stole my homework!" the other retorted.

She gave each of them a little shake. "Stop it right now!" Her hands flickered red, and a matching color rippled down the length of her hair before dissipating. "I want you both to apologize and go play."

"I'm sorry," the first grudgingly grumbled.

"Me too," the second sighed. "Let's go get snacks from Grandma!"

They zipped off as if there had been no fight, and Thom rubbed the side of his nose thoughtfully. "Well, well," he murmured. "Someone has mastered her Mood Magic on top of everything else. You did that very well. You will be in high demand as a Good Faerie with a skill such as that. I can't imagine any hero who wouldn't find the ability to control other emotions useful."

"I'm just happy I'm not as transparent as I always used to be."

"Unfortunately," he told her gently, "you are still quite transparent to those who know you well. You may hide your hair, but you can't hide your eyes. They have yet to change from black, Teydra. Your heart is broken."

She buried her face in her hands. "I messed up so badly!"

"It can't be that bad." He took a little breath when she looked at him miserably. "I see. Well." He sighed. "I want to be surprised, but

I truly can't be. It would be just like you to get yourself into this sort of a mess. You know that you will never live any sort of normal life like this. Faeries choose but one mate. You will have to be Cleansed of all memories in order to move on."

"He promised to come for me," she whispered. "If what he felt was real."

"How will he get here?" He groaned as he began to recognize what had happened. "You gave him magic."

"I couldn't control myself!" Her eyes widened. "You mean that I *actually* gave him magic? I know my magic is inside him, but you mean it's not just going to make him sensitive? He could use *actual* faerie magic?" She scowled as her hair flickered dark red with temper. "Dramatic is a word for it, I guess!"

There were some things an elder simply did not want to know. "Come with me, Teydra. You must prepare for the Cleansing."

A sudden commotion just outside the fence around the village had them turning quickly, and Teydra's eyes went wide. "Damian," she breathed. Gold and purple swept through her hair and eyes as she stared at him longingly.

Thom looked at her and then at the fence. He immediately spotted Vriya not on the side of the faeries keeping the prince out but instead on the side to let him in. Oddly, that did not much surprise him either. Teydra had an ability to touch others that had nothing to do with her Mood Magic. "What is the meaning of this?" he demanded.

Damian tried his hardest to push through the faeries determinedly blocking his way. "I want to see Teydra!" he demanded sharply. "I made her a vow that I will not break! I will have her for my queen or no one else!"

More than one jaw dropped, including Teydra's. "A prince can't marry a Good Faerie!" another elder protested. "It just doesn't happen!"

Damian held up the scroll where they could all see it. "You see this? It says that if Teydra loves me, she is mine to claim! It is overseen by a messenger of love, and it can and will be enforced!" His eyes met Teydra's, and his heart ached as he saw her obvious coloring. "I'm here," he told her softly. "I love you, Teydra."

She gave a hiccupping little sob and flew across the ground to throw herself into his arms. She wrapped her arms and wings around him as tightly as she could and clung on with all her strength. Each sob came with more force until she was wholeheartedly crying against the side of his neck. Her hair swept a bit wildly through half a dozen colors, but the gold undercoat remained the entire time. "I love you so much! Don't let me go!"

"Never!" He buried his face in her hair and held her closer.

The other faeries exchanged confused and uncertain looks. It certainly broke precedent for this to happen, yet the scroll he held was definitely familiar. Considering the fact that Good Faeries existed to help true lovers, it didn't quite seem right to break this set up just because 'it went against the rules.'

"Alright," Thom finally said. "Everyone back up a bit. Let Damian in." He almost smiled when Damian walked forward without putting Teydra down. "I think we had best treat you like we would treat anyone who sought to claim a faerie of Teydra's lineage. You must prove your worth in a magical capacity."

Teydra let go of Damian and whirled around. Distress turned her hair and eyes blue. "That's not fair, Elder Thom! He might have the ability, but he knows even less about magic than I did just a short time ago! You can't ask him to do something that he literally knows nothing about!"

"If he is the one for you, he will not need to study," the elder persisted. "Do you accept, Prince Damian?"

"In fact," came the cool retort, "I do not. You may seek to placate your people with that request, but you know as well as I do that this contract I carry is more than enough. I don't care for your acceptance, elder. As long as Teydra wants to be with me, then that is where she will be."

Teydra looked up at him in bemusement and wondered if he

had any idea how utterly *royal* he sounded. He had lost something of his 'ish' as well. "I want to be with you," she told him simply. "It's all I've wanted since I met you. I just didn't know it until I realized why I hated the idea of your journey."

Thom opened his mouth but the words he wanted to say never got voiced. An icy wind swept through the area and the trees rustled in agitation. A shadow crossed over the sun and seemed to cut off its heat and light from reaching within the Realm. A familiar acrid scent stung the air, and Damian took a sharp breath. "The evil," he whispered into the eerie silence. "It came here."

Disgusting tar began to drip down through the sky. It abruptly dropped in as a whole mass and splatted into the middle of the courtyard. Several faeries screamed. Most scrambled back out of the way. Evil was not common on Mirage because of its potent magic, but all knew it when they saw it. The blob burbled over itself, and a sinister, sibilant laugh rose on the air.

When it started to creep closer, Damian reacted instinctively. He shoved Thom safely to the side and drew the enchanted bow he had been given. "I'm immune to its magic!" he shouted. "I can distract it for you to kill!"

"Our magic isn't strong enough for that!" Thom protested.

"Mine is." Teydra stepped up beside Damian and smiled tremulously at him. "I guess maybe it's a good thing that I know just how far overboard I can go." She whirled and flew around to the other side of the blob. Fire swirled around her hands, and she hurled a massive fireball at its backside. The explosion of heat had the bystanders moving back even further. Jaws dropped again as they realized that she was more powerful than they had always suspected.

Teydra and Damian worked seamlessly without words to keep the blob trapped between them. Every magical blast and every arrow chipped away a little bit more at it. When it whipped around and suddenly lunged at Teydra, Damian reacted on sheer instinct. He reached out his left hand and felt a powerful surge of knowledge through his mind. A familiar fireball formed and flew from his palm at the evil. It yelped more than shrieked and swung around to focus on him again.

It turned out that he wasn't limited to one fireball. Anything Teydra could cast, he could cast as well as long as he watched her cast it first. Neither of them had any idea why, but they didn't exactly have time to dwell on it. And when a particularly strong blast blew a hole through the center of the blob, things got even worse.

It began to ooze and spread and greedily eat up the land. Faeries quickly flew off the ground to escape, and tendrils reached up to grab them. Their very lifeforce began to be sucked away, and it would only be minutes before someone died.

A misshapen head rose from within the center of the blob and looked around wildly. Damian felt a new presence and turned sharply to discover that the old peddler had somehow come up behind him. "You!"

Teydra felt movement at the same time and also turned around quickly. An unfamiliar woman with red hair stood just behind her. She wore clothes that didn't look at all like something from Mirage, and her black eyes held what seemed like literal sparks of temper. "Who are you?" Teydra demanded. She bit back a yelp as the woman calmly walked forward. "You're going to get killed!" she wailed.

In perfect harmony, the woman and the peddler lifted their left hands and pure white magic gathered at their palms. The two attacks shot forward and merged seamlessly in the air in a nearly sensual fusion. The combined blast struck the blob and . . . obliterated it. Without any ceremony or resistance, it exploded into bits of slime that splattered onto surfaces and disappeared.

The captured faeries were released yet no one could really move or find anything to say. The woman and the peddler looked at each other for a painfully long moment and then she started to step forward. His eyes closed and he immediately dissolved into the returning sunlight. "Just a shade," she whispered achingly. She took a long breath and looked around. "Is everyone alive?"

"We seem to be." Thom studied her for a moment. "You must be Rhianna Taber from Enforcers on Earth. I've never met you, but I've sent you the completed contracts that come through our hands."

She inclined her head. "I am, and yes you have. This was something I could not ignore." She turned to where Damian and Teydra stood together. Briskly, she said, "Damian has the right of it. He and Teydra are under contract, and indeed I will Enforce the terms and conditions. Yet it would seem he has also proven himself quite the magician thanks to his ability to pull knowledge from Teydra's mind through the hair she gave him. I think perhaps you can bend the rules a bit to let him and Teydra be together."

Not a single person there dared to tell her no. The power she possessed far, *far* outclassed anything any of them had ever witnessed. "I must concur," Thom said decisively. "Damian, you may take Teydra with you if that is so her wish."

Silver color swept through Teydra's hair and eyes alike as she flew into Damian's arms. "It is!" She burst into laughter as he picked her up, turned, and started walking away. "No, no! Give Rhianna the contract! She needs it for her files!"

He chucked it over his shoulder without looking and sighed contentedly as he walked out of the village with his prize. She opened a portal that he walked through, and he told her, "We can visit of course."

"Oh of course." She swung her feet. "I can walk or fly."

"I like carrying you. It's princely."

"Do carry on then." She put her head on his shoulder and wondered why she wasn't simply glowing with joy. "What will you tell your parents?"

"They said I couldn't come back without a bride. That's what I'm doing. And I think we need to plan a big wedding. A *big* wedding. And I feel like being very royal and bossy and picky about everything."

She started giggling. "I think we're going to have a very long and fun life together. Can I sew my own wedding dress?"

"Depends. Will it fit in a walnut?"

"How about a peanut?" She gave a breathless laugh as he swooped down and kissed her with a hunger she knew would never dim. He had enchanted her heart and soul, and she wanted it no other way. "Do you know who that woman was?" she whispered against his lips.

"No, who?"

"We faeries think she's one of the two deities who watch over true lovers. I think your peddler might be the other."

It wouldn't have surprised him at all if it was true. "So we get to live happily ever after now, right? Does that mean you won't cast that anti-fertility spell anymore? If you do, I bet I can unravel it."

"You'd chance having a miniature version of either of us running around? We'll be lucky if he or she survives to a third birthday!"

He grinned wickedly. "That's okay. I know an awesome healer."

# EPILOGUE

When Rhianna returned to her office in the Enforcers' Headquarters located within the 3rd District on Earth, she found her oldest friend and partner sitting behind her desk. He looked the picture of patience, but she recognized the tension in his body. She quietly shut the door behind her. "Well?"

Eric Mason got to his feet. "Are you ready to talk yet, Rhi?"

Her hesitation was obvious as she slowly sat down behind her desk. She unrolled the scroll she held and added notes to the bottom. She then slipped it into a folder that showed as 'Complete' across the front and added it to her drawer for Mirage. Aware that Eric intently watched her, she finally said, "No." She looked up at him and saw a trace of pain in his blue eyes. "You can't change anything, Riku. Talking about it right now will do nothing. I am still paying the price for the mistakes I made."

"What mistakes?" He raked his hands through his ash colored hair. "Damn it, Rhi! I just don't understand you anymore!"

Her pause was visible for a moment before she opened a small drawer in her desk. There, resting on a broken box, was a scroll written in Ancient Greek. She held it out to him calmly, though her fingers trembled lightly. "I want you to keep this for me. I don't . . . I don't know what will happen in the future. It's all grayed out around me. I only know that the end is finally coming. There will be redemption or there will be my final punishment."

He took the scroll and opened it. Though he could not read a single word of the main text, he very clearly could read the painfully bold red VOID that had been burned across the middle of the old paper. His heart began to beat harder and harder. "Does this have to do with . . . with whomever you're waiting for?"

"His spirit grows stronger." Her fingers dug into her temples to fight off an empathic and telepathic headache. The memories always overwhelmed her abilities. "I feel him all over Mirage. I saw his shade. I just don't know what I will do when—or even if—he returns to me." Her lips trembled when she tried to smile. "We didn't exactly part on good terms."

He looked down again at the VOID. "Yeah," he said very softly. "That seems to be one way of putting it."

*Status: File Complete*
*Analysis: It's easy to be enchanted when love is the magic being shared.*

Author Notes

Four books down, and one to go! I hope you loved the Lucino family as much as I did; they were a delight to write about. There's only one tale left to be told, and by now you should well know just what faerie tale Rhianna herself has been living out for so long! Look for THE TABER FILE in September 2017, and see how the penultimate happy ending is finally obtained—but possibly at a cost.

Coming at the same time as THE TABER FILE will be a bonus artbook that I have been working on since the first release. Tons of photographs, behind-the-scenes, and even some special pieces created by fellow artists. You won't want to miss it!

If you loved this story, or any of my stories, please leave me a review on Amazon! Reviews are the bread and butter of an author's life, and even a simple "More, please!" will keep us going.

You can keep up with me on www.facebook.com/stacyjgarrett or www.stacyjgarrett.com or follow my blog at stacyjgarrett.wordpress.com. I sometimes lurk on Twitter (@stacyjgarrett), and Tumblr as well (stacyjgarrett.tumblr.com).

I can't wait to see you again within my magical District! Until then, keep looking for those happy ever afters!

Stacy J Garrett

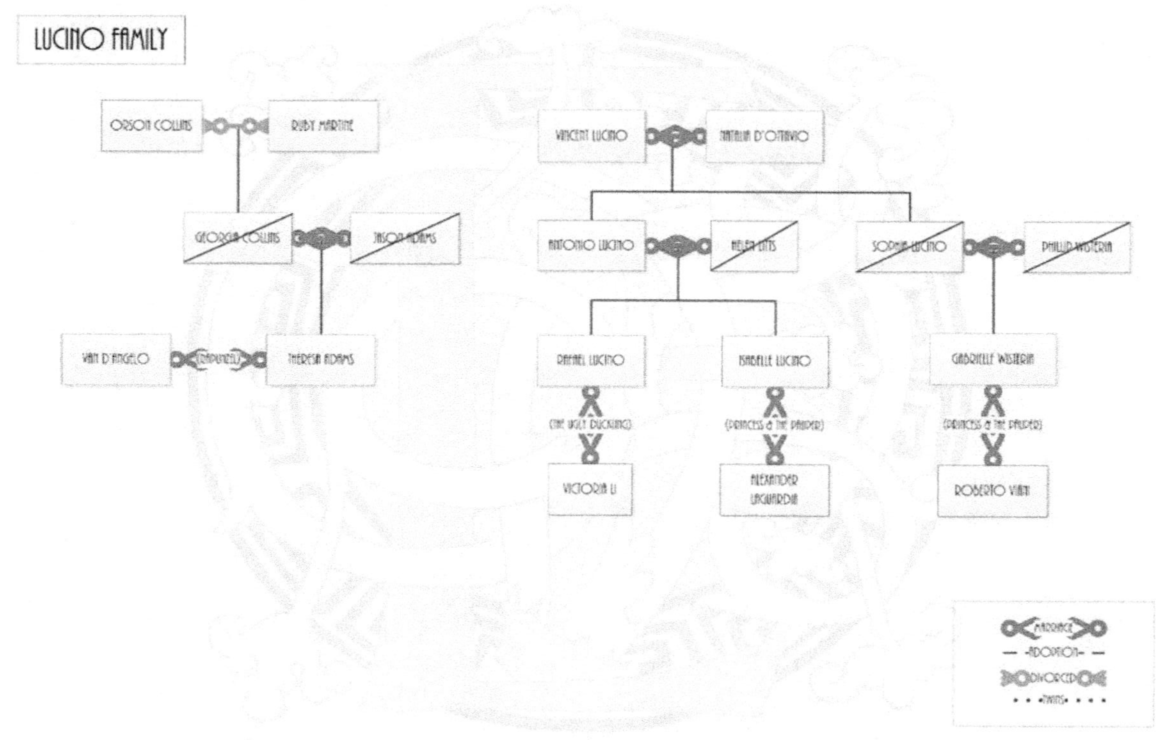

LUCINO FAMILY
ORSON COLLINS
RUBY MARTINE
GEORGIA COLLINS
JASON ADAMS
VAN D'ANGELO
(RAPUNZEL)
THERESA ADAMS
VINCENT LUCINO
NATALIA D'OTTAVIO
ANTONIO LUCINO
HELEN LITTS
SOPHIA LUCINO
PHILLIP WISTERIA
RAFAEL LUCINO
ISABELLE LUCINO
GABRIELLE WISTERIA
(THE UGLY DUCKLING)
(PRINCESS & THE PAUPER)
(PRINCESS & THE PAUPER)
VICTORIA LI
ALEXANDER LAGUARDIA
ROBERTO VIANI
MARRIAGE
-ADOPTION-
DIVORCED
•TWINS•

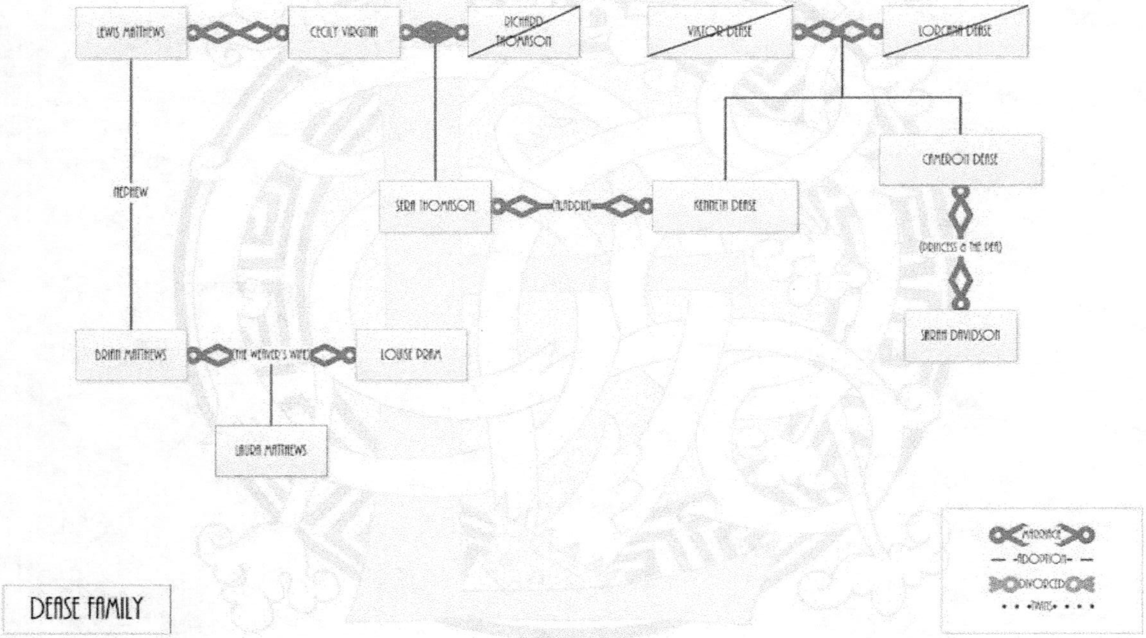

DEASE FAMILY

LEWIS MATTHEWS — CECILY VIRGINIA — RICHARD THOMPSON

VICTOR DEASE — LORCAN DEASE

NEPHEW

SERA THOMPSON — (ALADDIN) — KENNETH DEASE

CAMERON DEASE

(PRINCESS & THE PEA)

SARAH DAVIDSON

BRIAN MATTHEWS — (THE WEAVER'S WIFE) — LOUISE PRAM

LAURA MATTHEWS

MARRIAGE
— ADOPTION —
DIVORCED
· · · TWINS · · ·

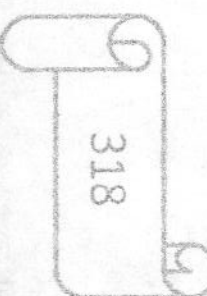

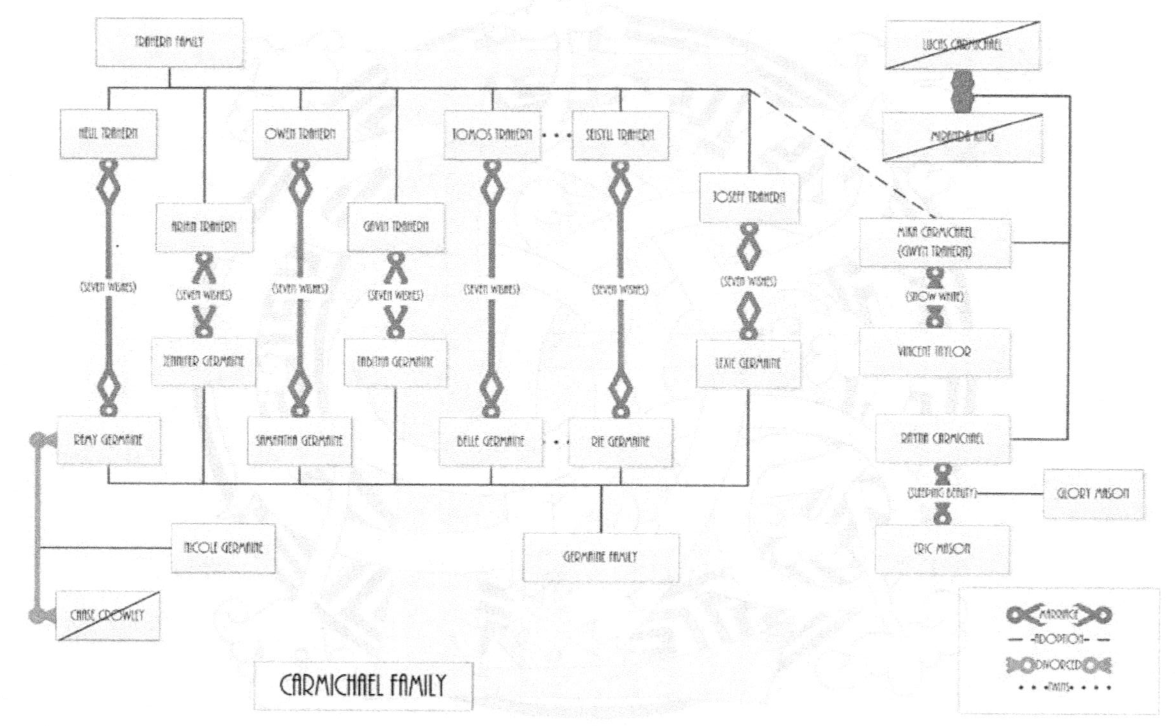

TRAHERN FAMILY
LUCAS CARMICHAEL
MICHELLE KING
NELL TRAHERN
OWEN TRAHERN
TOMOS TRAHERN
SEISYLL TRAHERN
ARTHA TRAHERN
GAVIN TRAHERN
JOSEFF TRAHERN
MIKA CARMICHAEL
(GWYN TRAHERN)
(SEVEN WISHES)
(SEVEN WISHES)
(SEVEN WISHES)
(SEVEN WISHES)
(SEVEN WISHES)
(SEVEN WISHES)
(SEVEN WISHES)
(SNOW WHITE)
JENNIFER GERMAINE
TABITHA GERMAINE
LEXIE GERMAINE
VINCENT TAYLOR
REMY GERMAINE
SAMANTHA GERMAINE
BELLE GERMAINE
RAE GERMAINE
RAYNA CARMICHAEL
(SLEEPING BEAUTY)
GLORY MASON
NICOLE GERMAINE
GERMAINE FAMILY
ERIC MASON
CHASE CROWLEY
CARMICHAEL FAMILY
MARRIAGE
ADOPTION
DIVORCED
TWINS

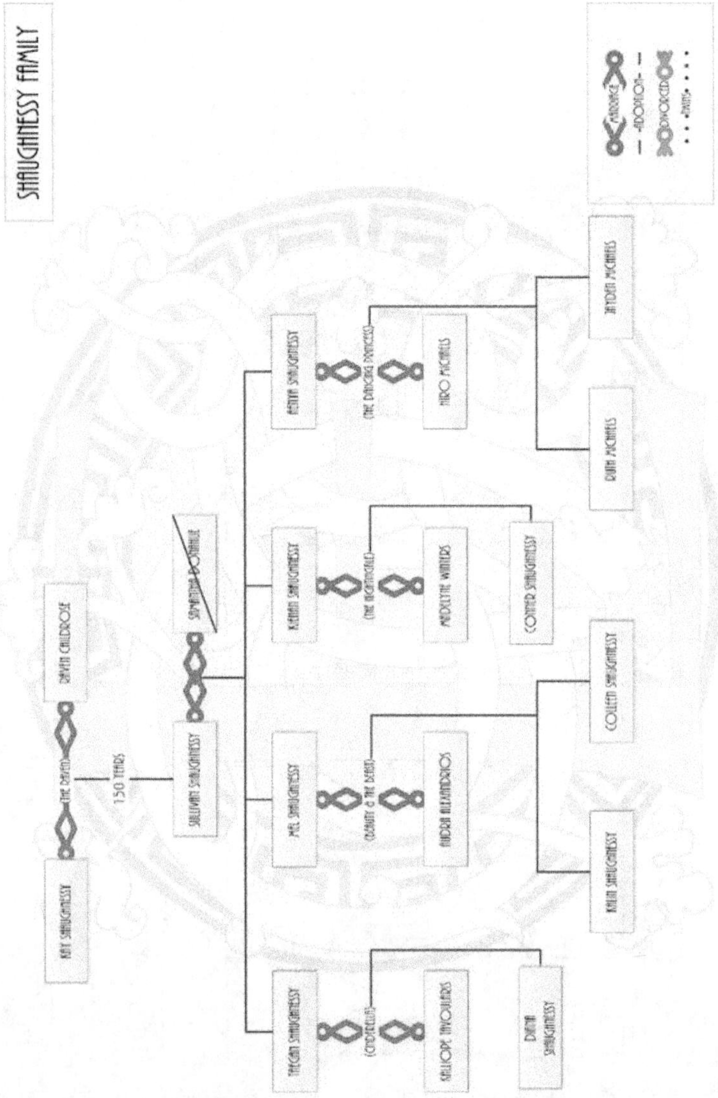

SHAUGHNESSY FAMILY

KAY SHAUGHNESSY — (THE RAVEN) — RAVEN CHILDROSE

150 YEARS

SULLIVAN SHAUGHNESSY — SAMANTHA DONAHUE

TAEGAN SHAUGHNESSY
(CINDERELLA)
KALLIOPE TAVOULARIS
DIANA SHAUGHNESSY

MEL SHAUGHNESSY
(BEAUTY & THE BEAST)
AUDRA ALEXANDRIOS

KIENAN SHAUGHNESSY
(THE NIGHTINGALE)
MADELYNE WINTERS
CONNER SHAUGHNESSY

AENYA SHAUGHNESSY
(THE DANCING PRINCESS)
HIRO MICHAELS

KALIN SHAUGHNESSY
COLLEEN SHAUGHNESSY
RUTH MICHAELS
JAYDEN MICHAELS

MARRIAGE
— ADOPTION —
DIVORCED
• • • TWINS • • •

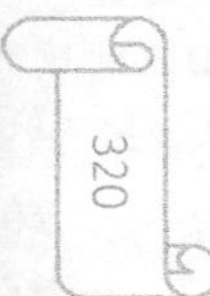

Stacy J. Garrett was made in England but born in Sacramento, California, and like the redwoods of the state, her roots have dug deep. Her destiny as a bard was somewhat inevitable. Little else can explain how she constantly told her mother tall tales so outlandish that she couldn't even get grounded for them. Her mother and grandmother had her reading by age three, and that love of a good story propelled her through so many books that Scholastic Books gave her a medal. A love of worlds created by others eventually brought out the desire to create her own, and she has never looked back.

Stacy has seen both good and evil in her life, and her stories, like life, have no half measures. Even in a fantasy world of dragons and faeries, even in a modern city where magic abounds, she knows that the constants of real emotion never change. Dreams come true, love can be found at first sight, princesses can rescue their princes, and maybe there really can be happily ever after. Her happy endings never come without cost, though, for she truly believes we can't appreciate the good and the joy without the bad and the pain along the way.

Her current haunt is a comfy house in her beloved Sacramento where she wrangles four feline fur-kids and consumes peppermints like mana in order to balance a calendar filled with more creative venues than a sane person should realistically undertake. If she's not chained to her desk, she's stomping through the scenery in search of equally fantastical photographs.